(continued from front flap)

women, not just to possess them. This is surely the reason that he is chosen to be the vehicle for Venus' rebirth, her protector in the hazardous ways of the twentieth-century world, and the recipient of her ample love.

The Man Who Liked Women is "an erotic novel which is, literally, enchanting, like the best Vercors," says Gore Vidal.

Marc Brandel lives in County Cork, Ireland. He is the author of several novels, including *Rain Before Seven* and *The Time of the Fire*, and is active in films and television as writer, editor and producer.

ALSO BY MARC BRANDEL

Marc Brandel, pseud.
THE MAN
WHO
LIKED WOMEN

SIMON AND SCHUSTER

NEW YORK

TO NAOMI
And to Antonia and Tara—for when they get bigger

In the domain of feeling, what is real is indistinguishable from what is imaginary.

—ANDRÉ GIDE

Ce n'est plus une ardeur dans mes veines cachée.
C'est Vénus toute entière à sa proie attachée.

—RACINE

1

CHAPTER

IT WAS OBVIOUS she had nothing on underneath. Going home in the taxi she wriggled affectionately in his arms and her tight little skirt slipped up the last inch of her thighs. She freed her hands and pulled it down. It wasn't a startled or reproving gesture. She might have been straightening the sheets on a bed. She smiled as he put his . . .

"You're not listening to me, Bascombe."

Bascombe Fletcher did not sit up with a start. He remained flopped like a thoughtful sheepdog. He had learned that when he was not listening and he sat up with a start, Mr. Mitchel said, "You see!"

"We've got to find a new approach shot to get us out of this rough."

Bascombe produced Mr. Mitchel's last few words without effort. He even reproduced the intonation of Mr. Mitchel's voice. He had discovered this aptitude in himself years ago in high school. He had been able to relax in the company of far more demanding bores than Mr. Mitchel ever since.

"Goddamn it, you never look as if you're listening to me, Bascombe."

"I was thinking—the best new approach might be the old approach. Nature. Nature's way. That town in Deaf Smith County. All the kids had teeth like crocodiles. Dentists were going out of business. Bankrupt. I don't think the English people over here know about that, Mr. Mitchel."

9

"I don't think you know about it either, Bascombe." Mr. Mitchel let out his breath in a long, artificial sigh. "Who wants teeth like crocodiles?"

Bascombe stirred contentedly, a dog in its sleep. Tomorrow Mr. Mitchel would start talking about nature, nature's way, that little town in Deaf Smith County, all those kids. He would never exactly claim he had thought of it himself, but there would be a disappointment in each (recalled) intonation, a reproof that Bascombe had not thought of it either. . . .

As soon as they got to her room, the moment he closed the door, she flopped down on the bed. This time her skirt withdrew to her waist. Her soft, bare little belly. When he kissed it, it was like licking cream.

"What do you do nights, Bascombe?"

"I've been trying to get to know the English people."

"How the hell do you manage to keep your weight down?"

"I walk home every evening."

Bascombe was lying. He never walked farther than the Underground station in Leicester Square.

In the three weeks he had been in London he had started to grade the streets: fantastic, great, fair, mixed, unreliable, pisspoor. The first lap of his walk to Leicester Square was along the Strand. The Strand was "okay" most of the time, and between five and six o'clock, when the offices closed, "remarkable."

They were all around him now as he started home, hundreds of them, striding to meet him, trotting ahead of him. Birds, the English called them. To Bascombe it was a surprise and delight, renewed each evening, that there should be so much pleasure in the world. Potential pleasure. Pleasure withheld. Pleasure briefly granted, like the loan of a glove. Best of all, pleasure to be shared.

Trafalgar Square at the top of the Strand was "unpredictable." Sometimes, if the spring weather was fine, they would be sitting in flocks around Nelson's Column, their shining legs dangling like gifts over the edge of the soot-dark stone. At rest like that they seemed, many of them, to be waiting, eager. It was rumor of this eagerness that had brought Bascombe to England. Not that there was anything wrong with American girls. But the facts of life in

America today precluded eagerness. To be open to adventure was to flirt with violence. The unknown was a synonym for the unspeakable. But even in the girls he had met at parties, through friends, under what they could presumably regard as reassuring circumstances, he had found a tendency to be cautious. They knew *he* had a great deal to be eager about. They made conditions, they bargained. Bascombe, longing to give everything to each of them in turn, found this haggling abrasive. About to disengage the hard cup of a bra from a superlative breast, he didn't want to be forced to repeat that he was serious.

The Underground was "sublime." Going down on the moving stairway they were below him with their breasts and above him with their thighs. Each time the train paused at a station they flocked variously aboard.

They sat opposite him on the padded benches. They glanced at him and kept their knees together. They forgot him and let their knees drift apart. They all seemed to wear tights, and as they moved their legs in their marvelously brief skirts they gave him glimpses of their flanks, their loins, the tender meeting of their thighs.

Bascombe got off at Earl's Court. The birds had thinned out a little by then, and the best of those remaining left the train there, too. They rode up to the exit, packed into the elevator with him, and scattered in front of him into the "greatest" street of all.

It was just chance, luck, that had brought him to live in this part of London. He had been sent here by a fruity girl in the real estate office where he had gone looking for a furnished apartment. She had only one vacant.

"It's in Earl's Court, Aim afraid. Aim not sure if you'll lake that neighborhood."

"Is there something wrong with it?"

Bascombe glanced at the fruity girl's legs extended toward him under the desk. Her knees were surprisingly rounded, dimpled, they smiled at him.

He looked at her face. She was about thirty, large gray eyes, good skin, marvelous neck. Her tongue was pressed against her lips, her mouth slightly pouted, as she wrote the address on a pad for him. Any moment, it seemed, the lips might part, the tongue win out, the tip of it appear, pink and personal. . . . Bascombe could feel the exact texture of it instantly, taste it on his own. He was as vividly aware of its first tentative movements, the later lingering explorations, as if he were actually kissing her now, laying her back in her swivel chair, putting his hand . . .

"A wouldn't say there was anything wrong with it, in fact."

For the first time since he had entered the office the fruity girl straightened her beautiful neck and looked directly at him. He looked back at her. Her voice and manner seemed so carefully assumed, it was difficult to believe they weren't, like her clothes, removable.

Bascombe had never been able to accept that anyone naturally talked or behaved the way so many of the professional, middle-class English did. Granted the parents had that accent, that intonation, it still seemed improbable that any child would develop it by unconscious imitation. The whole thing—the choked voice, the straining upward at the end of each syllable to add another one—"nee-ah"—"hee-ah"—"bee-ah"—the constantly averted eyes, the awkward, sudden self-conscious movements—could surely only be acquired by years of practice. And surely sometimes it must slip. Surely even to this girl would come a moment when she would gasp, "Yes." And the word then would be a single, natural syllable.

With a sudden, it seemed involuntary, jerk of her whole body she looked away from him again. She tore the page off the pad and gave it to Bascombe. She had nice hands, he noticed.

"And if you don't lake it, you can always come back."

He wished he could. If only there were world enough and time. Time to give to her. (To all of them.) Time to win her confidence and then her response. To strip off that artificiality with her tweed skirt and get to know the woman underneath.

"But then *you* may lake Earl's Court."

Bascombe adored it. It wasn't only the constant parade of birds there, up and down Earl's Court Road, at any time of the day or night, it was their prodigal variety. Tall girls, short girls, plump girls, slim girls. Vague-eyed girls. Girls with direct, knowing glances. Girls in saris and girls in jeans. Mysterious girls with skirts down to their ankles. Proud girls with thighs bare up to their hips. Girls with bellies like Buddhas and girls with waists like greyhounds. Girls with great round pumping bottoms and girls with deft, evasive little rumps.

Bascombe yearned to know them all. No longer in the mass, but one by one. Because that was the fantastic thing about them. Each one was unique. Each one was capable, with a simple nod, of granting him a quite different experience of almost unimaginable pleasure.

It was true, unfortunately, that the well-publicized rumor of their eagerness to share those pleasures, which had drawn him across the Atlantic, had turned out to be a little exaggerated now that he was here. In the three weeks he had been in London he had spent a distressing number of nights alone. English girls, he had found, could be cautious, bargaining, hung-up, too.

But they didn't *look* it. As he left the Underground and walked on to his apartment, his eyes, caught by the flare of a breast here, the gleam of a thigh there, goaded him with undaunted longing to experience, to understand in a way that could only come with physical accord, to *know* that girl who had just slipped past him. A tall girl in an airline uniform. My God, he thought, following her as though on a leash. My God, to make love to a girl like that. What would it be like?

It appalled Bascombe a little sometimes that he never willingly thought about anything else. All the supposed thinking he did at the office, the ideas, reports, promotional material, he produced for Mr. Mitchel in return for his fairly comfortable salary, were as effortless as automatic writing. It had always been that way. Although he had graduated from a Midwestern college with an engineering degree, found a job, kept it, earned small promotions, none of it had ever engaged his full attention for an instant. It had all been as much a means to an end, as passive as a bus ride to a football game. It was true he had planned it, as he had planned to become Mr. Mitchel's assistant as soon as he heard he was slated for the London job. But he had decided to become an engineer only because it had seemed to him a reasonably uninvolv-

13

ing way of earning enough to have an apartment of his own, money for restaurants, theater tickets, taxis, weekends in double rooms by the sea. He had no material ambitions, no interest in possessions. He had no interest in anything except the particular activity he thought of as "making love."

Bascombe was a fucking womanizer, in fact, as one of his college classmates had derided him. But he was also that rather rare thing, a man who liked women. He was no trophy hunter. He did not pursue girls like so much game to be bagged and counted. He neither reckoned his successes nor resented his failures. He never talked about either. To him the involvement, however illusory, was everything.

The preliminaries: the vivid meeting, the exchange of confidence, the mutual searching out of past and present. The telephone calls to secure further meetings, the caresses, the first long-anticipated, always faintly startling contact of nakedness.

And then the act itself. Prolonged, savored, repeated, varied.

And after that the no less perfect denouement: the languor, the gratitude, the tenderness and affection, the waking together no longer strangers.

It was all, all of it, marvelous to him. It was the only thing that interested him, the only thing in the world he had ever cared about.

Near the end of Earl's Court Road Bascombe turned off onto a side street and let himself into an ugly bay-windowed building halfway down the block. For all his devoted interest in the girls he had seen since leaving the office, none of them had taken much notice of him. Not one of them probably remembered having seen him. Outwardly there was nothing noticeable, nothing memorable about him.

Bascombe Helmut Fletcher, American, neatly dressed and in his right mind, twenty-three years old, six foot one, black spiky hair that would never stay down, dark eyes, thin slightly prominent nose, mouth too wide for his face, not good-looking enough to make any woman dislike him.

Distinguishing characteristics, none. And yet he was not a simple individual. Like a face formed by clouds, the outline only appeared straightforward. There is the eye, the nose, the chin. But seen from another angle that outline changes, and from another point of view the face itself is an illusion. Behind it are its elements, the shifting wind, the sun, the vapor risen from the sea.

At that moment as Bascombe climbed the stairs to his apartment to take a shower and change before going on to a party, all the elements that formed his nature were moving and gathering into a different pattern, a changed expression of themselves. Every single-minded moment of his life was contributing to reward him with one of the most extraordinary experiences that could happen to a man.

For several more hours he was unaware of it. He poured himself a drink and loosened his tie. He had a slight headache.

Only the real English would have called it a party, as Mrs. Waddington had. Bascombe had brought a letter of introduction to the Waddingtons from a mutual acquaintance in New York. "They're kind of boring," he had been warned. "But then they're English. You know, *real* English. If you're going to stay over there you ought to meet some of the real English."

Mrs. Waddington called him at the office the day after he mailed the letter to her.

"What luck! You're here now! We're having a party on Tuesday!" The exclamation points sounded in Bascombe's ears like the organ accompaniment to a television commercial. "Come at seven! Do!"

Bascombe arrived at half past. A short square woman answered the bell. She had what is aptly known as iron-gray hair and a probably unintentionally ecclesiastical appearance. Her long stiff robe hung on her like a bishop's, and the heavy layer of powder on her face caught and reflected the solemn purple. Her feet protruded beneath it like hassocks.

"Come in! Come in!" Bascombe recognized Mrs. Waddington's exclamatory tones, but she did not look in the least real to him.

"You're! Let me see!"

Clutching at his arm she hauled him into a dark hallway and peered up into his face.

"Bascombe Fletcher."

"Of course!" It was obvious the name meant nothing to her. Still holding him by the arm, Mrs. Waddington swung him around and pushed him forcefully away from her toward a doorway at the end of the hall.

"Go in! Go in! And join the party!"

Bascombe found himself in a narrow high-ceilinged room. Filled to the walls with gloomy confusion, it seemed intended, like a closet, to hide rather than display the accumulated possessions of the Waddingtons' lives. They had obviously traveled widely and in every country sought and acquired the worst of the typical local products. Machined brass from Benares; glass-eyed antelope heads from Nairobi; tassels from Turkey.

A dozen middle-aged people loitered among this rubbish like passengers waiting for an overdue train. Like English passengers they avoided each other's eyes. The few who seemed to notice Bascombe's entrance at all looked quickly away from him.

He hesitated a moment by the olivewood table from Valldemosa just inside the door, then reluctantly picked up one of the tiny glasses of sherry that were the only things on it. The lights had not yet been turned on in the room. The twilight of what had never been a very bright spring day filtered wearily through the windows, yellowing the averted faces around him. It revealed in each of them the same look of anger. Bascombe had noticed this anger before in the faces of English people. He had worried at first that it was personal. They hated him. For being an American? For being young? For being Bascombe? But he had come to understand that their anger was directionless. They resented everyone, even each other. It was as much a part of their present middle-class condition as enterprise had once been. It was all that was left to them from a century of abused privilege.

He carried his sherry to the nearest of the windows. He had known as soon as he entered Mrs. Waddington's front door that this was one of his American mistakes. It was the kind of mistake everyone makes his first few weeks in a foreign country. The empty restaurant whose waiters close in on you like process servers the moment you enter it. The wrong bus that finally lets you off

16

on the one-way turnpike. Half an hour? he wondered hopefully. If he made some excuse? His headache was getting worse. He had been having these headaches increasingly often lately. They came usually at this time of the evening and persisted for an hour or so, building with a curious breaking rhythm, like the tide coming in on a rough day. He did his best to ignore them. He had been ill so rarely he had never formed the habit of questioning his health. It had never occurred to him there could be anything wrong with him. It did not occur to him now.

He sipped his sherry. It was sharp with a lingering flavor of varnish. He put the glass down on a nearby tom-tom from Durban and leaned back more comfortably in the corner of the window alcove. . . .

As he cantered behind her along the shore the cleft roundness of her bottom was revealed, even emphasized by the straining whipcord of her riding pants. Her sweet full buttocks bounded ahead of him, now dipping out of sight below the rim of her saddle, now suddenly presented to him whole and enravishing. At the end of the beach they walked their horses for a few yards through the surf and entered a small deserted cove. He dismounted and helped her down from her horse. Her waist was incredibly delicate in contrast to the luxury of her hips. It was like holding a kitten, warm and boneless. She smiled . . .

"Are you the American?"

He turned toward the sound of the voice. A female of some kind was standing between him and the window. He could see nothing of her but a sphinx-like silhouette, a domed head, two wings of hair.

"I'm Hannah Cooper. I was invited to meet you. You're supposed to talk to me."

"I'm Bascombe Fletcher."

He held out his hand and then remembered, too late, that you weren't supposed to shake hands in England. The Italians and Germans shook hands. The French did it constantly. The English didn't.

Hannah Cooper did. She not only took Bascombe's hand, she held onto it while she drew him into an even darker corner of the room. They leaned there against a bamboo bookcase side by side.

"No, I don't," Bascombe was saying a few minutes later. "I don't think there's anything wrong with English food. And I don't mind the damp houses, either. I like it here."

"I wish I did."

"Why do you stay?"

"Where else is there to go?"

"Haven't you ever been to Europe?" He remembered the English called it abroad. "Haven't you ever been abroad?"

"It's probably even worse abroad."

It was rather fun, he thought, being free, in fact forced to imagine everything about her: her age, the color of her hair, her eyes. He liked her voice. It was friendly, with a faintly defensive note.

"What do you *like* about England?"

"The girls." He found it easy to be honest because it was like gambling in the dark, not knowing what the stakes were.

"What do you like about *them*?"

"Something, there's something very gentle about English girls." Bascombe hesitated, trying to say what he meant. "A lot of them look like, like nurses are supposed to look."

She laughed. She had a pleasant laugh.

"I don't."

"What do you look like?"

"Didn't you see me when I came in?"

"No."

"I saw *you*."

That was cheating. She was playing with a stacked deck. He started to reach for his cigarettes. Her hand touched his arm.

"No, you don't."

"Why not?"

"That's cheating."

"What?" He knew damned well what.

"Striking matches."

"Okay." She had won that hand. He dropped the cigarettes back into his pocket.

She was still holding his arm. Her fingers moved a little, kneading, pausing, creeping up to his shoulders. She was *feeling* him.

This was an even better game. He started with her wrist, stroking it lightly with the tips of his fingers, and then went on to her forearm. Her skin was beautifully smooth. His fingers lingered in the small tender hollow at the crook of her arm. He caressed it appreciatively.

It was at that moment Mrs. Waddington realized there was something wrong with her party. For some time now her guests, in motion if not in communication at last, had been blundering about, upsetting each other's drinks, tripping over each other's feet, apologizing to the stuffed heads. Mrs. Waddington, who had been hopefully mistaking confusion for revelry, now realized there was a simpler explanation. It was pitch dark in the room. She turned on the lights.

Bascombe dropped his hands to his sides. Hannah Cooper's fingers were snatched away just as quickly. They both leaned back against the bookcase again, side by side, not looking at each other.

"Oh, well." There was a note of surrender in her voice. She might have been saying it was bound to end sometime. For a few seconds longer Bascombe remained quite still. Supposing she had no nose? Would it really matter? God knows he had wanted her in the dark, all right. And confused with the memory of the desire was a familiar tenderness: it was almost gratitude.

He reached down and took her hand before he turned and looked at her.

Fair hair cut rather short. A small but definitely existent nose. Wide, grave, hazel eyes. Hannah Cooper was a dish. Even on Earl's Court Road she would have caught his attention. Even wearing a flannel skirt down to her knees as she was now. Even in the shapeless sweater she was wearing with it.

The first step was to get her out of here and into a restaurant, Bascombe decided immediately. Then later, warm with food and wine, out of the restaurant and into his apartment. Then later still, with luck, out of those awful clothes—

"You don't want to stick around any longer, do you?" he began.

She disengaged her hand and shook her head. The defensiveness was in her eyes now. " 'Bye."

She turned sharply and walked away across the room. He caught up with her by the drink table as she was forced to pause there to let someone pass. There was a single tiny glass of sherry on it now. He touched her arm. She looked at him blankly.

"What?"

"Could you—would you like to have dinner with me?"

"When?"

"Now."

"Now?" She might have been asking what the hell for.

"Aren't you hungry?"

"Yes."

"Well . . . good . . . wonderful." He guided her into the hallway. Mrs. Waddington was just closing the door. When she saw Bascombe and Hannah coming toward her she stood with her back to it and spread her arms. In her stiff robe she looked like a squat, playful Luther defending Church sanctuary.

"You're not leaving!"

"I'm afraid . . ."

"You can't!"

"I'm afraid we have to. We . . ."

"Why?"

There was one of those uneasy social pauses that seemed to be endemic in England. People very rarely asked you any questions here, but when they did they always seemed to be unanswerable.

"I know why!" Mrs. Waddington suddenly answered it for him. "I know why!" she repeated roguishly and, tottering forward a few steps from the door, seized Bascombe and hugged him. She was so short that her embracing arms circled his waist. She looked up at him with arch understanding. Bascombe did his best to smile down at her. Mrs. Waddington was stoned.

"It's sort of sad," he told Hannah half an hour later, after the waiter had brought their orders and the wine. "Don't you think it's sad?"

"What?"

"Mrs. Waddington, that whole . . . party. She must have hoped it was going to be fun and then when it wasn't. All those corpses standing around. So she got drunk."

"She's always drunk."

"What makes you think that?"

"She's my aunt."

That surprised him. Hannah seemed so young: he found it hard to associate her with that English middle class, those cold-blooded-British-shit-types, as Mr. Mitchel called them, who had been so ably represented at Mrs. Waddington's this evening. He remembered reading somewhere that for all the pretty girls of that class in England, there were very few pretty women. Past forty they were either dull and defeated or tough as old rope, all for hanging and flogging everyone in sight. Because so few men of their own social group really cared a damn about women. Recalling this, and looking at Hannah's face now, the defensive eyes, Bascombe felt a longing to change all that, at least for her. To make Hannah realize once and for all how much a man could care about her.

She was eating like a starved goat, forking in her veal and spaghetti, tossing down her wine, champing at her salad. It was a good sign. He watched her approvingly as she sopped up the last of her Bolognese with a hunk of French bread and popped it into her mouth.

"Would you like some more?"

"Food?"

"Yes." He handed her the menu and she chose a meringue. The waiter brought it with an Italian flourish.

"Everything is all right, Mr. Fletcher?"

"Fine. Thank you. Fine."

The waiter pranced off with an understanding smile.

"Do you bring all your girls here?"

It was an unfair question. He had brought three girls here in the past few weeks, but he had also eaten here quite often alone on those awful evenings when there was no girl to feed and talk to and discover.

"It must cost you a lot of money."

He shook his head.

"But I suppose some of them were worth it."

They had all been worth it in Bascombe's estimation. One of

them in particular, a tall Scots girl in London on a visit, had given him some astounding moments. Leaping around his apartment in the nude, wanting more and more and more. He kindled for an instant at the memory, but something in the tone of Hannah's remark had lodged in his mind. It worried him.

"Worth it—how?"

"You know how."

She had finished her meringue and was dabbing up the crumbs with the tip of her middle finger. Instead of warming her, the food and wine seemed only to have increased her defensiveness. The line of anxiety between her eyes was more noticeable now.

"Stuff them and bang them. Isn't that the idea?"

"No." Bascombe's denial was genuinely indignant. He had never banged a girl in his life. The idea was repugnant to him. He had made love to girls, certainly. He had laid them, yes. You might even say he had fucked them. But he had neither banged them nor screwed them.

"No," he repeated. "That's not the idea."

"You queer?" She looked at him searchingly. "You don't look queer," she conceded.

"Thank you."

"I expect it's pretty hard to get rid of some of them after you've banged them, isn't it?"

"Why should I want to get rid of them?"

"You couldn't pick up other girls at parties if you had one round your neck all the time. Banging *her* every night."

Bascombe wished to God she'd stop using that word. But he knew there was a twisted sliver of truth in her observation. It was true he had somehow managed to have eighty—he had never counted them—perhaps ninety affairs by now, without becoming inextricably involved in any of them. But he had never deliberately got rid of a girl. Some of his affairs had lasted for months without any wearying of his enthusiasm or desire. In each of those cases it had been the girl who had finally got rid of him. Because in the end she had demanded his exclusive enthusiasm, his undivided desire. And this he had never been able to promise.

It was raining lavishly as they came out of the restaurant. Neither of them was wearing a coat. They had not decided, nor even discussed where they were going next. They cowered in the doorway while the rain spattered off the sidewalk in front of them, watering their legs like a sprinkler.

"I'll get a taxi."

"You never will."

She was probably right. His apartment was only a few blocks away. It was worth suggesting.

"My apartment's only a few blocks away."

"So's mine."

She leaped out of the doorway and ran off down the street. He wasn't sure whether she intended him to follow her or not. But at the end of the block she half turned her head and waved at him in a vaguely directing way. He caught up with her halfway across the intersecting street. They reached the opposite sidewalk more or less together.

They stayed more or less together, dodging into doorways, panting, running on, splashing through puddles, dangerously skirting the rain-flecked lights of approaching cars, slipping and sidestepping and colliding with each other, through what seemed most of Kensington and Chelsea.

It could have been fun. Even with the rain gradually pasting his clothes to his body he might have enjoyed it. But there was a disturbing quality about Hannah's haste. She ran less as though leading Bascombe than being pursued by him. Even when she stopped and touched his elbow or his shoulder, made brief contact with him, she seemed only to be measuring the distance between them, reassuring herself that he hadn't quite caught her yet, before running on.

Bascombe's eagerness as a pursuer lessened with each of these encounters. He could understand Hannah being shy. But she didn't seem shy. She seemed angry. His headache had returned and with it an unusual objectivity. Sooner or later Hannah would reach her destination. There would be an apartment and somewhere in it the bed that had been his goal ever since he had met

23

her. There would be cajoling and reluctance. In the end, almost certainly, this girl with her anxious hostility would give in. It was possible, of course, that once he was physically close to her he might be able to rouse her beyond acceptance to willingness. Somewhere inside her there must be a woman who could respond directly, freely . . .

For the first time in his life Bascombe suddenly found he had no desire to search out that woman any further. Those elements that formed his nature had already started to shift in the past few hours. They were gathering now into that different pattern, that changed expression of themselves.

His headache was worse than it had ever been before. Something seemed to be probing at the inside of his skull as though it were trying to find a way out. It kept gouging away in short desperate bursts of energy and then pausing for a little while to let the agony sink in.

He turned and started home. He turned, inevitably, in the wrong direction. It wasn't until he reached the King's Road that he realized he was heading away from his apartment. There were no birds on the King's Road at this hour and he wouldn't have been interested in them if there had been. For the first time in his adult life he wanted only to be alone in his own bed.

It was still raining, although more thinly now. He stood at the curb, facing hopefully toward Sloane Square and trying to ignore his headache, until a cab finally picked him up.

In the taxi he was seized by a sense of urgency. He found himself counting aloud between the spasms of pain. He was obsessed by the idea that if one spasm succeeded the last before he got to ten, something disastrous, something hideously inappropriate would happen right here in the cab.

Back in his own apartment at last, he peeled off all his clothes as soon as he had closed the door behind him. He could not stoop to pick them up. Any movement hurt his head too much. The pain behind his eyes was so intense he could barely see his way to the bedroom.

Getting the door open, stumbling around it, was the hardest

labor he had ever done. His scalp seemed to be literally tearing apart as he crept toward the bed.

He never reached it. When he was still ten feet away something gave, like a dam, between his temples. The inside of his crown seemed to flood with warm liquid.

Bascombe swayed, half turned, and fell to the floor, unconscious.

2

CHAPTER

IT WAS JUST getting light when Bascombe woke up. The air had cleared with the night's rain and there was a freshness in the sky: that sense of a new beginning, a rebirth one can feel, even in cities, on some early mornings in May.

Bascombe felt it at once. His headache was gone. He was surprised to find himself lying naked on the floor. He had no recollection of his painful labor, his collapse the night before. He stared up at the ceiling, relaxed, relieved, as though some pressing demand that had driven him all his life had been taken off his mind while he slept. He could remember standing on the King's Road in the rain and then, dimly, a taxi, his desperate urgency to get back here before something happened. What? He wasn't sure he had ever known. He started to get up.

He almost trod on her.

He did not realize all at once what it was he had almost trodden on. She was at that moment only some small white creature that moved on the carpet beside his foot. The movement startled him. He snatched his bare foot away as reflexively as he would have from an insect or a mouse. But it wasn't an insect. And it wasn't a mouse. Even standing up he could see that.

After a few seconds Bascombe knelt down. He bent forward. Slowly, compulsively, he lowered his head to the floor, resting his chin on the carpet and approaching his eyes as close to whatever it was as he could get them.

He closed his eyes. He recited his own full name, Bascombe

Helmut Fletcher, silently to himself. He opened them.

It was still there.

Almost imperceptibly, so as not to frighten it, Bascombe inched his finger toward it. He touched it.

It was as real as his own flesh.

He touched it again, stroking it with careful gentleness, with a wondering tenderness that was like awe.

It was unmistakably a human being, stark naked, evidently female, and standing proudly erect as she was now, about an inch and a half tall.

Bascombe's later relationship with this tiny creature was so intense, so engrossing and exclusive, that he was always glad to remember afterward that his first articulate thought about her was one of concern. He thought she must be cold.

He was still too unsure of her absolute reality to risk withdrawing his eyes from her long enough to find something warm, a sock or a handkerchief occurred to him first, to cover her with. Rounding his mouth like a man cleaning his glasses, he huffed a little warm air toward her instead.

She seemed to appreciate it. She parted her legs, standing astride, and putting her hands on her hips, threw back her head. She swiveled her shoulders and thrust her hips forward, sunning herself in the warmth of his breath.

It was such a familiar feminine posture, recalling so many pleasant memories of Fire Island, that it brought home to Bascombe fully for the first time just how physically complete she was. Her hair was so fine that it looked in the mass like a single strand. But it was a strand woven of shifting, changing threads of gold. Her arms were as slender as the pistils of a tulip, but they swelled slightly between the shoulder and the elbow and tapered to her wrist. Her breasts were no larger than two seed pearls, side by side, but each rose delicately to a point, and although they appeared colorless to the naked eye, he could just make out the two specks of her nipples.

She might be less than two inches tall, but she was no embryo and no infant. She was a fully grown, a perfectly developed woman.

Bascombe had run out of breath. She took her right hand from her hip, holding it up for a moment in surprise, and then began waving it imperiously under his nose. He could see that the hand was partly open, two fingers the thickness of eyelashes extended, the other two doubled back to the palm in the traditional Latin gesture of demand. He refilled his lungs, bent quickly forward, and began exhaling again.

Kneeling there, stark naked on his bedroom carpet, huffing at an equally naked woman who would have fitted comfortably into an eggshell, he was already too completely engrossed in her to feel there was anything strange about what he was doing. Once he had recovered from the first astonishment of discovery, he had simply accepted the whole situation. As she stopped waving at him and basked once more in his breath, he made a further discovery about her.

She did not find him strange. She was obviously not in the least frightened of him. Wherever she had come from, whatever kind of world she was used to, there must be people roughly like him there, too.

She appeared to feel now that she had warmed the front side of herself enough. She lifted one foot out of the pile of the carpet, turned, and presented her back to him. He was struck by the graceful ease of her action. There was none of that darting brisk- ness in her movements which he associated with more familiar creatures her size, tropical fish or hummingbirds or lizards.

He took another deep breath and slowly let it out again. Her buttocks were no larger than raindrops but each of them was a pear-shaped jewel, the hairline of the cleft between them dividing into two perfect arcs that underlined their oval symmetry. They might have been the buttocks of some peerless girl sunning her- self a hundred yards away down the beach. Bascombe could have stared at them all day.

She did not let him. With the same graceful fluency she turned and began waving her arms at him again. He started to breathe in. That wasn't, apparently, what she wanted this time. She walked toward him. The pile of the carpet came almost to her knees and it must, he thought, seem as resistant to her as gorse. She strode through it with careless ease. She was obviously very strong for her size. A dozen steps brought her to his chin, almost out of his sight. By rolling his eyes down until they hurt he could just see her beneath the double image of his nose. He felt a sharp prick at his lower lip. He jerked back his head. She had her right hand raised, the index finger pointed like a needle at his mouth, ready to jab him again. She wanted something and she wanted it now. But what?

She fluttered both hands impatiently and let them fall to her sides. He heard the thin, high-pitched sound of her palms slapping against her thighs. In spite of its faintness it was unmistakably the sound of flesh striking flesh. The implications of this fascinated him so much he missed her next movement. By the time he had brought his concentrated attention back to her, she was standing astride with her hands on her hips again, shaking her head at him in obvious irritation. He moved his face a little closer to her. She nodded encouragingly, then thrust her right hand pointedly toward her own mouth.

She was hungry.

Bascombe rose instantly, obediently, to his feet, but he could not imagine what to feed her. There was some fruit in a bowl in the living room, but it seemed to him that if he managed to cut an apple or a pear into pieces small enough to fit into her mouth, its consistency would still be too coarse for her to swallow. Even put through a blender it would seem as thick as pitch to her. She might even choke on it.

It was the idea of the blender that suggested milk. The bottle in the refrigerator felt inappropriately cold for a naked woman's first meal of the day. He put it to warm in a saucepan while he washed and dried the smallest saucer he could find.

She was sitting cross-legged like a guru, facing the door, when he returned to the bedroom. From a distance of more than a few feet it was impossible for him with his rather clumsy human vision to discern the expression on her face. But as he knelt to put down the saucer he saw a tiny crescent of white between her lips. It was the first time she had smiled at him. He felt as proud as a new father. He smiled back and slid the saucer toward her.

She forgot him instantly. He remained kneeling, watching her, fascinated, as she strode over to her breakfast. The rim of the saucer reached exactly to the tiny golden triangle at the vertex of her thighs.

She paddled her fingers experimentally in the milk first, then cupped her hand and raised it to her mouth. It surprised him that milk with its high surface tension could form a drop small enough to fit into her palm. But she seemed to be drinking all right. It was several seconds before she lowered her hand again. She would have to swallow it slowly, he thought, like vichyssoise.

She rested a moment. He saw those pearl-like breasts rise and fall as she took a deep breath. Then, instead of scooping up another handful, she vaulted lightly over the rim of the saucer and began splashing around in it, kicking the milk up with her toes until the carpet was speckled with white beads. He could *see* now how small a drop of milk could be.

He was struck by the silence of her performance. The slap of her hands against her thighs had just carried to him. But her splashing was noiseless to his ear. It occurred to him that because of her size she probably lived within a different decibel range from his own. She might be able to hear all kinds of things he never could. A butterfly landing on the grass. A bud unfurling. The lapping of the milk against her face now as she knelt and drank with her lips to the surface. He was just thinking that if this were true his own movements must sound monstrous to her, when a noise exploded from behind his head that startled even him.

It was the telephone. He had time to see her raise her hands to her ears before he leaped back and, falling across the bed, snatched up the receiver. He looked at her. She had climbed out of the saucer and was standing in her familiar legs astride position, shaking her head at him reprovingly. He pressed the cup of the phone tight against his lips.

"Hullo."

"Bascombe?"

"Yes."

"Where the hell are you?"

30

Mr. Mitchel's question did not seem as idiotic as it might have another morning. As she jumped back into the saucer of milk and floated lightly on her back in it, it was even faintly reassuring to have it confirmed that he was still in the same world as Mr. Mitchel.

"Where do *you* think I am?" Bascombe really wanted to know.

"What are you whispering for?"

"I've got a sore throat, Mr. Mitchel."

"I can hardly hear you."

"I've got a sore throat, Mr. Mitchel."

"You just told me that."

She had turned over and was floating on her belly. Her specific gravity was not great enough to submerge her in milk. Not only her bottom but her shoulders and the backs of her thighs remained clear of the surface. She obviously had no difficulty keeping her head up either.

"—that bastard you dug up. So you'd better meet me at the restaurant."

Bascombe had missed the first part of Mr. Mitchel's last sentence. He hung up and reproduced the sound of it in his mind.

"Don't forget we're having lunch at Paolo's with that bastard you dug up."

Bascombe had forgotten. That bastard was Stanley Nolan, a Labour Member of Parliament, who had been eluding Mr. Mitchel for weeks. Bascombe had finally nailed him at his club by pretending to be Nolan's answering service. After relaying several invented messages, he had then deftly cut in on himself, impersonating Mr. Mitchel, and surprised Nolan into agreeing to a lunch date today.

Oh, shit, Bascombe thought. If he had played it right, he could probably have gotten out of it. If he had (hoarsely) defended Nolan, exaggerating the importance of the meeting and his own achievement in arranging it, Mr. Mitchel would have told him to stay in bed and take care of his throat. But it was too late now. Now that Mr. Mitchel had his cumbersome mind set on the expectation—it was almost the image, of having him there, at the lunch table, at Paolo's—nothing short of Bascombe's sudden death could deflect him. That was the way Mr. Mitchel's mind worked. It was one of the reasons he had been put in charge of the London office.

She had climbed out of the saucer and was standing on the carpet, one knee gracefully inclined toward the other, smoothing the milk off her arms with her hands. Bascombe crossed to the wardrobe and took a thin silk handkerchief out of the breast pocket of one of his suits. He bit through the hem and tore at the handkerchief until he had detached a square about the size of his palm.

He knelt down and held it out to her. That tiny white crescent showed between her lips again. She took the shred of silk and draped it over her shoulders. It reached down to her ankles, enfolding her like a Turkish towel.

Bathed, fed, clothed, and smiling, she seemed to have everything she wanted for the moment. But he couldn't leave her there on the bedroom carpet while he went out to lunch. Although he could now accept his guest as calmly as a mother giraffe her foal, without any sense of the little being's objective oddness, he could hardly expect his cleaning woman to feel the same way.

Bascombe's cleaning woman came with the apartment, and she came on impulse. Some weeks he would return home three evenings in a row to find his bed made and his coffeepot washed, some weeks not for days on end, and then suddenly on Friday. This was just as likely as not to be one of her days.

He looked around the room. There was a chest of drawers between the windows but he had never had a key to it, and from the state of his belongings after his cleaning woman's days he guessed that her curiosity was as impulsive as her work habits.

He took his empty suitcase down from the top of the closet and opened it on the bed. It was a bulky leather case over two feet long and about a foot deep. Bascombe had never had any interest in physics or engineering, but he had a natural aptitude for working out practical problems. Supposing his guest's height to be about one forty-fifth of the normal average, he figured she would have the equivalent of almost half a million cubic feet of air to breathe inside the case. As much as an ordinary-sized woman locked up in an indoor tennis court.

He put the open suitcase on the floor beside her and began to furnish it as comfortably as he could. A cashmere sweater pressed down flat for a carpet. The surgical cotton from a bottle of vitamins for a bed. The remains of the silk handkerchief cut into half a dozen more strips for sheets and towels. He hesitated over the question of a light. To be locked up in the dark, even in an indoor tennis court, could be a disconcerting experience. There was a pocket flashlight in the drawer of the night table. But he was afraid the metal casing would warm up after a while, and it seemed reasonable that the thinness of her skin should be proportionate to her size. If she touched the flashlight she might burn herself.

On the other hand, he thought, she had enjoyed the warm milk, so perhaps it wasn't a question of being thin- or thick-skinned, but of body temperature. If a moth could settle on a lighted bulb . . . But he realized he knew very little about the body temperature of moths.

In the end he found some Band-aids in the night table and taped the flashlight inside the lid of the suitcase where she couldn't reach it. He tried it out, almost closing the lid and then peering in through the crack. It looked shockingly bright in there. He taped one of the strips of silk over the lens of the flashlight and tried it again. It was quite cozy now. He put in the saucer of milk, wedging it into a corner with a fold of the sweater.

Everything was ready for her. All he had to do was get her inside.

She was sitting cross-legged on the floor, her hands raised to the back of her head. It was a moment before he realized what she was doing. She had pulled a thread out of the piece of silk he had given her and was binding up her hair with it. He could see her fingers moving deftly in and out as she gathered her hair into a glistening knot, the size of a match head, at the nape of her neck.

He was delighted by what he thought of as her cleverness: this proof that her mind worked like his own. He waited respectfully until she finished, before moving her into her new home. She gave her gathered hair a final touch. He reached down to pick her up.

He didn't touch her. It suddenly seemed so rude: to take her body between his finger and thumb, to move her like a chess piece into the suitcase. He laid his hand flat on the carpet beside her, inviting her to climb onto it.

"Up?" he whispered, remembering her decibel range.

She rose to her feet, letting the square of silk drop from her shoulder. But she ignored his hand.

Her head tilted slowly backward, returned to a level position, tilted back once more. He recognized instantly what she was doing. He had seen tourists go through the same motions when confronted by some sight familiar to them from their guidebooks. She was having a leisurely, critical look at him as he knelt, as naked as she was, in front of her, appraising him detail by detail and then as a whole.

Although he had never been interested in field sports, Bascombe had the natural slender grace of an athlete. His body, smooth-skinned and hard, had reminded several girls in the past of their first prurient awareness of male nudity: that disturbing interest they had felt as children in the classical sculpture sections of their home-town museums. She continued to look at him intently. She strode forward. His knees were slightly parted. She marched into the gap between them. There was nothing idle about her progress. She was unmistakably a sightseer with an objective. She reached the narrowest point of the canyon. The head of his cock blocked her path like a boulder. She raised her hand. She patted it. Bascombe could have sworn she patted it approvingly.

The touch of her hand was as light as a blade of grass. It tickled slightly and not at all unpleasantly. Bascombe felt some response was demanded of him. He curved the tip of his finger around her and stroked the small of her back. He could feel the two little mounds of her buttocks. He thought he could even feel their softness. She moved her hips slowly from side to side in response to his caress.

In spite of her size it did not once cross his mind that there was anything unnatural in this sudden physical intimacy between them. He was already too much aware of her as a woman.

34

It obviously hadn't crossed her mind either. She stretched her arms around the head of his cock and rubbed her cheek against it. She smiled up at him. Then with a quick light spring she gained a foothold on the rim of the inverted dome and began to swarm up the column.

It was an incomparable sensation. Bascombe's response to it this time was involuntary. Instead of climbing she was suddenly sitting astride. She gripped with her knees like a practiced horse-woman. She patted him again. There was no mistaking her approval this time.

She stood upright and advanced toward him, putting one foot directly in front of the other, as though balancing on a log. She halted an inch from his groin and looked up at his face. Her right hand rose to her mouth, paused there an instant, and then moved on in an arc, her fingers open, her arm flung wide.

She had blown him a kiss. It was a sportive salute to him, a token both of appreciation and promise. She repeated it, rising on her toes in her enthusiasm. Then she leaped onto his thigh, ran down to his knee, and, gathering herself in midstride, jumped straight into the suitcase.

Granted that his cashmere sweater had softened her fall, it was still an astonishing feat, Bascombe thought half an hour later, wandering into Paolo's restaurant. She had not only dropped at least eight times her own height and landed on her toes without losing her balance, she had also broad-jumped her equivalent of about twenty-five yards from his knee to the suitcase.

"Mr. Mitchel, please."

"Mister . . ." The headwaiter looked at his list. ". . . Mitchel."

"Thank you." Bascombe wondered what the Olympic broad-jump record was as he followed a Neapolitan in a San Tropez T-shirt to a corner table. He had an idea it was less than ten yards, anyway.

"Would you care for a drink while you're waiting, sir?"

"No, thank you." Bascombe hadn't had anything to eat since the evening before. He wished, too late, he had asked for a tomato juice. He crumbled a roll and put a piece of it in his mouth.

There was, he recalled from Physics 1, a simple reason for her astonishing prowess. The cubic relationship between size and weight. If you made something twice as big, you made it eight times as heavy. Equally, if you made anything—including, presumably, a human being—ten times as small, you made it a thousand times lighter. The bones and sinews and muscles were then a hundred times better fitted to cope with their own weight. It was one of the reasons the dinosaurs had failed, their limbs growing finally almost too heavy to move, and why insects had flourished. An ant could lift the equivalent of an oak tree and a cricket or even a cat could jump . . .

"Starting without us?" Mr. Mitchel was heavily good-humored as he patted Stanley Nolan toward the banquette beside Bascombe.

Bascombe swallowed the scrap of roll in his mouth and stood up.

"This is the Honourable Stanley Nolan."

"No, I'm not."

"Not what?"

"Not Honourable." Nolan slid down onto the base of his spine on the banquette and stretched his short legs under the table.

"I thought you British Members of Parliament . . ."

"Only when we're insulting each other. If you want to stand up in the House and call someone a shit, you refer to him as the Honourable Member for Huyton." Nolan looked up at Bascombe with melancholy friendliness. The irises of his eyes were so dark they looked black. "But you introduce him to other people as plain Mr. Shit."

Bascombe slid down onto the banquette beside Nolan. Mr. Mitchel took the chair facing them. Nolan crumbled a roll. The waiter gave them each a large gold-printed menu. There was a long silence.

Stanley Nolan was a surprise to Bascombe. He had expected a Labour Member of Parliament to look more or less like his Uncle Gerhard, who worked for the U.S. Employment Service in St. Louis. Bascombe's Uncle Gerhard was above all functional. Everything about him, his clothes, his manner, his opinions, were as carefully adapted to his function as a school bus. Slow, shabby, obviously durable. But Stanley Nolan was none of these things. In spite of the streaks of cigarette ash on his suit there was something defiantly elegant about him. Although he had not moved since the waiter had handed him the menu, he gave an impression of restlessness. Nolan was, above all, unpredictable, Bascombe thought.

"How about a drink?" The heavy good humor was back in Mr. Mitchel's voice.

"Large whiskey," Nolan told the waiter.

"Soda or water, sir? Ice?"

"No."

Mr. Mitchel ordered a Gibson on the rocks and explained to the waiter in detail how to make it. Bascombe got his tomato juice at last.

"I guess being a Member of Parliament . . ." Mr. Mitchel was off on his plodding roundabout course toward the Objective. "I guess you get a lot of crackpots asking you to lunch?"

Nolan did not contradict him. He did not even appear to have heard. He sat up suddenly and rested his elbows on the table.

"Do you think Johnson'll run again next year?" There was an irresistible deference in his manner. He might have been paying to consult Mr. Mitchel.

"Sure. Sure, he will." In that spring of 1967 almost any American in Mr. Mitchel's position would have given the same regretful, wrong answer.

"You don't like him?"

"I . . . " Mr. Mitchel dangled for an instant between honesty and tact. Nolan as a Labour bastard could be expected to approve, at least officially, of the Democratic Party. "I wouldn't say that . . ."

"You wouldn't? Pity." Nolan picked up his whiskey and slumped back in his seat. Bascombe waited. He had a feeling Nolan was about to dig a pit for Mr. Mitchel and that Mr. Mitchel was going to fall into it like a blind bear. But he had no impulse to stop him. In a minute, if he was right, Mr. Mitchel would be off on his most predictable monologue, the whole purpose of the meeting with Nolan would be screwed, and Bascombe could relax undisturbed for the rest of the meal. He finished his tomato juice.

"There's a general feeling in some quarters of our government." Nolan's night-colored eyes were focused on his own lap. "There's an increasingly strong body of opinion, in fact, that it would be a good thing if your Republicans got in next time."

"Yeah?" Bascombe could feel the brief struggle taking place on the other side of the table between the acquired suspicion Mr. Mitchel called Training and the outraged self-interest he called Conviction. He knew Mr. Mitchel too well to have any doubts about the outcome. It would all come rolling out in a moment. The whole tragic progression of undeserved injustice. Wall Street. Hoover. Depression. Roosevelt. New Deal. Wartime measures. Bretton Woods. Truman. Foreign aid. Planned economy. GOD-DAMNED GOVERNMENT INTERFERENCE.

Mr. Mitchel was headed straight for Nolan's bear pit, all right. Bascombe relaxed . . .

As soon as he had closed the lid of the suitcase behind him, she sat up on the huge pile of cotton she had been using for a bed and swung her legs over the side. She smiled. He started toward her. The tendrils of the cashmere came up to his shins, thick and resistant as corn stalks. He strode through them with careless ease. He was so strong he could have reached her in a single leap. She stood up to meet him as he approached her. Their naked bodies brushed lightly against each other. He raised his hands to her waist. Her skin was warm from the heat of the enormous light taped to the leather ceiling above them, her flesh so yielding he felt he could join his fingers around her waist. The top of her head was just below the level of his eyes. Her hair blazed in the light, a thousand varying shades of copper and gold. She lifted her mouth. Her tongue darted out, lingered, explored. They fell together onto the huge bed of coarse cotton. He slipped his hand . . .

"In Texas, Bascombe?"

"Deaf Smith County, Mr. Mitchel." Bascombe was as careful as usual not to sit up with a start, but he was a little surprised to discover he had almost finished his côte de veau. Mr. Mitchel must have come to the end of his monologue some time ago and was now approaching his pitch. He realized from Mr. Mitchel's encouraging smile he was expected to join him in making it. He turned toward Nolan.

"There was a natural deposit of calcium fluoride in the water."

Nolan looked at him with startled interest. "I didn't think you were listening."

"The local dentist discovered it."

"It's incredible."

"A man called George Heard."

"How do you do it?"

"Simple chemical formula. To every million parts of water . . ." Mr. Mitchel had taken over again. He outlined the chemical and mechanical process of fluoridating a public water supply. He outlined it firmly and persuasively. Nolan ignored him. He continued to watch Bascombe as he finished his veal.

"Do you think you could show *me* how to do it?" Nolan asked as soon as Mr. Mitchel had stopped talking.

"That's what we're here for. Our American company . . ."

Bascombe shrugged. He knew what Nolan was talking about even if Mr. Mitchel didn't.

"It'd be bloody useful in the House."

"Better to do it on a nationwide scale. Our company's prepared . . ."

Oh, shit, Bascombe thought. He wanted only to get back into that suitcase, onto that coarse cotton bed, between those thighs. But he knew Nolan was still watching him, waiting for him to relax so that he could lug him back out of it with another question, to test him, to see if he could do it again.

Mr. Mitchel and Nolan ordered brandy and cigars. Bascombe had some coffee. Mr. Mitchel continued to talk about calcium fluoride, its dental benefits, its incredible cheapness. For the first time in months Bascombe almost listened to him. That is, he actually consciously heard several words at the moment Mr. Mitchel spoke them.

"I don't pretend to understand the intricacies . . . Your British political system . . . I believe only a few M.P.'s . . . Each session of Parliament . . . Private Member's Bill . . . Your turn comes up next fall, I mean autumn. Right?"

Bascombe was suddenly reminded of his childhood. Coming out of a movie house into the daylight of a city street, still somehow physically captive to a world of highlighted tits, satin-sheened rumps, husky-voiced women who always finally said, "Mmm." Moving slowly, lightheadedly back into a world of perspiration, dirt, the wrinkled arm of the woman in the seat next to him on the bus, all the indignities of childhood waiting for him at home. Not absolutely certain yet which of the two was the more unreal.

The memory filled him with a sudden painful doubt. Had she really floated in that saucer of milk? Sported on his cock? Was she really there now in that suitcase on top of his closet? Or had he imagined the whole thing? Had she only been as much a creature of his own fantasy as the girl cantering ahead of him along the shore? Her sweet full buttocks now dipping out of sight, now suddenly presented to him whole . . .

"Goldwater, Mr. Fletcher?"

"No." Bascombe turned his head so that he was looking directly into Nolan's challenging eyes. "No, I was too young to vote in sixty-four."

Nolan smiled at him approvingly. He had passed the test.

Bascombe finished his coffee. He felt a faint momentary regret that he had lied to Nolan. His birthday was in September: he had not been too young to vote. Although he had never had any more interest in American politics than in fluoridating England, he had felt that, faced with the usual rival-gangs-of-identical-shits situation, any sensible citizen had a responsibility not to vote. He had an odd suspicion that even though Nolan was a Member of Parliament, he would understand this, might even agree with him.

"You must come and have a drink with me at the House one evening." Nolan was speaking to him again. "Please." He obviously meant it.

Bascombe thanked him absently. His regret had passed. It would have taken too long to be candid with Nolan, and impossible in front of Mr. Mitchel, anyway. While Nolan had been talking, his mind had returned to more immediate concerns. He thought he had never wanted anything so urgently in his life as he wanted at that moment to be back in his apartment; to take down that suitcase and see if she were really there.

"One evening next week?"

"Thank you." Still absently.

"You handled that okay," Mr. Mitchel admitted as they walked back toward the office after leaving Nolan. "He wants to get you alone. Pick your brains. Get the inside on our fluoridation project. You just keep playing it cool, Bascombe, and I think we've got him."

"I will."

"Just keep playing it cool." Mr. Mitchel skirted a woman with an indignantly leashed dog and plodded on in silence on his flat feet for a few yards.

"He's not such a bastard as I expected," he decided, stopping obediently for a red light at a deserted intersection. "Basically, he thinks like we do. He practically admitted he was a Republican, didn't he?"

The lights changed to green. The street in front of them flooded at once with cars making left turns. Bascombe didn't answer. He was quite sure Nolan was not a Republican, or a Democrat, or a Liberal, or a Conservative, or a Labour Bastard, or Anything Else. He was too intelligent for that brand-name crap. He had admitted nothing. He had sucked Mr. Mitchel into making admissions. At the first unwelcome pressure, the first direct request for official backing on the fluoride project, Nolan would simply recite Mr. Mitchel's monologue back at him. It was one of the contradictions in Mr. Mitchel's character that he could not see that his favorite monologue was the best possible argument against Goddamned Government Interference in such a private matter as the public water supply.

Bascombe touched Mr. Mitchel's elbow and led him safely through the momentarily stalled traffic to the opposite sidewalk. He had no intention of explaining any of this to Mr. Mitchel. He had no intention of wasting any more time even thinking about it. It had suddenly, disturbingly occurred to him that even if he went back to his apartment and opened that suitcase and found her there, it would prove nothing. He still couldn't be sure he wasn't imagining her, that she wasn't even then a creature of his own fantasy.

"I can't get used to it, the way these British cars come at you on the wrong side of the road."

The obvious way of testing her objective existence was to show her to someone else. But even if he hadn't felt so reluctant to reveal her, to share her with anyone anywhere, Bascombe couldn't think of anyone here in London to show her to. Mrs. Waddington? Hannah Cooper? Mr. Mitchel!

"Why the hell can't they drive on the same side as everyone else?"

Bascombe had a sudden gift of an idea. There was one way of testing at least her visual reality without involving anyone. He could do it now, this afternoon.

"The Japanese drive on the left, Mr. Mitchel."

"I can't hear you, Bascombe."

"So do the Irish."

"Stop whispering, goddamn it."

"I've got a sore throat."

"You smoke too much."

Bascombe shook his head. He sniffed. "I'm afraid I'm getting a cold," he lied hoarsely.

They walked on. Mr. Mitchel widened the distance between them a little. Ever since he had come to England Mr. Mitchel had been terrified of getting a cold. He had an almost superstitious idea that English colds were quite different from American ones, that what with the damp and all, you could practically die of a cold in England. Bascombe knew this. He walked on, waiting.

"Bascombe." Mr. Mitchel stopped and faced him across the full width of the sidewalk. He kept his hand in front of his mouth, speaking through his fingers. "Bascombe, maybe you better. You go on home, Bascombe. Straight home, you hear?"

Bascombe didn't walk to Leicester Square that day. He had lost all interest in the Strand, in the Underground, even in Earl's Court Road. But he didn't go straight home. He hurried instead to a camera shop he had noticed not far from Paolo's.

It was a small cluttered place that sold all sorts of photographic and optical equipment. Developers, tripods, enlargers, microscopes were stacked on top of each other like kindling. Bascombe asked for a Polaroid camera. He watched the clerk abstractedly as he searched for one. The impetus of the idea that had brought him here was waning fast. He was beginning to feel there was a certain treachery in what he was doing.

"I can let you have a nice secondhand Japanese Leica."

Bascombe shook his head. It had to be a Polaroid. Quite apart from the question of time, he had no intention of trusting any photographs of her to the prurience of a commercial lab.

"I know I've got one somewhere."

He would only take one picture, Bascombe excused himself. Just glance at it, make certain her image had registered, and then tear it up. He might have been promising his conscience he would only deflower the girl once and burn the bed afterward. His guilt, his treachery lay in the motive, the doubt.

"Here we are, then." The clerk wiped some of the dust off the box with the back of his hand and held it out to him. He didn't take it.

Christ, he thought. If Mr. Mitchel was real, she certainly was.

Outside on the street he changed his mind again. He went back into the shop. He picked up another box that had caught his attention. He held it out to the clerk.

"I'll take this instead."

"You sure now?"

Bascombe was quite sure. He paid the clerk for it and hurried back into the street. A taxi was just turning with awkward dignity, like a hippopotamus, at the corner. He caught it at the next stop light. As soon as the driver had closed the glass panel between them, Bascombe opened the box and took out the thing inside. It had cost almost twenty dollars, but it was worth it. It was well made, very powerful, and as he could see, testing it on his thumbnail, extremely accurate. But its real value, like that of gold, was symbolic. It was a token of his faith in her. Bascombe put the magnifying glass back in its box.

His cleaning woman had felt no impulse to work that day. Bascombe could see the still rumpled bed through the open door of his bedroom as he entered the apartment. He closed it behind him and pulled a chair over to the closet. He was careful not to tilt the case as he lifted it down. With the same concern he set it gently on the floor. He had the key ready in his hand. He slipped it into the lock at once. The slightest hesitation would have been a betrayal. He opened the lid.

She was there, all right. She was sitting up on her bed, yawning. She lifted her arms, stretching her whole body with the heedless discovery of a child waking from sleep. She stretched until she had composed herself to movement. Then she slipped down off the little pad of cotton and sauntered over to the saucer of milk in the opposite corner of the suitcase.

Bascombe was a little hurt; he had been looking forward so much to seeing her again; it was disappointing to be ignored. It had not yet occurred to him that because of her size, her defenselessness, she was forced to accept some of the conditions of childhood, and that a child's strongest weapon is acceptance, trust. He frowned reprovingly at her naked back.

But halfway to the saucer she paused and looked up at him. She smiled. She waved. It was more like a wink than a greeting. Instantly delighted, Bascombe smiled back. She walked on to the saucer and, cupping her hands, began to bathe her face in the milk. He took out the magnifying glass.

Her hips swam into focus: suddenly, as it seemed to him, almost life-size. He resisted the temptation to shift the lens at once to the pearl-like breasts, to discover those seemingly colorless nipples. There was plenty of time. He dwelt for several admiring moments on the perfect oval between her waist and her thighs, the graceful convexity between thigh and loin. He had been right this morning: every glorious detail, every shifting subtlety of a woman's body was present in miniature. He could see now that the golden triangle he had marveled at earlier was in fact composed of silken curls.

Bascombe snatched the glass aside. She was standing erect beside the saucer, rubbing milk into her cheeks. He brought the

44

glass back to her again. He watched her waist, her hips, her thighs move quickly in and out of focus. The sprinkling of curls appeared again. A moment of adjustment and they were sharp and clear.

Bascombe put the magnifying glass down on the carpet beside him. He almost stopped breathing in his excitement. He blinked. But there was no mistaking it. He could see it now with his naked eye. The rim of the saucer no longer reached to the vertex of her thighs. It was just below it.

There seemed to be only one possible explanation. In the few hours he had been away, her legs had gotten longer.

She was growing.

3

CHAPTER

"IN DREAMS begin responsibilities." Bascombe had forgotten where he had heard that phrase, but in the next few days he discovered the truth of it.

Like many of his generation he had always been a bit of a stranger. It wasn't only that possessions, status, God, all the things that had interested earlier Americans, had always either bored or disgusted him. He had never committed himself emotionally to anything else either. His only engagement had been in his surrender to affection: that gratitude he felt for the transcending moments he had shared with a variety of consenting young women.

Because of that he had almost no experience of the loss of freedom involved in being responsible for someone else. There had been a girl in New York once whom he had helped over an abortion. Although he was not the author of her condition, he had stayed in her apartment for a week, cooking her meals, fetching her milk and orange juice. He had known all along it was only a temporary situation, a role he was playing. At the end of the week the girl's mother had called her from Connecticut, and that same evening, coming home from the office to meet the mother, to have dinner with the two of them, Bascombe had gotten entangled instead with a plump secretary on the crosstown bus. He had never realized before how deliciously complaisant being overweight could make some women.

Now with the guest living in his suitcase Bascombe was no longer playing a role.

It was on a Wednesday she had appeared for the first time and he hurried back from lunch with Nolan to find she had grown. The next two mornings he called Mr. Mitchel at the office, sniffed and rasped at him over the phone, and was told to stay in bed. With the weekend he had four full days to spend with her.

It was during those four days Bascombe lost his freedom.

He no longer cared whether she existed outside his own mind or not. She was in the suitcase every morning when he opened it. She was *there* every second he was in a position to see her. She moved, she acted quite independently of him, and to that extent she also existed in her own right.

At the same time, because of her size, her obvious unfamiliarity with the customs and components of his world, she was dependent on him for everything she needed. For food, for warmth, for clothing, for cleanliness, above all for protection against the uncomprehended dangers of his apartment.

She could jump without hurting herself from the living room table to the floor. But she didn't understand about the hinges of doors, or hot water taps, or gas stoves, or refrigerators. She was an adventurous and fearless explorer, and it was appalling how many murderous traps for her his apartment contained. Things that could fall and crush. Things that could burn. Things that could smother. Things that could poison. She had a childlike tendency the first day or so to test the edibility of objects by eating them. As soon as he discovered this, he had to make a tour of the rooms, locking away matches, soap, cigarettes, shaving lotion, pepper, iodine, lighter fluid, disinfectant, aspirin, detergent, and so on, safely out of her reach.

He hated to curtail her physical freedom. He loved following her from room to room, watching her leap onto chairs, run across table tops, slide down cushions. But after he had followed her into the bathroom the first day just too late to stop her diving into the toilet bowl for a morning swim, he kept that door closed to her altogether.

And then there were the electric light sockets. They were just intriguing tunnels to her. She kept poking her head and her arms into them. Fortunately, he found, it was impossible for her to

47

force her hands far enough into the two contacts at once to electrocute herself.

The gas stove was another matter. It was no trick for her to hang by her hands from the rim of the stove and, swinging her legs, kick on one burner after the other. He kept lifting her down. He shook his head at her.

"No," he whispered. He was still careful to remember about her decibel range.

It was difficult to tell whether she understood him or not. Certain gestures were obviously meaningful to her: she used them herself. She shrugged. She nodded. She raised both hands in exasperation whenever Bascombe was slow about understanding her. But when he lifted her down from the stove and shook his head, she either didn't understand, or, and he thought this increasingly probable, she understood all right but was in no mood to obey him. As Bascombe soon realized, she was a willful creature, and with a strong sense of her own dignity.

She could be positively imperious. When he was sleeping alone, Bascombe usually wore pajamas. On Thursday morning, as soon as he woke up he rushed to the suitcase on the floor by the foot of the bed and flung it open. She seemed glad to see him at first. She had been lying in the milk saucer taking a bath, and she climbed out at once and jumped out of the suitcase onto his knee. She strolled up his thigh. Something seemed to be bothering her. She knelt down and scratched at the material of his pajamas stretched tightly over his thigh by his squatting position. She plucked at it, trying to get a firm hold on it to pull it clear of his leg. When she found this beyond her, she stood upright again and advanced to the intersection of his leg and hip where the cloth had bunched into folds below the waistband. She grasped one of these folds with both hands and pulled. It may not have seemed so to her, full of confidence in her own strength, but it was a reckless thing to do because she was so light.

The elastic waistband of his pajamas yielded to her tug and then snapped back into place. She was catapulted into the air and landed precariously on his shoulder.

She was furious. He could just see her out of the corner of his eye, hands on hips, scowling at him.

He held up his finger for her to step onto, to put her back on his knee. She refused his assistance. She slid down the piped edge of his pajama jacket like a sailor down a rope, dropped onto the carpet, and stepped back a few inches so that he had a clear view of her.

She began, still plainly tense with anger, to try to convey to him in gestures what she was after.

It was one of the times he was slow about understanding her. With mounting exasperation she kept touching her hands together in front of her almost imperceptible navel and then tearing them apart. She abandoned that effort finally in the face of his obtuseness, and tried little plucking motions at her breasts instead.

Bascombe still didn't get it. He was perhaps being unusually stupid, but he had only known her for twenty-four hours, and in spite of their brief intimacy the day before, he had very little insight yet into her wants and values. His own mind was still moving along practical lines—food, water, warmth—in his efforts to understand her.

It wasn't until she jumped back into the suitcase, picked up one of the scraps of silk he had given her, and went through the performance of first casually dressing and then explicitly undressing herself that he realized what she wanted.

She wanted him to take those freaking pajamas off.

He obeyed her at once. She rewarded him with a smile and one of her approving pats on his cock. After that, whenever he was with her in the apartment, Bascombe went around as naked as she did.

She preferred to be naked most of the time. Occasionally she would take one of those scraps of silk and drape it around her waist, folding it over and tucking in the loose end so that it hung from her hips like a skirt.

The first time she did this, on Thursday morning after her milk bath, Bascombe was watching her through the magnifying

49

glass. She had her hands raised to the back of her neck, gathering her hair. Both her arms were hidden from him by the loose tresses that still fell over her shoulders. Her weight was on her right leg, that hip slightly protruded, the other knee bent. For a moment there was something hauntingly familiar to him about her, about the way she was standing, the set of her head, the folds of the silk as they were draped over her left thigh.

The association, whatever it was, was lost as soon as she moved. Bascombe tried to recapture it several times, but it eluded him, maddeningly, like a name.

And all the time she was growing. By Friday morning the rim of the saucer was a full eighth of an inch below her tiny golden pussy. Bascombe tried not to put too much hope in the implications of this. Because she had grown perhaps a quarter of an inch in two days, it did not necessarily follow that she would go on growing at that rate. Mice, kittens grew very quickly at first but at a certain point they stopped. She might very well reach her full height at three inches, or six, or perhaps even a foot, or . . .

Or she might not. But the prospect that she might one day become a full-grown woman in his own human terms was too dazzling to think about. It was like staring into the sun.

He could wait for the future. There was enough wonder in the moment to keep him entranced, and more than busy. By Friday morning he had started to introduce a rough routine into their life together.

Because he dared not leave her alone with the full run of the apartment, and because she protested so indignantly at being locked back into the suitcase when he had to go out to buy her milk, or apple juice, or new batteries for the flashlight, he didn't open the suitcase on Friday morning until he got back from his errands. After that, when he had changed her milk and her bedding, and she had had her bath in one saucer and her breakfast in another, he watched her through the glass while she arranged her hair.

There was a strong natural wave in it. Even when she drew it back to her nape and plaited and bound it into a knot there, it would not lie flat but rippled and curled back from her brow. She had a fine forehead and a straight high-bridged nose. The kind of nose that has come to be associated in the English language with some idealized imaginary aristocracy. Her mouth was full and, even in repose, vividly expressive. There was a serenity in the set of the lips and at the same time an awareness, an understanding, and a suggestion of amusement. The modeling of her cheeks was extraordinary: the planes merged so subtly into each other that seen from any frontal angle the lower half of her face was a perfect ellipse.

It took her only a few minutes to dress her hair. Bascombe wished it took longer. It was almost the only time she stood still enough for him to get her into accurate focus through the lens and look at her at his pleasure. Her nipples were not colorless but a very pale rose, as poignantly delicate as the eyelids of a child.

A final touch to her hair and she was off into the living room with Bascombe still hopefully carrying the magnifying glass after her. There was an antique couch under the living room window, rather surprisingly upholstered in blue satin. She made straight for it, bounding across the carpet with six-inch strides. Arrived on its worn surface, she stood waiting for Bascombe to catch up with her. She pointed to the unoccupied area of the couch, as vast and open to her as a public square. She wanted him to sit beside her.

For half an hour or so she gave him her concentrated attention as she explored his naked body. She made him lie down, and curling up on his nipple, rubbed her cheek and, as he could just see, her mouth against it, until the tip of it swelled to the size of her own head. This amused her enormously. She had still never made any vocal sounds that he could hear. But it was obvious from the bobbing of her firm little breasts that she was breathless with laughter.

She stood up and loitered for a while around his navel, stepping down into the crater and then back onto the rim like a child playing in a sandbox.

She appeared to consider his other nipple. But then turned her back on it and made instead for the shrubbery of his pubic hair. She walked through it like an Amazon, parting the bushes with her hands as she advanced and letting them spring back into place behind her. She reached the base of his cock. She sat down there for a moment with her feet on either side of it. Then, launching herself forward, half slid, half swarmed down the trunk until she reached the head. Still dangling face downwards, gripping tightly with her arms and thighs, she rubbed her breasts and belly against it until it began, inevitably, to respond to her attentions.

It rose gradually, like a tree being hauled upright for planting. She still clung to the trunk with arms and thighs, but she was no longer upside-down now. She turned her head. He caught a glimpse of her face. She was smiling delightedly.

She resumed the quick sinuous motion of her hips. Bascombe could only stand it for a few seconds. Although she was gripping him with all her considerable strength, the friction of her body was so light, so delicate, that it was torture.

He put out his hand to restrain her, to lift her off him, if he could. And then suddenly started upright off the couch altogether.

There was a second clicking sound from the front door of the apartment. The latch snapped back, the door started to swing open.

Bascombe glanced quickly, anxiously down. His leap off the couch had not dislodged her. She was still clinging to him like a shipwrecked sailor to a spar. He cupped his hand gently around her and ran for the bedroom, as a middle-aged woman carrying a string bag entered through the front door.

His cleaning woman had had one of her impulses.

Bascombe slammed the bedroom door closed behind him and stood quite still, listening, figuring. She had probably had a fairly clear view of his naked back as he fled across the living room, but he did not think she could have seen more than that from the front door. Even if she had caught a glimpse of his cock, she could not possibly have had time to distinguish the little figure clinging to it.

Relieved, Bascombe sat down cautiously on the bed. He held his hand under his groin, praying this would not be one of the times when she was in no mood to obey him. It wasn't. She dropped instantly into his palm. He lifted her to his mouth.

"Listen," he whispered. "You've got to go back in the suitcase. Back in the suitcase. Until she's gone. Please."

He never knew whether she understood him or not, because at that moment there was a knock on the door, and she reacted instantly to that in her usual way. She frowned at him reprovingly and covered her ears with her hands. The open suitcase was only a foot away on the floor. Bascombe took advantage of her momentary unwariness to reach out and topple her gently into it. He closed the lid after her.

"Are you home, sir?" Whatever she had seen of him, his cleaning woman had evidently decided to play it cool.

"Yes. Just a minute." He pushed the suitcase half under the bed with his foot and looked around for some clothes. He snatched up a pair of trousers and a shirt.

One of the comparatively ordinary, but still complicating factors about the present situation was that Bascombe had never until then set eyes on his cleaning woman. She worked for the people who owned the apartment; she was paid by the agency out of the rent; he had never been home before when she came.

He buttoned his shirt and opened the bedroom door. She was standing just the other side of it.

Inevitably in the weeks he had lived there he had formed a rough mental image of the woman. She was an excellent cleaner in her impulsive way, thorough with a duster, and given to rearranging his personal things, the clothes in his drawers, the letters on his mantelpiece into symmetrical patterns. And, as he had always thought, having a good look at them in the process. Because of this he had pictured her as thin, long-nosed: one of that bedraggled army of English women who had been defeated by peace and were to be found in any station buffet, slopping cups of tea at you as if they hoped they might poison you.

He had been dead wrong. The woman facing him was, perhaps, forty-five, stout without being fat, handsome, immaculately groomed, and supremely sure of herself. She looked a little like the Queen Mother.

"How do you do, sir. I'm Mrs. Charrington."

"How do you do." Bascombe went through his usual moment of American uncertainty about holding out his hand and finally did. She shook it.

"I'm sorry. I wasn't feeling well. I had a cold. So I stayed home today."

"I'm very glad to meet you at last, sir. I've been hoping we could have a little talk."

"Wouldn't you like to sit down?"

Mrs. Charrington's manner was so overwhelmingly gracious that after she had considered this suggestion and finally settled herself bolt upright on the couch, Bascombe himself remained standing in her presence. He wondered what she wanted to talk to him about. About having girls up here? That leaping Scot had probably left traces of her London visit.

"It's about your shirts, sir."

"My shirts?"

"I notice you've been sending them to the Millstream Laundry."

Bascombe nodded. The Millstream Laundry had come with the apartment, too. It came every Monday morning and woke him up: a mild little man with a cardboard suitcase who waited patiently while Bascombe collected and stuffed his dirty clothes into it.

"The Millstream Laundry are quite satisfactory for under-things, sir. But I think you should send your dress shirts to a hand laundry."

"Of course. Whatever you like." It was all a deep mystery to Bascombe. Why the hell should she care where he sent his shirts? He had never met anyone like Mrs. Charrington before, and it was to be a long time before he understood the answer to that question. "Was that all you wanted to talk to me about?" he asked hopefully.

Mrs. Charrington smiled and stood up. The audience was at an end. Bascombe stepped automatically aside as she sailed past him into the bedroom.

He caught up with her just inside the door. He glanced instantly at the suitcase projecting from beneath the bed. Mrs. Charrington glanced at it, too. Its asymmetrical position obviously offended her. She stooped.

To straighten it? To put it back on top of the closet? Bascombe didn't wait to find out. He managed to reach it first. He slid it toward him, holding the lid down with his fingers. He went on sliding it along the floor, until he had it in the living room. Mrs. Charrington was starting to pull the sheets off his bed as he closed the door on her.

He waited a moment and then cautiously pushed back the lid. The cashmere sweater, the little pad of surgical cotton, the two saucers were all in their usual places. But they were the only things in the suitcase. In his startled haste he had forgotten to lock it, and she had somehow managed to raise a corner of the lid and escape.

The full horror of this took an instant to hit him. The full horror of it was that she was now somewhere in the bedroom with Mrs. Charrington.

The next moment Bascombe was in there with them. He looked desperately around. Mrs. Charrington straightened from the half-made bed.

"Have you misplaced something, sir?"

"No." It must have been obvious to her he was lying. His glance kept moving about the room as if he expected a misplaced tiger to jump out of a corner at him. Mrs. Charrington's puzzled eyes searched the room, too.

It was Bascombe who saw her first. She was standing on top of the chest of drawers. For some reason, from some sudden sense of modesty, she had brought one of the scraps of silk out of the suitcase with her and was draping it in her usual fashion around her hips. The next instant Mrs. Charrington saw her.

Bascombe moved instinctively, protectively toward her. Mrs. Charrington followed him and stood looking over his shoulder at the tiny figure standing between his hairbrush and his cufflinks.

She might not understand about gas stoves or refrigerators but she certainly understood about people. She did the only thing she could possibly have done to protect herself against Mrs. Charrington's curiosity. She kept perfectly still.

She was standing in one of her habitual positions. The weight on her right leg, that hip slightly protruded. The draped silk falling across her left knee. Her head serenely, proudly level.

"It's very pretty, sir. Such pretty colors."

Bascombe turned and looked at Mrs. Charrington. She was smiling, obviously intrigued.

"I've seen one of those before, sir," she explained calmly. "One of my other gentlemen had one." She studied the little motionless figure in silence. She seemed puzzled by something about it.

"But his was different, sir." Her voice had regained its gracious certainty.

"The other gentleman's didn't have any arms."

In a single sentence Mrs. Charrington had answered the two questions that had been nagging Bascombe. She had confirmed the objective reality of his guest: he was not the only one who could see her. And she had explained why she was so hauntingly familiar to him.

From then on Bascombe, too, always thought of her as Venus.

4

CHAPTER

AFTER MRS. CHARRINGTON had left with a parcel of his dirty shirts that Friday afternoon, Venus was in an unusually serious mood. She had something on her mind, and as soon as she had gotten him undressed again she set out to convey it to him.

They were in the living room. He had pulled a chair up to the table and, resting his chin on his hands, was ready to give her his full attention. She started to strut up and down in front of him. She puffed out her cheeks and, cupping her hands under her breasts, protruded her belly.

Bascombe nodded encouragingly. The first part of the message was "Mrs. Charrington."

Venus turned and faced him. She lifted her hand, finger extended, and waved it under his nose like a windshield wiper. Bascombe got that at once, too. He had seen women make that gesture to their kids in Little Italy: "Forbidden."

He nodded again and waited for the next bit.

Venus put her hands on her hips. He watched her intently. She kept her hands on her hips. He realized with dismay that that was all there was. That was the message: no more Mrs. Charrington. Venus wasn't going to have cleaning women busting in on them like that.

Bascombe agreed with her. But he didn't see what he could do about it. He couldn't fire Mrs. Charrington. And once he went back to work he couldn't stop her popping in whenever she happened to feel like it.

Worst of all, he couldn't think of any way of explaining this to Venus. There was no sign language he could devise for, "She doesn't work for me. She's paid by the agency." He tried whispering it several times slowly in English, but it was clear from Venus' reaction he was not getting through to her. She kept waving her finger at him. Bascombe nodded and shrugged to convey his helplessness. As often happens between two people, even when they speak the same language, the harder each tried to get his separate message across, the more separated they became. Until in the end Venus stalked off into the suitcase and went to sleep.

Bascombe drifted into the kitchen and fried himself some eggs. He had had nothing to eat yet that day. He felt guilty and depressed as he ate them.

He could protect Venus from Mrs. Charrington's curiosity easily enough for a while. He could stay home with the chain on the door and get her safely out of the way each time before he let Mrs. Charrington in. But that was only postponing decision. Another few days of hoarse telephone excuses and Mr. Mitchel would be calling the Embassy for an American doctor. Then he would either have to go back to work or quit his job.

That was where the guilt came in. Bascombe was afraid of quitting his job. He was not prepared to cut himself off from everything he rejected. The whole boring, irrelevant world of Mr. Mitchel was too necessary to him. It was the base camp from which he set out on his own voyages of discovery.

He knew, of course, that millions of other young men were discovering they could get all the sex and most of the other things they wanted with no base, no supplies except a handful of beads and a faceful of hair. But that required a certain holy arrogance which he lacked. In his pursuit of happiness he had always had to rely on the trappings of eligibility. As Hannah Cooper had guessed, taking girls out to dinner cost him a lot of money.

As he made himself some coffee, he excused himself with the thought that he had no intention, no desire to take any girls out to dinner now. He wanted to hang onto his job only for Venus. She needed a home, a settled refuge, regular meals.

He poured the coffee and took it into the bedroom. She slept all lax, splayed out like a child. Through the magnifying glass he could see the tip of her tongue lying over her teeth as limply as velvet. If he could only explain things to her, he thought. She might not mind so much being locked up in the suitcase if she understood why he had to do it. That was the real problem. As Mr. Mitchel would have put it, they had a communications hangup.

It was not until a week later, on the following Friday, that Bascombe discovered, through a series of further misunderstandings, how to solve the problem.

Venus was almost three inches tall by then. He had surreptitiously measured her the night before while she was lying on his thigh. She had grown a full inch in a week.

He spent a relaxed Friday at the office savoring the implications of that. An inch a week. At that rate she would reach five feet, his arbitrary threshold of nubility, in fifty-seven weeks. Unless, of course, she stopped growing altogether at some point. Bascombe no longer believed she would. He was becoming addicted to staring into the sun. He looked at his calendar. May 19, 1967. Add fifty-seven weeks. He pulled a scratch pad toward him and wrote "Saturday, June 22, 1968" on it in large festive letters. It did not seem impossibly far away . . .

It was a beautiful morning. He had been sleeping on the couch in the living room for the past few months so that Venus could have the double bed to herself. The sun woke him early. It was like a birthday in childhood, or the first day of the summer holidays. As soon as he opened his eyes every part of his body was suffused with awareness that this was the day. He made her some coffee and took it into her. Although her eyes were closed she was not asleep. She smiled as he put the cup down on the night table. There was no need for speech, for any further communication between them. She pulled her hands out from under the bedclothes, stretching her parted arms to him. The sheet slipped off her breasts. She kicked the rest of the bedclothes aside. The proportions of her body were so perfectly balanced that lying there naked she looked much taller than five feet . . .

"June the twenty-second, Bascombe?"

"It's my mother's anniversary, Mr. Mitchel."

"I thought your mother was dead."

"My father's dead. My mother's in St. Louis."

"That report I asked you for about our meeting with Nolan, goddamn it."

"It's in my out basket." Although he had no recollection of having written it, he could see it there through the wire mesh.

Mr. Mitchel, who had recently succumbed to the inefficient English grandeur of having things hand-made for him, had an appointment with "his little shirt man" at five. Bascombe left the office by the next elevator.

He no longer walked to Leicester Square these days. He ran to the nearest subway station, Temple, went straight to Earl's Court on the District Line, standing by the door all the way, leaped up the station stairs, and sprinted home down Earl's Court Road without a glance at the parade of birds along it.

He could see before he entered the apartment that it had been one of Mrs. Charrington's days. Every morning before he went to work that week he had left a message for her, thumbtacked to the outside of the front door: "Please do not disturb suitcase on top of closet. It contains bowls of fermenting yogurt and must not be tilted. Thank you. B. Fletcher."

The note was gone at last. The bed looked as though it had been made by a pastry cook. There was a pile of immaculate shirts on the chest of drawers. He glanced hurriedly at the note pinned to them: "I hope you will find these more satisfactory, sir. I am afraid mice have got into your yogurt. I heard them distinctly. But I did not disturb them regarding your instructions. Mrs. Charrington."

Bascombe lifted the suitcase carefully down onto the bed. Venus had obviously been waiting for her release for some time. And not patiently. She gave him a look of reproach as he pushed back the lid. He couldn't blame her. Because of the harrowing difficulty of getting her back into the suitcase before he left for work he had stopped letting her out in the mornings lately. She had been locked up since he had gone to bed, just after midnight. Almost eighteen hours. And today she had had the further irritation of

60

hearing Mrs. Charrington treading majestically around outside her prison.

"It's Friday night." Bascombe tried to propitiate her with whispered promises as he changed her bedding. "We've got two whole days. You won't have to be shut in. All day tomorrow and Sunday. You'll be absolutely free."

She paid no attention to him. After that first accusing look, she jumped out of the suitcase and strolled away from him across the counterpane, glancing about her at the hill of the pillows, the distant architecture of the chest of drawers, with indifferent suffrance. Except for her nakedness she might have been a tourist strolling across the piazza outside her hotel, wondering how to put in a couple of hours before plane time, bored, aimless, resolved only to ignore the importuning natives.

He longed to go after her, to catch her hand, turn her toward him, put his arms around her and hold her. He stretched out his finger instead and touched the small of her back. The little lobes of her bottom reminded him of the wild white grapes that used to grow along the river banks when he was a child.

She stopped. She looked at him over her shoulder. She had expected to be subjected to these insufferable familiarities in this godforsaken place. She stalked on across the piazza and jumped down onto the carpet.

Bascombe sighed and went back to his chores. He had furnished a corner of Venus' living quarters with the plastic cap from a bottle of Vieux Ceps, and she was scrupulous about using it. He emptied the droppings in it—they were the size of birdseed—down his own john, and washed it carefully under the hot tap before putting it back in the suitcase.

He picked up the two milk saucers and took them into the kitchen and washed them too. But when he went to refill them he found the bottle in the refrigerator was empty.

Oh, screw Mrs. Charrington, Bascombe thought. She had gone and drunk a whole pint of Venus' milk. The appalling thing was that if Venus was to have any dinner tonight he would have to get her into that suitcase again so that he could go out and buy some more. Miserably, apprehensively, already hating himself for

61

the deed before he had accomplished it, he returned to the bedroom.

Venus was sitting cross-legged on the chest of drawers. She had pulled a bristle out of his clothes brush and she appeared to be cleaning her toenails with it. She did not look up at him as he hovered in front of her.

It had sometimes happened to Bascombe when he was sleeping with a girl, "banging her every night" as Hannah Cooper had put it, that the very intensity of their pleasure in each other had aroused that contrary mood in her, that impulse to end what (surely?) cannot last which is such a common American reaction to happiness. Silence, sullenness, accusations had followed. Bascombe had never been able to tolerate this. At the first sign of a sulk he had always fled.

The extraordinary thing now was that, faced with Venus' scowls, the idea of flight never crossed his mind. He wanted only to placate her, to win her back somehow, *anyhow,* to her usual serenity.

At the same time he was puzzled. There had been a hint of reproach from her every evening this week when he had freed her from her hours of confinement. But her ill-humor had soon passed; she had quickly recovered her high spirits; and last night she had been particularly jocund.

He continued to hover in front of her. She continued with her pedicure.

He wondered anxiously if there was anything wrong with her physically. It had been worrying him that, as she grew, there was proportionately less and less air for her in the suitcase. Already, at three inches tall, she had the equivalent of only half an indoor tennis court to breathe in. He would drill some holes in it this weekend, he decided, or maybe take the whole back off and replace it with wire mesh.

She had finished with her toes. She threw the bristle aside, and, without once looking at him, walked over to the soft leather box in which he sometimes remembered to keep his cufflinks. She pushed back the lid and began to rummage through the things inside. Bascombe craned forward to see if there was anything she could hurt herself with. There did not seem to be: a couple of tie clips he had been given and never wore; a paper fastener; a squashed Ping-Pong ball; an American penny and three French francs; an assortment of those removable plastic collar struts which he never wore either.

She took these things up one by one. The French franc became a dinner tray in her hands. She examined each of them with her usual curiosity. She threw them all back except one of the collar struts. Balancing that over her shoulder like a plank, she carried it to the edge of the chest of drawers and hurled it into space. It dropped onto the carpet. She bent her knees slightly and swung back her arms, ready to jump after it.

Bascombe held out his hand to help her down. As soon as she stepped onto his palm he was going to grasp her by the hips and put her back in prison. She was going to struggle and kick and flail at his fingers with her petal-light hands. His only consolation was that the pitch of her voice was still beyond the range of his ear: he wouldn't be able to hear her screams. He hoped to God she would ignore his proffered, treacherous assistance.

She didn't. She shrugged: "Oh, well." She looked at him. She smiled. She stepped onto his palm.

Bascombe set her gently down on the carpet.

As he slipped out of the room, closing the door carefully behind him, and ran into the hall and down the stairs to the street, he reassured himself with the thought that she *had* seemed to be learning from experience lately. She stayed clear of the gas stove now. She avoided door hinges. She seemed to have lost all interest in light sockets.

There was a delicatessen halfway up Earl's Court Road that was open. He thrust a two-shilling piece into the girl's hand for the milk and didn't wait for the change. He was panting slightly as he opened the bedroom door.

He did not see her at first. He put the milk down on the chest of drawers and searched the carpet in front of him before stepping any further into the room. She wasn't on the bed either. Something glinted on the mantelpiece.

Bascombe had once seen a woman run out of a tenement on

63

Third Avenue and snatch a child out of the path of a skidding taxi. The woman had gasped in exactly the same furious way as he did now.

But he didn't run to Venus. He forced himself to walk over to the mantelpiece. A single startled movement and she would cleave herself on the razor blade she was balancing between her legs. He grasped her gently by the waist from behind and very slowly lifted her clear of the blade's edge until it toppled sideways and fell flat.

A minute later, after he had locked it away in the bathroom cabinet, he felt so weak he had to sit down on the rim of the bath to recover before he went back into the bedroom.

Venus was still on the mantelpiece, standing in front of the mirror. She had what looked like a white stick about the size of a tea leaf in her hand and was rubbing her head with it.

Bascombe watched her irritably. He resented that instant of terror Venus had caused him. He wanted to make her aware of his resentment. But she was so absorbed in dabbing at her hair that he was at first even more irritated; then puzzled and intrigued. Finally he began to share her absorption. He got the magnifying glass to see more clearly what she was up to.

He brought her moving hand into focus. He watched it, astounded, through the glass. He saw what she was doing. He realized what she had done.

It was one of those sudden moments of understanding that advances the relationship between two people onto a different plane. For all the physical candor between them, his awareness of her as a woman, his dreams of treating her like one, Bascombe had never really regarded Venus as an equal. Because of her size, her dependence on him, he had persisted, in many ways, in thinking of her as a child.

Now all was instantly changed between them, changed forever.

She had not been playing with that razor blade on the mantelpiece. She had not chosen that collar strut idly as a toy. Holding the blade between her knees, she had pared off a sliver of the plastic; then she had cut regular wedge-shaped incisions in the paring to form teeth. She had made herself a perfect miniature comb, and she was combing her hair with it.

It made Bascombe realize, as perhaps nothing else could have done, that he was dealing with a deliberate, inventive, adult intelligence. He was dealing with a mind not similar but equal to his own.

She paused and looked at him in the mirror. He was still wearing his gray office suit. She raised her hand curtly to her breast as though fingering a lapel and went back to her combing.

As he undressed Bascombe was shocked by his own stupidity. All her swinging from the gas stove, her probing of the light sockets, had been not play but experiment: logical efforts to familiarize herself with a new world. He should have realized this the first time he saw her bind up her hair with a thread pulled out of that square of silk he had given her. But his stupidity was natural enough, he supposed. Whole generations of Europeans confronted with unfamiliar equals had persisted willfully in regarding them, at best, as inferior children. Millions still did.

He glanced at her guiltily, surreptitiously. Her hair was growing, too. Combed out, it reached below her shoulder blades now. He had always liked girls with long hair. By the time Venus was five feet tall it would be down to her waist, a great plume of gold.

He restrained his galloping imagination. It was just as bad to think of her like that, as a promised event, a kind of movable feast.

He sat there penitent and naked on the bed, determined from now on to consider her as an equal individual.

It simplified their domestic arrangements immediately. As an adult, Venus could safely be left alone in the apartment, or in the bedroom anyway, now that she had familiarized herself with its hazards. She could sleep in the open suitcase at night and return to it during the day whenever she was hungry or felt like a bath or a rest.

There remained only the problem of Mrs. Charrington. And he could see how to solve that easily enough. If he rigged up some kind of warning signal that operated as soon as Mrs. Charrington unlocked the front door, Venus would have plenty of time to hide before Mrs. Charrington got to the bedroom. Instead of leaving the suitcase open, he could cut a little door in the back of it for her, and she could hide in the case, among the not-to-be-tilted-please-do-not-disturb yogurt, until Mrs. Charrington left.

He got up and walked across the living room to the front door. It was fitted with the usual type of snap lock. He turned the knob and opened the door a few inches. It would be simple enough to wire the latch to the front doorbell, so that when it was drawn back the bell would ring in the apartment. He didn't think it would sound frighteningly loud, through the closed bedroom door, even to Venus. He stepped out into the corridor and tried it.

"Wednesday would be super."

For an instant the two of them confronted each other: the girl in the fringed leather dress who had just come out of the apartment across the hall and the naked Bascombe ringing his own front doorbell. She didn't start. She didn't pretend he wasn't there. Her glance slid over him as gently as a feather duster.

"Wednesday would be super," she repeated enthusiastically to someone out of sight in the apartment. She reached behind her and delicately, firmly closed the door. She walked off down the hall.

There were times when there was a lot to be said for the English cool, Bascombe thought, slipping back into his living room. He would go out and buy the wire and the fittings for the alarm system tomorrow morning and install it over the weekend.

Venus had finished with her hair and was glad to see him back. It wasn't until he was lying on the bed and she was curled up on his chest that the one great flaw in his idea hit him. How was he going to explain to Venus what the bell meant?

It would have been easier if he hadn't been so determined to treat her as an adult individual. Pets could be conditioned to jump through hoops at the ringing of a bell. But Bascombe was enthralled with Venus' new image in his mind. The more rationally and deliberately she acted, the more unpredictable and exciting she was to him. Now when she stood up and began to saunter down toward his groin, she wasn't merely bent on pleasuring him, she was paying him an extraordinary compliment. She was doing it because she wanted to.

Any communication between them must be on that level. She must not be trained to react to the bell; she must understand what it meant. Brr-brr means Mrs. Charrington. Without speech, how could one adult convey that concept to another adult? Bascombe raised his head. In a moment Venus would reach her objective, and he would no longer be able to think coherently about anything. He forced his mind to the problem in the moment that remained. Brr-brr equals Mrs. Charrington. It wasn't a concept. It was an equation. It could be expressed in symbols. Pictures.

Three minutes later Bascombe was sitting at the living room table with a pad of paper in front of him and a pencil in his hand. Venus was standing a little grumpily where he had set her down at the edge of the pad. He reached around her and began.

He could draw quite well in an untaught way. He started to sketch a stout middle-aged woman carrying a string bag. Venus' grumpiness disappeared at once. He held her interest from the first line. He extended the woman's right arm from her shoulder. He projected a key from her hand. He roughed in the outline of a door. Halfway down the edge of it he drew an explicitly detailed lock, a keyhole. He paused.

Venus turned and looked at him. There was no crescent of white between her lips; her eyes were almost hidden by her frown. She pointed to the drawing. She raised her index finger and waved it back and forth. She had identified the woman as Mrs. Charrington. He felt like clapping his hands. She continued to wave her finger at him. Forbidden. He held up his palm. Wait.

He boxed off the first drawing and started another one beside it. With his technical education he had no trouble sketching a bell: the magnetic coil, the gong, the striker. He had reached the most difficult part, to express the sound. Recalling the language of comic books, he drew jagged lines of lightning spreading out from the edge of the gong where the striker touched it. He paused again.

Venus remained quite still, watching the pad. It was impossible to tell from her back, the set of her head, whether she understood or not. Without any real hope of clarifying his meaning, more as an embellishment than anything else, he wrote, "B-r-r! B-r-r!" among the lightning.

Venus craned quickly forward. He held his breath. She turned and faced him. The frown was still there, but it was no longer forbidding. It was a frown of incomprehension.

Exasperated with himself for not having thought of it before, Bascombe ran to the front door. This time he opened it only just wide enough to slide his hand out and reach the bell. He pressed it. He looked at Venus.

She didn't seem to have heard a sound. She was completely absorbed in playing with the pencil. She had lifted it from the table, managed to stand it upright, and was holding it like a pole vaulter ready to start his run.

He kicked the door closed and hurried back to her. He had been as wrong about the pencil as he had about the razor blade. She had the point pressed against the pad and was moving it carefully and methodically over the paper. She was trying to draw something with it.

Considering that the pencil was twice as tall as she was and as big around as her thigh, she was managing surprisingly well. She could control the motion of the enormous thing but not the pressure. The lead skittered so lightly across the surface of the pad that it left almost no impression behind it.

Bascombe grasped the pencil and started to pull it away from her. She resisted indignantly, glaring up at him over her shoulder. He gave her a reassuring smile, tugging a little harder, until she yielded. He bit into the sharpened end and gnawed it open. With his fingernail he pried a half-inch of lead out of the groove. He presented it to Venus.

She smiled. She nodded her congratulations. Kneeling on the pad and holding the piece of lead in her clenched fist like a pestle, she began to pull it firmly across the paper.

It was one of the great moments of Bascombe's life. Ten years ago in a locked physics lab in Missouri he had felt something of the same awed sense of anticipation, of imminent discovery, watching a senior named Louise Pringle unzip her blue-jeans realizing that the time of speculation and fancy was almost over at last: within a few seconds he was finally going to *know* what it was like.

Venus worked rapidly with the stub of lead. As an illustrator she appeared to be more of an impressionist than he was. She showed little concern with details. The swift, looping, unbroken line she began with was recognizable as a fish, but she didn't bother to give it an eye or to complete its tail. She was already busy erecting a pagoda beside it. A flat roof with wide eaves. No windows or door. Bascombe watched her intently, beginning to be a little puzzled, as she dashed off what might have been a swan beside the pagoda. Still kneeling, she sprawled across the swan to reach a clear space on the paper beyond it, and her next effort was hidden from him by her bottom, but whatever it was it took her only a moment to complete it.

She rose to her feet and stepped down from the pad. There was an element of challenge in the way she swung around, hands on hips, waiting for his reaction. But Bascombe was only tenuously aware of that: he was too fascinated by the finished work in front of him. He saw it now for the first time as a whole.

απιτω

He understood its significance at once. The mathematical symbol pi, π, was as familiar to him as a dollar sign. He recognized the fish now, too. It was an alpha. A Greek "a."

Bascombe's heart was pulsing as excitedly as it ever had in that physics lab. The whole realm of connection, of revelation and discovery, was open to them now. There was no longer any need for pictures, for signs. Venus could write. She had just written him a message. It was there on the paper in front of him, as startling as truth. απιτω. There was only one problem still to be faced. She had written to him in Greek, and he couldn't read a word of the language.

He looked at Venus. They looked at each other. He saw the challenge in her eyes quite clearly this time, but he interpreted it as an appeal. He still knew very little of the workings of her mind and naturally ascribed his own mental processes to her. He was intent only on breaking through that last frail barrier of language between them, on communicating with her, communicating anything. It did not occur to him that Venus was ahead of him, that she might have something to say and that all *her* will was concentrated on saying it.

He snatched up the pencil and chewed the broken end until he had bared enough of the lead to write with. Several other letters of the Greek alphabet were commonly used in mathematics, phi, theta, and so on. And although he had steered clear of all fraternities in college, he had spent many happy hours in various sorority houses, and he remembered some of the Greek capitals, Sigma, Kappa, Delta, Beta, Chi, which had adorned their porches. This gave him perhaps a dozen Greek letters to work with. He also knew there were several Greek words that had filtered down into the English language pretty much unchanged. If he could find one of those words which contained enough of the Greek letters he could write, Venus might recognize it. They would still not have found a common language, but like two ships hooting at each other through a fog they would have at least established mutual contact. Tomorrow he would buy a Greek dictionary and send her more articulate signals.

Words derived from the Greek: he searched the closets of his memory where such impractical scraps of knowledge might be stored. *Psyche, cinema, aphorism, clitoris* came tumbling out into the daylight of his consciousness. He rejected them, but only because of their spelling, not their irrelevance. Their meaning was of no more concern to him than the actual message on the Rosetta Stone had been to Champollion. Any word would do to provide the first key to communication. *Dyspepsia, zoo, erotic, hypnosis.* None of these seemed to contain quite enough of the Greek letters he knew, either.

Aphrodisiac.

Bascombe had no idea why the word appealed to him at once. He was certainly not aware it had any association in his mind with Venus. It struck him only that it began with a letter which he knew, alpha, and contained also a phi, a delta, a sigma, and a kappa. There was a clear space on the pad beneath his drawing of Mrs. Charrington. He reached around Venus with the pencil and carefully and rather laboriously began to inscribe ΑΦΡΟΔΙΣΙΑΚ there.

He had only got as far as ΑΦΡΟΔΙ when something hit him in the face. It was the back of Venus' hand. He had seen her angry before, but nothing to compare with this. She wrestled the pencil out of his hand and stabbed him in the nose with it. The point was fortunately blunt, but the jolt was enough to make him jerk his head back and sit upright in his chair. She hurled the pencil at him like a spear and leaped after it. The spear glanced off his cheek. Venus landed on his chin, reached wildly for the nearest handhold, and thrust her hands up to the wrist into his nostrils. Her fingers, the length and thickness of a cat's claws, sank into the membrane inside his nose. Bascombe tried quite reflexively to withdraw his head still further. The chair overbalanced. He fell on his back onto the floor.

Venus had him now. She clambered to her feet on his chin and began kicking at his mouth. She did not do it haphazardly. She took a step forward for each kick, balanced herself on the ball of her left foot, and swung away with the full force of her right leg. Apart from the bruising impact of her foot, he could feel her newly pedicured toenails tearing at his upper lip like thorns. He reached for her with his right hand. She stopped kicking him just long enough to bend down and sink her teeth into the tender skin between his parted thumb and forefinger. He snatched his hand away. She went back to kicking him. He could taste the blood on his upper lip now. He opened his mouth to lick it away.

She must have seen the warning gleam of his teeth, because she stopped in mid-stride with her knee bent, considering the damage to her bare foot if it struck them, and jumped onto his cheek instead. Arrived there, she ran up and down his face, stamping on him.

It was laughter that saved him from any further injury. Kicking, clawing, or biting, she was formidable, but she was too light to stamp effectively. Her running feet, the spasmodic tap of her heel against his cheek only tickled him. For once Bascombe forgot her decibel range. He let out a howl of laughter.

She was gone from him instantly. When he raised his head she was standing several feet away on the carpet, her hands pressed against her ears in her usual protesting way.

He stood up and righted the chair. What in God's name had detonated that explosion? He looked down at the pad of paper on the table, trying to figure it out. His drawing of Mrs. Charrington had obviously annoyed her, but she had cooled down again after that. The bell had apparently meant nothing to her—although he saw it was his own "B-r-r! B-r-r!" with its Greek beta and gamma that had both puzzled her and made her think he could write Greek. She had answered it instantly with her own mysterious απιτω. It was just after that, while he was writing *aphrodisiac* . . . A drop of blood splashed onto Mrs. Charrington's leg. His lip was still bleeding. He went into the bedroom for a handkerchief.

By the time he returned, holding it to his mouth, Venus was back on the table, sitting cross-legged on Mrs. Charrington's face. She had never been a girl to nurse a grudge. She was obviously cheerfully prepared to resume their efforts to understand each other. Bascombe found the pencil and sat down.

It seemed to him the next best step would be to try to convey his own ignorance to her, that he didn't understand Greek.

He tapped her απιτω word with the blunt end of the pencil. He raised his left eyebrow and pulled down the corners of his mouth. He opened his eyes so wide that his vision lost all focus for a moment. Finally, he raised both shoulders.

He relaxed his eyelids and brought Venus back into focus. She had her back to him and appeared to have ignored the whole performance. All her attention was on the pencil. She grabbed it out of his hand and dropped it on the table. It was hexagonal and rolled pendulously away from her. She was after it at once and, bending over it, rolled it back toward her until the lettered side was uppermost.

She straightened slowly and looked up at Bascombe. He might have been some total stranger who had just presented her with a diamond necklace.

He could understand her surprise and gratification. He hadn't noticed it himself until that moment, but there it was, in gold letters on the green-patterned pencil, her own name, Venus. He nodded, smiling foolishly, an involuntary philanthropist telling her not to worry, the necklace was real. He stopped nodding or smiling.

How did she know he called her Venus?

He realized that cajoling her back into the suitcase, or summoning her to her dinner or bath, he might have whispered, "Come on, Venus," "Here, Venus," "There, Venus," at one time or another. But he had never thought she could hear his voice except as a dull, indefinite booming. It was wonderful to know she had not only heard but distinguished his name for her.

It was even more wonderful, now that he came to think of it, that she could recognize it in Roman letters.

He picked up the pencil to see whether there were other words she might recognize if he printed them out for her. *Milk? Bath? Suitcase?* But once again Venus was ahead of him. She had already torn off the top sheet of paper to give herself a full clean page and was working away with her own scrap of lead, writing him another message.

Physically the process, watched from behind, was rather like someone scrubbing a floor. She knelt in the same way, supporting her weight on her left hand and pounding away with her right.

It took her perhaps two minutes to complete the job, and by that time she had covered the whole sheet of paper. She stood up and tossed the scrap of lead aside. She brushed the palms of her hands against each other in a gesture of finality. "All right," she might have been saying. "That's it. Read it."

Bascombe did his best.

All the letters at least were clear to him this time. They were large Roman capitals.

S O L A
A P H R O D I T E
S U M.
N U L L A S
A L I A S   D E A S
H A B E T O.

It was after midnight when Bascombe left the House of Commons. He had been right in following the hunch that had sent him there. Nolan knew no Greek, but one of the Other Lot, as he called them, did, and in the curiously "matey" atmosphere of the Strangers' Bar he had found the answer to all his questions.

He walked home through the deserted streets of Pimlico considering those answers. He was a little shaken by them. They had revealed to him at last the magnitude, the enormity of that communications hangup between himself and Venus.

There was no exact English counterpart to the Greek word απιτω—he pronounced it "apito"—the Conservative Member for East Anglia had told him, but what it meant, approximately, was, "Away with her!" "Out!"

Now, recalling the challenging way she had turned on him after writing it, Bascombe could see why Venus had been so incensed by his reply. She thought he was writing Aphrodite under his drawing of Mrs. Charrington, paying the woman the greatest flattery in an ancient Greek's vocabulary, according to the Conservative M.P., calling her his love goddess.

She thought Mrs. Charrington was his mistress.

This was clear to Bascombe from Nolan's translation of the first part of Venus' Latin message. "I am the only Aphrodite."

But it was even clearer from the somewhat Biblical command with which she had completed that message.

"Thou shalt have no other goddesses but me."

5

CHAPTER

"ALWAYS READING that goddamn dictionary?"

"I'm trying to broaden my education."

"What the hell use is Latin ever going to be?"

"Fluoridation's a Latin word."

"Yeah? How were their teeth?" Mr. Mitchel sat down in the armchair facing Bascombe's desk. It was an expensive, welcoming leather chair, presumably chosen to sweeten visitors who had business with Bascombe. No one had ever sat in it except Mr. Mitchel.

"It comes from the Latin word *fluens,* a flowing, a flux."

"What's a flux?" Mr. Mitchel didn't really want to know. He picked up a message slip from the In basket. It was one of several Bascombe had received in the past few days. Stanley Nolan called. Mr. Mitchel nodded approvingly.

"Still playing it cool?"

"M-n-b." One of those totally noncommittal sounds he had learned to use with Mr. Mitchel.

Mr. Mitchel began to tear the corners off the message slip, roll them into spirals, and drop them into the ashtray. He did it slowly, giving his full attention to the job.

"Maybe we're playing it a bit too cool."

Bascombe made a gesture of pushing the Latin dictionary away from him, as though preparing to give his full attention to Mr. Mitchel. If he looked thoughtfully off into the middle distance he could just read the left-hand page without moving his head. *Fatigatio*—Fatigue. *Blandus*—Fawning. *Insulsus*—Fatuous. He was trying to memorize twenty new words every day.

"How do you figure him, Bascombe?"

Pennatus—Feathered. Bascombe had never tried to figure Nolan. He liked him better as he was, unpredictable. He had only seen him once since his visit to the Stranger's Bar. He had taken Nolan out to lunch to thank him for his help with the Latin, and Nolan had been friendly and restless and unexpectedly inquisitive. He had spent the meal cross-examining Bascombe on his attitude to a wide variety of subjects, from the American Constitution (numb) to Women's Lib (enthusiastic). It had been Bascombe's impression, in fact, that for some unpredictable reason of his own Nolan was trying to figure him. A stir of air from the window ruffled the pages of the dictionary. *Scitus*—Shrewd. It seemed as good an answer as any.

"I figure he's pretty shrewd, Mr. Mitchel."

"Is he going to play ball? That Private Member's act or whatever the hell they call it. Is he going to carry a banner for fluoridation? That's the point."

Scortum—A harlot. Since that first ridiculous lunch with Mr. Mitchel, neither Bascombe nor Nolan had ever once mentioned fluoride to each other.

"Keep after him. Get his measure pinned out." Mr. Mitchel was acquiring odds and ends of new jargon from his little shirt man. He rocked himself slowly out of the armchair and padded back to his own office.

Copulare—To couple. Venus was six inches tall now. His hope that she was growing an inch a week had been too pessimistic. She had grown three inches in the last eighteen days. She was big enough to wrap her arms around his cock now and clasp her hands together so that he could not dislodge her except at her pleasure. Not that he any longer tried to. In the past few days he had surrendered unequivocally to her dallying.

He had first succumbed to it last Saturday. It was warm for an English June evening. He was lying naked on the bed with the windows open and the curtains drawn back. The twilit room was full of the summer sounds of a city. Indistinguishable questions from beyond other open windows. A plaintive, self-conscious cry

76

of "Taxi! Taxi!" from Earl's Court Road. The monotonous rise and fall of Australian voices singing their single, endless, indigenous song in the beer cellar on the corner. His own phonograph was playing in the next room. He had adjusted it for Venus. She could hear and enjoyed music if it was played softly enough. Her tastes were catholic, eccentric, and untouched by fashion. One track of a group's latest L.P. would make her smile, sometimes even dance, and the next, which sounded much the same to Bascombe, would send her burrowing under a cushion until only her protesting, kicking feet could be seen. He had gradually winnowed out half a dozen sides with no tracks that offended her and had put them all on the spindle. From time to time he was briefly aware of the throb of a guitar among the other sounds in the room.

Venus was lying across his cheek. Her dangling feet brushed his throat. Her left breast was pressed against the bone of his nose. Her face was so close to the pupil of his eye that it had lost all proportion. It might have been the face of a woman of any size, immeasurable, like a close-up on a movie screen.

She was separating the lashes on his lower lid, and putting them, one at a time, into her mouth. The movements of her hands and lips, firm and assured enough not to tickle, caused him an extraordinary sensation in the back of his mouth. He had never felt anything exactly like it before, although it recalled both the pleasure of swallowing good wine and that urgent tightening of his throat he had sometimes experienced an instant before copulation. It was not a continuous pleasure. It kept overcoming him and then lessening, vanishing altogether. At the same time he felt a recurrent impulse to put an end to it, to complete it in some way. He was not sure how.

It was Venus who showed him. She had reached the last lash at the inner corner of his eye. She sat up and straddled the bridge of his nose, looking down the narrowing vista of his torso. He could no longer see her, except as a white blur between his eyes, but he could feel her body trembling in that spasmodic way he had come to recognize as a symptom of laughter. He raised his head slowly, careful not to topple her off his nose, and had a look

77

too. He hadn't been aware of it before, but he could feel as well as see now what had caused her amusement.

She was on it in a single leap. He barely felt her land at its base, but as she swung her left leg astride it, mounting what a strategist might have called its soft underbelly, and began to wriggle her body slowly, lingeringly against it, he felt that tightening of his throat again. Far more urgently now. This time, he knew, it could only end in completion. He might as well enjoy it.

That seemed to be Venus' plan, too. She was facing toward him, her loose hair falling over the absurdly heart-shaped tip of his cock. Bascombe had never noticed it was that shape before, but he had seen that private, expectant smile on several other girls' faces. And he had seen it change after a time to a sudden protesting astonishment as the expected happened to them. He let his head drop back on the pillow. In the throes of the pleasure she was giving him, he was delighted Venus was also taking pleasure for herself.

She was in no hurry about it. Instead of quickening the movements of her hips she gradually slowed them, drawing out each wriggle into a deliberate motion. Bascombe's legs were writhing now, the muscles of his thighs twisting and stretching independently as though trying to raise him by their own sympathetic efforts to the final relieving summit of feeling.

He was almost there: so close it was impossible to believe the delight of anticipating, striving toward it could last another instant.

Venus stopped moving altogether.

He almost cried out aloud in protest.

She made a quick brushing motion of her hips against him. His whole body strained to raise him that last immeasurable fraction to attainment. Venus lay quite still against him again. This time an audible, pleading gasp escaped him. Another feather-light movement. A responsive, desperate reaching upward. Suddenly he was there.

For what seemed a considerable length of time then, Bascombe was not aware of anything at all in ordinary, everyday terms of awareness. Everything he felt was reflexive, beyond his control. It was like the blind, floating reaction to an injection. Everything was happening *to* him, inside him. It was ecstatic, overwhelming.

When he opened his eyes at last he was lying so limply on the bed he could feel the pressure of the sheet against every part of his back and the underside of his legs. He had once been told such total physical relaxation was excellent therapy, but he had never been able to achieve it at will. He lay there benefiting from it a little longer.

Venus was resting too, lying on his thigh, her arms folded under her chin like a girl on a beach. He could feel the flushed warmth of her body against his skin. As he moved at last she lifted her hand to her mouth and blew him a kiss. It was different from the sportive, promissory kisses she had blown him before. The action was affirmative this time: the stamp on an agreement, on an understanding.

Bascombe's relations with Venus had changed in other ways too this past week. He had scattered scraps of lead and writing pads all over the apartment like ashtrays, and with the help of his dictionary and a Latin grammar they were able to communicate quite freely. The surprising thing, now that they could understand each other, was how little they needed to say. When he got home in the evening it never occurred to him to write *Ave* (Hello) on a pad, nor if it was a warm night, *Nox calida est*. It confirmed what Bascombe had always suspected, how much of human speech is unnecessary.

He had gotten things straight about Mrs. Charrington now, too. He had explained to Venus that Mrs. Charrington was his cleaning woman. (The only Latin equivalent seemed to be *famula*, a handmaid, a slave, *f.*) She was a dangerous gossip (*lingulaca periculosa*). And whenever Venus heard the sound of the bell he had rigged up, she should take to the suitcase and stay there until the *famula* had finished her *famulatum* and gone home.

He knew he was being unfair to Mrs. Charrington. He found he had also been unfair to her in the matter of the missing pint of milk. Far from drinking it herself, Mrs. Charrington was fermenting a new batch of yogurt for him out-of-mouse-reach in the linen closet. But it seemed to him essential to keep Venus out of Mrs.

Charrington's sight. He didn't know exactly why he felt this. He was sure Mrs. Charrington was not a *lingulaca,* dangerous or otherwise. It was, rather, an immediate feeling he had about most people of Mrs. Charrington's generation. Anything that was personally important to him must be hidden from them, because they lived in a world of interpreted experience that did not touch his at a single point. It wasn't only imbeciles like Mr. Mitchel or those guests at Mrs. Waddington's party. The more intelligent the stranger from the past, the longer it took to establish their mutual lack of understanding, that was all. The simplest words, "good," "change," "dirty," "normal," had completely different meanings for them, and no matter how many dictionaries he or they referred to, that would always be true.

Bascombe had realized this for years. It didn't bother him. He could see why other people his age had been driven to resort to obscenities in their efforts to get something across to their elders, particularly to those who claimed authority. It was only in expressions of motherfucking abuse they could hope to find any common language with them. But for himself he had chosen a less wearying solution. He had clammed up years ago. He almost never listened to anything anyone from that other world said. Above all he did not trust them.

It wasn't always immediately possible to identify these other-world people. He was too open-minded to apply a strict age rule, and Nolan, for instance, was for the present a borderline case. But Mrs. Charrington wasn't. He was convinced Mrs. Charrington would not understand Venus. A six-inch woman, particularly a naked one, would seem strange to her. If she found one in Bascombe's apartment she would do something extraordinary about it. Scream. Call the newspapers. Complain to somebody.

The very fact that Bascombe, himself, found nothing strange in Venus and something extraordinary in Mrs. Charrington's anticipated reaction to her was a revealing example of his lack of contact with that other world. As Nolan had remarked during their lunch together, "The thing that fascinates me about you young people is that you can accept anything except the everyday. Put you in a cave in Benares, with a living skeleton who hasn't uncrossed his legs for thirty years, and it's great, you're at home with him at once. Shove you into a perfectly ordinary university, an office, a factory, and it's all a monstrous nightmare to you."

Bascombe pulled the typewriter stand toward him. Surfacing for a moment into the everyday world of his office, he found he had just called Nolan. They had had quite a long talk over the phone while he was thinking about Venus and Mrs. Charrington. He lapsed back into automatic activity and began to write Mr. Mitchel a memo reporting the substance of that conversation.

He was almost finished with it five unremembered minutes later when the door opened and Mr. Mitchel flopped into the visitor's chair again.

"I've been thinking. Why don't you call Nolan?"

Bascombe typed on for a line without replying, then pulled the blue memo sheet out of the machine, detached the carbon, and handed the top copy to Mr. Mitchel.

Mr. Mitchel did not move his lips when he read. But watching him was like tending a Xerox machine; you could follow the gradual process of assimilation and reproduction quite plainly.

Bascombe did not watch. *Pestis*—Ruin. *Perversus*—Perverse. *Pervungere*—Smear all over.

"He's going to Los Angeles! Tonight!"

"Parliament's recessed until fall."

Mr. Mitchel was silent, processing this. *Pervagari*—To Roam.

"It's those bastards in our West Coast office. They're after him."

"He's got a sister in Los Angeles. She lives in Topanga Canyon. It's all in that memo." *Pervigilare*—To stay awake all night.

"That's a lot of shit, Bascombe."

"Her name's Mrs. Munnings. She's married to a veterinary."
Bascombe pursed his lips, let out his breath, and carefully blew over a few pages of the dictionary. *Scobis*—Sawdust.

Mr. Mitchel got out of the chair and stood rocking slightly on his flat feet. It was a sign he was thinking.

"He's playing ball with those bastards out there. Why not? A free trip. Hollywood. Topless restaurants. Abalone steaks. Heated

81

pools. Go-go girls." Mr. Mitchel's associations were enlighteningly wistful at times. "Then if that Private Member's act goes through, they get all the credit."

Bascombe did not bother to answer. He huffed over another page. *Perturpis*—Scandalous.

"You're going too!"

For once in his association with Mr. Mitchel Bascombe sat up with a start.

"To Los Angeles?"

"That's it. You're going to fly out to the Coast first thing in the morning. Stick with him. Let those bastards see you around. That'll fix them."

"Fly? To Los Angeles? Tomorrow?"

"Damn right, Bascombe."

Bascombe leaned forward with his elbows on his desk. He was thinking, too. *Cogitare*—To ponder, to make plans.

6

CHAPTER

"Take that too, shall I?"

"No, thank you." Bascombe followed the porter into the international departures hall carrying his own briefcase.

He had managed to delay his departure until early evening by explaining to Mr. Mitchel that he would actually lose no time in Los Angeles that way. Mr. Mitchel had never really got it straight about time differences, and it had been easy to persuade him that the morning flight would get to California in the middle of the night. This had given Bascombe time to make careful preparations for the journey. He had bought the briefcase in Bond Street that morning. It was the old-fashioned kind, of expensive, hand-stitched leather, with a flat base and tall sides rounding in toward the handle on top. He had calculated its internal capacity at six hundred and sixty-one cubic inches, which meant that Venus had as much air to breathe as Bascombe would have had in a hotel bedroom, about ten feet by eight with an eight-foot-high ceiling and no window. He had considered boring holes in the leather, but after taping a pencil flashlight inside, he had realized that a briefcase spangled with pinpricks of light would attract unwelcome attention, and he had finally decided that the light was more essential to Venus' comfort than the ventilation.

He had lined the floor and walls of her traveling quarters with fur, two rabbitskin muffs he had bought in the King's Road, cut up and laboriously stitched together. A separate compartment inside the case contained her supplies for the journey: flasks of milk, apple juice; a plastic container of Mrs. Carrington's yogurt; silk sheets and towels; spare batteries for the flashlight; leads and paper for messages. Taped to a corner of the rabbit-skin carpet was a teacup from a child's toy set with a cardboard cover he had made for it. Venus had outgrown the Vieux Ceps cap now.

Bascombe followed the porter to the check-in desk, carrying his briefcase through the crowd like a chalice.

"Do you have any hand luggage?" The check-in clerk was dressed in a mud-brown uniform and a rounded fez with a badge on it. There were three short curling hairs sprouting out of a mole on the left side of her chin. They were the only personal things about her.

Bascombe turned from paying the porter and very carefully lifted the briefcase so that she could see it.

"You'll have to weigh it in." Her voice sounded as though it came from a tape recorder in her throat.

Bascombe set it delicately on the scale. The indicator registered less than another three kilos. The clerk seemed disappointed by its lightness; she left the case standing on the scale while she fiddled disapprovingly with his ticket, tearing pieces out of it and pushing them aside. He lifted the case gently off the scale.

She had finished with the ticket. She picked up a baggage label and held out her hand for the case. Bascombe held out his hand for the label. For a moment as they faced each other across the counter she actually looked him in the eyes: they might almost have been a man and a woman. Then she slapped the label down where he could reach it and Bascombe tied it to the handle of his briefcase. She pushed the diminished ticket back across the counter to him.

"Can I reserve an aisle seat, please?"

She did not look at him again, but a faint gleam of triumph flickered in her eyes.

"You'll have to ask the reservation clerk that."

"Where?"

She had already transferred her attention to a phone. She was dialing a number, keeping her finger in the hole as the dial swung back before moving it to another hole. Bascombe watched, waiting until she had finished and was listening attentively to the ringing at the other end.

"Where can I find the reservation clerk, please?"

"At the reservation desk." Ask a silly question.

"Where's that?"

"Over there." She was careful not to raise her eyes or indicate in any way where "there" might be.

Bascombe thanked her and set out into the enormous hall in search of the reservation desk. He held his briefcase against his chest with both hands. He was not in the least ruffled. He had had a fairly wide experience of air travel and felt he understood the theory on which airports were run.

They were called airports because it sounded more enticing, but they were in effect conditioning centers. The uniformed professionals who ran them were only ostensibly there to ticket and label you and herd you onto the right plane. Their real function was psychological and far more complex than that. It was their job to get you into a frame of mind where anything, even being imprisoned in a pressurized metal box for eleven hours, *anything* was a longed-for relief from the purgatory of the airport.

They induced this state of mind in a variety of subtle ways. They never let you relax for an instant, relaying a constant flow of inaudible announcements, any one of which might turn out, too late, to be the one you had been waiting for. They kept you guessing about excess luggage, letting you think you were going to get away with it, and then suddenly demanding, with well-trained clairvoyance, a few francs or pfennigs or drachmas more than you had left and refusing to accept any other currency. Above all they treated you with a brusque contempt calculated to make you feel like a sordid nuisance, and became absolutely inaccessible when the treatment began to work and you tried to reach them with panic questions about gate numbers or departure times.

Bascombe understood all this and had learned to roll with it. Within just over an hour of his arrival at Heathrow, he had strapped himself into an aisle seat in the particular metal box scheduled to arrive in Los Angeles eleven hours later. He held his briefcase on his knees.

"Will you place your hand baggage under your seat, please." A tall girl in an identical mud-brown uniform and fez, but without a mole, was leaning over him. She made a grab for the handle of the briefcase. Bascombe resisted her, putting the case on the floor in front of him, holding it steady between his ankles. The tall girl moved on up the aisle, swinging her ample, girdled bottom, and pausing from seat to seat to reprimand other passengers about their hand baggage or their seat belts. Bascombe slipped his Latin dictionary out of his pocket and began to compose a message for Venus.

There was, of course, no Latin for airplane, only for flight (*volatus*) which was presumably natural, birdlike. Rather than try to explain the process of mechanical levitation to her, he had decided to ignore that whole aspect of the journey and treat the plane in its simplest functional terms. "The vehicle (*vehiculum*) has started now," he wrote in Latin. "Is there anything you . . ." He stopped to look up "want." It was a word that had meant many different things to the Romans, to lack, to need, to wish, to desire.

To desire, Bascombe thought. Is there anything you desire? But the Romans had conceived of various kinds of desire, too: appetite and avarice and (sexual) cupidity and, more subtly, uncontrolled desire (libido). Uncontrolled? Or surrendered to? This time next year Venus would be fully grown. She could be sitting beside him, her marvelous legs gleaming against the tired gray of the seat. The night before while she was lying briefly spent on his thigh he had had a chance to appreciate her legs through the magnifying glass. They were perfect. Full, rounded, graceful, slender, delicate in turn, as he moved the glass slowly down from hip to ankle. In a few months he would be moving his hands, his lips . . .

For the present Bascombe controlled his desire. "Is there anything you lack?" he wrote in Latin.

"You speak English?"

Bascombe hesitated. He had a wild impulse to shake his head. He could speak a certain amount of French and German—his maternal grandparents had commonly used the one and his paternal grandparents the other—enough probably to get away with it if the man next to him spoke neither. But he would have to keep up the pretense with the hostesses when they came around to take his order for drinks, to ask if he wanted the luke-warm Filet Bearnaise or the stone-cold Hawaiian Ham for his dinner. And one of the hostesses might even *be* French or German.

He nodded vaguely, trying to suggest that he might or might not have understood the question.

"I noticed you studying that Italian dictionary."

He nodded again.

"Going to L.A.?"

The freaking plane was going there, wasn't it? He lifted the briefcase onto his knee and began to slip his message to Venus in through the crack under the rim.

"That your home?" The message was three-quarters of the way in. The last inch of it zipped suddenly out of sight as Venus grasped the dangling sheet of paper from inside. Bascombe glanced at his interrogator.

He was quite young, about thirty, good-looking in a modest way, with fair hair that was neither long nor short enough to be an emblem. There was no declaration in his choice of clothes, either: charcoal slacks, a dark cotton jacket, and, as a compromise, a plain shirt open at the throat to display an Italian silk scarf. Nothing in his appearance affirmed his values or criticized other people's. He was as neutral as an astronaut.

"No," Bascombe told him.

"Just going for a visit?"

"Yes."

"Business?"

Bascombe hesitated again. That bland, noncommittal appearance, the eager questioning had alerted him. His neighbor had all the characteristics of a devoted, perhaps even a rabid word-game player.

There were three main word games in Bascombe's experience: "What I Like For Breakfast," "See What I've Got," and "I've Got More Than You Have." And with eleven hours in front of them they would have time for them all. "Breakfast," the usual opening game, was harmless and uncompetitive. You simply chose some subject—your job, your best round of golf, the town you lived in, your health, some hobby, a recurrent dream, what you liked for breakfast—that gave you a personal, self-indulgent pleasure to dwell on but that could not conceivably interest anyone else, and each player in turn was allowed to talk about it. He was allowed to describe his daily routine at work, his sinus condition, to relive his enjoyment of scrambled eggs or cornflakes. There was nothing in the rules that compelled the second player to listen. He was quite free to use the other's talk-time rehearsing for his own turn. But he must not yawn or fidget or interrupt, and a cooperative player would try to *look* as if he were listening, even interject a short question or some vague prompting sound from time to time.

The other two games, "See What I've Got" and "I've Got More Than You Have," were essentially developments of the first, but introduced a competitive element, each player in "See" describing something he owned and at the same time searching out his opponent's lacks, in preparation for the third game, "More." "More" was unashamedly competitive and played by a master could be brilliantly destructive, leaving the defeated player with a lost, naked sense that he lived nowhere, might just as well be unemployed, had never enjoyed his breakfast, and owned nothing of any value.

In asking him if he were going to Los Angeles on business, his neighbor was tacitly suggesting they play "Breakfast." If Bascombe said "Yes," he would then ask him what kind of business he was in, and the game could start. It would be Bascombe's turn first to talk about "My Job."

Bascombe was prepared to cooperate. He had had very little social contact with the everyday world these last few weeks, and it would be good practice for Los Angeles where "See" and "More," in particular, were played almost as a religion. The trouble was that his job seemed to him so boring that the mere anticipation of talking about it out loud reduced him to leaden apathy. What was there to say? I work for a metal company. We're trying to get the British government to fluoridate public water supplies so we can sell them some of our waste products. I . . .

"No," Bascombe said firmly. "I'm not going on business. I'm just going for a visit."

There was a silence. Bascombe realized it was his turn to ask a question. He could not think of anything he genuinely wanted to know, so he repeated one of the questions that had already been put to him.

"You live in Los Angeles?"

The bland eyes brightened at once. "It's my home. *Now*. I've got a home in Westwood. I don't know if you know Westwood."

This wasn't a question, but Bascombe shook his head helpfully.

"It's kind of a nice neighborhood. For Los Angeles. I don't get much time to spend at home there. *Unfortunately*." He had a way of isolating occasional words and giving them a staccato emphasis, as though his thoughts, searching ahead for his meaning, kept unearthing unexpected nuggets of truth, holding them up for him to exclaim at. "My home office is in Los Angeles, too, so you'd think I'd be home quite a bit, but my job keeps me in Europe a lot of the time. It's just south of Wilshire. My home. They say the *south* side of Wilshire is the un*couth* side of Wilshire." He rhymed the two words, excusing his modest joke with his apologetic smile. "But the street where I have my home. It's kind of a nice neighborhood. *For instance*. We have an eight-foot-wide sidewalk in front of my . . ."

Home, Bascombe thought. Home. Home. Home. Jesus! What in hell was he going to say when his turn came? Ranch houses in Westwood or motels in Turkey were all one to him. The only nostalgia he had ever felt had been for some warm and eager girl. And it had never mattered to him where she came from either. There was a soft scratching sound from the briefcase on his knee. Venus had a message for him.

He could slide a sheet of paper into the case without opening it, but she could not reach to push one back to him through the same crack under the rim. He pressed the brass catch and opened the case just wide enough to get his hand in. He dangled his parted fingers inside waiting for Venus to put her message between them.

"There's a light in there." The evocation of home broke off in sudden surprise.

"Yes." He withdrew his hand pulling out the sheet of paper. His neighbor, rigid with curiosity, was obviously waiting to see what he was going to do about the light.

Bascombe snapped the case shut. "It goes off when you close it," he invented rapidly. "Like a refrigerator."

"Hey. That's great. That's a great idea."

"Yes." He put the case back on the floor between his feet before the other could ask to see how it worked. He opened Venus' message. It was only two words long. "Me libra." He didn't have to look at the dictionary. He knew what that meant. "Let me out."

"Excuse me." Bascombe picked up the case again, and holding it carefully against him, made his way to the toilets at the rear of the plane. There were three of them. He looked hopefully at the three doors in turn. A lighted Occupied sign disappointed him each time.

"They're all busy." The tall hostess who had reprimanded him earlier about his hand baggage was stacking bottles and glasses on a trolley. She had taken off her uniform jacket and her cotton blouse revealed that her front was as ample and as firmly supported as her behind. Five weeks ago Bascombe would have yearned for her. Dreams of ungirdling those hips, shelling those breasts would have goaded him for the rest of the journey. He would have angled endlessly to get to know her, make a date with her in Los Angeles. He would have grabbed at this chance to talk to her now.

"Yes." He turned his eyes back to the toilet doors.

"You must have a million bucks in that thing."

"What?"

90

"The way you never let it out of your hands."

"Oh. Yes." Bascombe smiled back at her. But the smile was reluctant: a ransom payment. He saw her copious presence only as a menace to him. He planned to take his briefcase to the toilet —to give Venus some air and a change of scene—at least once an hour until the end of the flight, and he couldn't afford to arouse any officious curiosity about what he had inside it. His imagination was working rapidly again.

"Sinus," he explained.

"Pardon?"

"My sinus." He thickened his voice as though speaking through a gauze mask. "I have to go—I have to use this nasal spray." He indicated the briefcase. "I have to spray my sinus passages every hour."

"That's terrible." He saw with relief she had lost any interest she had ever had in him. If she gets nosy again, he thought, as one of the toilet doors opened at last, I'll tell her about the time I had to have sunlamp treatment.

Please lock the door, the sign said in four languages. Bascombe didn't need any reminding. He pushed home the bolt and tested it before opening the briefcase.

Venus had nothing on but a pair of felt earmuffs he had made to protect her against the noise of the plane. They were kept in place by black elastic, fitting over her crown and under her chin, and with her titian hair pulled back in a pony tail they gave a perverse emphasis to her nakedness. He stroked her back and she dallied affectionately against his finger as usual, but she had other things on her mind. She indicated she wanted to write, and he got the paper and leads out for her.

He had brought the dictionary along with him and translated the message as she wrote it. He had expected some practical request and her question came as a double surprise to him.

"Why didn't you tell me we were going to fly?"

He got out his own pencil. She watched as he started to compose his answer, and then jumped onto the rim of the washbasin. She tried each of the sample bottles of after-shave lotion in turn, taking off the caps and sniffing them until she found the one she liked best; then she made herself a spill from a strip of Kleenex and dabbed a drop behind each ear.

"I thought perhaps you would not understand about flying vehicles." He handed her his finished message. She glanced at it and scribbled her answer.

"They go past us constantly. Some of them go backwards."

Bascombe assumed she meant past Earl's Court. She must have seen them circling, waiting to land at Heathrow, from the window of the apartment. Before he had time to try to figure out why she thought some of them were flying backwards, Venus claimed his attention again. She scribbled a few more words and he went back to his dictionary while she jumped onto the towel rack. Someone rattled the door.

"I've always wanted to fly in one." When he looked up from translating this second part of the message she was standing on the ledge under the wall mirror, rearranging her pony tail. The mirror was made of some kind of amber glass that was supposed to make you look tanned, younger. Her jaundiced complexion bothered her for a moment until she compared the back of her hand with its reflection. She returned to her hair.

Someone rattled the door again. He glanced at his watch. They had been in the toilet almost ten minutes. He had his next Latin message ready in his pocket; it was another of the preparations he had made for the journey. He took it out and showed it to Venus.

"We must return to our seats now. According to the law. We will come back here hourly."

She took a last look in the mirror and then returned to the briefcase willingly enough. He gathered up the rest of the things. A middle-aged woman was standing just outside the door. She bristled slightly as he walked past her. Five weeks ago he might have apologized for keeping her waiting. Life with Venus had changed him in other ways beside his new-found indifference to random enticement. It had hardened him, made him ruthless in the way he supposed some married men with children must become ruthless.

The man from Westwood was reading *Life* magazine. Bascombe tried not to distract him from it as he slid into his seat.

92

He felt in his pocket for his dictionary. It wasn't there.

At first he thought he might have left it in the toilet, but he remembered picking it up with the pad and the grammar and Venus' leads. None of these things were in his pockets either. Shit, Bascombe thought. He'd put them all back in the briefcase. He glanced quickly at his neighbor and lifted it onto his knee.

"It goes on when you open it?" The man from Westwood had abandoned *Life* magazine. His whole attention was on the briefcase, waiting for it to light up.

"Yes." He would have to open it several inches to peer inside, locate the dictionary, fish it out. From where he sat his neighbor would be able to see right into it. Venus might be standing up, moving around, combing her hair. He decided not to risk it. He put the briefcase back on the floor.

"Sinuses holding up all right?" The tall hostess had stopped beside him with the trolley of drinks.

"Yes, thank you." Bascombe ordered a double vodka.

"You got sinus trouble?" The man from Westwood seized his chance to resume playing Breakfast.

"Yes." Bascombe thickened his voice a little again. "I've had it all my life."

"What do you do for it?"

"Spray. I have to go and use my nasal spray every hour." He might as well get that clear all around, anyway.

"You watch that sign in the toilet now. If that sign goes on, you come right back to your seat, you hear." The tall hostess pushed her trolley on to the next row, bending to the cash tray, presenting her captive bottom to him. It was almost against his face, as immediate as a shop window. Thank God he hadn't pretended to be German, Bascombe thought. She would probably have bawled him out for losing the war.

"That's no good, nasal spray." The man from Westwood was off. "I had sinuses. *Bad.* The last time I was home. The only thing that cleared them up. In the *end.* The only thing was sunlamp treatment."

He was playing out of turn, but Bascombe did not interrupt him, as he went on to recall how much he had paid for his sunlamp, how many minutes he had spent under it each day, the way it had seemed *at first* to give him dandruff.

Bascombe did not listen, but he made no effort to claim his next turn either. He had as little urge to talk about the functions or malfunctions of his body as about his job. It wasn't only that he knew (as well as the man from Westwood did) that they were matters which could never interest anyone else. They didn't interest him either.

He was fascinated and absorbed by the question of how Venus had known they were on a plane. She had seen nothing but the inside of the briefcase between Earl's Court and the toilet. Could her eardrums, her diaphragm have told her she was flying? Only if she had flown before. Where? When?

He understood that in trying to answer these questions he was forcing himself to examine the whole greater enigma of her existence. Who was she? Where had she come from with her Latin and her Greek? And those were questions he had almost consciously decided not to ask the first morning he had discovered her on his bedroom carpet. There seemed to him a disloyalty, a meanness in such probing. She had given him a sense of exuberance and purpose that he had never imagined experiencing. It would be the greediest ingratitude not to accept that without query. As Nolan had guessed, Bascombe belonged to that clan which did not question sunlight; or copulation; or visions, however induced; or any other sensual experiences. They only questioned the denial, the withholding of them.

"We make fibers. All *kinds* of fibers. We're a worl'wide company." The man from Westwood had exhausted his own interest in his scalp. "For instance I've just been in Norway. They've got hundreds of miles of fir trees up there. That's where *we* come in. In the resin. The gum. We're planning to build a factory for them. But the Norwegians can't see it. They sell those firs. They sell them for *Christmas* trees. Now, what I told them." His voice, no longer modest, was shrill with recalled enthusiasm. "What I've been trying to persuade those Norwegians. It so happens one of the things we use that gum for is making artificial Christmas trees."

There was a soft scratching sound from the briefcase. Bascombe leaned forward eagerly. The hour wasn't up yet, but if Venus wanted an outing he would be delighted to take her along to the sanctuary of the toilet at once. He let the side of his jacket dangle over the case to shield it from his neighbor's curiosity and slipped his hand in for the message.

It was not a request to be liberated this time. "I SLEEP NOW," she had written in letters an inch high. But Bascombe's disappointment was remitted by surprise. Venus had not been wasting her time with his grammar and dictionary. The message was in English.

"I told them, our artificial trees. They're noninflammable, for one thing. Nonperishable. And they're *totally* nonallergic. You can clean them, too. A small one, I told them, you can put it in the *dishwasher*."

Bascombe had purposely not brought a book to read on the flight, determined to devote the time to his dictionary, and he was less fortunate than Venus. He could not stretch out on a fur rug and sleep. He had another drink and the hostess brought him his regulation dinner. It did not look as if it were intended to be eaten. The perfectly circular disk of ham, the three blanched fingers of asparagus, the glossy saffron wheel of pineapple, the vacant eggshell of bread had a mock appearance, like something served on a stage to give the actors business between their lines. But he ate some of it anyway to pass the time. And a little later there was the movie.

He paid his two-fifty for the earphones willingly. They were worth it as muffs against the staccato intrusions of the man from Westwood. He plugged them into his seat. But he did not turn them on. He thought about Los Angeles.

In most ways it should be better for them there than in London. He would have practically nothing mindless to do. An occasional phone call to Nolan. Daily fictional reports to Mr. Mitchel. Token appearances at a few company "think" sessions. He would not have to go to an office every morning. He could spend whole days with Venus. He did not see why he could not take her for rides in the car. They might even find an undeveloped stretch of beach somewhere within a hundred miles of Santa Monica. And in less than six weeks time she would be a foot tall. Then his own hands would be smaller, more delicate, better fitted to caress and pleasure her. He sat there with the plastic stethoscope, sanitized for his protection, hanging rather painfully from his ears, and thought about that.

When he surfaced again and looked at the screen a bulky girl in very tight shorts was running round and round a sports field. A sparse crowd of very clean-looking people was silently shouting at her. A middle-aged man silently blew his nose to hide whatever emotions he was supposed to be feeling. A high school band was silently playing. And then quite suddenly everybody—the girl, the middle-aged man, the crowd, the band—everybody was smiling as though they'd all been simultaneously gassed with pot. The movie was over.

Bascombe took the stethoscope out of his ears.

"We've built an extension. A *wing*. You'd have to call it a wing, out over the carport . . ."

Bascombe put the stethoscope back. The man from Westwood was playing "See What I've Got" with his neighbor on the other side. Even if he hadn't been so alert to any future signals from Venus, he knew there was no hope of getting to sleep. The delegates to the international conference who had determined the legal minimum space between economy class seats had all been short, thin, supple men. Bascombe's legs felt as though he had been kneeling in penance on a stone floor for six hours. He managed with some pain to get his feet out of the trap that had been set for them under the seat in front of him and stretched them into the aisle.

"You be sure someone doesn't fall over your legs now." The tall hostess thrust a small hard slippery pillow into the nape of his neck and swung on up the aisle. Bascombe returned his legs to their penance. Glancing to his right he could see the man from Westwood's lips still moving. He disengaged one earphone for a moment.

"I have a lovely wife and two lovely children, and *one* thing we've got, we've got a real relationship . . ."

He let the plug snap back into his ear. I have a lovely wife and two lovely children. He had heard Mr. Mitchel voice exactly those same words to some stranger in a bar, in a hotel lobby. He had never believed him. It was true, of course, that Mr. Mitchel was married and that there were two children living or at least sleeping in his house in New Jersey. But as far as he could see, Mr. Mitchel did not *have* them in any of the accepted definitions of that word. He did not have them "to hold." Both Mr. and Mrs. Mitchel, and possibly the children too, had devoted a great deal of their imagination these last three months to inventing excuses for not getting together in England. He did not "own them or possess them as something at his disposal." He obviously had no control over any of them. And from things Mr. Mitchel had said, he did not "enjoy them carnally" (at least not Mrs. Mitchel). The truth was he did not either have them or want them. They existed for him only as an expense, a noise, or a hazard. The younger child gave him hives. And yet in a way they were important to him. They were a vital part of his fantasy world. They were as lovely and true and commendable as the benefits of fluoride—when he talked about them.

And that, Bascombe saw with sudden clarity and dismay, was exactly why he was sitting here now. Because for hours every day he, too, was a creature of Mr. Mitchel's fantasy: "Bascombe, my assistant, bright ambitious kid, been training him to take some of the legwork off my shoulders." In flying six miles high over the North Pole at this instant, he was fulfilling Mr. Mitchel's imagined role of "Bascombe" as surely as any actor in an author's play.

Shit, Bascombe thought. Shit on him. He did not mind so much for himself. But it seemed to him intolerable that Venus' life, her well-being, even her whereabouts should be affected in any way by Mr. Mitchel's fantasies.

Because she was a conception of his own mind, his own wishful dreams? He refused to believe that. Venus existed absolutely, in her own right, independently of him or anyone else. Only then could the wonder she had already brought him be an outright gift, and when she was bigger. . . . His thoughts loitered pleasurably off into the future, into sunlight and beaches and afternoon bedrooms and intimate night.

There was a scratching sound from the briefcase. Bascombe looked at his watch. Venus had had a good long sleep. He did not pause to open the case for her message. He reached his bundled raincoat down from the rack and stuffed it under his arm. It was as bulky as a parcel of laundry, its pockets filled with the preparations he had made for the final and most dangerous stage of the journey.

He picked up the case and hurried down the aisle to the toilets. At this hour the whole plane had the appearance, the weary smell of a first aid station. Gaping passengers lay strewn about the seats like accident cases. The rumpled hostesses in their mud-brown uniforms were loading breakfast trays onto a trolley as though they were kits of sterilized instruments bound for surgery. The tall hostess gave Bascombe a startled glance: she might have been surprised to see him ambulatory.

He bolted past her with his case and raincoat and locked himself into the first toilet he came to. He had a great deal to do to put into action the careful plans he had made before leaving London. And he hadn't much time now. In less than an hour they would be landing in Los Angeles.

In Los Angeles he would be entering the United States. He would have to smuggle Venus in through customs.

7
CHAPTER

THERE WAS the world outside like the breath of an engine room; then instantaneously, as he stepped indoors again, the chemical cold and that familiar, but forgotten, tuneful tinkling indigenous to American public buildings. There was a measureless corridor flanked with mosaics that seemed to have been assembled by a computer. There was Immigration: "Welcome back." And Health: "How are *you* today?" There was a long wait before his own estranged suitcase lurched out of a hatch and ambled toward him like something alive.

Bascombe considered the four customs inspection channels. There were several passengers ahead of him and he had time to choose. One of the inspectors was a woman. He was immediately inclined to chance his luck with her. But then it occurred to him that a woman customs inspector was likely to be more efficient, sharper than a man. She would have to be to get the job.

Two of the others could be ruled out at once. Their uniforms fitted too well. They blatantly enjoyed wearing them: the anonymous license of badge and strap. The fourth looked Irish, dulled with years of fingering other peoples' possessions. Bascombe chose him finally for his obvious lack of curiosity.

As he took his place in the line the tall hostess was just leaving the building. There was something ritualized about the way she swung her hips. She might have been shaking dice. He watched her pause to talk to someone at the exit, a bald young man in a loose cotton suit. She kept her bottom moving even when she was standing still. She turned her head to glance in Bascombe's direction and out bulged the right buttock like a cornering tire. She turned back to the bald young man and out bulged the left. Bascombe lifted his suitcase onto the counter and placed his briefcase beside it.

"That all you got?"

"Yes."

"No liquor?"

"No."

It was difficult to tell whether the slight pursing of the tired lips was an expression of disbelief or reproof. "I didn't have time to buy any liquor," Bascombe explained. "They didn't announce our flight—"

"Did you buy anything while you were over?" He wasn't paid to listen to complaints.

"A magnifying glass."

Bascombe lifted the lid of his suitcase. It was lying on top of his hand-laundered shirts. The Inspector ignored it. Bascombe closed the suitcase. He started to pull it off the counter, picking up his briefcase with the other hand.

"What you got in there?"

"Papers."

"What else?"

It was a moment of decision. If he lied, "Nothing else," and the old bastard went through the briefcase anyway, his inspection of its actual contents would be all the more suspicious and thorough.

"A couple of dolls."

"Dolls?"

Bascombe opened the briefcase and lifted one of them out from beneath the sheaf of loose papers he had spread over it. It was less a doll than a figurine, a Piccadilly flower girl, a beautiful little thing of Victorian porcelain with a marvelously lifelike, adult face, a large velvet hat, and an ankle-length skirt. After searching unavailingly through several toy departments he had found two of them in an antique shop in Knightsbridge.

100

"It's a present for my niece, my sister's kid."

He lied fluently now. "She's married to a veterinary in Westwood. That's a great place to bring up kids, Westwood." He put the doll gently down on the counter. "South of Wilshire, that is. Wilshire Bullvard? Near the veterans' cemetery? For instance—" With any luck if he kept this up, he could bore the man into letting him through. "For instance, my sister, they've got an eight-foot-wide sidewalk in front of the house, and at Christmastime they have these artificial trees—"

It worked. The tired eyes puckered; the man waved his hand as though physically trying to dispel the fog of words. He moved on to the next passenger.

Bascombe put the doll precisely back into the briefcase, lifted his luggage off the counter, and made for the exit. His careful planning had paid off.

Venus had entered the United States.

The tall hostess had gone, but the bald young man was still hanging around. Probably waiting for one of the other hostesses, Bascombe thought as he passed him. Maybe he likes them less mobile.

"Mr. Fletcher."

The bald young man stood balancing lightly on his toes, his shoulders hunched. A smile was fastened to his face like a false moustache.

"What?" It was all he could think of to say.

The young man—he must be in his early thirties, Bascombe could see now—reached out and grasped his arm just above the elbow. He did it without haste, almost casually, but his grip was as hard as a shackle.

"Let's go this way."

This time Bascombe said nothing; he did not even nod. He walked down a short carpeted corridor, carrying his luggage, with the man beside him, gripping his arm. He wasn't frightened or even particularly worried. He had, by choice, had very little previous contact with the representatives of law and order. His class at college had preceded active protest. His reaction now

101

came not from experience but out of his whole character and values. He felt a tight, unyielding contempt for the bald young man.

"Let's go in here, shall we?" He might have been suggesting a good place for a hamburger. He threw open a door, stepped in first, and drew Bascombe into a small musty office. There was a bare desk, three chairs, a green filing cabinet, and on the wall above it a framed photocolor portrait of General Douglas MacArthur. He closed the door, let go of Bascombe's arm, and crossed to the desk. Bascombe dropped his suitcase and kept his briefcase in his hand.

The bald young man was searching for something in the filing cabinet. He pulled out several plastic signs and shuffled through them until he found the one he wanted. He fitted it into a little stand on the desk, as though planting a flag. "Chester Q. Voigt," the sign said.

"Would you pull your sleeve up, Mr. Fletcher. Your left sleeve." Chester Voigt moved around the end of the desk in his balanced, athletic way and stopped a foot from him. "Unless you're left-handed. Are you?"

"No." Bascombe pulled up the left sleeve of his jacket.

"And the shirt, too."

Bascombe bared his arm to the elbow. That cow, he thought, as Voigt examined his forearm. That stupid, rubber-girdled snoop. She must have thought he'd been going to the toilet for a fix.

"Okay." Voigt let go of his wrist. Bascombe pulled down his sleeve.

"Okay, let's have a look in that briefcase now, shall we?"

For a moment Bascombe thought of refusing. Not because he imagined he had any legal right to do so; Voigt presumably had as much authority to search his belongings as any customs inspector. But because the simple act of refusal would have been so satisfying. It would have relieved him, however briefly, of his scorn: that sickened sense of accusation he felt against all Chester Voigts and their bland assurance of their own ultimate force. He had never shouted "Pig" at a policeman, but he suddenly understood why people did.

Bascombe opened his briefcase. Moving away from Voigt he quickly lifted out the things inside and displayed them on the desk, the sheaf of papers, a couple of pencils, five rubber bands, a handful of paper clips, other carefully chosen emblems of authenticity, and finally the two dolls. He set the dolls side by side, the arm and shoulder of the one he had already shown customs partly covering the other so that anyone would naturally pick up the top one first.

Voigt went back to the other side of the desk. He lifted the briefcase and peered into it. It was empty. On his last trip to the toilet Bascombe had stuffed all Venus' supplies for the journey, the flask of milk, her yogurt, her rabbit furs into the used-towel receptacle.

Voigt explored the inside with his fingers. He held up the open case and punched his fist into it. Nothing happened. No false bottom gave way. He did it again. He was obviously a man who enjoyed violent movement. He put the case back on the desk.

Bascombe had pointedly selected the sheaf of papers from his files at the office. There were buck-passing memos from Mr. Mitchel, rapacious urgings from the head office of the company, shameless invitations from advertising agencies. A glance at them would have persuaded anyone he was a paid-up supporter of all the traditional American values. Voigt showed no interest in them. He picked up the top doll.

He lifted its skirt and examined its legs. He pulled down its pantalettes and tapped its bottom with his fingernail. He held the half-naked doll in both hands as though testing its weight. Then he seemed to fumble. He grabbed at the doll and quickly, sharply twisted his wrists.

It was neatly done: it could have been an accident. The doll broke cleanly in half at the waist. Voigt smiled at Bascombe. It was the apologetic smile of a professional fighter who has just got away with a kidney punch. He poked his finger into the hollow torso of the doll. He found nothing. He sniffed his finger. It apparently smelled only of what it usually smelled of. Voigt dropped the broken pieces back into the briefcase. He was ready to give his attention to the second doll.

Before leaving the plane Bascombe had shown Venus a prepared statement explaining they were entering hostile territory. Latin was rich in bellicose terminology, and he had let himself go in describing the barbaric malevolence of the enemy whose lines they were crossing. His warning had taken effect. In her ankle-length skirt and wide flower-girl hat, Venus lay rigidly, palely motionless on Voigt's desk. She did not betray by the faintest breath that she was anything but another porcelain figurine.

Voigt reached out to pick her up.

Several things happened inside Bascombe at once. He noticed that Voigt bit his nails. He remembered the exact moist brittle feel of a boy named Ernest Carter's mouth against his knuckles nine years ago, the last time he had hit anyone. He decided coolly to kill Chester Voigt if he touched Venus.

Everything seemed to be moving slowly and very distinctly. Voigt's hand was still descending through space. Bascombe stepped forward with his left foot.

Voigt's hand never reached Venus. He smacked it suddenly against his own chest. He clasped it there with his other hand.

"Jesus," he whispered. "Jesus Kay Riced. Isn't she cute?"

He bowed his head, looking down at her, his tough, dull face collapsed like a tent. He was smiling helplessly, with the same proud idiocy as the high school band, the clean spectators in the movie on the plane.

"You know. You know something." The muscles of Voigt's face were so relaxed with good humor he could hardly move his mouth to form words. "I've never seen anything so cute in my life. My whole life."

Bascombe reached out decisively and picked up Venus. He did not know how she had done it, or even exactly what she had done. But there was a look in Voigt's eyes he had seen before: in the eyes of girls at pop concerts, of grandmothers babbling over baby carriages, of Englishmen greeted at the front door by a bounding mongrel.

Voigt was infatuated. (From the Latin *fatuus,* adj., foolish.) Bascombe decided to move now while the spell lasted. He stuffed the papers and the other things back into the briefcase with one hand and crunched them into a loose nest for Venus to lie in. He was about to set her in it when Voigt touched his shoulder.

"Could I? Please? Would you mind?" He was holding out his nail-bitten finger as though for Bascombe's blessing. He was begging to be allowed to touch Venus with it.

"All right. But just once," Bascombe told him sharply.

Voigt nodded. His finger trembled as it moved slowly toward Venus. He dabbed once, tentatively at her hair, and then snatched his hand back and put it away like a souvenir in his pocket. He was still smiling in the same moonstruck way as Bascombe closed the door on him and made quickly for the exit sign across the main hall.

He was smiling, too, by the time he reached it. He felt physically light with pride and relief. It was not pride in anything he had done. All his careful camouflage and deception had in the end been neither effective nor necessary. He was proud of Venus.

8

CHAPTER

PEOPLE OFTEN SAID some other place—Durban, South Africa, Sydney, Australia, parts of Long Island, the road to the airport, any airport—was like Los Angeles. But it was impossible to say Los Angeles was like any of those places. Going there for the first time was as close to entering a new world as one's first experience of flying, or diving, or anæsthesia. Even people who had been there for years still couldn't talk about anything else.

You could live in Dayton, Ohio, all your life without anyone wanting to know how you liked it. But you couldn't stay in Los Angeles a day without being pestered for your opinion of it.

"How do you like it here?" waitresses greeted you with bright indifference across drugstore counters. "You *like* it here?" retired salesmen echoed each other's doubts on the park benches of Santa Monica. Serious, gray-haired men probed you defensively in their Dufy-papered living rooms: "Do you really like it here?"

Bascombe who had been sent out to the Coast office on various errands half a dozen times in the last two years had gotten as bored as everyone else trying to answer this question. On his third trip he had resorted to the device of saying, "Why not?" and then switching off and thinking about something else until the other person had stopped telling him why not. He continued to do this now, partly out of habit, but mostly because he had made a discovery these last few weeks that was too personal to explain.

He loved Los Angeles. It was the perfect place for him and Venus.

106

All the things most people deplored about the area, the lack of personal contacts, the guarded indifference, the eerie vacancy of the streets, all contributed to form the ideal conditions for their life together. He could walk out of his hotel in the morning, down the cracked, crazily tilted sidewalk, past the secretive motel apartments and the Midwestern frame houses, past the jungle-encroached cottages, without seeing a single other pedestrian. He could loaf down to Hollywood Boulevard with Venus, naked except for a head scarf, on his shoulder, straphanging from his ear, without the least fear of being noticed. If he ever did meet anyone else on foot, the other—man, woman, or child—would look instantly away, afraid of being sucked in, trapped by the least flicker of interest. ("Only four ninety-five, friend!") It was one of the greatest things about Los Angeles, this universal certainty that there was a catch to everything. Stop, look, listen, and you'd had it. You'd get conned or sued, or find yourself liable for twenty-four monthly payments on an encyclopedia. Worst of all—most amorphous and terrifying of conditions—you'd get involved.

Turning onto Hollywood Boulevard, Bascombe popped Venus inside his shirt. Legs astride, balanced on the ledge of his belt, she leaned her chin in the open V of his collar, holding onto the cloth on either side of her face, like an actress peering out at the audience on opening night. But there was no audience. Even the group of shaven-headed young men tinkling their bells and burning their joss sticks outside the Pickwick Bookstore knew better than to give her a second glance. For all their cult of innocence and simplicity they weren't naïve enough to be caught that easily. The various elderly men aping Buffalo Bill or Robin Hood further along the Boulevard were just as cagey. They knew a shill when they saw one, too. And in all the three weeks he had been in Los Angeles, Bascombe had never yet met a woman's eyes on the street.

One morning when he was having breakfast in a drugstore, he lifted Venus out of his shirt front and set her on the counter. She was nine inches tall by then, her breasts the size of cherries, her thighs like subtly tapering candles. He helped her lift his glass of orange juice and she had a sip of it. The man and woman on either side of him instantly averted their eyes. Venus was tasting the syrup on his waffle when the waitress hurried over to him.

"You'd better put that away," she warned him. "The manager catches you trying to hustle novelties in here, he'll call the cops."

Bascombe thanked her and put Venus back inside his shirt. The man on his left paid his check. It was only when he had his change and had slipped off his stool, with a clear line of flight all the way to the street, that he risked a look at Bascombe.

"Works with a battery. Huh? I know."

"Transistors," Bascombe corrected him firmly.

In other ways, too, Bascombe hadn't felt so blissfully untrammeled since college. Almost all his time was his own. Since no one at the Coast office knew what he was supposed to be doing there, and it was no part of Mr. Mitchel's plan to inform them, he had been greeted at the beginning with a deferential curiosity which had gradually soured into suspicion. They supposed he was doing *something*, and after an inquiry had revealed that his salary and expenses were being paid by the New York office, a private memo was immediately circulated to the heads of all departments in Los Angeles that B. H. Fletcher was to be granted "minimal cooperation." After that they did not call him and Bascombe, gratefully, did not call them.

He had not seen Nolan yet. But he felt as though he had. He wrote Mr. Mitchel long almost daily reports about him, about their encounters, Nolan's ambivalence, his suspected treachery, his own rising and sinking hopes of keeping him from making a deal with the Coast office. As he was forced to read the carbons of these reports in his efforts to make sense of Mr. Mitchel's replies to them, Nolan assumed a vivid reality to him, a dramatic identity which he had never had in life.

He kept intending to call the actual Nolan. But the long hot empty days with Venus were so engrossing he couldn't bring himself to interrupt them.

He had rented a car his first morning in L.A., a two-year-old Pontiac. "Transportation," the clerk in the rental office had called it contemptuously, trying to steer him toward a new Mustang. "It's got more status."

But Bascombe had no illusions about cars. He found it impossible to regard a metal contraption—lethal as a gun and destructive as a locust—as an enviable possession. All cars were transportation to him. There was no other excuse for them. He chose the Pontiac because it had a wide, well-padded ledge above the dashboard. Lying on it Venus had a clear view through the windshield when they drove down to the ocean or up into the hills.

He had found a place in Topanga Canyon where he could leave the car on the verge and, following a dirt road, climb to a pine clearing overlooking the Pacific. It did not seem to be part of anyone's estate, and no one else ever seemed to come there.

He took Venus there that morning after leaving the drugstore. It was the end of June, with the temperature in the nineties. He stripped off his T-shirt and lay down on the ground. Venus jumped onto his stomach and started to tug at his belt to undo it. He had left the Latin dictionary at the hotel. He no longer had any need of it. Venus had worked her way through it within a few days of their arrival, memorizing a page at a time, and after a few further hours with the grammar, had begun to write English far more fluently than he would ever be able to write Latin. "It is most easy," she had explained in one of her early messages. "Like the Teutonic language." He had brought a small scratch pad and a pencil with him, and he reached for them now to explain to her that here in this country it was against the law to be naked in the open air.

She had his belt undone by this time, and he decided to forget the message and the law. He kicked off his moccasins, slipped out of his jeans, and turned over on his chest. It was deliciously liberating to lie there naked in the sun. Even a bikini, even the narrowest of jock straps would have spoiled it. He wondered lazily why. Because the sense of liberation came from breaking an acquired inhibition?

Venus was pulling gently at his earlobe. He guessed she wanted him the other way up. He rolled over on his back and turned his face toward her. She wasn't absolutely naked. She still had her bandanna over her head, knotted under her chin. He smiled at her, smoothing her back with the tip of his finger. She moved closer to him, leaned forward, and stretched herself across his face. Her breasts were against his right cheek. He could just feel her nipples pressing into his skin. It was like being prodded with daisy stems. She lowered her mouth to the corner of his eye, licking the tender juncture of his lids. Something brushed against his lips as lightly as a puff ball, too silky and fragile for any reminder of hair. He extended the tip of his tongue and felt an answering fleck of moisture. Her left leg was straddled across his chin, her right pressed against his cheek and neck. He reached his hand around her and stroked her bottom. She wasn't actively stimulating any part of him except his eyelids. But he could feel the response converging from every part of his body to a single central point between his thighs. She was moving her hips more quickly now, that fleck of sweet moisture darting over his tongue.

My God, he thought, without even knowing he thought it, I'm going to—

"Comb."

He was so startled that all the gathering excitement drained out of him as abruptly as the wine out of a shattered bottle.

"Comb. Comb on, comb."

This time Bascombe couldn't help it, he sat up. Venus slithered down his face and landed on his chest. He looked around. The small clearing was as empty, as still as it had always been.

"Yow villain." The voice was so light it seemed to come from a great distance, a sigh on the wind. It was only when the sigh was repeated with a sharp accompanying scratch across his neck that he realized it had come from his chest.

Bascombe was so astonished and delighted he ignored Venus' anger altogether. He picked her up and kissed the top of her head. He stroked her back. He whispered exultantly in her ear, "Venus. Venus. Venus." The stage in her development he had been anticipating so eagerly had taken place at last. Her voice had entered his decibel range.

"Yow pute me doven."

It took him a moment to translate that, to realize that she had no guide to the pronunciation of English except what she had referred to as the Teutonic language. But he still didn't put her

110

down. He was too happy. He lay back on the ground. He sat her astride his mouth. He held her there against his darting tongue until she ceased struggling, until she began to writhe instead, until he felt her tremble with pleasure and she tumbled forward across his face.

"All rigt. Nov I shov yow."

Even from a distance of a few inches the thin sighing sounds barely carried to his ear.

He smiled. "All right," he whispered back. "Now you show me." He felt her rise to her knees on his cheek. He felt her feet run lightly over his chest. In a moment their rhythm would quicken as she gathered herself for the final leap onto her objective. Instead the tap of them against his skin stopped altogether. He raised his head.

She was kneeling motionless on his stomach. There was no need for words. From the attitude of her body he could tell at once that something had alarmed her. She had heard something he couldn't.

She jumped down to the ground and he snatched up his shirt and put it protectively over her, holding it there, ready to pick her up in it if anyone came. Then he heard it, too. The still distant but approaching yelp of bloodhounds.

They were coming on fast. He only just had time to lift Venus, loosely wrapped in his shirt, into the crook of a tree before the lead hound undulated briskly into the clearing. It was followed by fifteen or twenty others. They swarmed around Bascombe, sniffing and howling at him. They did not seem particularly unfriendly. He did not know enough about bloodhounds to be sure whether they were or not. But standing naked in the midst of them, he found their snuffling, shameless interest in him unpleasantly threatening. He had never realized before how wet dogs' tongues were. It was like being daubed all over with warm paintbrushes. He tried to find his underpants beneath the turmoil of dog flesh around him. Two of the hounds had found them first and were now mournfully challenging each other for the last torn shreds. Pushing with his palms at the nearest muzzles, he managed after a minute to reach his jeans, which he had hooked over a branch. He struggled to keep his balance, hopping on his left foot, and got the right leg into them.

"Heel. Heel, I say."

It was as though the waters had parted. The frisking bodies receded instantly. Freed of their resistance he half fell against the tree. He was still trying to get his left foot into his jeans when a woman in Western boots strode into the clearing. He snatched up the loose trouser leg and held it inadequately over his crotch.

"I wondered what they were after."

She was about thirty-five, blonde, with her hair combed tightly back into a bun. She would not have jolted him to a dead stop on the Earl's Court Road two months ago, but sitting opposite her on the subway he would have found food for fantasy in her. There was a boneless quality about her body, an eel-like slenderness that was perversely intriguing. His senses were still prickling from his uncompleted passage with Venus and his exposure to the dogs. He reacted involuntarily. That provocative question which had once been habitual crossed his mind. What would it be like?

She stood quite still, looking at him. She took her time about it, starting at his knees, one trousered and the other not, and letting her glance wander up over his thighs, his hips, his bare chest, to his face. She nodded. She might have been complimenting a waiter on the sip of wine he had just poured for her.

"You'd better put the rest of those trousers on."

"Thanks."

He still had something of an erection, and there didn't seem to be any way he could get the other leg into his jeans without her seeing it. He dropped the waistband of his trousers, got his left foot into them, and pulled them up again. The tip of his cock had recalcitrantly popped out of his fly. He had to stuff it back in before he could do up the zipper.

"Careful."

She wasn't smiling. She had merely issued a warning, as she might have called "timber" if a tree had toppled toward him. He found himself liking her for this indiscriminate concern.

"Thanks," he repeated. He fastened his belt.

"What were you doing here?" It was partly all those hounds,

grouped obediently behind her, partly the way she stood, her long, waistless body as still as a tree, that gave the question an irresistible authority.

"Sunbathing."

"Alone?"

"Yes." He glanced at his bundled shirt on the branch above him.

"I suppose you know you're trespassing."

"No, I didn't."

"This whole ridge belongs to us."

"I'm sorry."

"Haven't you got any shoes?"

He looked around for his moccasins. Some scraps of leather among the pine needles showed they had gone the way of his underpants.

"No."

"You walked up here from the beach barefoot?"

"I left my car down in the canyon."

"That blue Cadillac?"

It was the thing that had been puzzling him about her. Although she had no identifiable accent, she didn't talk like an American. Now he was sure she couldn't be. Any American woman who owned the whole ridge would have known a Cadillac only when she saw one.

"It is blue," he admitted.

"Oh." She seemed disappointed. "I thought you were a hippie."

"No. No, I'm sorry."

She turned away, swiping at the hounds with her crop, driving them into a torrent before her as she walked off down the path. Her knitted silk shirt and Western riding pants lay as flat against her body as a coat of paint.

He reached up for his T-shirt and carefully unwrapped Venus. She beckoned to him to lower his head.

"Yow like her."

"No."

"Yow vant her." Her voice was so soft, so thin, it was difficult to tell whether it was an accusation or a question.

113

"No."

"Do you drink?"

The blonde woman was back, pliantly still at the edge of the clearing. She wasn't as flat in front as behind, he noticed. He could see her breasts, like nippled saucers, only slightly blurred by the tight silk of her shirt.

"Sometimes."

"I'm Nora . . . Nora. We live over there." She waved her crop toward the evening sun. "If you drive on up the canyon and take the second turning to the left you can't miss it." She nodded to him over her shoulder as she slipped back into the trees. "Come over, if you feel like it."

"I don't feel like it. I don't want to go." Bascombe unwrapped Venus and set her in her usual place above the dashboard. "I don't vant to go," he repeated, respecting her Teutonic w's. He started the car.

"Yow go."

"What about you? Vot about yow?"

"I comb, too."

She was smiling. He realized she did want to go. After their isolated life together in London, her sight of people in California had whetted her curiosity about them. She wanted to meet some.

"I'll take yow if yow like," he agreed. "But I'll haf to hide yow."

She considered that. He had managed to convey to her by now some of the strangeness, the extraordinary character of five- to six-foot human beings. They would gratefully mistake her for a doll or a mechanical toy. But if they were forced to realize she was alive and exactly like them in every way except her size, they would not accept her. They would be frightened by her at first, and then recovering from that, they would insist on isolating her from their own kind. They would examine her endlessly, analyze her blood and her urine, put scrapings of her skin under microscopes. They would test her reflexes and her I.Q. and the electrical impulses of her brain. Worst of all, they would fight for possession of her. They would argue over her for years in law courts, wrangling to define her rights and status, the extent of her

114

financial responsibility. Because there would be money in her. They would soon see that. Someone stood to make a fortune out of showing her off to everybody else.

Venus shrugged. She appeared to understand and accept all this. "All rigt, yow hide me."

Bascombe took the second turning to the left. The blonde woman, Nora, had been right, he couldn't miss the place. It was a long low house, set just over the crest of the ridge, the usual Californian jumble of wood and concrete. What made it unmistakable were the noise and the smell.

Bayings, barkings, roarings, neighings, screechings, howlings greeted him as he got out of the car. And underlying this din was that associated odor he recalled instantly from childhood, a mixture of peanuts, raw meat, cabbage, and piss: the smell of a zoo. He could see some of the animal houses among the trees, long sheds with tar-paper roofs.

She came out of the house to meet him as he crossed the drive. "Hullo." She glanced at the rolled towel he was carrying but she did not comment on it.

"Hullo."

"Would you like to look round first?"

"Sure."

"Most people do."

He walked beside her toward the sheds. "You're English, aren't you?" he asked. It was the way she had said "look round" not "around" that had made him guess this.

She stopped and faced him. "Let's not ask each other a lot of questions about each other. All right?"

They walked on in silence until they reached the sheds.

"I expect Daniel's in with the lions."

He looked at her. She didn't appear to feel she had said anything humorous. She led the way to a door at the end of one of the buildings, shorter and squatter than the rest.

There were two lions in there, a male and a female in separate cages. A tall, bony man in his late thirties was kneeling over the female as she lay on her side, playfully rubbing her belly. There

115

was an open tin box on the floor beside him, and he had a hypodermic syringe in one hand. As Bascombe watched him, he stuck the needle into the lioness' haunch and pumped a syringeful of milky fluid into her. He straightened up and saw Bascombe.

"Hi." He withdrew the needle, put the syringe back into the box, and held out his hand through the bars of the cage. "I'm Daniel."

"Hi." Bascombe shook his head.

"Haven't you got any shoes?"

"No."

"That's great." Daniel looked approvingly at Nora. "I guess you found him on the beach."

"No."

"Wait a minute till I get out of here." He picked up the tin box and let himself out of the cage, locking the door after him. "I'm always glad to get the hell out of there," he admitted cheerfully. "To tell you the truth, we don't get too many lions. And that one—I have to give her three shots a day, Vitamin B, just to keep her going. She's not as young as she was in *Ben Hur*, and not everybody knows this, but it's only old lions that eat human flesh. Nora and I—"

"I haven't told him anything about us."

"Okay." Daniel looked at Bascombe's feet again, his T-shirt, the rolled towel he was carrying. "I guess Nora found you on the beach."

"No—"

"He's not a hippie."

"Oh." He sounded as disappointed as Nora had. "My wife and I sort of hoped—"

"It doesn't matter, Daniel. I mean, he'll do, won't he?"

"Sure." He seemed relieved by his wife's tolerant attitude. "Sure, he'll do fine. Let's all go up to the house and have a drink."

They had several drinks in almost total silence, sitting on separate couches at one end of the long living room. It was not for Bascombe an uncomfortable silence: it was simply a pause. Nora half lay with her boneless legs and her Western boots

116

tucked under her and looked at Bascombe in her candid, exploratory way. Daniel sat down and stood up and roamed around, refilling their glasses. They both seemed to be waiting for something.

"Dinner?" Daniel was on his feet again. Nora nodded. Bascombe made a polite effort to leave. They insisted he stay.

"You're the whole point," Nora persuaded him.

He had kept his rolled towel on his lap during the drinks, but alone, while the dinner was being prepared, he looked around for a safer and more comfortable place for Venus. Between the windows that overlooked the drive was an old-fashioned bookcase with glass doors. It was surmounted by an ornate wooden frieze. He pulled a chair over to it and found, as he had expected, that the top was hollow. It was a perfect place. Venus could sit in this hollow, as he might have sat on a terrace, and command a view of the whole room between the carved minarets and pierced scrolls of the frieze without any fear of being seen.

"All rigt?" He unwound the loosely rolled towel and set her down.

She nodded, stretching her arms. "Yow vant her nov?"

"No."

"She vant—" Bascombe didn't have time to hear the rest of it. He jumped down from the chair and pushed it back into place as Daniel returned with the great slabs of steak he had been scorching outside. Nora brought in a salad. They ate off paper plates on their knees, sitting on separate couches at the other end of the room.

There was a surprising number of couches in the house. Besides the eight in the living room, the whole ground floor was choked with them. He could see two, a Recamier chaise longue and a reclining beach chair, in the alcove leading to the kitchen, and the hallway next to it was lined down one side with narrowly spaced divans, like a hospital ward. He began, absently, to count all the couches in sight. Thirteen. Fourteen.

"You'd better tell him now, Daniel."

Fifteen. Bascombe looked at his host.

"Let him finish his steak first."

"The others'll be here any minute, and you've still got to feed the camel."

"Not this Friday, Nora."

"It's not my turn to feed that bloody beast."

"You promised—" Bascombe watched the argument volley between them until it was finally agreed that the camel could wait.

He had almost finished his steak. The paper plate, soaked with warm blood and furrowed by his knife, had begun to intrude itself into each mouthful. He put it aside.

"All right, I'll tell him." Nora was leaning pliantly toward him. She stood up without appearing to stiffen, like an eel lifted by its gills. "Daniel and I have been married for nine years, and I don't know how long you've been in California, but there's an awful lot of divorce out here. Practically everyone we know—"

"Practically everyone we know has been divorced three or four times. I'll tell him, Nora." Daniel was on his feet, too. "And we think one of the reasons for this. Well, frankly, it's because people get bored with each other, and—"

"And they start to have affairs—"

"Not that there's anything wrong with that—"

"Unless they get serious—"

"Then they want to make it stick—"

"So they get divorced—"

"And it starts all over—"

"Do you know what I mean?"

Bascombe turned his attention finally back to Nora. He nodded. "Is it going to be general?"

"What?" This time they spoke together.

"The party."

"How?"

"Are they all swingers?"

Daniel smiled. Now that the word was out at last, they were both blatantly relieved. Nora reclined again on her couch. Daniel remained standing, his clenched hands on his hips, an umpire laying down the rules of the game.

"Sure. It's a love-in, not a circus. I mean we all feel the safest way to preserve a marriage is to change partners occasionally, so everybody joins in. If they feel like it. That's up to you. You can do anything you like but you don't have to do anything. That's very important. There's no compulsion. Of course, naturally, Nora, I mean, I, we hope you . . . if you want to."

"Do you?"

Looking at Nora, Bascombe realized he did. In that position on the couch, her legs and neck arched back, she appeared to be all of one piece, uncleft, like a mermaid. He couldn't help it, he felt curious about her. Would her body be soft to the touch or tight and slippery, like one of those airline pillows? His hesitation was only because of Venus. For the first time in his life he sensed the lure of fidelity. He remembered how, back in the clearing, she had guessed at once: "Yow vant her." She hadn't seemed to mind. It was she who had insisted on coming here. He half turned his head and glanced up at the top of the bookcase. He could just see her shadowed face, framed in one of the carved scrolls, but he could not distinguish the expression on it. He was still hesitating when for no reason he could understand the image of Chester Voigt came to his mind. Voigt stretching out his hand to pick her up. And then Voigt suddenly smiling, helpless: Voigt incapable of doing anything against her wishes.

"Sure." Bascombe found he was smiling, too. "Sure, I'd like to."

"Great."

"All right." Nora was more temperate in her outward enthusiasm than her husband.

"Oh, there's just one thing." Daniel was back in his umpire's attitude as the wheels of a car sounded on the drive outside. "No . . . no consequences."

"No follow-ups," Nora prompted him. "None of that I'll-meet-you-in-a-motel-next-week."

"No dates. No dates anywhere," Daniel concluded firmly as he paused by the door and carefully dimmed all the lights in the room before welcoming his first guests.

The love-in, as Daniel had called it, was like most parties Bascombe had been to in one respect. It was in three acts. Although the host's usual problem, to get his guests on their feet, was reversed, the first act was sticky. Daniel did his best. He threaded his way between the dozen couples and one single girl who gradually assembled in his living room, refilling their glasses, patting the women with his long dry hands and urging everyone to sit down. "Come on, Suzie, over here." "Why don't you make yourself comfortable, Clara?" "For God's sake, relax, Betty."

Bascombe stood with his back to the bookcase, sipping a large vodka on the rocks. Accustomed to blend easily, unconsciously with his surroundings, it was a new experience to feel so out of place. Most of the guests were, to him, vaguely middle-aged, in their late thirties, and they were all impeccably dressed. They would, most of them, he supposed, later shed some of their clothes, but for the moment this group of executive types in their polished shoes, their neatly pressed slacks and jackets, made him uncomfortably conscious of his own bare feet. He felt on display, like a symbol of some kind—like the token Negro he had met at so many prosperous middle-class parties.

That was exactly how they treated him. They were overfriendly, overanxious to make him feel one of them, no different from anyone else. Each of the men made a point of approaching him and shaking his hand. Each of the women forced her face into a smile as she met his eyes. And then Bascombe recognized a more subtle similarity between his position here and that of a single black in a roomful of whites. There was a derogatory envy in the way the men looked at him, a hint of expectation behind the women's smiles. Tanned, barefoot, in his hipster jeans, he was expected to be one hell of a performer.

There were signs he was expected to start performing any minute now. The party was beginning to slip into its second act. The men were no longer segregated from the women. The female voices were shriller, the male less self-consciously cheerful. The glances in Bascombe's direction were becoming more frequent and more frankly expectant.

There was nothing to stop him standing here for the rest of the evening doing absolutely nothing, Bascombe told himself. He looked around for Nora.

She had her back to him, leaning forward over the arm of a

sofa as a man lit her cigarette, her Western pants cupping her almost imperceptibly separate buttocks. In spite of himself he felt a stir of excitement. He finished his vodka and went in search of another drink.

As he replaced the bottle on the bar, someone tapped him on the shoulder. It was a woman he had noticed earlier because she was the only one in shorts. Knee-length white shorts, white sports shirt, immaculate white sneakers. She looked as though she had stepped straight off a tennis court, and this impression was strengthened by her figure. Her arms and legs were tanned and lean, her shoulders austerely right-angled. Even her breasts seemed pared down to essentials.

"So you're the hippie."

Bascombe decided impulsively not to contradict her.

"Nora found me on the beach."

"I guess you get a lot of excercise living like that."

"I surf."

"I don't mean that kind of exercise." She was drinking low-calorie orange juice out of the bottle. She rinsed her mouth with it and swallowed. "You kids—all you do is screw each other all the time. Right?"

He was surprised by the disapproval in her tone. That was, after all, what this party was supposed to be for.

"Aren't you going to join in?" He did not intend it as an invitation. She was attractive enough in her athletic way, but she was the kind of girl who would only copulate if they made it competitive: the best of three falls.

"Listen." She tapped his chest with a hard forefinger. "I used to be a nurse. I know something about it."

"About what?"

"You kids—I bet you haven't changed those jeans in a month."

He had put them on fresh out of the laundry that morning, but again he didn't contradict her.

"And you haven't got any underpants on. Right?"

There seemed no point in telling her that Nora's hounds had eaten them. He nodded.

"Listen." The hard tapping finger again. "It's just simple

121

hygiene. I wouldn't touch you with a pair of forceps." She rinsed again and moved briskly away from him. He felt a flush of anger, but it was not against her. It was like that moment on the plane when he had realized to what extent his actions were dictated by Mr. Mitchel's fantasies. He was aware of being the creature of these people around him now, type-cast by their fantasies because of his appearance—his clothes, really. He looked up at the frieze above the bookcase. Venus was the only person in his life who had ever taken him as he was, without trying to make him fit into some image in her own mind. And yet she had changed him more than anyone he had ever known. He seemed to himself to be a different person from the Bascombe of seven weeks ago, of that party at the Waddingtons', the dinner with Hannah Cooper. His anger had passed. It was replaced by eagerness. He found a chair and carried it to the bookcase. They'd get the hell out of here together. Right now.

"Vat's vrong vith yow?" She was kneeling, her chin resting on her hands in a curl of the frieze. "Vy don't yow haf her?"

"Don't you want to go. Don't yow—"

She shook her head. "Yow haf her."

"The Japanese ones are the best."

Nora was sitting on the floor, peering up at him in the half light. He jumped down off the chair. "If you're interested in that kind of thing."

"Japanese?"

"Pornography." She stood up and pointed to the top shelf of books. He pushed the chair quickly back against the wall before she could climb onto it.

"No. No, I'm not. I was looking at the wood carving."

"You are an odd young man. Wood carving! All these creatures." She gestured fluidly toward the sprinkling of still unoccupied women about the room. "They're all mad for you to do them."

"She isn't." He indicated the tennis-playing nurse.

"You don't want *her!*"

"What about you?"

"Later." She took him by the wrist and led him into the hall.

122

"Wait here for me." She slipped away toward the stairs. Bascombe realized without either excitement or regret that he had committed himself now. He waited, leaning against the wall, looking into the half-darkened living room.

The third act had begun. Most of the guests were at it now: the women with their skirts up to their waists; the men with their trousers down to their knees; both pumping and thrusting with little gasps of achievement. It was admirable, really, Bascombe thought. How could any roomful of business executives be less harmfully employed? Make love not money. Even the most overfed of them seemed to him less grotesque, engaged in this odd friendly act, than they would have sitting behind a desk. There was something sensible at least about what they were doing now. No steambath, no other sport in the world would make them feel so physically restful afterward, so purged of aggression and insecurity.

"All right." Nora was back. For a moment he wasn't sure what was different about her. "I'm ready now." She had taken off her riding pants. Her clinging silk shirt reached to the top of her thighs. Below that she was wearing nothing but her Western boots.

"Come on." She led him into the living room. There was no spotlight, no announcement, but it was as though she were leading him onto a dance floor: it was time for their number.

She stopped in front of a deep, square-backed velvet couch. The sides were held up by cords looped over wooden posts. She slipped them off, letting the sides down to the floor, creating plenty of room for free play at both ends of the long seat, setting the stage.

She stood and faced him just out of his reach and unfastened the three buttons of her shirt. She was going to do her specialty first. She pulled the open neck of her shirt down over her shoulders and began to wriggle her way out of it as though casting her skin. Her breasts emerged above the tightly stretched silk. They were, as Bascombe had guessed in the clearing, as shallow as saucers, but quite large in diameter and in no need of support. The neck of the shirt had reached her hips. There was nothing to stop it there. A last wriggle and it fell in a ring around her heels. She stepped out of it.

There was no applause. But Bascombe was aware of a murmur of approval from the group of people who had gathered around the couch. He caught sight of Daniel's bony face among them, the tanned figure of the tennis-playing nurse.

Nora was standing close in front of him. She rolled his T-shirt slowly up to his armpits, and as he raised his hands, pulled it off over his head. She unfastened the buckle of his belt.

His jeans fell in a rumple around his ankles. He kicked them off. Nora stepped forward and pressed herself flat against him, close as a Band-aid, from knee to mouth. In the moment before they moved to the couch together he wished she'd take those freaking boots off. He was still the only barefoot person in the room.

Most of the watching guests later agreed that Nora and Bascombe gave a great performance. Their bodies fitted and complemented each other like well-rehearsed dancers in a *pas de deux*. In the first, or missionary position, in particular, their timing was so perfect, they worked so closely together that they moved as a single body. In the intertwinement of arms and legs it was difficult to tell where Nora left off and Bascombe began.

In the second, or Roman position, as Nora rolled on top of him and doubling her legs beneath her, knelt astride him, Bascombe faltered for an instant in his response. He was slow to bring his knees up. But the basic rhythm of their pelvic action was not altered or interrupted by this.

She leaned slowly away from him. He seesawed with her so that he came to be kneeling beneath her hips, her legs extended on either side of him like the shafts of a plow. He watched the stem of his penis lengthen and shorten as he partly uprooted and then replanted it in the sparse blonde patch presented to him. He was surprised how monotonous he found the sight.

He sensed from the tightening of Nora's body that she was deliberately holding herself back now. She wanted to prolong their acrobatics before returning to the first position, but with their heads at the other end of the couch this time, for the climax, the finale.

The hell with it, Bascombe thought. He pulled her legs down, clutched her behind, and drove his pelvis against hers until she couldn't hold herself back any longer.

He kept her oh-ing and ah-ing for what seemed a charitable length of time and then got to his feet. Stooping for his jeans, he pulled them on with his back to her so that she shouldn't see he hadn't come. He felt no resentment against her. She had put him on exhibition no more than she had herself. He was confused and disturbed by his own feelings. He had thought he wanted her.

Their audience had moved like a single person to the bar. She was wriggling back into her shirt. He waited until she had it settled, then touched her lightly at the waist and brushed his lips against her cheek.

"Are you going now?"

"Yes."

She hesitated for an instant. "There's a place I know, a sort of motel—"

"No."

"Perhaps you're right."

"Good-bye, Nora."

Venus was asleep, stretched out on the towel, her cheek resting on her forearm. He wrapped the towel around her and lifted her down, trying not to awaken her. The tennis-playing nurse was standing in the archway that led to the front hall. She dodged playfully in front of him.

"Listen . . ."

"No."

He did not look at her as he let himself out. His car was at the head of a long line, its front bumper within a foot of the wall at the end of the drive. But each of the arriving guests had left enough space for the one in front to back out. Bascombe was impressed by the consideration this showed. They would not have done that at most parties. It was the kind of politeness people usually only displayed at Sunday morning church or a funeral. Those ritual spaces between the cars seemed to express the whole spirit of the evening.

He settled Venus, still wrapped in the towel, above the dashboard and started the engine, glancing in the mirror as he prepared to back out.

Bascombe switched off the ignition. There was a man lying on the back seat. He leaned over to look at him. The man was stretched out, face up, with his head on the armrest and his short legs almost straight. He was wearing a light gray suit and no hat. It was Nolan.

During the past few weeks Nolan had become so exclusively the product of Bascombe's imagination, it was like finding the emptied shell of his body there. He was instantly, irrationally convinced Nolan must be dead. He wasn't; he was asleep and sat up with a start when Bascombe touched him.

"Hullo." It took him a few seconds before he recognized Bascombe, and then he was understandably surprised, too. "What are you doing here?"

"I've been out here for weeks."

"Oh." Nolan absorbed this slowly. It didn't seem to make any sense to him. "Here?"

"In Hollywood." Bascombe's defensiveness had nothing to do with his recent activities. He felt he should have called Nolan: he had had no right to invent him without even seeing him.

"Oh." Nolan started to get out of the car. Something still seemed to be puzzling him. He walked around to Bascombe's side and leaned in the window.

"I don't— What are you doing *here*?"

"They— Some people here had a party."

"Oh." There was a roar from the lion house among the trees. It was answered by an indignant bleat from the unfed camel. Nolan had to raise his voice for the next question.

"You've been to the party?"

"Yes."

"Did you—Did you join in, I mean?"

"Yes."

"With my sister?"

The aging lioness; Vitamin B; Topanga Canyon; the English idioms; "She's married to a veterinary"; all fell into place in Bascombe's mind.

126

"Did you—with Nora?" Nolan persisted.

"Yes."

Bascombe had always thought Nolan was unpredictable, and he confirmed it now. He burst out laughing. He held on to the door of the car and laughed. Bascombe began to laugh, too.

"Where are you staying?" Nolan asked, when he had finished laughing.

Bascombe found Venus' leads in his pockets and wrote the name of his hotel inside a matchbook.

"Are they still . . . at it, do you know?" Nolan put the matches away. He looked hesitantly toward the house.

"I shouldn't think so."

"I don't—I never thought I had any prejudice about things like that. But it's funny. It's funny when it's your sister."

"Yes."

Venus had woken up. Bascombe started the car and backed it across the drive. She sat up and arranged the towel over her shoulders as he turned onto the Pacific Coast Highway.

"Did yow haf her?"

"Yes."

"Did yow like her?"

"No."

"Vy not?"

"It was boring."

"Vy?"

Bascombe still didn't know the answer to that. He shrugged.

"I knov." Venus nodded understandingly. "I could not keep my eyes open."

She was silent, watching the lights of Wilshire Boulevard rush toward them and sweep by in an indistinguishable flare of cars and neon and civilization. It was not until they reached Westwood that she spoke again.

"Love-in!" she said contemptuously. "All they did vas fuck."

9

CHAPTER

"Gloria Stuart." Nolan stopped, looking down at the name with its brass-rimmed, pink star set in the sidewalk. "I don't suppose you remember Gloria Stuart."

"No."

They walked on down Hollywood Boulevard toward Grauman's Chinese.

"She was marvelous, all sort of cuddly, and she seemed like such a nice girl. *The Old Dark House* with Boris Karloff. There was a scene where she sat on the stairs with her husband. They'd had a row and they were going to break up. I thought he was a right idiot. My God. How could anyone even think of leaving Gloria Stuart? I was only about ten but I used to imagine *I* was married to her, protecting her. You don't remember her at all?"

"No."

"You could go to the cinema for sixpence in those days. It was warm in there if you kept your overcoat on, and sitting in the dark watching Gloria Stuart you could forget everything. All the misery outside."

"I know." Bascombe, at ten, had felt the same way about Kim Novak.

"I used to nick empty beer bottles from the pubs, and then take them to the brewery across the river and get a penny back on them—"

They had met several times since the night of the party. The other, potentially double-dealing Nolan, the Nolan of his letters

128

to Mr. Mitchel, had remained unchanged by these meetings. Nolan had simply become two people to him, the one more or less factual, the other more or less fictional.

Bascombe had never quite got around to explaining to the physical Nolan his reason for being in California. He had not told him he had been ordered to follow one or other (or perhaps both) of the Nolans there. (It was difficult to say which of the two Mr. Mitchel had had in mind.) Fluoride was never mentioned between them. They would meet for lunch at Musso and Frank's and then walk up and down Hollywood Boulevard playing a nostalgic form of "Breakfast" together. He had heard a great deal about Nolan's childhood in Liverpool, how his father beat him, how he ran away. Nolan's voice would recapture a slight Mersey accent when he talked about it. He would reuse the idioms of his youth.

"I never spent a penny of it on anything except cinema," he went on now. "I'd bugger off straight from school to the Prince's or the Royal. I used to take our Nora with me when she was old enough to sit quiet—"

Don Ameche, Deanna Durbin, Edmund Lowe passed under Bascombe's feet. None of the names meant anything to him.

Venus was home watching television in their apartment hotel. She had developed a great interest in it lately.

"It's new, isn't it?" she asked one morning in the middle of a shameless talk show.

The program? The set? The avid self-exposure of the guests being interviewed? The process of visual transmission? Bascombe wasn't sure which she meant.

"Yes," he agreed doubtfully.

She nodded, satisfied. "I never saw it anywhere before." She had lost her Teutonic accent by now, replacing it with the rootless network American, occasionally leavened by a Western vowel, which she had picked up from the box. "You've got a lot of new things."

It was one of those remarks she made occasionally which he found himself reluctantly examining later. Who was "you"? Himself? Americans? The human race? And what did she mean by "new"? New since when? He had no desire to examine Venus' blood or test the electrical impulses of her brain, and he didn't really want to answer those questions either. But he was forced to admit they suggested an interesting contradiction to something she had scribbled to him on the plane. "They fly past us constantly. Some of them go backwards."

He realized that viewed from beyond man's normal perspective a Western flying plane could be said to be traveling backwards. But if she were accustomed to seeing things from such an outward, elevated point of view, how did she know what was new here and what wasn't? And where had she picked up her Teutonic and Greek and Latin? And her tacit acceptance of so many things about the present-day world and its people? The first trousered woman she had seen on Hollywood Boulevard had not surprised her in the least; neither had the first Afro haircut; nor the Buddhists in their saffron robes, although she had seemed to resent the Buddhists a little.

"I managed to get her a job with the Board of Trade. I was in the House by then and we used to meet for coffee at an expresso bar near Victoria. Expresso bars were the big thing in those days. I gave her Keynes and John Strachey to read. I never thought she'd end up married to a vet." Nolan stopped to face him.

Bascombe, who had not anticipated the sudden halt, went on alone for a few steps and then returned. Taking a walk with Nolan was filled with minor hazards. His physical restlessness made him a bad pedestrian. He would come to a dead stop without looking behind him, shoot out his arms as though making signals, accelerate without warning, and bump into someone ahead of him.

"I'm sorry." He was not apologizing for his impulsive halt: he did not appear to be aware of it. "I don't know why it is. I never seem to talk about anything except the past these days."

"Maybe it's this place," Bascombe suggested as they walked on. "Hollywood. It's a freaking National Monument."

"How?"

"All these names on the roll of honor. Maps to show you where

130

Marilyn Monroe died, Jean Harlow's tomb, the back lot where Griffith made his last stand for Intolerance. It's like Gettysburg."

"I suppose in a way." Nolan thought about it as far as the next cross street. "Except it's a monument to something that never happened. Vivien Leigh didn't watch Atlanta burning. Greer Garson's husband didn't sail back from Dunkirk."

"Millions of people think they did." Bascombe got Nolan safely across with the green light.

"Yes, but Gettysburg, the people involved there, Robert E. Lee wasn't just playing a part in a made-up story."

Bascombe didn't agree. General Lee had always seemed to him the most fictional of characters. "It's all a made-up story now," he argued. "The peach orchard, Pickett's charge, the whole thing. It only happened the way *we* think it did—the way we've made it up from letters, diaries, books, Mathew Brady's photographs, a couple of movies we've seen about it."

"Do you really believe that? There's no actual past, only what we imagine?"

"Yes." It seemed to Bascombe to be just as true of the present if there were such a thing. All events were obviously indefinite, subjective. No two people could ever agree about what had taken place even an instant before.

"Then what's real?" Nolan persisted.

Real. That word again. It was becoming as meaningless with abuse as "love." People talked about having a real relationship with their wives. Out here they were always saying someone was a real human bean.

"Whatever you think is real, I guess. Like Gloria Stuart being a nice girl."

They had reached the end of the Boulevard. They crossed to the opposite sidewalk and started back toward Vine. Lily Pons. Norma Shearer. Alice Faye.

It was surprising how much Venus did know. As he had guessed that first morning when she had shown no fear of him, she had obviously lived for some time in a world that was at least similar to this one. Now that she could hear and understand English, she could anticipate the plot of any television film in a way that showed an easy familiarity with all the props of Western dramatic narrative.

Some of Venus' reactions to the box were all her own. "What are they doing with their clothes on?" she would ask, watching a suburban family sit down to their canned soup. And her attitude toward good and evil was even more eccentric than television's own code. The moment some dog-eared villain appeared on the screen she would throw up her hands and condemn him to his fate. "That one will get killed," she would predict with unfaltering accuracy. "He is too proud." And once when the hero, having turned down the heroine and slaughtered everyone else in sight, rode off into the foothills of next week's episode, Venus jumped to her feet and shook her finger at him. "You'll be struck down, too," she warned him. "They won't let you go on like that, you conceited idiot." As it happened she was right, because the series was canceled. But Bascombe had a feeling that when she said *"They* won't let you go on," she was not referring to the network executives.

"You've got to admit someone like . . . President Johnson is more real than—" Nolan glanced down at the sidewalk—"than Tom Mix."

Bascombe had never seen Tom Mix. He had never seen Johnson either. All he knew of him was some selective, largely fabricated image that had been presented to the public under that name. He could see no essential difference between politicians and actors except that politicians were worse paid and more dangerous.

"Why?" he asked.

"Why? Why?" Nolan raised his arms in a sideways flapping gesture of disparagement and struck a young woman coming out of the Roosevelt Hotel a sharp blow in the ribs.

"Why? That's the new politics, isn't it?" he continued, after he had apologized. "No one ever asks *how* any more. It's a kind of philosophical anarchy. You're determined to ignore the world as it exists." His voice had lost all trace of its Mersey sound. "You refuse to work with the materials you have." He halted

132

again, facing Bascombe. "Don't you want to do anything with your life?"

Bascombe didn't answer. It seemed to him an absurd question. Obviously he wanted to do something with his life. He wanted to live it. They walked on in silence as far as Las Palmas.

"When I was young." Nolan quickened his pace a little. "When I was twenty, twenty-one, I wanted to *do* so much. I wanted . . . I wanted to change things as they were. I wanted to make the ordinary man's life—"

Venus was over a foot tall now, and a few days ago Bascombe had made a wonderful discovery about that. Her rate of growth had accelerated slightly. She was adding an inch to her height every five and a half days.

The proportions of her head and body were still classically perfect. She did not grow like a child, irregularly, arms and legs thinning and lengthening and then gradually reacquiring fullness. Venus' whole body simply, beautifully enlarged, as though a camera were being brought closer and closer to her. At the present rate, Bascombe had figured, she would be five feet tall by the beginning of next April.

"—Prescription charges, education, housing, all down the drain already. This may come as a surprise to you, but I think the man's a posturing ass, an unprincipled liar, and a self-seeking shit."

Nolan was waving his arms like a birdman. They had reached the corner of Vine Street. He quieted a little as they crossed the Boulevard again and started back toward Musso and Frank's. To Bascombe the only surprising thing about Nolan's outburst was that he should have expected anyone to be surprised by it.

"Sure. They're all shits," he agreed cheerfully.

"Who?"

"Johnson, Wilson, de Gaulle, Gomulka, Brezhnev, Eshkol, Mao, Chiang, Nasser, Hussein . . ." No other heads of state came immediately to Bascombe's mind. He fell back on the current gang of Presidential hopefuls in that summer of sixty-seven. "Humphrey, Nixon, Rockefeller, Symington, Kennedy, Stanton . . ."

"All of them?"

"Sure."

"How?" He apparently had surprised Nolan. "I mean what do you mean by a shit, exactly?"

It was an arresting question. Bascombe knew what he meant, but he had never been asked to put it into words before.

"Anyone . . ." he began.

Anyone who believes he's on the right side, he thought, and wants other people to recognize it. That is, anyone who believes in capital punishment, or any sort of punishment, or in America my country right or wrong, or in the Soviet Union, or General Motors, or white supremacy, or the class system, or status, or privilege, or any kind of pecking order. Anyone who wants to be a big deal . . : He suddenly saw how he could define it all in a few words.

"Anyone who wants or expects more from society than he does from life," he told Nolan.

"Is a shit?"

"Sure."

"How?"

"Because anyone who expects society to protect his interests and promote and reward him is going to make other people's lives miserable. And that's being a shit."

"It's too simple." Nolan made one of his unscheduled stops. "It won't work."

"I know."

"It's too impractical. It'll never work."

"I know."

They walked on and crossed Wilcox in silent agreement. Now that they were nearing home, Bascombe quickened his pace a little.

In a few minutes he would be letting himself into the hotel room. Venus would be lying naked on the couch. She would climb on the stool he had arranged for her and turn off the television set while he undressed. There was an alcove kitchen off the room and he would cook dinner for her. She could eat meat now and was particularly fond of poultry and game. He had a *poussin* in the icebox for her tonight. And after she had eaten they would lie on the bed together. He would caress her and they would talk and she would reveal a little more of her unfathomable self to him.

Bascombe knew that for the past few weeks he had experienced that most fragile of all human conditions. He had been happy.

He was not sure whether he ought to tell Venus so. She had her own ideas about happiness. One morning he had been typing a letter to Mr. Mitchel. Venus was sitting cross-legged on the arm of the chair, watching the box and doing an intricate sequence of breathing exercises she had picked up somewhere.

"Why is that man so happy?" She paused with her arms extended in front of her.

Bascombe glanced at the screen. A youngish man in a toupé was beaming at him from behind a desk. He listened for a moment.

"That's Boxo. B.O.X.O. Boxo. So next time you're in your neighborhood supermarket—"

"Because he's selling dog food."

Bascombe went back to his letter. "Nolan is disturbed by the possibility that any large-scale plan to introduce chemical solubles . . ."

"He's brave."

Bascombe typed a few more mindless words and then stopped and looked at her.

"He has reckless courage," Venus explained. "It's dangerous to flaunt his happiness like that."

"What about you?" They had reached the corner of Las Palmas where they usually parted. Bascombe's hotel was at the top of the hill and Nolan's car was parked in the lot across the street.

"Me?"

"That company you work for—don't you want to get ahead?"

"No."

"Don't you want to fluoridize, fluoridate, whatever it is, England?"

"No."

"You don't think it'd be good for children's teeth?"

135

"As far as my job's concerned, that's got nothing to do with it."

"No. I suppose not." Nolan touched his arm. "If you feel like that, why don't you quit?"

Bascombe didn't answer at once. Nolan was confronting him with the moral dilemma that had been nagging him for some time. He looked down at the sidewalk. Hedy Lamarr. He remembered her only as a faceless name.

"I guess I want a comfortable place to live. I don't want to be a hippie. I'd rather . . ." He shrugged.

"You're tacitly condoning everything you reject. You know that, don't you?"

"Yes."

The frankness of the admission robbed Nolan's indignation of any further purpose. He smiled.

"Well—" Like all people of Irish origin, he was bad at saying good-bye. "Well, let's get together again soon."

"Sure."

"Nora asked if you'd come out to dinner—"

"No."

"We'd better have lunch then."

"Yes."

"How long are you staying out here?"

It was a curious moment. For a fraction of a second the two Nolans were one: the man who had been walking up and down Hollywood Boulevard with him; and the quarry of Mr. Mitchel's carefully fed fantasies and ambitions. Bascombe was tempted to tell one or the other (or both) of them the truth (it was difficult to say which of them the information actually concerned), to say he would be staying out here as long as "Nolan" did. But he saw that in admitting this he would become subject to Nolan's fantasy. Nolan could play with the idea of leaving tomorrow, of going to New York, anywhere in the world, and know that "Bascombe" would have to follow him there.

"I don't know," he said truthfully.

"Some time next week, then. I'll call you." Nolan was still finding it difficult to take the decisive step of parting. He glanced down at the sidewalk.

"Hedy Lamarr," Nolan read. "I never really liked her. She never . . ." He raised his hand, fingering the air as though sifting it for the right words.

"She never seemed quite real." He snatched himself away at last and zigzagged across the street to the parking lot.

Bascombe hurried home to Venus.

10

CHAPTER

BASCOMBE had been right about the fragility of his happiness. One morning toward the middle of August, Nolan called him to say good-bye.

For a minute, while Nolan told him he was leaving the next day and hoped they would see each other again somewhere, sometime, he was tempted to respond in the same vague terms. But he saw it would be impossible for him to stay on in California after the physical Nolan had returned to London. He could go on spinning out fiction for Mr. Mitchel easily enough; but Nolan was after all a Member of Parliament; he might make a speech, be interviewed on television, get his name in the papers in a dozen ways; Mr. Mitchel was sure to find out he was back.

"I'll see you in London," he assured Nolan. "I'll be following you in a few days."

Nolan's obviously genuine pleasure at this news still surprised and touched him a little after he had hung up. He had always devoted so much of his free time to the company of women that he had had few friends of his own sex, and although he had inspired more than his share of affection in his time, that response, from girls, had been almost consciously earned. It did not occur to him that to a man like Nolan his own undemanding friendliness had come as an equally unexpected pleasure.

Venus was sitting on the windowsill. She had lost interest in television lately and had taken up reading. She read very quickly, sitting cross-legged, the book flat on the sill in front of her, flipping over the pages with the same brisk authority as Mrs. Charrington turning the sheets on the bed.

"We're going to have to leave here, Venus."

She extended her right leg, marking her place on the page with her foot.

"Why don't we go to Paris," she suggested. "It sounds interesting." She pushed her loose hair back from her cheek. "Except for these extraordinary Americans."

Like many of her remarks this puzzled him for a second. He leaned over to see what she was reading: Hemingway's *The Sun Also Rises*.

"Do you think they're extraordinary?"

"All this nonsense about being *men*."

Bascombe's preparations for the return journey were far less elaborate than they had been for the voyage out. He had been on expenses for the ten weeks he had been in California and he could afford to fly back to London first class. The rules about hand luggage were less strictly enforced for first-class passengers. Bascombe bought the largest, loosely woven Mexican basket he could find, lined the bottom of it with padded silk, and arranged a billow of muslin over the top. He did not dare risk a light for Venus to read by, but it was only a few steps from his seat to the toilet, and accustomed to the self-concern of the rich, none of the hostesses questioned his lie about his kidneys.

He had arranged his flight to arrive in London on Friday afternoon so that he and Venus could have two free days together before he had to report to Mr. Mitchel at the office. Since he laid no claims to being a British subject, there were no difficulties with the Immigration authorities. When he reached customs he simply lifted Venus out of the basket and she stood motionless, gracefully poised on the counter.

Her beauty in the red silk sari he had bought her seemed to light up that whole area of the building. The young customs inspector's eyes went to her like a child's to a Christmas tree. His face melted into the same idiot's delight as Chester Voigt's had in Los Angeles.

"Would you say she was a work of art or an antique, sir?"

"She's a doll," Bascombe told him, replacing her tenderly in the basket.

Mrs. Charrington had been characteristically conscientious in her impulsive way. The apartment was immaculate. For a moment, as Bascombe put down his suitcase and locked the door behind him, nothing seemed changed. It was good to be back in this familiar place where Venus had first entered his life, where she had bathed in a milk saucer, written her first words to him.

But then Venus, who had gone ahead of him into the bedroom, reappeared in the doorway, and he knew everything had changed.

She had been only six inches high when they left for California —mute, dependent on him for everything. She was just over a foot and a half tall now, accustomed to sun and freedom, to the varied sight and sounds of human life, to his own constant companionship. How could she stay locked up alone in this pokey little flat nine hours a day while he was at the office?

There was no longer any physical reason why she could not roam all over London by herself, take taxis or buses, shop, eat in restaurants. But there were other reasons why she couldn't.

They discussed them while they took a bath together. In spite of her occasionally eccentric viewpoint, Venus had a sharp understanding of the world around her by now. There was no need to explain to her that walking about the streets of a modern city she would attract dangerous attention. People would not only stare and follow her, they would demand explanation. Who was she—*what* was she, nineteen inches tall and as lovely as the moon? The first policeman who saw her attracting a crowd would take her into custody for her own protection. And then the press would get onto it.

Venus understood this. Bascombe explained to her now that her particular power of enchantment, her ability to infatuate any male on sight would not help her. It might be an adoring crowd that mobbed her, but adoring crowds had proved often enough they could be as dangerous as a lynching party.

Venus held out her hand. She wanted the soap. Bascombe passed it to her. They were both hot and sticky after the journey, and he had run the bath tepid and not too deep so he could laze at one end while Venus floated or swam or stood and soaped herself at the other.

"In California, they mistook me for a doll with—what was it?"

"Transistors."

"So many new things."

"In California, I was with you and we had the car." When she had grown too big to put inside his shirt he had carried her down to the hotel parking lot, or from the car to the beach, in a cellophane box he had bought from a florist. Except for that one occasion in the drugstore, she had never walked about in public.

Venus tossed the soap back onto his chest and submerged. For a second only her marvelous legs showed, ruffling above the surface. He soaped himself until she was upright again.

Standing up to her waist in the water she pushed her wet hair back from her face. He had been wondering whether she could somehow be dressed to pass for a child, but he could see, all the more clearly with her hair damply flattened, that her proportions were unmistakably adult. A child her height would have had a head twice as large as hers.

"You're still rather small for a child, anyway," he told her regretfully. "For a child old enough to walk around the streets alone."

"We could try it together." Venus swam forward to retrieve the soap. She began to wash him, kneeling on his chest, working up a lather, moving down past his navel.

"We could buy some kids' clothes and see how you look in them," Bascombe agreed. "Oh. Oh, Christ. Oh, Jesus. Venus!"

The girl in "Children's Wear, fourth floor and to your left" had a great deal on her mind. The store closed at one o'clock on Saturdays, and she was concerned about her nails, her hair, the fact that she had finally, almost definitely decided she was wearing the wrong shade of tights for those boots, and most of all about getting to the pub around the corner in time to be included in a party of Hurray Henrys who were driving down to Goodwood for the races that afternoon. She was not concerned about children's wear.

"What size-ish is she?" she asked Bascombe indifferently.

"She's about . . . about two feet tall now."

"Really?"

That seemed to be that. She showed no further curiosity. She privately thought Bascombe was quite dishy, but if he had a two-foot child he was probably *married*. She went back to worrying about her tights. She was wearing practically no skirt so she had plenty of flesh-colored thigh to compare with beige-colored boot.

"What size—what size-ish would a two-foot child take?"

"I couldn't say."

Bascombe looked at her. She was what the leaping Scot used to call a debby little bitch, he thought. "Couldn't you guess?" he asked.

"Actually, I couldn't, in fact. No."

"Try."

She sauntered out from behind the counter and led him aimlessly to a rack. Lifting her hand she ran it along the row of hanging clothes as though plucking a harp, then relapsed into her limp, waiting attitude.

"You might find something there, I suppose."

Bascombe settled the Mexican basket carefully on a chair and tried. There were some that looked short enough, but there was another problem he hadn't anticipated. The smaller a child's dress, the more nearly square its shape. He had brought a pull-out metal tape measure and he measured the smallest. It was twelve inches long and eleven inches wide at the shoulder. He had never realized before what squat little bodies children must have. Cut almost rectangular, the dress was apparently designed to fit a grotesque 20-20-20 figure. Venus, who in full womanhood would be a magnificent 38-24-38, was at the moment a perfect 11-6-11. The stupid thing would hang on her like a yoke. It would also reveal her arms and legs, which were slender and graceful and would look like reeds in that thing.

The thought of her legs raised another problem, shoes. There were some children's play shoes on a nearby counter. The smallest of them was over four inches long. Venus' feet, which were as delicate as her hands, not the sturdy wedges children used for standing on, were less than three inches from heel to toe.

He replaced the shoe and, still carrying the dress, went back to the deb. She had found an emery board and was improving her nails with it.

"Are they all like this?"

"Some of them have pleats, actually."

"This *shape*."

His slightly raised voice got her head up again. "What shape is your child?"

She reminded him of the fruity girl in the real estate office who had told him he might like Earl's Court. But he had no desire to strip off this girl's artificiality with her clothes and get to know the woman underneath. It astonished him he could ever have been that naïve. She would be as spurious in bed as she was in children's wear.

Bascombe hung the dress back on the rack and left her there with her nails and her hair and the wrong tights. Like everyone else, she had her own life to live.

On his way to the elevator there was a scratching sound from the Mexican basket. He put it on his shoulder so that Venus could talk to him through the rushwork.

"Look at him. He's small."

He turned around in time to see a woman and a boy disappearing into the piano department. He went after them. Venus had been right. The kid was minute. A peaked white face, eyes like caves, a stem of a neck. But he could walk all right. While Bascombe watched him he trotted over to a Bechstein grand and began prodding at the keys with his pistil fingers.

"I could wear that."

He had kept the basket on his shoulder. He murmured agreement. The little boy was wearing a one-piece boiler suit with a pointed hood hanging down the back.

"I'll see how tall he is," Bascombe whispered.

He edged over to the Bechstein, but before he could get into position to measure him the kid had climbed onto the piano stool. Kneeling over the keys he tapped out the opening notes of the "Moonlight Sonata." He tapped them out correctly.

"Nobody's paying any attention to *him*."

It was true. Two feet away a stout woman with a Scottish terrier cuddled the animal more closely against her as though to protect it from the influence of the alien music. But she barely glanced at the child who was playing it.

"*Angelo, vieni qui! Vede questo!*"

The boy's enormous eyes turned toward his mother. He played a few last self-assertive notes and slithered off the stool. Bascombe stepped in front of him. The kid bumped against his thighs.

"I'm sorry." Bascombe patted the top of the boy's head and moved aside, keeping his hand pressed against his own leg to mark the level of the pat. He took the metal tape measure out of his pocket and extended it down to the floor from his palm. He look at the figure on the rule.

It seemed incredible, but there it was. The little bastard, the smallest self-propelled child he had ever seen, was thirty-two inches tall.

"Put more in."

Venus slid the hook back from her head and Bascombe stuffed another piece of muslin inside it. After buying the smallest one-piece suit he could find, he had gone to the furniture department for a square of foam rubber. By cutting platforms out of this to fit into the feet of the suit, he had managed to raise Venus' height to twenty-one and a half inches. Padded all over with crumpled muslin and zipped up the front, she looked all right, by human child standards, up to the collar. Above it her lovely head stood poised like a bubble risen from a vat.

She pulled the hood on again and he fastened it under her chin. Bulged out at the sides, with only her features showing, it brought her head into acceptable, childlike proportion to her body. Its peak added a further illusory two or three inches to her height.

"Can you walk?"

She could. Although she had lost some of her prowess as she grew bigger, she was so light—she weighed less than five pounds—that she was still extremely strong for her size. She could no longer leap twenty times her own height, but she could spring onto the mantelpiece without the least effort. The padded boiler suit was no burden to her. She strode into the bedroom as though she were walking in space.

Bascombe followed her. She wanted to look at herself in the mirror. As he lifted it down from the wall he found himself seeing her for the first time, not as his accomplice in an amusing masquerade, but as she would see herself in a moment: squat, stuffed, distorted. He felt he hated the whole human race. It was people, with their rigid, narrow minds, who were forcing her to wear that grotesque uniform. Why the hell couldn't she walk around as she was? Just because she was smaller than they were.

He propped the mirror upright on the floor so she could see her whole reflection in it. He watched her as she turned and looked.

It didn't anger Venus. It amused her. He realized that her sense of her own dignity was too great to be disturbed by any artificial disfigurement. Dipped in tar and feathered, she would still have known herself to be beautiful. He knelt beside her and kissed her forehead.

"Ready?" he asked.

"Can you go out like that?"

"No." He had taken all his clothes off, as usual, as soon as he came home. He would have to disguise himself for the streets, too.

The Earl's Court Road was crowded with Saturday afternoon youth. It was not a fashion parade as it was in Chelsea. Here the young milled and gathered and darted from one group to another like messengers. They might have been assembling for a mass demonstration. Bascombe knew from his own experience they weren't. They were simply, individually, trying to get fixed up for the evening so they wouldn't have to spend it alone, each in his own miserable bed-sitter.

He was afraid to set Venus down in this throng. She sat astride the back of his neck, her feet clutched in his hands, her arms resting on the top of his head. Most of the other young men who had children carried them the same way. The girls had theirs slung on their backs. The couples walked with their arms around each other's shoulders. Even in reserved England, physical contact had become a fashionable appetite.

"It's like Hollywood. Nobody looks at me here, either."

It was true. They had reached the halfway mark of the post office and no one had so much as glanced at her. The few girls who had considered Bascombe had stopped their inspection just short of the child on his back. The two little legs hanging down over his shoulders had been enough to end their interest.

"Why not?" Venus didn't seem put out, only curious.

"I don't know—the English don't seem to care about children much. I guess they're just not interested in them."

"Who are the English?"

Bascombe had forgotten: they hadn't been able to talk to each other when they were in London before. He had never explained to her about England as he had tried to explain about America. She had never watched television here.

He didn't know where to start. America was comparatively simple: it had once been the New World (except to the Indians who lived there); Europeans (she seemed to know all about Europeans) had gradually forcibly occupied it. But he had very little understanding of how England had been populated. He remembered that Caesar had conquered the island. He thought it had been known as Britannia in those days.

"They're Britannians?" he suggested.

"Celts?" She sounded intrigued.

"No. I don't think so. Anglo-Saxons?"

"Saxons!" She might have been saying "Horses!" But she perked up a moment later at the sight of a dark young man with chestnut eyes. "They don't look like Saxons."

"They're all mixed up by now."

"Are they interested in making love?"

"They're supposed to be much more interested than they used to be. Some of the young ones are quite . . ." He tried to find the right word, thinking of the young people he had known over here. The leaping Scot sprang to his mind. ". . . quite impulsive."

"The girls, too?"

"Mostly the girls."

The crowd thinned north of the post office. He set Venus down and she strolled beside him. He had never been for a walk hand-in-hand with a child. It surprised him how much stooping and kneeling to hear what was said it entailed. Each time he bent and looked at her, her lovely face framed in that puffed-out hood, her body submerged in stuffing, he felt a fresh sense of outrage. He couldn't accept the affront to her dignity as blithely as she could. He hated to see her disfigured like this. After a few minutes he seized a street crossing as an excuse to put her back on his shoulders.

They circled home the back way. In the squares and residential streets, preparations for Saturday night were more visibly practical. Young men with their heads inside the engines of sports cars. Girls lugging stereo sets and gallon cans of beer, and some of them sleeping bags, up the front steps of the houses.

"Let's go in the field."

They had reached the square behind the street where they lived. In the center was a rectangle of overgrown garden, surrounded by iron railings. There were several fine trees, a dilapidated rustic hut, the vestiges of gravel paths, and, as Venus had accurately described it, a field, although it had probably once been a lawn.

Bascombe crossed to the nearest gate in the railings. It was locked. He had scarcely ever walked this way before, but he remembered, when he had first taken the apartment, the fruity girl had said something about "a key to the square" being included in the rent. He had an idea it was hanging somewhere in the kitchen.

"I could come *here* alone."

There was no one in the gardens. It did not look as though there ever had been. If Venus came here in her child's disguise, he didn't see why she shouldn't be safe. She could sit under the trees, read; there might even be sunshine before the end of August.

"I've got a key. Do you think you could reach the lock?"

"I don't need a key."

"Somebody might be looking out of the window. If they saw a child jump over a five-foot railing, they'd—" He wasn't sure what they would do, but he didn't want to take the chance of finding out.

"I could go in between the posts."

Bascombe put her down to see if she could. Her body could have slipped between much narrower railings; the muslin padding yielded easily. She turned and looked up at him through the bars.

"Go and see what it's like in there," he suggested.

"You come in, too?"

He could have climbed over the gate, but he was afraid of attracting attention.

"I'll wait for you here." He watched her with sudden sadness as she moved off through the grass. They had been separated so seldom these past ten weeks. Now, starting on Monday, they would be separated all day, five days a week.

Screw Mr. Mitchel!

"Welcome back, stranger."

Bascombe had scarcely put his feet on his desk Monday morning before he had to take them down again. He stood up as Mr. Mitchel closed the office door behind him. He was surprised how short and gray Mr. Mitchel was. The man to whom he had written his letters had acquired an independent image in his mind, larger, more colorful than the one facing him now.

"How did you make out with the go-go girls?"

They shook hands and Mr. Mitchel sat down in the visitor's chair. Bascombe didn't answer. He knew that when Mr. Mitchel was playfully facetious it meant he had something on his mind. He waited without interest to hear what it was.

"I got your letters."

Bascombe knew that already from Mr. Mitchel's answers to them. He continued to wait.

"Nolan." He might have been saying "war" or "sewage." He was not identifying a man but a topic. "I won't tell you what the latest developments are here until you've told me what the latest developments are there. So don't interrupt me until you've an-

148

swered one question."

Bascombe had no intention of interrupting. He had no intention of saying a word until he was forced to. He had taken Venus to the gardens that morning in her child's disguise. It was a mild, unthreatening summer's day. She had a pocketbook and an apple and some chicken breast wrapped in tinfoil. She had seemed quite content at the prospect of spending the whole day there. He was looking forward to meeting her under the trees this evening. He hoped to be out of here by five at the latest.

"Is he or isn't he, Bascombe?"

He didn't answer at once. In spite of the inflexible way Mr. Mitchel had asked it, it was not a question that had to be answered yes or no. He could say Nolan was still *considering* fluoridation as the subject of a Private Member's bill, but on the other hand there *were* certain imponderables . . . and all that shit. He could string the whole thing along for another two or three months if he felt like it, so long as he kept Nolan and Mr. Mitchel apart, and he didn't think he would have any trouble doing that. Nolan found Mr. Mitchel as boring as he did.

"No, he isn't. Bascombe wasn't sure why he said it, but the moment he had, he felt relieved. He was sick of making up stories for Mr. Mitchel. He had always been able to justify these fictions in the past on the grounds that they were nothing compared to the fictions with which the company sought to justify *its* actions. Service. Progress. A cleaner America. But now he was suddenly as tired of his own lies as he was of other people's.

"Nolan isn't going to do a damn thing about fluoride," he added firmly.

"Bascombe." Mr. Mitchel came up slowly out of the chair. His flabby face was expressionless from the shock. He put both hands on the desk and leaned forward. "Bascombe, you screwed it up."

"Yes."

"Thank God." Mr. Mitchel let out a cackle of laughter. "That leaves their ball right on the green, six inches from the hole. And —They—Won't—Sink—It." He brought out the last five words with the panting glee of a child jumping on another child's sand castle, and sank back into the visitor's chair. "Now, I'm going to put you right square in the picture, Bascombe."

He didn't see how any harm could come to her in the gardens. There had been no one there when he let her in this morning. The ground was so overgrown with weeds and bushes that there were plenty of places where she could stay comfortably out of sight of the street. If some woman did look out of her kitchen window and see a small, a very small child in a boiler suit sitting under a tree reading a book, saw the child still there three or four hours later, was there any reason why she should do anything about it? He didn't think a woman, in England, would do anything about it.

"I'm having lunch with him." Bascombe cut through the fog of Mr. Mitchel's metaphors at the mention of Nolan's name.

"You get a letter from that son of a bitch."

"I'll talk to him."

"Get him to write you a letter."

Mr. Mitchel was at the door at last. Four minutes of repetitious jargon later he was out of it. Bascombe put his feet back up on the desk. If he made some excuse to get away from Nolan by two o'clock, he could go to the gardens and make sure she was all right before returning to the office.

The sun had dispersed the morning's haze. It was a hot day by London standards. They had lunch on the terrace of the Houses of Parliament. The food was bad and the service perfunctory, but there was a festive compensation in a city in just eating out of doors within sight of a river. Nolan had shaken off his nostalgia now that he was home again. He was cheerful and inquisitive. He wanted to know about Bascombe's job, about Mr. Mitchel, about the company's activities. If Bascombe had planned the whole conversation, he couldn't have contrived a better opportunity to ask Nolan for the letter Mr. Mitchel wanted from him. It wasn't even as though he would be asking much of a favor. Nolan would have understood the situation at once.

Cleared of golfing metaphors, the situation was this: The Cleveland office of the company, who had been so exclusively occupied with waste disposal in the past that there was not so much as a living newt left in Lake Erie, had been arguing for some time that the fluoride project was rightfully their baby. The New York office had finally agreed with them. Mr. Mitchel and Bascombe were being taken off fluoride and put onto something else. ("When I tell you *what*," Mr. Mitchel had inaccurately assured Bascombe several times, "you'll be so excited you won't sleep.") Cleveland was setting up its own London office. ("After we've done all the groundwork for them, goddamn it.") Cleveland would inherit, among other things, Stanley Nolan, M.P., and the Private Member's bill. And that was the whole point, as Mr. Mitchel saw it. Cleveland must inherit a situation that *seemed* so close to success that a talking dog couldn't fail to push it through. And then—Mr. Mitchel had repeated this many times, too—and then, Cleveland must be the ones to screw things up. Nolan, robbed of the persuasive cooperation of his friends Newton R. Mitchel and Bascombe H. Fletcher, must suddenly seem to change his mind. That was where the letter from Nolan came in: a friendly, hopeful letter, filled with goodwill toward Mitchel and Fletcher, toward the company, toward the whole fluoride project. ("The bastard doesn't have to *commit* himself to anything.") That letter, dated just before the Cleveland takeover, would go into the New York files. It would remain there forever, the last pre-mortem X-ray of the corpse, token of Mr. Mitchel's success, proof of Cleveland's hopeless incompetence.

It was the kind of situation that was so routine that after two years with the company, Bascombe was sometimes surprised that its factories ever did actually produce anything.

"What were you supposed to be doing in Los Angeles?" Nolan picked a piece of grit off his ham with the end of his knife. "I mean, why did your firm send you out there?"

There it was, another opening. His relations with Nolan were so easy by now that if he told him the truth they could have what the English called "a good giggle" about it. Then they could go on to Nolan's office and concoct the letter between them.

"Nothing. Just a lot of office politics," he told Nolan truthfully. He didn't say any more.

"Were you supposed to be lobbying me?"

"Yes." Bascombe didn't know how Nolan had guessed, but he

151

was not surprised he had.

"About fluoride?"

"Yes."

He had been right. Nolan did think it was funny. He pushed his gritty ham away from him. "Why didn't you?"

"I don't know."

"Are you supposed to be lobbying me now?"

"Yes."

"What about? I mean, what do they want from me exactly?"

"A letter. They want you to write me a letter." Bascombe was beginning to think it was funny, too.

"What do they want me to say?"

"Nothing."

"I'll do it if I can."

"I know. Thanks." Bascombe shook his head.

"Why not?"

"Because . . . screw it."

The waitress brought them some soot-flecked ice cream. They were busy scraping it with their spoons for a minute. A small madness had overtaken them both. They had to keep pausing; they put their spoons down while they trembled with almost silent laughter. The ice cream, never very firm, melted into a gray mess on their plates.

"You're a stubborn bastard, aren't you?"

"I don't know." They were beginning to recover from their childish hilarity. "It's just lately. It never seemed to matter before. It all seems so stupid."

"Will you get fired?" Nolan was serious, concerned.

Would he? Bascombe wondered. It was almost a hope. But he didn't belong to a generation that got fired. Passed over; demoted; locked out of the toilet; shifted to a suboffice; replaced by automation; laid off because of a change in policy, the curtailment of defense spending; but not fired.

"No."

Nolan guided him back through the fake-medieval passages to the street. Beyond the rush of traffic Richard the Lion Heart beamed at them from the back of his unlikely-looking horse.

"If you change your mind—if you want me to write that letter . . ." Nolan was having his usual trouble saying good-bye.

"Thanks." Bascombe stopped a cab. "Thanks," he called again through the window.

The moment the taxi dropped him in the square he knew something was wrong. A tall, thin woman in hair curlers was standing on the steps of the corner house, gazing into the gardens. There was a classic quality about her attitude: a sea captain's wife watching her husband's ship founder in the bay. Bascombe followed the direction of her gaze. A dozen men and women were grouped under the trees, their heads lifted, their bodies held in the same fraught stillness. Here and there in open windows on every side of the square arrested figures stood staring down.

"What is it? *What's happened?*" He had to shout at the woman to get in touch with her.

"Oh, isn't it terrible!" It was a lament, not a question. "Trapped up in the tree!"

"What is? *What is?*"

"The poor little thing." She did not look at him. She could not bear to interrupt her attention to the tragedy. "The poor little thing."

Bascombe ran to the gate. He had the key out of his pocket before he reached it. The rusted lock caught and would not turn. He used it as a foothold and jumped over the railings. He was running again as he landed, racing through the grass toward the trees. Long before he reached them he saw the small still thing under the elm, the peaked hood face downward. He slithered to his knees beside it and gently, with a sense of sickened terror, turned it over. It was empty. He looked up into the densely leafed tangle of branches.

"What's happened? Where is she?" He was shouting again. "Is she hurt?"

He was instantly the center, not so much of attention as of averted sympathy. Not a head was shifted from its rapt, tilted position, but several voices answered him at once.

"I don't think she's hurt, in fact, no."

153

"She can jump about all right."

"I saw her distinctly. Jumping like anything."

"She's just frightened, I expect."

"We've been trying to coax her down."

"She just keeps climbing further up."

"Poor little thing."

"Are you the owner?"

Bascombe had been acutely relieved by the assurance that "the poor little thing" could "jump about all right." But it was the last question that put him, as Mr. Mitchel would have said, right square in the picture. As he pulled off his jacket and dropped it on the ground he realized he should have guessed the truth from the beginning. There was only one object that could have commanded such unanimous concern from this group of middle-class English people. He had been more than willing a moment before, when he thought Venus was in physical danger, to expose her to the less immediate threat of human curiosity. But he saw now there was still a chance of saving her from that, too. He moved quickly to the base of the tree. If he could get a grip on the lowest branch he could climb the rest of the way easily enough. He stretched his arms upward, judging the necessary spring, then stepped back a few feet.

"We've sent for a ladder."

"Better leave it to them."

"The Royal Society are so awfully reliable."

"Poor little thing."

He ran forward, jumped, got his right foot against a knot a third of the way up the trunk, and kicking back, jumped again. His hands grasped the branch at its thickest part. The bark was deeply ridged and firm. He held on, swinging from side to side, advancing his fingers ridge by ridge until they met. His arms circled the branch. He swung his legs, got one foot over and straddled it.

"Jolly good."

"Well done."

He began to climb. Above him the branches curving out from the trunk provided him with a rough spiral staircase. Below him a breathless silence encouraged his ascent. "Venus," he called softly. "Venus." He was partly hidden from the ground now. "Venus."

She was almost at the top, sitting in the cleft from which the last slender boughs forked up toward the light. She was stark naked and not in the least frightened.

"You're early!" she greeted him happily.

"Venus." He rested on the branch below her. He reached up and touched her hand. He was so glad to see her: concern, anger, reproof vanished like shadows in the blaze of his relief.

"Are those idiots still there?"

"Yes."

"I was just climbing down when a woman started shouting at me. I thought I'd better keep away from her. Then all those others came over. So I climbed back up here."

"They can't see you up here."

Venus slipped lightly down onto his shoulder. "It was hot sitting under the tree in that thing."

"I know." He didn't blame her at all. There was nothing unreasonable about her behavior.

"If we stay here for a little time, do you think they'll go away?"

"No." He stroked her ankle, trying to decide whether to tell her the truth. In spite of her indestructible dignity, he couldn't be sure she would find it amusing.

"Have you got her?" It was a man's voice from below. The question was followed by a chorus of inquiries in which the words "poor little thing" stood out most clearly.

"They sound quite friendly," Venus commented. She swung her leg over his shoulder, sitting astride the back of his neck. "Let's go down. Come on."

"I'll have to hide you."

"It's too late for that now." She rubbed her cheek against his hair. "Bring my book."

He reached the book down from the branch above and slipped it into his back pocket. She clasped him firmly around the neck waiting for him to start down. He stayed where he was.

"I'll have to hide you, Venus."

"It's too late." She had always hated having to repeat anything. "That woman's already seen me."

"She thinks—they all think . . ." He was going to have to tell her the truth. The R.S.P.C.A. would be arriving any minute with their ladder.

"They think you're an animal."

He couldn't see her face. There was no immediate reaction he could feel in her attitude. "She just caught a glimpse of you," he hurried on. "And she made up her mind that's what she saw. That's why they're all waiting down there. They're all worried to death about some goddamned animal."

It was all right. He could feel it now, in her arms, in her breasts pressed against his head, the tremor of laughter. He undid his tie and the top two buttons of his shirt. She slipped inside it next to his skin, wrapping herself around his waist. He tightened his belt to secure his shirt more firmly and started down.

"Got her?"

"Jolly good."

"Well done."

They did not exactly crowd around him as he dropped to the ground, but they circled him in their own reserved way. He put one arm protectively around his bulging shirt to show he had no intention of letting the poor little thing escape again, and snatched up the hooded suit from the grass under the tree. But he wasn't to get away quite so easily. Their concern had earned them the right to curiosity, even at the dreaded English risk of seeming nosy.

"Is she all right?"

"She's awfully quiet."

"She was awfully quiet when she was up the tree."

"What is she, actually?" It was the man who had led the chorus all along. He had a moustache and gray hair and a look of suspicious disdain that was as unchanging as a birthmark.

Bascombe crumpled the boiler suit under his arm. He looked at the circle of waiting faces. What the hell kind of animal could there be that looked even remotely like Venus in the nude?

"She's a chihuahua!" There was the mistaken conviction of the eye-witness in the woman's raised voice. A murmured chorus of disbelief did nothing to shake it.

"I saw her distinctly," she repeated several times.

"Sure." Bascombe decided to take her side against the others. It sounded as reasonable to him as anything he could think of. "That's what she is. A chihuahua."

He started forward and they parted to let him through, but another chorus of murmurs followed him to the gate. They were neither curious nor approving now. They were angrily suspicious.

"Rot," he heard the moustached man say. "Owned dogs all my life. And one thing I can tell you. They don't damn well climb trees."

It was after three, Bascombe saw, as he let himself into the apartment. He helped Venus out of his shirt and dropped her suit onto a chair. Mr. Mitchel would be waiting for him at the office, waiting impatiently to hear whether he had gotten the letter from Nolan. He undid his belt and pulled off his soiled shirt.

"Do you have to go back to your work?" Venus stopped and looked at him from the bedroom doorway.

"No." He kicked off his shoes.

"Not till tomorrow?" She was delighted.

"No." He followed her into the bedroom. She jumped onto the bed. He slipped off his trousers and lay down beside her. She knelt over him and stroked his spiky hair back from his forehead.

"Do you think it'll be safe for me to return to that field tomorrow?" She rested her face close to his cheek. "I'll keep my clothes on this time." She was not being contrite; she was only being practical. "Even if it's hot."

"It doesn't matter." He realized he had made a decision at last. "I'm not going to work tomorrow, either." He turned and stroked her shoulder. Her closeness stirred the skin of his lips like a touch.

"I'm not going back to work at all. The hell with the freaking job."

11

CHAPTER

TWENTY-FOUR AND EIGHT: thirty-two; and two: thirty-four. Bascombe was going through his checkbook. Counting some savings
bonds an aunt had left him, he figured he had three thousand,
four hundred and eighty dollars in the world.

It was the end of August and he was free. He had spent several
mindless sessions with Mr. Mitchel trying to persuade him first
that he meant it; then that he couldn't be bribed to change his
mind; and finally that he was not betraying a man who had
treated him like his own son, selling himself and his inside info
to another company; he was not playing ball with anyone anywhere; he was just quitting. Mr. Mitchel had at last accepted his
decision but not his innocence. Arrived at this expedient misun-
derstanding, he suddenly changed into a different person, cold,
practical, and efficient. He arranged for Bascombe's final salary
and expense check to be paid to him at once, and ordered him
to pack up his things and be out of the building within an hour.
Bascombe was out of it within a minute. He was not one of those
men who make a second home of their offices. There were no half-
empty packages of breakfast cereal, no unanswered letters from
mother, no broken alarm clocks or odd socks in the drawers of
his desk. He had nothing to pack up but the paperback copy of
Darkness at Noon which he had brought to work with him that
morning.

Venus was lying on the blue couch reading it now. Out of deference to Mrs. Charrington, who was cleaning the bedroom, she

was wearing one of her California saris. She looked exquisite in it. One inch every five and a half days . . .

Bascombe figured it would be the beginning of March before Venus was four foot eight or nine, tall enough in high heels to lead an unremarked, independent existence. As soon as she reached that stage he could start looking for another job. Because of Home Office restrictions it might be difficult for him to find one in England, and once she was too big to travel in a basket he would have to face the problem of getting her a passport (Date and country of birth? Full names of parents?) if they went back to America. But he was too resilient to worry about that now. When the time came that she was free to live her own life, to spend her days safely, as she pleased, without him, he would find some kind of job somewhere to support her.

Meanwhile they had about three thousand dollars to last them for the next six months. A hundred and twenty dollars a week. The rent was paid in advance until the twentieth of October and would be three hundred dollars a month from then on. Electricity, gas, and phone were separate. There was food, laundry, transportation, which almost unavoidably meant cabs in the city with Venus . . .

Mrs. Charrington passed silently through the room into the kitchen. Venus gave her a smile and went back to her book. The change in Venus' attitude toward the *lingulaca periculosa* since their return from America had been complete. Bascombe had come back from one of his early sessions with Mr. Mitchel to find them together. Venus had been waiting for him to take her out for a walk and was dressed in her child's costume but without the hood. Mrs. Charrington was making the bed. Venus was sitting on the chest of drawers, watching her.

"This is my niece," Bascombe explained hastily and unconvincingly. "From America. My daughter—my sister's daughter. She's staying with me for . . . a while."

"Yes, sir." Mrs. Charrington included them both in her gracious smile. "We've already introduced ourselves."

It was always impossible to tell what was going on behind that majestic calm, but Bascombe had the impression Mrs. Charrington did not believe him for a moment, that she and Venus had already arrived at some far more mysterious and truthful understanding of the situation. If they had, Mrs. Charrington had never revealed what it was, and Venus was equally silent about it.

"She's okay," she said with one of her drifts into network American, when Bascombe asked her about the incident. "She won't talk."

"We have ways of making her talk," Bascombe kidded her, trying to extend the discussion. But Venus pretended she didn't understand the joke, and he couldn't get any more out of her.

Since then, Mrs. Charrington had treated Venus with the same courteous condescension as she treated Bascombe and, he supposed, everyone else. But there were moments when he felt something tacit and inexplicable in the way they smiled at each other; something close to regard in Mrs. Charrington's manner toward Venus.

"Where is this terrible place?" Venus had finished *Darkness at Noon*. She flicked it shut with her foot. "Russia?"

He pushed aside his figures as she jumped onto the table. "It's one of . . . It's east of Gaul."

"They're mad. All of them. They've all been struck mad."

"Worse than the Americans?" She had once said roughly the same thing about the Americans after watching a documentary advocating better things for better living through chemistry.

"Different." She came over and put her arms around his neck. He had always found it one of the loveliest things about her, the spontaneous, almost casual way she had of showing and claiming affection. "That sort of nonsense, politics, has never been any of my business, thank heaven," she admitted cryptically. "But it's so obvious— You should try to organize those things so you can live—so you can forget everything except living. Those madmen—" She gestured toward the novel on the couch. "You'd think they only wanted to live so they can organize. They've got it all backwards."

He thought of what he had said to Nolan: his definition of a shit. The sense of it was very close to what Venus was saying.

"What's this?" She was examining the figures he had written.

160

"All these numbers?"

"Money."

"Oh." There was sadness and a touch of pity in the way she looked at him. "That's one of the ways you've organized things, isn't it?" She might have been saying she had forgotten he was crippled by that, too.

"Yes."

"Everywhere now?"

Maybe there were Indians up the Amazon who hadn't. "Almost everywhere."

"Oh, well." She obviously wasn't going to take money too seriously. He drew her toward him and kissed the top of her head. Although she was still less than two feet tall, and her arm from shoulder to wrist was shorter than his hand, he had no sense of her smallness when they were close to each other. The aura of her presence overwhelmed all other awareness.

"I'll take your dress shirts to the laundry on my way home, sir." Mrs. Charrington was wearing her hat and coat. She picked up her bag from its usual place by the front door.

"Good night, Mrs. Charrington." Bascombe stood up. He had never been able to address her sitting down.

"Good night, sir." Mrs. Charrington's glance moved to the table. Venus was reclining on it, supported by one arm, her sari falling in graceful folds over her knees. As Mrs. Charrington looked at her, Venus inclined her head slightly. Mrs. Charrington smiled. Bascombe was sure there was a glimpse of gratitude in the smile.

"Good night, madam." Mrs. Charrington's voice lost none of its graciousness in its momentary deference.

As soon as the door closed softly behind her, Venus wound off her sari. She had never shown any trace of woman's fondness for clothes. She seemed to regard them rather as a disfigurement of her beauty than an adornment to it. Bascombe undressed, too. They moved at once by unspoken agreement into the bedroom.

Their physical intimacy had developed into an endlessly searching progression of caresses. Bascombe no longer thought of the day when she would be grown enough to make love to—as he

161

would have once expressed it—"properly." He no longer looked forward to some climactic wedding night. He clung to each stage of her capacity to exchange embraces, knowing it was irretrievable.

Lying on his back he could taste her mouth like the flesh of a wild strawberry on his tongue. His throat was between her breasts. Her spread thighs clasped his ribs. He circled her hips with his hands. Her buttocks were no larger than pears, but so delicately yielding that his fingers, like his eyes, had no sense of their smallness. They were the tangible perfection of every bottom he had ever yearned after in his life.

She began stroking his eyelids with her fingers, parting and ruffling the lashes. At the same time she shifted slightly and moved her hips in a slow circle against his chest. He felt a familiar stirring. Her tongue prickled his lips. He slipped his finger between her legs until he found the parting there, tiny and sensitive as a kitten's eye.

His throat ached. He let out a pleading gasp. Usually when he did this she would dart down to his groin and clasp and relieve him between her thighs. But this time she kept her hips against his chest. Her arms hugged his cheeks. His hips began to move in the same slow circles as hers. Time had ceased as abruptly as the beating of a stifled heart. He had no awareness of anything except the caressing pressure of her body and hands and lips, and his own striving for release as he kept thrusting wildly into nothing, into the images her closeness lighted in his mind.

And then suddenly it happened. He felt the trembling tenseness of her body, and his own answered it. She relapsed into delighted murmuring laughter as his semen showered onto her back.

"Ah." Her voice was like a promise in his ear. "Ah, you see?"

When he could think again, when he could move and reach for a handkerchief and dry her, he thought for a moment that perhaps he could. He could understand at least a spark of what she was trying to teach him. He remembered what she had said after the party in Topanga Canyon. "All they did was fuck."

"It's lovely now that we can be together in the daytime." They were lying side by side, companionable and content, talking in that fragmented way intimacy sometimes causes. Bascombe agreed with her. It was perfect. He wanted nothing but to spend every day for the rest of his life with her. But at the same time her remark brought his mind back to problems he had entirely forgotten during the past two hours. It wasn't the money. He thought they could manage on what they had. The acute problem was people. Even now that he was free to go everywhere with Venus, there still seemed nowhere they could go without her having to wear that wretched disguise.

Last week, having a free day between his sessions with Mr. Mitchel, he had rented a car to take Venus into the country. He had no specific objective. It was one of those August days which come as such a luxuriant surprise in Northern Europe. He thought vaguely of finding some empty stretch of hill or meadow or woodland where Venus could take off her boiler suit and they could laze together in the sun. He drove west toward Heathrow Airport and then, instinctively avoiding Slough, turned southward into Hampshire.

Hartley Wintney, Hook and Basingstoke: in the funeral procession of cars he had joined it was difficult to tell where one town ended and the next began. He looked at his map. He was on the North Downs. He had been attracted by the promising sound of those words earlier. But now that he was there, there seemed no there to be. He kept pulling into what the English called "lay-bys" (another promising sound) and climbing through hedges or over brick walls. His efforts only landed him in someone's back yard. Where there were fields there were crops and barbed wire and No Trespassing signs. He took to back roads that skirted holiday camps. He turned down winding country lanes that led to housing estates. He found a wood at last, and carrying Venus on his shoulders tramped hopefully into it. In a well-ordered maze of paths and trees, long family lines were queuing for their turns at the rustic picnic tables.

He thought of the sea. It was less than thirty miles away on the map. About two hours' hard driving, he figured from recent experience. Portsmouth sounded grim, an English San Diego, but Selsey Bill looked remote and there was something charming about that "Bill," with its invocation of wild birds.

The sun sparkled from a thousand facets beyond the point. He thought at first it was the prismatic effect of the sea. But it was the windows of the massed cars in the parking lots that produced such magic.

He turned east toward Littlehampton. *Little*hampton, he thought, with his last hope of the day. At Littlehampton there were people queuing to get onto the beach.

Angmering, Goring-by-Sea, Worthing, South Lancing, Shoreham-by-Sea, Southwick, Portslade-by-Sea, Hove were strung along the fifteen miles of coast road to Brighton like worry beads. At Brighton he gave up and joined the car queue to London.

There was, of course, nothing to keep them in England. If they left within the next couple of weeks he could take her back to California in the Mexican basket. North of San Francisco they could probably find reasonably comfortable isolation. But there was a hazard about returning to the United States at once. Bascombe was twenty-three years old. As an engineering student and later working for a company with "defense" contracts, he had never yet come in conflict with his draft board. Once he was employed again, rendering assistance of national importance to some other Mr. Mitchel, he could probably avoid a showdown indefinitely. But to spend six months in America doing nothing was like asking to be called. And Canada was so damn cold; all fur boots and lumber jackets; he didn't think Venus would enjoy their consequent exile there.

It was Nolan who suggested a possible solution. Bascombe met him for lunch a few days later at a pizza place in Fulham Road. He was not surprised Bascombe had quit his job. From a political point of view he approved the decision. "Philosophical anarchy's wasted on a company like that." But the practical side of his character was also roused.

"Will you stay in England? Can you find something here? What would you like to do now?"

"Nothing."

"I thought you didn't want to be a hippie."

"I don't have to be a hippie." He wondered how he could explain his quandary to Nolan without mentioning Venus. "I just want to live for six months. Without going to an office."

"Then you'll stay in London?" Nolan was pleased.

"I don't know." His tongue was still smarting from his first slice of pizza. The last remaining wedge was cold and limp in his fingers. "I've got enough money. It isn't that. I'd like to go somewhere—where there aren't any people."

"Today!" It was an expression of despair.

"I know."

They talked about that for a while. Nolan knew much more about it than he did. He knew all the terrifying statistics. "—one point seven percent per year," "—in South America alone since nineteen-twenty," "—by the year two thousand and twenty-three," "—that means about nine square yards," "China—"

"There is one place—perhaps—by September . . ." He returned to Bascombe's immediate problem before they parted. "You could try it, anyway. The west coast of Ireland."

Venus had never heard of Ireland. After their walk on the Earl's Court Road, Bascombe had bought her a plastic globe so that she could see for herself what the present-day world looked like. He pointed out Ireland on it to her. It looked very small but she recognized it at once.

"Ierne!"

Bascombe had never heard of Ierne.

"Hibernia?" she suggested.

"Yes." He remembered that vaguely from St. Louis; the Hibernian Society; large florid men, uneasy allies of the Bavarians in city politics and the saloon business. "Would you like to go?"

Venus looked at the globe again. "Are the Celts still living there?"

"I guess so." He wondered what it was about the Celts, what intriguing part they had played in her experience; but he was still reluctant to ask her questions about her past. "We could go and see."

He could take her there by plane in the basket, but if they

stayed any time it might be difficult to get her back into England. He wondered if it would be any easier if she pretended to be a child accompanied by an adult. He figured that by March, at four foot nine, Venus could still be dressed up to look less than twelve years old if necessary. He called the Irish Embassy. A girl's voice that managed to sound direct without being rude asked if she could help him.

"I'm an American citizen," he explained. "I'm traveling with my niece. She's—eleven years old. So she hasn't got a passport yet." It sounded hopeless, even to him. "I wanted to know if I could take her to Ireland."

"You can, of course."

"Yeah? Good. I see . . . But if I stay there for six months can I bring her back?"

"You can, of course."

"She isn't—she hasn't got any passport." He wasn't sure she had understood about that. He wanted to make it absolutely clear to her. "Can she come back here?"

"She can, of course." She seemed to think he was a bit of an idiot. "If you're traveling between this country and the Republic of Ireland, you don't need a passport at all."

Bascombe thanked her and hung up. He looked at Venus. She could travel *with* him in her boiler suit. If they stayed until March he would no longer have to disguise her. She could come back in any clothes she liked, in a mini-skirt or a sari. He was beginning to like the sound of Ireland. He had a wild idea that if he had asked that girl whether Venus could run naked through the fields of Mayo she would have told him the same thing, in the same level tone.

"She can, of course."

12

CHAPTER

THE FIRST THING that struck Bascombe about Ireland was that it was a foreign country. It was impossible to be educated in the United States without anticipating England: visiting it was like a *déjà vu*. But all his expectations about Ireland were mistaken. The country itself had no connection with any picture he had formed of it from books or movies or from Third Avenue, New York.

Driving west from Cork Airport along the empty roads was like traveling back into an unknown past. To someone born in the nineteen-forties, any period before the First World War seems as dark as an engraving. But here that darkness was in the present. It was in the bloody carcasses hanging from their gibbets in the butchers' doorways. In the dim, stone-floored shops. In the silent, watchful faces. By the time they reached Skibbereen, fifty miles to the west, Bascombe was inclined to turn around and flee. If it was as sinister as this on a sunny day in September, in the full dusk of winter Ireland must be terrifying.

It was the emptiness that lured him on. There were miles of solitude between the villages; they were scarcely towns; stretches of moors and hills and bleak tidal estuaries in which a single house, a single figure surprised the eye.

"Are you very hungry, Venus?"

She was. So was he. At the approach of each dot on the map they had promised themselves they would stop and have lunch there. But Timoleague, Clonakilty, Rosscarberry, Leap had come and gone without a sign that said "Restaurant" or even

"Cafe." There were hotels, rambling buildings with a confusion of doors, but if they served food they kept that secret to themselves.

It was after two when they reached Skibbereen. In a few minutes, Bascombe thought, accustomed to England, any restaurant they might find here would close firmly until six. He parked the car behind a monument inscribed with Gaelic letters and surmounted by a sad stout woman clutching a shamrock to her breast. They walked down the main street, looking for anything that suggested the possibility of a meal.

Venus was no longer wearing her boiler suit. These last few weeks before leaving London, while Bascombe was subletting the apartment and arranging about a house and a rented car in Ireland, she and Mrs. Charrington had been busy assembling a wardrobe for her. It had been Mrs. Charrington's suggestion. "Madam will need warm clothes in Ireland." And she had proved both inventive and practical about it. Venus now had a whole collection of children's wear, dresses and sweaters and tights and jeans which had been so skillfully taken in that they almost fitted her. With a knitted hood, only slightly padded, she no longer looked as if she were submerged in a space suit. She looked like a very beautiful, very thin, very small girl.

Bascombe had carried her on and off the plane and held her on his lap during the flight, so that their walk together down the Main Street of Skibbereen was her first full-length exposure to the public in her new clothes. He watched anxiously to see whether she would attract attention.

She did; and yet it wasn't exactly attention. People watched her as she passed: women with coveys of shy-eyed children; men in somber clothes loitering so inanimately in the doorways that they seemed to be part of the building. It was difficult to define or interpret their watchfulness. There was sympathy and a strange awareness in it that was close to understanding.

"*They're* interested in children." Bascombe had to stoop to hear what Venus said.

"Are they Celts?" He couldn't resist asking while he was crouching beside her.

"They're all mixed up."

"Like the English?"

"No." Her small voice was positive. "Not like the English."

The street crossed a stream. On the bridge a man with two brass lamps and half a dozen mackerel for sale was deep in conversation with a young priest. Beyond the bridge every doorway led into a shop. Regan and Kelly and O'Mahoney and Sullivan, the ancient lettering said. Often the only things in the windows were a few bars of putty-colored soap, or some cans of peas, or a single pitchfork. One in three had a handpainted sign above the door mentioning that the owner was licensed to sell wines and spirits "on or off the premises." None of them gave any indication of serving meals.

Bascombe gave up before he reached the bridge on the way back. He bought a loaf of bread and some butter and cheese and sardines and then, unexpectedly, was able to buy a breadknife and two forks and a blue china plate in the same shop. He asked the woman behind the counter if she had any milk.

Instead of answering she turned and disappeared behind a curtain. There was the sound of unintelligible whispering, a soft clink, and a little girl of about eight shot out of the darkness and whisked past him into the street. The woman returned to the counter. She had not brought any milk with her, and she did not seem to feel that Bascombe's question about it required an answer. She had said nothing while she was getting him the other things, searching out the sardines under a pile of woolen socks, and she said nothing now. She stood and looked at Venus and waited.

It was like the party at Nora's; Bascombe felt as though he were in the grip of some ritual; he wondered what he was supposed to do next. He asked the woman how much he owed her.

"Won't you be wanting the milk?"

"Yes, I didn't realize—I didn't know if you had any."

"Jo won't be long gone."

This conveyed nothing to him at all. The woman continued to look at Venus. There was the same sympathy in her eyes he had noticed on the street. She dipped under the counter and came up with a bar of chocolate. Peeling the wrapping and foil off one end she held it out to Venus. It was a practical, unemotional gesture; she might have been opening a door for her.

"Thank you." Venus took the chocolate and bit it. Silence returned like a familiar shade. It was broken by the little girl whisking back into the shop. She was carrying a bottle of milk and four pennies. She put them all on the counter and vanished.

"Now so." The woman started writing figures on the back of her hand. She was making out Bascombe's bill. She charged him eightpence for the milk, which was evidently what the little girl had paid for it in another shop.

"They're not very talkative." Bascombe and Venus were eating in the car behind the Gaelic monument. The bread was delicious, soft and dark with a brisk crust to it. "They're supposed to be so garrulous."

"They were always an unpredictable people."

Bascombe hesitated. He was dying to ask how, and yet afraid to. He finished his mouthful of bread and cheese.

"How?"

Venus smiled. "When they sacked Delphi—" She gestured toward the Gaelic plinth. "What do you call those things?"

"Monuments."

"They didn't touch my monument."

Beyond Skibbereen the landscape hardened. The fields were scarred with ridges of gray rock, and their green was broken by tough yellow-flowered gorse. The house was at the end of a promontory overlooking Roaring Water Bay. It was over three miles from the nearest village, and the road leading to it was unmarked and unpaved.

It belonged to a journalist friend of Nolan's. "He only uses it in the summer," Nolan had told him, and their first days there Bascombe understood the warning note in Nolan's voice when he said it. They had arrived just in time for the equinoctial gales. For three days wind and rain besieged the house with a fury that seemed animated by hatred. It was unthinkable to step out of doors. It was impossible to force the front door open. Bascombe had fortunately driven into the village the first evening and, ignoring the silence with which he was met there, had gone from shop to shop loading the car with food and whiskey and milk and electric light bulbs and bundles of processed turf for the fire, and blankets and a kettle—and all the other things that a brief tour of the house had shown him they could not survive without.

The house was of stone with three-foot-thick walls, and it was drafty and damp and haphazardly furnished with incongruous folding things. But it was stacked with books and it had that greatest of all obsolete luxuries, a fireplace in the bedroom. It was like experiencing some legend of childhood to lie there under the sheets and blankets with real firelight flickering on the ceiling.

For three days they spent most of their time in bed. Like invalids they made it the center of their lives, gradually accumulating around it more and more of their requirements, books and glasses and bottles and plates and trays. They read and they talked and they ate and they made love and they listened to the storm.

On the fourth day they awoke to an eerie stillness. It was like finding themselves in the eye of a hurricane. Bascombe went to the window and drew back the curtains. From the upstairs room he could see for miles across the bay to Cape Clear and the Fastnet lighthouse. The sea was the improbable blue of a postcard from Cannes. The sun was shining.

They dressed and ran out of the house at once. They spent the morning exploring the cove at the end of the promontory. There was an island that could be reached by a causeway of rocks. There were mussel beds and shrilling gulls and on the island narrow tunnels in the soil that Bascombe thought might be otter holes. It was warm enough to take off most of their clothes. Venus taught Bascombe a game with shells. She called it Nim's game. "The Northmen used to play it." She beat him at it every time. They saw no one.

In the afternoon they drove around the bay to the land's end.

The Atlantic was an improbable mauve. They scurried, awed, along the brink of the monstrous cliffs. There was nothing between them and Newfoundland.

On the way home they turned off the coast road and found themselves in a wide valley. The land was divided into innumerable fields by crooked walls made of great random stones piled and balanced against each other. There were two farmhouses in the whole length of the valley, a few lean trees bowed to the east, and in one of the fields a sparse gathering of cows, head down in the bracken. There was not a man-made sound to be heard.

They left the car and, climbing the stone walls, walked across the land toward a stream at the base of the valley. It was hard going. They had to follow the winding trails, marked by cow pats, that the animals had forced between the gorse bushes in their search for grass. Here and there at the corners of fields were clumps of loose stones, a solitary gable bound with ivy, a chimney stack.

"They're all gone."

Bascombe was carrying Venus on his shoulders. He stopped.

"Who?"

"All the people and the children. It was like a town. There was a house and a family in every field."

"How do you know?" He didn't disbelieve her for a second.

"They weren't all Christians." She accentuated the last word with the same resentment as she had shown toward the Buddhists on Hollywood Boulevard. "And they weren't madmen organizing everyone to death. They knew living was an aim in itself. And some of them . . ." Her voice rose into laughter. "Some of them believed in me."

Bascombe did not answer. He was afraid to prompt her. He was frightened of her telling him, inescapably, what she meant by believing in her. It was part of that whole area—the planes flying backwards, her monument at Delphi, her origin onto his bedroom carpet—that he did not want to explore.

"Grand day." He was startled to hear a human voice, to see

the man walking across the field toward them.

"Yes. It's great, isn't it?"

"What we call a pet day." The man stopped a few feet from him. He was wearing heavy boots and a collarless shirt held together at the neck by a brass stud. "Taking a walk, are you?"

"Yes."

The man was looking at Venus in that same watchful way. He did not seem inquisitive or unfriendly: he seemed serious.

"Is this your land?" Bascombe tried to distract him.

"It is."

"I guess we're trespassing."

The man shook his head as though he didn't understand.

"I guess we're trespassing," Bascombe apologized more loudly.

"Everyone has the right of way." He spoke with the patience of a man arguing the obvious. He raised his hand briefly. "Grand day." He was gone as abruptly as he had appeared.

Bascombe carried Venus back to the car. "Is that true?" he asked her, as they drove away. There was no need to explain the question; she always knew what he was talking about.

Venus nodded, looking back over the valley. He wondered if she were remembering the swarming families who had once peopled it, but her thoughts had gone even farther back in time.

"The Celts always went anywhere they liked."

Bascombe was not particularly cowardly. He had no more than the usual tendency to evade the disturbing. After that walk into the valley with Venus, he knew it was only a question of days before he would have to face all those questions about her he had been avoiding for so long.

The moment came sooner than he had expected. It came that night. There was no moon. They had to pick out the path with a flashlight to find their way down to the cove after dinner. It was warm enough to sit on the beach. The sea was so still there was no breaking rim of white. The faint gray of the sand simply vanished at its edge. Beyond it was blackness.

"Do they still call it after me?"

He could just see her on the sand beside him. She was resting back on her elbows, looking up at the sky. He raised his eyes, too. He didn't know much about space, but he could recognize the planet Venus when he saw it.

"Yes."

She nodded. It was impossible to make out the expression on her face. She lifted a shell and stroked it against her cheek. He waited. He could hardly breathe.

"Does everyone call me Venus now?"

He didn't have to ask her what she meant. It was like one of those moments that are supposed to result from analysis, when a whole subconscious area of knowledge is painfully exposed.

"Most people," he admitted reluctantly.

"They don't remember me by any of my other names?"

He didn't want to answer her. Once admitted, the knowledge could never be forgotten. She could never again be the same Venus to him, the playful, intimate companion. But he was honest enough to see that it would be absurd, demeaning, to try to evade the truth any longer, to continue treating her as something she wasn't—*his* Venus. It was like refusing to let a child grow up or denying that a woman was an individual. He recalled that first message she had written to him, "Thou shalt have no other goddesses but me," and how stubbornly he had misinterpreted it even after it had been translated for him.

"Some people remember you as Aphrodite." He might have been pronouncing his own doom.

"Ishtar? Ashtoreth? Astarte? Freyja?"

"No." None of the names meant anything to him. "Don't you like being called Venus?"

"I never cared for the Romans much. They were a gross, cruel people. It was almost a relief when they turned to Christianity."

"Don't you think it's a lovely name—Venus?" He was clinging to the shreds of his illusory well-being.

"Okay." She dropped the shell into the pocket of her cardigan. "You can go on calling me Venus if you like."

He looked at her timidly. She did not seem any different. Her bare legs, faintly paler than the sand, had the same human beauty they had always had. He was sure that if he touched her she would respond with her usual quick affection. For a moment it seemed possible that nothing had changed after all. But in spite of himself he could not leave it at that.

"Why me?" he demanded. "Why was I lucky enough to find you in *my* apartment?"

"I don't know." She fingered the shell in her pocket. "Suddenly there seemed to be a lot of people who wanted me again. People like you," she admitted frankly. "It was my father's idea I should be reborn in that way. And it had to be someone." There was a quirk of amusement in her voice. "Someone with a practical side, too."

She reached up and touched the top of his head.

"Did it hurt much?"

"What?"

"When I was reborn."

"That's where you came from!"

He was on his feet in a single spring. He started to run up and down the beach, jumping onto the rocks and back into the sand. What he had been so frightened of losing was not possession but responsibility. He could never lose his responsibility for Venus now. Out of all the millions in the world, she had chosen his head to spring from. He wanted to rush out into the sea and match his happiness against its darkness.

Venus laughed as he stopped again beside her. She seemed touched by his pride. She stretched herself with her heedless grace, composing herself to pleasure.

13
CHAPTER

ALTHOUGH BASCOMBE thought of himself as an atheist and had lost all recognizable faith as a child, he had never quite accepted the position that a belief in gods (or even in God) was a form of legalized insanity. He was neutral: as indifferent to religion as to technology. Both seemed to him uninteresting, "all right in theory." It was only what people had done with them, the personal ends they had used them for, that made them both such sores.

Now, finding he was living with a goddess, he was forced to reconsider the whole subject. The first thing he had to do was try to find out what gods were.

Venus did her best to help him.

"They're what you believe they are," she told him over her scrambled eggs the next morning. "That's all any god can tell you, because you've never invented any words to imagine us."

"None?"

"Divine, sacred, holy—do they really help you to understand anything?"

After an incomparable half hour on the beach, they had spent an affectionate night together in the double bed. As she sat facing him across the breakfast table, his awareness of her physical presence kept breaking in on his thoughts like the beam of a lighthouse.

"What about images?" he suggested. "Paintings, statues?"

"They're all what *you* think we are, idealized versions of yourselves. The Greeks used to say that if donkeys were religious, they'd picture their gods as donkeys."

He remembered his conversation with Nolan about Tom Mix and the President on Hollywood Boulevard. Although actors and politicians were largely—deliberately—what other people believed them to be, even a movie star, even a head of state had some consciousness of his existence apart from his public image. He felt at least pain, if he felt nothing else.

"Okay, gods are what I believe they are—to me. But what are they to themselves?" he demanded.

"What *they* believe they are. That's what makes them gods."

He could see what she meant: it did seem to set gods apart. However dismaying his illusion of omnipotence, there were things about himself no President could change.

"Is it important to you what people believe about you?"

Venus wanted the marmalade. He passed it to her. She shook her head as she spread it on her buttered toast.

"It's only important to you. It won't change me—what you believe—but it will change you."

She seemed to be warning him that every human was at least three people. What he was to himself, what he was to others, and what his gods or lack of gods were to him.

Venus, as he realized more and more clearly in the days that followed, was a single being. She tolerated others' conception of her, but it did not affect her. When he found a paperback copy of *The Iliad* among the books in the house and showed her Aphrodite's biography in the glossary of gods, she did not deny she was the daughter of Zeus and Dione, that she had been married, not very happily, to Hephaestus, that Paris had been her favorite, and Ares her lover. She did not deny any of it. But she did not admit it either. "That's what the Greeks thought," she agreed cheerfully. "They were a wonderful people. I always liked the Greeks."

In only one respect would she concede any vulnerability.

"Have you always existed?" Bascombe asked her one night when they were lying in bed; and then, feeling that "existed" sounded rude: "I mean, have you lived forever?"

"Only since—" He could not see her but he could feel her shrug. "I don't know how long it is now. Long before the Greeks. Long before the Sumerians or the Aegeans."

"Will you go on living forever?"

"Not in this body."

That seemed to him a tragedy. Her body was perfect. Her skin was so smooth that it seemed liquid to the touch. She was still so light he could barely feel the weight of her on his arm. But there was such vitality in her every movement that if she so much as stirred it was like a caress.

She stirred now and his skin quickened responsively.

"I'll never grow any older and I shall go on living as long as there are two people left in the world."

It was then she made her single concession.

"But when they're all dead, I shall die, too."

He had to be content with that much help from her for the present. But he continued to think about it.

The truth was he had always believed in Venus, Aphrodite, Ishtar, Ashtoreth, Astarte, Freyja. As the deification of a way of living, an ideal, she was all that he ever had believed in. He felt he had made a wise, or perhaps merely fortunate choice, too. In contrast to the homogenized deity of Christian mythology—one part jealous patriot, one part golden bearded hermaphrodite, one part ineffable oblong blur—she seemed to him a radiant and credible figure. He did not regret his lack of interest in any of the other Greek gods or goddesses either. They had all fallen pretty low in the present-day world. The cult of Pallas Athene had been reduced to the dull follies of politicians. The disciples of Hera to the disasters of the feminine mystique. The followers of Hephaestus had become qualified vandals masquerading as architects and engineers. Ares was the Pentagon. Hermes, Foggy Bottom and the dead hand of John Foster Dulles; Apollo, Mantan and the Gallup Poll; Asclepius, the A.M.A.; Demeter, no-calorie food. Of all the gods and goddesses of Olympus, the only one whose image had not been totally discredited in Western society was Aphrodite. To believe in her still promised some hope.

Living with her was a delight.

Nolan had been a sound guide. They had all the privacy they wanted; no one ever came near the house; and at this time of year they seemed to have the whole outdoors to themselves, too. Even the roads were deserted: there were more horses and carts than there were cars; a lurching tractor on its way to the creamery with a load of conical milk cans; lethargic cows feeding on the grass verge. There were occasional gales and other days of soft mist; but there were also, all through the winter, those sudden pet days when the metalled bay seemed to have been refilled overnight from the Mediterranean, and it was warm enough to laze on the beach.

A small group of retired English people had settled in the area. They sat around the bars, embalmed in self-importance. Venus and Bascombe avoided them. They explored the country and they gradually discovered the Irish. There were two sisters, Anne and Geraldine, who kept a pub in the village. They were in their forties, handsome women who must have been very pretty girls. Out of some instinctive feminism, neither of them had ever married. It was not that they disliked men; it seemed, rather, that they could not be bothered with all the added nonsense that made men male. In the ancient complex pattern of village society, this was an acceptable choice. There was no shame about remaining a spinster or bachelor.

Bascombe and Venus first happened into their pub in early October. On a sunny morning the single street of the village was like an illustration from an instructive children's book. Everybody was doing what they did. The baker was baking, the smith shoeing horses, the postman delivering letters, the milkman milk. The post office was out of eggs that day. "You could try the Regans," the little girl there suggested.

Anne Regan was alone in the bar. There was the usual waiting silence while she looked at Venus and then at Bascombe. Bascombe had begun to understand by now there was nothing hostile about this silence. It was not the silence of the Westerner confronted by a stranger. In that sense he and Venus had never been strangers in the village, anyway. From the hour they moved into their rented house, all the local people had known about them. They knew their names, where they lived, that Bascombe was an American, that Venus was "his small sister's child," that he was staying for the winter. They recognized his car. He did not understand how they knew all these things, but there was no mistaking they did.

"They told me at the post office you might have some eggs."

"I do, of course." Anne Regan came out from behind the bar and moved to the counter at the other end of the shop. She kept her eyes on Venus while she counted out a dozen eggs and fitted them precariously into a paper bag. There was a shadow of concern in her eyes.

All size is an illusion—a form of prejudice. Isolate anything and its bigness or smallness vanishes. Familiarity can have the same effect. A new coat may be shorter or longer than the old one; after being worn a few times it seems the only natural length. Bascombe had forgotten Venus was still not as tall as an average two-year-old child.

That day she was wearing woolen tights, a pair of rubber boots with platforms inside them, a short dress, a heavy knitted cardigan, and her slightly padded hood. Her waist was less than ten inches around. Even in the cardigan it was apparent he could span it with his fingers, like a teacup, without touching it at any point. Her arms and legs were in adult proportion to it. With the help of the platforms in her boots the top of her peaked hood was just level with the shop counter. Suddenly, in response to Anne Regan's concern, Bascombe saw all this.

He paid for the eggs and turned to leave.

"You'll have a glass of milk, girl."

Anne Regan had Venus by the hand. She led her into the kitchen behind the shop. He followed them.

Geraldine was in there, hovering over the stove. A high stool was brought to the table for Venus. She was lifted onto it. Roast beef and potatoes, bread and butter and milk were placed in front of her. Venus, with all her growing, had an impulsive appetite at any time and was more than ready for her lunch. She began to eat.

Bascombe managed to persuade the two sisters he wasn't hungry. He sat on a ruined leather sofa and watched them as they waited on Venus. They asked no questions. They said very little. "Here, girl," the salt. "There, girl," another potato. "Now, so," a slice of cake.

When she had finished Venus climbed down from the stool and thanked them both gravely. Anne followed her to the door of the shop. She evidently had something she wanted to say to Bascombe. He waited for it, lifting Venus in his arms as he reached for the door handle.

"Mrs. Daley's child was terrible thin when she was small."

"They think I'm starving you." Bascombe fitted Venus into the baby chair attached to the front seat of the car. She was too big for the dashboard now.

"The younger one's a good cook."

Bascombe turned off onto the rutted road to the house.

"Did you do anything to them?"

He meant, like Voigt. Like Mrs. Charrington, too, he suspected.

"No." Venus looked at the sea. "They'd feed anyone they thought needed it."

After that they got into the habit of going into Anne and Geraldine's almost every day. There was no objection to children in Irish pubs. Venus would have a glass of stout—she preferred wine, but Geraldine thought stout was better for her—and sometimes in the evening they would watch television in the kitchen. They never left without one of the sisters putting a loaf of bread, a breast of cold chicken, or a slice of cake into Venus' hands. It was impossible to refuse these gifts. It obviously gave the Regans pleasure to make them, and yet they did it as naturally, in the same practical way, as they gave Bascombe his change when he paid for a drink. They never threw in any sympathy with the food. They were incapable of such falsities as "poor little thing." It was simply, as Venus had said, that they thought thin children needed feeding.

It was through Anne and Geraldine and one or two others in the village that Bascombe began to understand something about the Irish, about their silences and their directness. In spite of all the myths and music that had been fashioned for them by expatriates and strangers, they were in their own country a kind, naturally generous, but totally unsentimental people. In more traveled districts they might play the maudlin fool for foreigners, Uncle-Tom them to tears if they felt it was expected of them. Left to themselves they were as realistic as cats. Their only criterion of behavior was what seemed sensible to them.

This practical attitude made things much easier for him and Venus. It helped solve what might otherwise have been a threatening problem. Venus was growing six inches a month. It was impossible to disguise that fact. By Christmas she was three and a half feet tall, as big as an average six-year-old. By human standards she had aged four years in three months.

"Aged" was, of course, a loose way of describing it. Except to enlarge, she had not changed at all. Her beautiful features, the straight nose, the round chin, and unfathomable violet eyes were the same. She still wore the same kind of children's clothes in public. They made a trip into Cork in early November and bought a whole range of sizes in tights, dresses, shoes, cardigans. Looked at objectively, in fact, it was less as though Venus had grown than everything around her, doors, furniture, clothes, other people, had shrunk.

But still, there she was, in a little village in Ireland, and almost twice as big as she had been when she arrived. Bascombe waited uneasily for someone to remark on it.

No one did.

He began, like a man with a too obvious wig, to feel called upon to mention it himself.

"She's growing fast, isn't she?" he announced with fake casualness to the baker's wife one morning.

Mrs. Sullivan considered Venus, who had found a copy of *Newsweek* among a pile of *Catholic Heralds* and was reading the book reviews by the window. She might have been considering the weather.

"She is."

He brought the matter up again at Anne and Geraldine's a few evenings later. Venus was sitting cross-legged on the sofa, watching a horserace on television. She had refused a cushion; she no longer needed one to see over the top of the table.

"She's getting big," Bascombe told Anne with the same bogus objectivity.

" 'Tis great."

He and Venus had reached such an easy friendly relationship with the Regan sisters by this time that he was about to push the question further, to ask Anne frankly if she didn't think Venus' progress was surprising. But Venus shushed him. She wanted to hear the winners of the earlier races. She marked them off in the newspaper as they were announced.

"It's incredible," he told her as they drove home that night. "It isn't only that they never say anything about you. They never ask anything, either. They've never asked me about my sister, who your father is, why you're here with me. They've never even asked me how old you are. Any of them."

"Their country was occupied by a foreign enemy for almost seven hundred years."

A tradition of not asking personal questions could easily grow out of a national experience of that kind.

"Do you suppose they talk about us among themselves?"

"Of course."

"What do you think they say?"

"What Mrs. Sullivan said in the bakery when you told her I was growing."

"She didn't say anything."

"She agreed with you."

He could see what she meant. They probably did talk about Venus, in much the same way as they talked about Din Jo Kelly's wife, who had cancer, or the butcher's little boy who had been born without ears. They said Mrs. Kelly was dying, or that the boy was being sent to the Sisters in Clonakilty. With that rationalism that was so much a part of their character, they knew the only tenable attitude toward any phenomenon was to accept it.

"Geraldine makes wonderful cake." Venus borrowed his handkerchief and wiped her hands. As she gave it back, her fingers touched his. He began to drive faster. The sooner they got home, the sooner they would be naked in the warm double bed.

That night, as they usually did, they kept the light on. It seemed almost perverted to exclude any of his senses from his delight in her. They made love with their hands, their mouths, their skins. She gratified him once between her thighs and then a second time, in the way she was gradually coaxing him to prefer, without any conventional sexual contact at all, by stimulating his senses with her barely moving closeness until he exploded out of pent-up desire.

After that he lay back, content, with her breasts against his side and his arm under her waist. Something brushed his neck. It was the newspaper she had been referring to in Anne and Geraldine's while she watched the horseraces. He pushed it onto the floor as he turned off the light. But when he got up in the morning, after a lingering lie-in with Venus, he unfolded the newspaper and looked at it.

She had made a neat circle on the left-hand side of the entries column against her favorite horse in each race. On the right-hand side she had made a circle against the winner as it was announced on television. The circles corresponded five times out of six. She had picked five winners.

"How do you do it?" he asked her over breakfast.

"Your future's always more or less predictable."

He had learned by now that when she said "your" in that particular way, she meant ordinary, earthbound people. She was too considerate to use words like "mortal."

"Why? How is it predictable?"

"It already exists."

"Definitely? Unchangeably?" He did not want to believe that.

Venus was eating fish. She had her own way of doing it. She did not pick at it in little pieces. She cut it open and took all the bones out and then enjoyed it without interruption. She had taken all the bones out of her herring now and he had to wait for an answer until she had finished it. He waited with slight apprehension.

"No. Not definitely. Not absolutely, unalterably. There are

184

usually several possibilities. But some of them . . ." She changed her plate and took a piece of toast. "Some of them are more probable than others."

"How can you judge those probabilities?" He had never seen Venus reading a racing form.

"It's difficult with the distant future. There are so many things that could happen that they're all rather faint. But as you move closer to any moment, some of the possibilities are lost altogether and others get clearer."

He imagined that seeing the future, as he did not for a moment doubt she could, was like looking at a series of photographs. As any human action in the present set up its own chain of consequences, some of those photographs faded altogether. The events they depicted were no longer possible. A particular child could no longer be born if someone tomorrow napalmed his mother. A likely horse would not win if its owner gave it tranquilizers before the race.

He was instantly eager to explore their own future.

"What about us? Can you see what's going to happen to us?"

"Of course not." Venus seemed a little shocked.

"Why not?"

"Because *we* can decide our own future."

He looked away from her, suddenly saddened. She might have been including Pallas Athene, her lover Ares, and her husband Hephaestus in that "we"; but she had certainly not been including him.

She had not been including the Christian gods either. As Christmas approached, she refused to take any part in the customary celebrations of "that upstart's birthday," as she called it.

"He wasn't born at this time of year, anyway," she said coldly and accurately. "Those early Christians stole the whole thing from us. It used to be my grandfather's feast, the turn of the year after the shortest day."

It was a long day for Bascombe. They were, fortunately, out of earshot of the nearest church bells. But as though some malignant spirit were abroad, Venus refused to go outdoors. She stayed in bed reading Proust ("At least he wasn't a Christian") and for the first time since he had known her was cold and passive when he tried to make love to her.

"Go and kiss *his* feet," she told him. "That's what they do, isn't it? Silly masochistic nonsense."

She was over it the next day and made amends to him the moment she woke up with uncharacteristically famished eroticism. Later that afternoon Bascombe cooked a turkey and chilled a bottle of champagne he had originally bought Venus as a Christmas present. Then, since it was the last day of her grandfather's feast, they celebrated it in traditional style in front of a Yule fire.

They were living quite cheaply in Ireland. Their only luxuries were heat—they were both naked so much of the time, they had to keep fires in every room—the rented car, and wine. But by the end of January, Bascombe was down to his last thousand dollars.

Venus was just over four feet tall then, as big as an average eight-year-old child. Her features had always been adult, but her skin was so clear and unlined, with the soft patina of youth, that she still looked a little too young to wander freely around a city on her own. Her beauty would always attract attention; her smallness might still attract inquiry. Bascombe thought it would be better to stay in Ireland another month until she was a safe four feet six before he took her back to London and started to try to find a job. It meant they would be returning with less than five hundred dollars.

He did not mention any of this to Venus. She suggested a possible answer to the problem spontaneously.

"Are there any horseraces near here?" she asked, one morning when they were walking down to the cove.

Bascombe didn't know. Mr. Sullivan, the baker, looked it up in Old Moore's almanac. There was a race meeting in County Tipperary the first week in February.

It was a four-hour drive. During the whole of those four hours, as they moved out of West Cork into the softer, more domesticated country of central Ireland, Bascombe struggled with a decision. He had two hundred pounds in his pocket, almost five hundred dollars. On his own he would have been willing to bet it all, go for broke. But as he had understood in the first few days of Venus' life with him, he was no longer on his own. If they got back to London without enough for the rent on the apartment, Venus— He could not even finish the thought. For the first time in his life he found himself experiencing the peculiar ravages of worrying about money. Anxiety fed on itself, distorting its own terrors, depriving his mind of all common sense, all power of decision.

Better play it safe, he kept thinking, put aside forty or fifty pounds to bet with, no more— And despised himself for his caution, for his lack of faith in Venus' powers.

Trust her, risk it all, he thought, and found himself back facing the unthinkable: Venus in a dirty little furnished room; Venus without enough to eat.

He had still not reached a decision when the horses cantered out onto the track for the first race.

"Let's not bet on this one," Venus suggested, prolonging his torment. "I want to see how it works."

It did not work like any horserace Bascombe had ever been to in the United States. There was no parimutuel. The space in front of the rough wooden grandstand was crowded with individual bookmakers, close-eyed, raincoated men with collapsible stands, great leatherbound ledgers, and Gladstone bags stuffed with pound notes. They chalked the horses and the odds on children's school slates. The bets were written into the ledger and the horseplayer given a dirty pasteboard card with "Shaun Kelly" or "Tim Devlin" printed on it, "Licensed Turf Accountant."

The odds on the slates were changed constantly until the start of the race. By picking your moment to bet, shopping around, you could make a big difference to how much you could win. Although not, Bascombe thought with a return of anxiety, to how much you could lose.

Standing at the rail near the finish post with Venus on his shoulders, he watched the dozen horses in the first race file, as it seemed, in slow motion along the far side of the grass track. The distant line shook itself like an awkward chain as the horses braced themselves for the first jump, topped it, landed splay-legged, and cantered on. Two of them stumbled and fell, their riders somersaulting over their necks and crouching on the ground until the others had hoofed clear.

By the time they were over the third jump one of the horses had pulled lengths ahead of the others. Bascombe thought it had made its move too soon; it would tire and fall back. It didn't. Rounding the turn it might have been running in a separate race. He could see its number now. He looked at his program. Marius. He remembered the name: it had been at the top of every slate. Marius took its ease at the last four jumps, gliding over them as though practicing for future, higher hurdles. It finished twenty yards ahead of the rest. Bascombe checked the odds on the nearest slate. Two to nine. It took him a moment to figure that out, and then he realized that if he had bet his bundle, his whole two hundred pounds on the beast, he would be a clear forty-four pounds richer. Even if Venus' powers were infallible, it looked like being a long, anxious afternoon before he so much as doubled his money.

"You can put me down now." He helped her gratefully off his shoulders. She had weighed fifty-two pounds on the chemist's penny-in-the-slot machine in Skibbereen last week. They walked over to the paddock together. The entries for the next race were being mounted, beginning their slow, neck-stretching walk around the enclosure. Venus watched them carefully for several minutes, occasionally checking their names on her program; then she hurried Bascombe back to the winning post.

She stood there, gravely abstracted, briefly closing her eyes.

She was projecting her vision into the future, seeing the finish of the next race, he thought admiringly. As the minutes passed she was evidently seeing it more than once. Finish after finish must be taking place in front of her with now this horse, now that one ahead, while she compared the succeeding images for their firmness and clarity. He prayed, impulsively picking her father as the god to appeal to, that she would get one good clear final picture while there was still time to bet—the horses were cantering toward the start now—and that whichever animal was in front would pay better than even.

Venus shook her head. "It's either Zero or Fusilier, but it's not clear enough which one. It depends on too many things."

"What?" For a moment he forgot his anxiety. He was fascinated by this glimpse of the workings of cause and effect. He wanted to learn more about it.

"I can't see either of them fall at any of the jumps. I've tried that." Venus raised her hands in her familiar gesture of dismissal. "But between now and the end of the race, something's going to happen to one of them."

"But—" His apprehension returned like night. "But, then, how can you *ever* be sure? Something could happen in *any* race."

"Most things that happen are already decided."

"But this time, this race, it isn't?"

"It may be decided, but not definitely yet."

That seemed to Bascombe a subtle distinction. As he helped Venus onto his shoulders again, his own picture of the future, a dank little bed-sitter, Venus eating cold beans out of a can, was so clear it obscured every inch of the present.

"It's decided now. You see?"

He looked toward the starting line and, as he watched, it happened. The starter literally dropped his flag. It slipped out of his hand. The horses broke the tape and were off. The starter hesitated an instant, seemed about to call them back, and then decided to make the best of it. It wasn't an indefensible decision. All but one of the horses had got off to a fair start. The single exception had its rump to the others. It was Fusilier.

Zero won at one to three. If Bascombe had bet it he would have made a clear sixty-six pounds. As Venus decided to pass up the next race as well, gloom settled on him, irrevocable as old age. Even if Venus got the clearest picture since Lumière, he didn't see how it was going to help them much. The favorite, or near-favorite, won every time. No horse paid as much as a dollar for a dollar.

"You can bet on number three." They were back at the winning post before the start of the fifth race. He looked at his program. Number three was a twelve-year-old mare named Semolina, ridden and trained by its owner, Mr. Finbar O'Mahoney. From the triple zero in front of its name it had evidently been some time since Semolina had had a glimpse of victory. Bascombe determined not to say, "Are you sure?"

"Semolina?" he asked instead.

Venus nodded. He looked at his program again. There were only six horses in the race. He remembered Semolina vividly now. There had been a second in the paddock while its rider was mounting it when it had seemed doubtful if it could stand his weight.

"That brown and white mare?" he reminded Venus.

"With the big jockey in the black cap."

Bascombe fingered the twenty ten-pound notes in his pocket. The words "Are you sure?" were throbbing in his head like some awful, unforgettable song. Keeping his mouth firmly closed, he wondered if Venus realized how much was at stake, how much the loss of the two hundred pounds between his fingers could mean to her welfare and comfort, could mean to her *nourishment* in a few weeks' time.

"How much shall I bet?"

"As much as you like."

He saw she was testing him, but it did not seem to him a fair test. It wasn't a question of believing in her, only in her powers of prediction. He had read enough Homer by now to know Aphrodite had never claimed to be an oracle. That was not, as she would have been the first to admit, her specialty.

But then, because he knew and understood at least some aspects of her by now, it occurred to him it was not his faith she was testing. She was testing him, Bascombe. His character. His courage. It still did not seem to him a fair test because he had no fears for himself. He would have cheerfully shared a grotto with her, eaten uncooked roots, clothed himself in woven grass. Only the thought of her possible privation terrified him.

It was Homer in the end who decided Bascombe. Remembering what Venus had said, "I always liked the Greeks," he thought of those characters in *The Iliad*. There was no question what that crowd of roistering braggarts would have done in a situation like this. With that curious combination of fatalism and rebellion against fate, they would have laid their whole families, their ancestors and heirs, on the line for Semolina.

"Okay."

There were still five minutes before the start of the race; time to shop around for the best odds. He approached Joseph Murphy, a severely dressed, pious-faced bookmaker whom he had noted earlier as the most dependable-looking of an uninspiring bunch. He looked at Murphy's slate. It was worse than he had expected. Semolina, the bottom of the six horses, was at twenty to one. The favorite, Herod, was at one to five; Patsygirl, the second favorite, one to three. Joseph Murphy obviously had little expectation of Semolina beating either of them. Bascombe pulled out his wad of ten-pound notes.

"No. No-no-no. No. No-no." As though still afraid he had not made his refusal clear enough, Joseph Murphy shook his head emphatically. "I'll not take more than the ten pounds on Herod. Ten quid's the limit."

"I don't want to bet on Herod."

"Patsygirl, is it?"

"Semolina."

The single word had an extraordinary effect. Although Bascombe had not raised his voice, it carried instantly to every bookmaker in the neighborhood. The next second they were all around him, pulling at his arms, grabbing at his shoulders, begging for his business.

"Twenty-five to one."

"Thirty."

"Thirty-five."

They were screaming in their eagerness to accept his bet.

"Okay!" he told them.

"Forty."

"Forty, I'll give you."

"*Okay!*" he shouted back at the ring of avid faces. "I'll share it out between you."

It took some time, handing them twenty pounds each, seeing the bet recorded in ten separate ledgers, "Semolina. 40-1," collecting his handful of dirty pasteboard cards. When he got back to Venus the horses were already on the track going to the starting post. Semolina was the last out of the paddock. Watching the brown and white mare as it ambled after the others, Bascombe briefly forgot his concern about its chances of winning. The question occupying all his attention at that moment was whether it would make it as far as the starting line.

It did. It even got off to a recognizable start. It was facing in the right direction when the flag went down, and as the other horses broke away, Semolina followed them.

For once the two favorites did not have it all their own way. At the third hurdle the lead horses were still a close flurry of pecking heads. It was still not clear which of them was in front. The only certain thing about the race at that point was Semolina's position.

Like a weight at the end of a line that was being paid out behind the others, Semolina bumped along the track and over the hurdles, first ten, then twenty, then thirty yards in the rear.

So now he had less than five hundred dollars left, Bascombe conceded. All sight of the present had vanished again, obscured by his vision of the future. With luck, with care, they might get back to London at the beginning of March with about fifty pounds. He would get a job at once, any job. The London Underground stations were always plastered with want ads for drivers, station attendants, guards. He remembered being struck by how little the jobs paid, but anyone willing to work enough overtime, which he was, should be able to take home about twenty pounds a week. Surely? He could get a reasonable furnished room for six or seven. If he ate nothing but canned spaghetti—with maybe two apples a week to stave off scurvy—that would leave about ten pounds for Venus to feed, clothe, keep her warm. Thank god summer was coming . . .

It started almost as a sigh, was recognizable as a gasp, then swelled up to a moan, and finally a roar of dismay. The roar brought Bascombe back to the present. His eyes were still on the far side of the track. It wasn't until he turned his head that he saw what had caused the outcry. Fifty yards away, just his side of the last hurdle, a riderless horse jerked itself to its feet. A jockey ran blindly for the rail. Two other horses lay awkwardly on their sides, levering convulsively at the ground with their shoulders, trying to get themselves upright. Another riderless horse kicked up its heels and trotted playfully into the crowd. Two jockeys knelt on the grass like Muslims at prayer, their hands clasped over their heads.

Four, Bascombe counted automatically. Four down, and then triumphantly, as Patsygirl cantered past him to the winning post, its stirrups swinging from its empty saddle—*five!*

He looked back down the course. A hundred yards away, just rounding the turn, its black-capped rider hunched over its neck, Semolina was plodding gamely toward the last hurdle. It had all the time in the world now. The only horse left in the race, all it had to do was finish. All it had to do was clear that last jump and canter, trot, *walk* if it wanted to, the last fifty yards to the post.

It was obviously going to be a close thing. Semolina had already heaved itself and its massive owner over nine hurdles in the past few minutes and it was showing the strain of it as it approached the tenth. It no longer had the wind to leap a blade of grass, and it knew it. But the animal had determination if it had nothing else. Unable to jump, it simply straddled the hurdle. It got its front legs over first, planted its hooves firmly on the ground, and then hauled its hind legs over after them.

A nervous fifteen seconds later, Semolina was home, the winner.

Bascombe had won eight thousand pounds.

It took him some time to collect it. Venus waited for him in the car while he went from bookie to bookie, presenting his pasteboard cards and standing, the center of a fast-growing crowd, while one after the other grudgingly counted out to him eight hundred and twenty pounds in crumpled bills. When he reached his third bookie he had no pockets left into which to stuff the things. He had to take off his raincoat and lay it on the ground, bundling it around the money and dragging it like a sack from stand to stand.

By then every man, woman, and child at the track seemed to have heard of his win. For the first time in his life Bascombe knew what it was like to be a celebrity, to be surrounded and stared at and talked about as though he existed on a separate, un-hearing, unfeeling level from everyone else. There were those in the crowd who assumed he was the beneficiary of a miracle, a sort of repetition of the loaves and fishes that was taking place in Tip-perary. This section loudly resented him. Several elderly people were only restrained from grabbing their share of the miracle off his raincoat by a larger younger group who felt he was a de-serving crook entitled to his loot. Only the man who had rigged the race himself would have bet that much money on Semolina. There was a moment when these two groups almost came to blows. But then, magically, the word "Yank" fluttered through the crowd. Americans were not exactly unpopular in Ireland. In-dividual Americans were generally accepted at their own worth. But in the abstract they were regarded, much as the Irish had been in the United States a hundred years before, as objects of ridicule. They were known to be noisy, gullible, absurd. As soon as Bascombe was identified as a Yank, the mood of the crowd changed. He became the butt of a joke that had been played on him by the cannier locals. A damn fool American had bet his damn fool money on a damn fool horse. The best part of the joke was that the clown had won. Now he was being paid off for his folly in this hilarious way. Every soiled pound note laid on his raincoat was like a custard pie in his face. The crowd roared with derision.

By the time he had collected his last pound, bundled up his raincoat, and knotted the sleeves together, he was close to being an object of sympathy. The crowd that followed him to the car was in a penitent, "don't take it too hard" mood. A faint, encour-aging cheer sounded behind him as he drove out onto the road.

He glanced at Venus. She did not look proud of herself. She did not say, "See. I told you so," or even ask him how much he had won. She was silent until they had crossed back into County Cork. Then she pulled her legs up, knelt on the seat beside him, and kissed his cheek.

He stopped the car. She put her arms around his neck. He held her against him. Anyone passing them, seeing his face, the small figure clutched in his arms, might have thought they had just escaped some near-fatal accident.

Apart from his gratitude to Venus for saving herself from that dank furnished room, the money meant nothing to him yet. He had no plans for it. It wasn't until late that night, when they were home in bed together, that it struck him how much he could *do* for her with all that crumpled wealth still tied up in his raincoat.

He was kissing her breasts, marveling at the proportions of her body, the gentle dale between her ribs that ran down to her navel, when, perhaps through the association of the word valley, perhaps because silken and satin were such a poor description of her skin, the name Balenciaga floated into his mind.

"When we get back to London you can go to any dressmaker you like."

"Do you want me to wear clothes?"

"No." Her belly was like nothing in the world, not even like a heap of wheat set about with lilies. It was incomparable: delight made flesh, flesh made delight. "But you'll have to wear something when we go out. Now you can wear beautiful things."

Nothing could ever be as beautiful as her skin: so immaculate it seemed poreless to the eye. He had always thought he found the blemishes on girls' bodies endearing. But that had been mere expedience, self-compensation. Venus had no blemishes. Their absence gave her another dimension of wonder. It was like being told as a child that the sky went on forever. He could never *quite* believe it.

His mouth was between her thighs, his tongue searching the soft fur. After a minute her thighs began to move, clasping and caressing his cheeks. She reached down and touched his shoulder. It was an implicit signal between them. She rolled over on top of him, drawing her body down until her lips were against his chest.

They had satisfied each other so often like this. She was so skillful at clenching and stroking his erection between her thighs that he was not immediately aware she had changed from her usual way of making love. It was only when he felt her parted knees on either side of him that he realized he had entered her.

The moment, the event which he had once spent whole days dreaming about, had arrived without any action on his part. She had taken him into her body as naturally and casually as she had patted his cock that first morning after her bath in the milk saucer.

He fondled her back and her hips, striving to express the startled tenderness he felt, to direct it all into the movements of his fingers over her skin.

She was scarcely moving, her lips plucking at his chest, her body not so much pressed as released against his. He drifted, gliding in a dream of feeling. He knew nothing, thought nothing. His mind, habitual interpreter of his senses, had ceased to exist. The wordless, imageless experience of his body had replaced all consciousness. There was no light, no sound, no purpose, no present. There was only sweet pain, unbearable pleasure. It was impossible that it should continue. It was unimaginable that it should end.

He had no recognizable awareness of its ending. There was no moment at which his body's experience of hers seemed to reach completion. There was only a long, imperceptible reawakening, a gradual return of light and sound and finally of thought. The light was the blaze of Venus' hair; the sound was her laughter; the thought a realization that her body was a separate presence. For some minutes now, it almost seemed always, she had been as much a part of him as if they had been enclosed in each other's skins.

She raised herself and kissed him on the lips. He could feel her amusement exploding inside his mouth. It didn't wound him. There was mockery, but no malice in her laughter. It made him laugh, too. They had done such a comic, triumphant thing together. What they had accomplished was as transient as a poem, a song, a swim in clear water; but it had raised them for a time into a realm of infinite experience. With no aim, no audience, with no stimulant but each other, they had created something out of themselves. They had made love.

He rolled her off his chest. She held onto his shoulder, curling up beside him as he pulled the sheets and blankets over her. She was still smiling as he turned off the light, and then as suddenly as a child, she fell asleep.

Bascombe lay awake for some time, restful, wondering. Phrases that had once challenged his adolescence drifted through his mind. He had made it. Got inside her pants. Had her ass. Laid her. He had never identified with the attitude behind those words, but he could not rid himself of the ridiculous feeling that in actually entering Venus at last he had crossed some more than physical threshold. He had accomplished something. He had scored. He tried to figure out why in hell he should feel that way.

They had made love so often, in so many other ways. What was so special about (okay!) fucking her? They had given each other pleasure, satisfaction, *everything* for months. Why should he feel so pleased with himself because tonight, finally, for the first time, they had copulated in the conventional way? Was there some mystical quality about coitus, absent from cunnilingus, fellatio, *soixante-neuf?* If not mystical, something animal, instinctive, that could not be expressed in any other way?

The more he thought about it, the less it seemed to matter. As he lay beside his fifty-inch goddess, almost ready at last to make her unequivocal entry into human society, he knew with the force of a discovery that he was happy. Before in California, here in Ireland, he had only recognized happiness as a gilding of time past. Now he was aware of it as the color of the present. He was happy as unquestionably as he was young.

Boxo, Bascombe thought incoherently, just before he fell asleep. That's B.O.X.O. Boxo. He's brave. He has a toupé. He has reckless courage. It's dangerous to flaunt his happiness like that.

14

CHAPTER

THE TELEPHONE was ringing again. Usually in the mornings and always at night they left the damn thing off the hook. It always started ringing the instant they replaced it. But this morning Bascombe was expecting a call from Nolan. Mrs. Charrington went into the bedroom to answer it.

Venus was standing in her slip in the living room, being measured by a gaily plumaged young man who wanted to create gear for her from head to foot.

"Madam *has* grown," Mrs. Charrington had greeted her with majestic cordiality when they returned to the London apartment at the beginning of March. Venus had more than doubled in size during their absence, but Mrs. Charrington made no further comment. She no longer came impulsively; she came every day. In her devotion to Venus she seemed to have found a central purpose which her life had lacked. She tended and arranged her as she had once tended and arranged other people's apartments.

Venus was still growing. Now, at the end of April, she was five foot six. By the time the young man presently draping her with lengths of velvet had created a single trouser suit for her, she would have outgrown it.

"It's a young lady from the Burne-Jones Agency," Mrs. Charrington announced from the bedroom doorway. "Do you wish to speak to her, sir?"

"No, thank you." Bascombe had had several idiotic conversations with the young lady from Burne-Jones in the past few days, and he didn't feel like having any more. She wanted him and Venus to have lunch with her, "One day soonish." She had a way of saying "lunch" as though it were a minor religion. Bascombe suspected she was one of the growing crowd of nuisances who wanted to put Venus under contract, not with any specific idea of organizing a career for her, just in case someone else came along with one.

"Beautiful. Beautiful." The young man had relieved Venus of the lengths of velvet. He was gazing at her in her slip with that helpless imbecility which had become all too familiar to Bascombe these past few weeks.

Venus smiled at him and walked through into the bedroom. She had no vanity; she knew she was beautiful; she did not need anyone to tell her so. She smiled at the young man as she smiled at the gaggle of fixated teen-agers who waited outside the house all day for a glimpse of her, not because she was flattered by their adoration, but because she was kind.

Bascombe dropped the obscene letter he was reading back into the suitcase filled with unanswered letters. They came, fifty or sixty a day, shameless, abusive, exhorting, appealing, imploring. He got up off the couch to let the young man out. He went about it cautiously, opening the door on the chain and taking a look out before opening it any further. Most mornings there were salesmen, hairdressers' representatives, promoters of implausible showbiz schemes, free-lance photographers, strip-club managers, and indefinable lunatics camping outside the apartment. They got tired of knocking; he had long ago disconnected the bell; but they never seemed to get tired of being there in the corridor. They brought tea and sandwiches, rugs; they squatted in strict order of precedence on the floor. They had the English passion for forming queues; but it had struck Bascombe at first how un-English, as he had experienced the English character, their behavior was in every other way. The instant, opening the door, he gave them a glimpse of their goal, the inside of the apartment, they clamored, they howled, they shouted questions and accusations at him as they threw themselves into the breach.

This morning when he drew back the door a hand was instantly thrust into the opening. Bascombe waited a second. There was no sound from the corridor; the hand slid a little further into the room. It was followed by a bony wrist, a Mickey Mouse watch, a pinstriped sleeve.

The phone was ringing again. Mrs. Charrington came out of the kitchen, ignored the hand, tapped discreetly at the bedroom door, and went on in to answer it. The hand clawed at the air like a separate famished being. Bascombe could not ignore it. Except for the Mickey Mouse watch, it reminded him of a concentration camp newsreel he had seen as a child in St. Louis. He opened the door to the full extent of the chain and looked into the corridor.

There was only a single squatter there this morning. A thin-faced man with gray hair cut in a page-boy bob, a ruffled shirt, and the pinstriped suit.

"My name's Igor Wessex." At least Bascombe thought he said Igor Wessex. "I want to talk to you."

"You'll have to take your hand out of the door first."

"I insist on talking to you." He had a precise way of speaking that was out of keeping with the watch. It went better with the suit.

"I can't open the door unless you take your hand out."

"I don't believe you."

"It's on a chain."

The thin face hesitated; the hand acted. It groped around the corner of the door. It found the chain. It withdrew into the corridor.

"Mr. Stanley Nolan's on the telephone. Do you wish to speak to him, sir?"

"Yes." As Bascombe passed Mrs. Charrington in the bedroom doorway, he told her about the owner of the hand. She agreed to show this gentleman out and the other gentleman in, sir.

Venus was standing in front of the mirror, combing her hair. It reached down below her waist: the golden plume he had once imagined. She still had nothing on but her slip and a pair of sheer tights. She never wore a bra. He didn't even glance at the telephone. He went straight over to her and kissed her back, sliding the ribbon of her slip off her shoulder with his lips. She turned to him at once. Her nipple was so delicate it filled him with a kind of anguish. It was impossible to look at anything so perfect without instantly fearing for it, too. He looked up at Venus' eyes. They were smiling at him.

He knew he only had to say a few words and she would be on the bed with him, utterly willing. He couldn't think of any reason in the world not to say them.

"I'll lock the door." She said them for him. As he pulled off his jacket, he saw the telephone and remembered Nolan.

"Hullo."

"Bascombe?"

"Yes."

"Nolan."

"Yes."

Venus was standing naked at the end of the bed. She leaned down to take off his socks and shoes. Her hair fell forward across her shoulders, misting her breasts in a haze of gold.

"Bascombe?"

"Yes?"

"About tonight?"

Bascombe stopped listening. It didn't matter. He would be able to recall what Nolan had said later. Venus was stripping off his trousers and underpants, unbuttoning his shirt, slipping it off his shoulders. He could already feel in anticipation the first breathless contact of her body against his.

"—at the bar, Bascombe."

"Bye, Nolan."

He lowered the receiver but he still had just enough awareness of the everyday world not to replace it on its stand. The gaggle of teen-agers in the street outside, the salesmen, the hairdressers, the promoters, the agents, the lunatics, the gaily plumaged young men, the suitcase full of unopened letters, Igor Wessex waiting in the next room—all vanished so completely from his mind they might never have existed.

Half an hour later when he returned to the living room, they gradually began to reappear. Igor Wessex was the first. He was sitting on the couch with his hands on his knees as Bascombe came out of the bedroom. He stood up.

"You are Mr. Fletcher, I suppose."

"Yes." Bascombe felt so happy he missed the hostility in the other's voice. "Sorry I kept you waiting."

"It wasn't very nice."

"I'm sorry."

"Sitting here waiting while you were screwing that girl."

Oh, shit, Bascombe thought, he's one of the lunatics. He tried to assume the brisk manner he had found worked best with them. "What do you want?"

"I don't want to screw her, if that's what you're thinking. I want to take some photographs."

"Photographs?"

"Pho-to-graphs. Pictures. Snaps to you, probably."

"Are you a photographer?"

"I'm the best photographer in London. In the world," he corrected himself hastily. "I'm also the rudest. I'm as famous for my rudeness as you are for your—I don't know what the hell you're famous for. I told Philip, *Prince* Philip, one night . . ." He went on and on about what he had told Prince Philip. Bascombe didn't listen. He played back his conversation with Nolan in his mind and found they had arranged to meet at Parkes' restaurant at nine. In the bar.

"I want you to bring that girl to my studio."

"No."

It was disconcerting how suddenly the one word defeated Igor Wessex. He slumped down on the sofa, resting his elbows on his knees and his head on his hands. "Why not?" he asked humbly.

"She doesn't want to be photographed. She's sick of being photographed. It's a bloody bore. And now you can get out—"

"I'm so confused."

"What?"

"I told my wife it wouldn't work. I hate this watch." Wessex took his head out of his hands and waved his thin wrist at Bascombe. "Mickey Mouse! At my age! I had a very nice trade in Knightsbridge. Debutantes. They weren't really debutantes, of

202

course, but some of them *had* been to boarding school. Eight and a half by eleven matte prints. A choice of six poses, fifteen guineas."

"Would you like a drink?"

"I'm not an alcoholic." There was no indignation; there was even a mild regret in the denial. "It wasn't drink. It was all that business about Profumo and then the Beatles and the Great Train Robbery. That's when everything started to change. What's so old-fashioned about lighting a girl so that you can see her face? That's what photography's for. There's not much point in having a picture of someone if you can't even recognize who it is. Is there?"

"No."

"My wife *made* me buy this wig. My head gets so hot when I turn the studio lights on, the sweat absolutely blinds me and then it fogs up the eyepiece." He lifted his fingers to the bridge of his nose, and for a horrible moment Bascombe thought he was going to burst into tears. "Where's your studio?" he asked quickly.

Igor Wessex handed him a card. The Knightsbridge address printed on it had been scratched out and a number in Fulham Road written in underneath.

"I'm terribly sorry what I said about you and that—you and the young lady. I don't like language like that. Will you really let me photograph her?"

Bascombe said he would. They arranged an appointment, four o'clock that afternoon. Igor Wessex was trembling slightly as Bascombe eased him out of the door.

"It isn't the fifteen guineas. It's the—"

"I know." It was the publicity.

Bascombe bolted and chained the door after him. It was the publicity that had led to his whole present way of living, to the routine with the door chain, the phone that rang every time he replaced the receiver, to Igor Wessex himself.

He knew he should have anticipated it. It had all started so naturally; and yet so inevitably. They had returned to London flushed and eager. Venus was just under five feet tall, free at last, as he imagined, to go where she pleased, do as she liked. The

203

first thing was to get her some adult clothes. He had bought several fashion magazines at Cork Airport, and that evening she showed him the dresses she liked in them.

"The romantic leads in chiffon, organza, and georgette," Bascombe read from the paragraph snaking down the side of the page. "The art, the heart of romantic fashion. Soft. Sheer. Beautiful. With color used to add a dimension . . ." His eyes skipped another six inches of this quaint cajolery. "From Willa Carter. To Order."

Bascombe's conception of a fashionable dressmaker's establishment had been formed several years ago from Hollywood movies: acres of vacant carpet, marble steps, thin chic vendeuses gliding forward, snapping their fingers, "Yvette! M'sya le Cont is ear." Willa Carter's was three narrow rooms one above the other in a house that looked as if it had been built by someone who hated daylight. No one could have glided an inch in it. You could barely edge and sidle your way between the rails of clothes, the mirrors, the bolts of material, up and down the pinched stairs. No one called for Yvette as Venus and Bascombe entered. Everyone was busy saying, "Excuse me," "May I?" "Do you mind?" "*So* sorry."

Venus, still less than five feet tall then, was wearing a flannel skirt and a white lambswool sweater. Her hair was in a pony tail down her back. She looked at first glance like a well-brought-up schoolgirl in London on a visit. Bascombe followed her down the steps into the bottom room and stopped as she stopped on the edge of the preening, chirping crowd of customers.

That was the first time he saw it happen. Venus didn't do anything. She just stood there. A woman of about forty in a fur coat down to her ankles turned and glanced at her, a quick, dismissing glance. Her eyes met Venus' level gaze. The woman shook her head slightly, as if she didn't believe it. There was a man standing beside her. She reached out and touched his arm without taking her eyes off Venus. She might have been calling his attention to a star that would vanish if she let it out of her sight.

Several other people glanced at Venus. Not one of them looked away again. She held their attention by the force of her serenity, her assurance, her beauty. Bascombe was always sure of that: he never found it hard to believe or understand. What he had not anticipated was how impossible others would find it to accept such an obvious explanation. They refused to admit anything so unflattering to their own egos. It was like being forced to confess to a natural inferiority. There had to be some less disturbing explanation. Their interest must be attributed to the kind of specious, artificial deference they were used to. Softly, a polite whisper at first, Bascombe heard the words that were to follow Venus through London for the next few weeks.

"Who is she?"

And then immediately came the answers. They did not have to be true. They only had to seem to explain why some particular collection of successful, conceited people had suddenly paused, silent with fascination, to stare at her.

"She's that Belgian, Greek, Danish, What's-it-called Princess. That Earl of, Duke of, You-know-who-I-mean, *His* daughter. That Onassis, Rockefeller, Ford, Kennedy, Krupp girl."

That first morning in the crowded shop the explanations had descended no lower than Onassis when a strikingly attractive woman in her late twenties edged forward out of the whispering group. She was nearly as small as Venus, with a skin so pale it seemed faintly luminous.

"My dear, I don't know who you are," she said in a soft tentative voice, as she took Venus by the hand and led her toward the stairs. "But I'm Willa Carter, and I'd like to look after you myself."

That was the beginning, the "you-know-who-she-is-don't-you?" phase. Wherever she went, the attention Venus attracted by being herself was attributed to the fact that she was someone else. It couldn't last, because inevitably, and quite soon, the press got involved. Willa Carter asked Venus to let herself be photographed at the White Elephant one evening wearing one of the "free, ephemeral, Grecian" dresses she had created for her. Several of the papers, intrigued by this "mini-beauty," as two of them captioned her, printed the pictures. Reporters who had heard echoes of the "who-is-she?" whispers decided to find out who she actually was. They knew she wasn't Princess Anybody, or Lady Who-sits, or a Ford. They weren't interested in soothing their egos; they were on a job. The day the pictures appeared the phone started to ring.

Bascombe realized it could be dangerous. If he tried to fluff off the reporters, they might start digging in earnest; they might get at Mrs. Charrington, at Anne and Geraldine in West Cork; they might find out Venus had grown almost two feet in the past four months, that she had no birth certificate, no nationality, no parents. No explicable origin. Now that she was almost fully grown at last, she could still become the victim of that tribal curiosity he had been so careful to protect her against when she was nine inches tall.

He invited a group of reporters to the apartment. He gave them drinks. Venus entered in an Italian silk jersey dress that made him gasp. She let the photographers take all the pictures they wanted. She sat down on the couch; she looked at the reporters—she and Bascombe had agreed earlier that she would not infatuate them—she gave them a friendly smile. Bascombe stood up and told them who she was.

"She's Venus, Aphrodite, Ishtar, Ashtoreth, Astarte, Freyja, the Goddess of Love."

"How do you spell Ishtar?" a studious-looking girl in a cloche hat wanted to know.

"I.S.H.T.A.R."

She wrote it down.

"Ashtoreth?"

"A.S.H.T.O.R.E.T.H."

Most of them wrote that down, too.

A middle-aged man from one of the Sunday papers stood up. He had a tired, kind face. He glanced at Venus as he put his empty glass down on the table.

"In other words, it's a publicity stunt." It was obvious he spoke for all of them.

Bascombe let Venus answer that.

"It's whatever you believe." She said it with such candor that it impressed even them. Most of them printed the story straight.

"A very beautiful and charming girl who claims to be the goddess of love . . ." Only one paper spelled Freyja correctly.

After that the reporters left Venus in peace. Occasionally a free-lance feature writer would reveal she was actually Shirley Trent from Liverpool, or Irma Marks from Balham, in a special exclusive, imaginary interview. But as far as the working press was concerned, there was no story.

It was a different matter with the photographers. Venus soon began to attract not only attention but admirers, people who invited her and (sometimes reluctantly) Bascombe to their parties, to dinner here, to the theater, a horse show, a discothèque there. Some of these people were genuinely celebrated; they had actually done something. Some sought publicity as a means to getting something done; others as an end in itself. Venus, in their company, began to share their exposure to flashbulbs. She was so beautiful that the flattest lighting, the cheapest mass reproduction process could not obscure her radiance. It was impossible to take a dull picture of her; even the dullest photographers soon caught on to that. Gratefully they concentrated on her. Thanks to that news story she was easy to identify. The pictures were captioned "Venus." "Venus" at the opening of, "Venus" at a party for. The day a woman's page omitted the quotes (*Venus buys all her lingerie at . . .*) marked a public recognition that she had achieved the purest form of celebrity. She had become well-known for being well-known.

Celebrity, like anxiety, feeds on itself. The more she was sought after, the more sought after she became. When Venus and Bascombe got out of their rented chauffeur-driven car that evening in front of Parkes' restaurant, the photographers, tipped off by the secretary who had taken Bascombe's reservation, had been waiting for almost an hour. The photographers had attracted the usual crowd of gapers: Somebody was evidently expected. Rumors flourished like weeds. "I wish it *was* Maggie," one of the photographers complained to his assistant. "At least the police stop the buggers *shoving* when it's royalty."

It was less than ten feet from the car to the restaurant. It took them five minutes to make it. The photographers treated Venus as though they were paying her. "Turn this way." "Head up." "Now with the cape open." The crowd treated her as though she were deaf. "Look at her hair." "That's from Willa Carter, that dress." "They're not really real pearls." "Look at her *legs*." Venus treated everyone with her usual serenity. She was helpful to the photographers; she smiled at the crowd. But with the same authority, power of enchantment, whatever it was that had once arrested Chester Voigt's hand in mid-air, she stopped anyone except Bascombe touching her. When she had had enough of being photographed and discussed, she moved forward and the crowd got out of her way. It always fascinated Bascombe to watch her do this, but it did not surprise him. He still accepted her as unquestioningly as he had when she was living in his suitcase.

They were late. Nolan was on his third Scotch when they entered the bar. Bascombe introduced Venus. She was wearing one of her "Grecian" dresses, a simple length of silk held up by a brooch on her left shoulder and divided in front to reveal her legs up to the thigh. As she smiled at Nolan he jerked his head aside, glancing over his shoulder as though someone had jostled him from behind. Bascombe apologized for being late. "We went to the British Museum," he explained. "And got sort of held up."

It was only partly true. They had left the British Museum hours ago. It was later, when they were home undressing to take a shower, that they had got held up.

Nolan ordered drinks, white wine for Venus, vodka for Bascombe, another large Scotch for himself. He seemed to be having trouble thinking of anything to say. He kept trying not to look at Venus.

"What did you see at the museum?" He held his eyes fixed on her brooch.

"The encyclopedia."

"Who?"

"We didn't go to look at things," Bascombe explained. "We were in the reading room."

"Reading the encyclopedia?"

Venus nodded.

"How far did you get?"

"Inertia."

"Where?"

"It's Newton's First Law." Bascombe was beginning to feel like an interpreter.

"Are you reading the encyclopedia, too?"

"No." He had spent the afternoon delving into classical mythology.

"What's the law of inertia?" Nolan's eyes were back on Venus' brooch.

"Every body perseveres in its state of rest."

Nolan's didn't. He kept shifting about on his stool as though it were a bed of nails.

Things got a little easier over dinner. Nolan gave in, and sliding down in his seat, gazed up at Venus with the frank abandon of a small boy at the movies. Venus did most of the talking. She had a way at times of gathering a series of impressions into a judgment of some aspect of the present world.

"You don't care about your cities. There's no coherence in them," she told Nolan over her *steak au poivre*. "You cooperate with each other most of the time in the way you organize things. You distribute food and clothes to every district. You have buses and postmen. You're an orderly people in some ways. But you put up buildings as though you hated each other."

Later, Bascombe and Nolan were alone at the table for a few minutes.

"Where did you find her?"

"We met in Ireland." It was Bascombe's stock answer.

"She's not Irish!"

"No."

"Are you living together?"

"Yes."

"You're lucky."

"Yes."

Nolan suddenly dropped his chin onto his hands. "My God." There was a flash of pain in his eyes. "It's such a long time since it happened to me. I never thought it could happen again. The moment she walked in. It was like— When I was just a kid in

Liverpool— The way I used to feel about Gloria Stuart."

Bascombe nodded sympathetically. There didn't seem to be anything to say. It wasn't the first time in the past few weeks someone had fallen in love with Venus at first glance. Many of the letters that came every day were outpourings of passion, most of them sadistic, but some tender and moving.

Caught up in the squirrel cage of their social life, Bascombe had never really had time to come to terms with this quandary. He had never discussed it with Venus. There had been no cause to. She never gave him the least reason for jealousy. They were still almost never parted; at the longest, for an hour or two while she had a fitting at Willa Carter's. She loved to wander around out-of-the-way streets—Tooting Bec, the East End, Clapham Junction—where she was unlikely to be recognized. She always wanted him to go with her, to stroll hand in hand, inspect shop windows, answer her questions: "Is it a ceremony for women to come to these laundromats?" "Why don't people ever speak to each other on buses?" "Why are the people who seem to do all the hard work the only ones who ever smile in England?"

At parties they were usually separated by her admirers. But she never showed any sexual interest in other men. Sometimes she would let them take her arm, kiss her cheek in greeting, but most of the time, however amiably she treated them, she kept them at a physical distance, as she had that crowd outside the restaurant.

And always, when she had had enough of the actors and the politicians, she would come and find him and they would go home to bed together. Then for an hour or two before they fell asleep they might have been the only two beings alive.

There was a stirring of heads by the door to the lounge. Eyes followed Venus like compass needles as she returned to the table. Nolan stood up and did his best to look cheerful.

They took him on to one of the five parties they had been invited to that night. The host was a youngish American who had settled in London. He liked to tell you he had a Gatsby complex, but he was richer than Gatsby and his motive for giving parties less romantic. His analyst had revealed to him that he hated people; he hated his analyst; he devoted a great deal of money and a genuine flair for spotting next week's celebrities to refuting him.

It was not like the party at the Waddingtons: the hundred guests in the vast maze of a living room seemed to have been let loose on each other. Venus was instantly surrounded and escorted away by a group that included a guitarist, a hairdresser, and a junior cabinet minister. Nolan disconsolately followed them.

The room was gleaming with half-dressed girls. Several of them, knowing that any male at this party must be Somebody and pleased to see Somebody their own age, smiled at Bascombe. He got himself a drink from one of the three bars. He was thinking of what Nolan had said: "You're lucky." He knew it. He was perhaps the only person in the world, certainly the only person in this roomful of success-seekers, who had everything he wanted. What disturbed him sometimes was the feeling that Venus must want something more. She had never shown any sign that she did. She rarely expressed any but the most momentary desires. "I'd like to go to the Victoria and Albert Museum." "I'll have spaghetti and clam sauce." "Lock the door." "Where's Stonehenge?"

He could see now that all his anxiety about her at the races in County Tipperary had been ridiculous. There could never be any dank furnished rooms in her future. She could obviously have anything the world had to offer: diamonds, yachts, houses. She had only to ask the right man for them, or buy them herself. She had won three thousand pounds in a few minutes playing roulette two nights ago, and if she felt like dipping into the stock market, there was no end to the fortune she could acquire. Apart from clothes—and she still preferred being naked—she seemed to have no interest in material possessions. When Bascombe had suggested moving into a larger, more luxurious apartment she had shrugged, "It's all right here," and asked him who Cohn-Bendit was. Was it only for this the goddess Aphrodite had returned to the world: to be photographed and exclaimed over, explore Tooting Bec, go to parties and restaurants, read the Encyclopaedia Britannica, and make love with a totally undistinguished young American engineer?

It was in an attempt to answer this question that Bascombe had been delving into mythology that afternoon. He had been searching the past for some possible indication of Venus' plans for the future. He hadn't come up with much. It was surprising how little there was on record about her. There was the story from *The Odyssey* about her affair with Ares and the invisible net her jealous husband, Haphaestus, had made to trap them in bed together. There were references to her beauty and her marvelous hair, which was sometimes described as a golden crown. She was said to be amiable, laughter-loving, good-hearted—he knew that about her already. She had been loyal to Paris for his Judgment and had fought "not very effectively" on his side in the Trojan War. The Myrtle, the rose, the apple, the poppy, the sparrow, the dove, the swan, and the swallow were sacred to her. Her chief shrines had been on the islands of Cyprus and Kythera. She had power to bestow "the gift of irresistible charm" on anyone if she chose to.

The rest of the volumes the librarian had brought him had seemed to consist of not uninteresting descriptions of the varied rites that had been performed at her shrines at various times.

Bascombe's research had merely confirmed what Venus herself had told him. As far as humans were concerned, the goddess of love was whatever they believed her to be.

He knew what he believed her to be, what he had always believed her to be, the only ideal worth pursuing.

"*You* the guy who's handling that girl?"

Bascombe found he was sitting down. He had wandered over to a window seat and settled there. A tall man in his forties with a pale horse face was leaning over him. He recalled the man's words reluctantly to his mind. "Handling" was an expression he had heard too often in the past few weeks. The lets-have-lunch-soonish girl from Burne-Jones was not the only agent who wanted to "handle" Venus. He stood up.

"No."

"You're Bascombe Fletcher, aren't you?"

"Yes."

"Got you. What's your angle, Bascombe?"

"There's no angle." He recognized the man now. Ten years

ago Saul Franklin had been one of the New Wave film directors. The wave had washed over him, leaving him struggling to stay on his feet as a promoter, one of that interminable list of producers who would make any film he could get backing for.

"*No* angle?"

"No."

"For Christ sake." A spasm of irritation parted Franklin's drawn-in horse's lips, revealing a row of long lower teeth.

"Let's cut the Ping-Pong. How much do you want for her contract?"

"I don't want anything."

"Got you." Franklin nodded understandingly. "You keep the contract. I'll give you a one-shot deal." He was one of those men who felt he could not convince anyone of his sincerity without laying his hands on him. He kneaded Bascombe's shoulder. "You know who I am. You know how I stand with the studios." It was less a boast than the offer of a bribe.

Bascombe freed himself before answering. He realized he was going to have to resort to obscenities to get in touch with Franklin.

"I don't give a shit who you are."

"I've heard that crap before."

"It's not crap. It's true." He started toward the nearest bar. Franklin grabbed his arm just above the elbow. He pulled free again. At that moment he felt only a familiar weariness. It was like being back with Mr. Mitchel: he was going to be forced to listen, or pretend to listen, to the usual self-seeking chicanery, some scheme as senseless in the end, as grotesque as cutting down firs to make artificial Christmas trees.

"I've got a movie going in Spain in July. About the Cid. None of that Charlton Heston racism. We're on the side of the Moors. Two million eight below the line. You know what that means?"

"No." He meant: no, don't tell me.

"It means thirty thou for her. Second lead. Six weeks maximum. She gets a solo credit— And Introducing Venus As—"

"No."

"Forty."

213

"No."

"Fifty's the top figure."

"What are you asking me for? It's got nothing to do—"

"Cut that out." Bascombe got another look at Franklin's lower teeth. "Everyone in town knows you're running her."

"If you're making a movie and you want her to be in it—talk to her."

He meant no more than the words did. Venus was free to do anything she liked. But that wasn't the way Franklin took it. He grabbed it as an agreement that Venus' handler approved the deal in principle. He kneaded Bascombe's shoulder again and started to lay in the details.

"Three weeks location and we do the studio in Madrid. You're on expenses to keep her happy. But I've got that prick—" He mentioned the name of a Hollywood actor Bascombe had seen at several parties recently. "He's the one who suggested her, and he's the key to the package, so we might as well get things straight right now and avoid the kind of scene in Spain that's going to screw up the shooting schedule." His hand moved up toward Bascombe's neck, persuasively massaging the trapezoid muscles. "Hell. With that jerk it's not his id, it's his ego. If she gives him a blow job once a week, everybody's happy. Got me, Bascombe?"

Bascombe got him. Suddenly at that moment he got much more than Franklin. He got this whole roomful of people, all the other rooms and restaurants full of the people he had mingled with this past month. With a few exceptions like Willa Carter, who did something and cared about what she did, they were a collection of self-important locusts. They were classic examples of what he had told Nolan he meant by shits. They all believed in their own pecking order. Every last one of them wanted to be a big deal. It wasn't only that they were so avid for status, possessions, envy, all the things their society could give them. They did not believe there was anything else worth having.

Franklin was still waiting for his answer. Bascombe grabbed the hand on his shoulder and pulled it loose.

"Fuck off."

"Who are you telling—"

"I'm telling you, you poor miserable shit. Fuck off."

"Listen to him." A small group had gathered around them, attracted by the sound of obscenity, the chance of violence. Franklin turned, appealing to them, "Listen to this jerk, telling me to fuck off." He obviously felt it was a phenomenon worth broadcasting. "Do you know who he is, this—this nobody?"

Venus was sitting on a sofa by the fireplace. It took Bascombe a moment to work his way through the men around her.

"De Gaulle won't stand any nonsense from those students," a fat man in a tight suit was saying. "A good beating on their behinds, that's what—"

He never finished the sentence. Venus stood up, leaving him with his mouth open. Bascombe took her hand.

"Come on."

It was one of those times when they had arrived at the same mood independently. She didn't ask any questions; she didn't even pause to say goodnight to the men around the sofa. They went in search of Nolan.

He was not at any of the bars. Hand in hand they threaded their way in and out of knots of talking people, peering into strange faces. They found him at last in one of the bedrooms. He was unconscious drunk, lying amid a heap of mink and beaver and vicuña on a fourposter bed. He was smiling in his sleep. Was he dreaming of those days when he had given his young sister economics to read? Bascombe wondered. When he had wanted so much to change things as they were? They didn't try to wake him. There didn't seem to be anything they could do for him except leave him to dream.

Outside on the street they sent the car back to the garage. They walked out of Belgravia into Sloane Square and strolled along the King's Road. At that hour London was like a museum; they could hear their own footsteps. They talked very little. They both knew they had reached an end. Bascombe was waiting for Venus to tell him what the new beginning would be.

215

"They have no virtue," she said as they passed Peter Jones. "It's extraordinary. They've tried to create a whole society with no measure of worth except self-advancement."

Bascombe didn't argue with her. They walked on in silence.

"They don't believe in me," she announced flatly opposite Mary Quant's. "I thought at first they might. I let them make a show of me. But they have no gods. Only idols. They don't even have any anti-gods except that crab they're always talking about."

It took Bascombe as far as The Chelsea Potter to figure that out.

"Cancer?"

She nodded. "It's the only thing they ever mention with awe. What is it?"

"A disease."

"They do believe in you in a way," he tried to reassure her. "They love you. They want you."

"No." She was in no mood to accept that. "Most of them don't even desire me. They think it's a contest. If they fuck me, they win. And they only want to win so that other people will envy them."

Bascombe couldn't help it; he was delighted by this. Her attitude seemed to eliminate all possible competition. With her hand clasping his, she was excepting him from all the other men she knew.

"Of course, it isn't true of all of them," she admitted thoughtfully at the corner of Old Church Street. "Those sisters in Ireland, Anne and Geraldine, have virtue. So does Willa Carter and, I think, your friend Nolan, and some of the women in Tooting Bec in that laundromat. And Mrs. Charrington."

It was an opportunity Bascombe had been hoping for, to find out about Mrs. Charrington.

"Does she believe in you?" he asked. "Does she know you're a goddess?"

"She doesn't think about it. It doesn't matter to her. It's like the apartment. Like your shirts. Mrs. Charrington has a quest. When she was looking after all those other apartments she didn't ask who lived in them, she devoted herself to keeping them perfectly clean. Sometimes she would spend a whole week on one of them, sometimes only a day, whatever she thought was necessary." Venus raised her hand in that shrugging gesture. "When we came back from Ireland she decided to choose me as her task instead. A lot of the Greek women were like that. They used to tend all our shrines, but I think they only really believed in Hera."

As they turned onto the Fulham Road, Bascombe felt a stab of remorse. Igor Wessex. He had only made the appointment to get rid of him; but it was appalling to think of him waiting for them in his studio, sweating under his wig as he arranged his lights and camera, glancing again and again at his Mickey Mouse watch as the hands moved on to half-past four, to five, until (when? at five-thirty? at six?) he lost hope. It was nothing as easeful as pity Bascombe felt; it was cruelty remembered in tranquillity.

"We've got to get out of here." He spoke protestingly to shut out his own thoughts.

"Yes," Venus agreed at once. He wondered where she wanted to go. Anywhere outside of England or Ireland would raise the problem of a passport. Legally, in spite of her celebrity, she still had no existence. But now that she was an ordinary human size, he didn't think getting her a passport would be all that difficult. At the time the newspapers had first shown an interest in "Venus" and he had been worried about trying to establish an acceptable identity for her, he had made some cautious inquiries. It was surprisingly easy, he had found, to get a copy of a birth certificate in England. All you had to do was go to Somerset House and represent yourself as someone whose birth had been registered there. Besides a birth certificate, all you needed for a passport was a letter from a responsible citizen saying he had known you for two years. There were various categories of citizens who were regarded as responsible, doctors, lawyers, Members of Parliament . . . Nolan! Nolan, he was sure, would be glad to help them.

"Where do you want to go?" Bascombe asked.

She did not reply at once. He began to sort through his recollection of all the girls they had met these past few weeks for one whose identity Venus could borrow. Some girl in her early twenties with a fairly common name? There was only one other essential qualification. She must never have applied for a passport herself, never been abroad . . . The memory seemed to come out of the distant past, almost from his childhood: a darkened room and a girl's hand in his, a friendly, faintly defensive voice, "It's probably even worse abroad."

They were almost home before Venus told him her plans. "There are some people, I think, who do believe in me." Her voice had that searching, thoughtful quality it had when she was comparing images of the future. "That savage fat man at the party was talking about them, and I've been feeling more and more lately that many of them want me, that they're people like you, the ones I came back for."

"Who?" It was painful to lose his brief illusion that he was different from everyone else.

She put her arm around his shoulder. They climbed the stairs to their apartment.

"Where's the Sorbonne?" she asked as he opened the door for her.

15
CHAPTER

MEN'S ONLY boundaries are the limits of their imagination.

For three weeks in Paris that was almost true. Instead of asking, "How?" people began demanding, "Why?" and then, hopefully, proposing, "Why not—?" For a few days grocers, riveters, laborers, schoolteachers, waiters, even concierges came out and blinked in the sunlight of possibilities.

Venus and Bascombe arrived just before the beginning of those weeks. It was May 10, 1968, Venus' first birthday. A year ago she had appeared reborn, an inch and a half tall, into the modern world. She was five feet eight now, a woman of that world, traveled, well-read, but still infinitely curious. Riding in from Orly to their hotel in St. Germain, she watched Paris assemble around her with the same searching interest she had once shown in the light sockets, the plumbing, a box of matches in Bascombe's apartment.

The taxi driver hadn't started to blink yet. He had a bronchial condition and bubbled incessantly with phlegmy amusement. Bascombe had learned some Quebec French from his grandparents and understood about half the cause of the hilarity. He gathered that a rough kind of football game had been going on all week between the students and the police. So far the students, to the wheezing amusement of the taxi driver, appeared to be winning. A few nights ago they had had the whole field to themselves, charging up and down the Champs Élysées and celebrating their victory around the Arc de Triomphe.

"And the referee hasn't blown his whistle once yet," the man concluded, as Bascombe paid him off outside the hotel. "So far from De Gaulle—nothing but farts."

"Big Charlie'll have to get the hell off that pot. And the sooner the better."

Chuck Higgins didn't share the taxi driver's amusement. He was the Paris correspondent of an American newsmagazine and took a depressed view of the riots. "We're in the thick of it here," he went on, gazing across the river at the distant dome of the Panthéon. "If the police can't hold the bridges—I don't have to tell you how those students feel about Americans." He was a short, bulky man whose head was too big for his face; his features huddled around his nose as though for company. He closed the window and shifted his gaze to Venus' legs.

"How do they feel?" She had been given Higgins' name by a journalist in London and had called him from the hotel. Having read all the English newspaper reports on the situation she was anxious for factual information. "What do the Americans have to do with it?"

"This whole thing blew up from Vietnam."

"The *Times* said it was because of the segregation in the dormitories at Nanterre."

"Those fucking dormitories had nothing to do with it." Higgins had a carefully cultivated reputation for plain speaking. "Those kids were bombing every American building in Paris. That's how that mother, Cohn-Bendit, got started. Protesting against the arrest of the bastards who were doing it."

Venus stood up and walked across the large, expensively furnished room to the window. Higgins' eyes followed her. "You married?" he asked Bascombe.

"No."

"What do they want, Mr. Higgins—the students?"

"Call me Chuck." His nickname had been carefully cultivated, too.

Venus waited for the answer to her question.

"Right now their demands are get the *flics* out of the Latin

Quarter. All the arrested students out of the can. And reopen the universities."

"That's all?" Venus sounded disappointed.

"Right now, I said." He moved over to the window beside her. "Later it'll be our turn. Run all Americans the hell out of Europe. That's what they really want." He took his eyes off Venus for a moment, looking toward the Sorbonne a mile away on the opposite bank. "I only hope the cops can hold those fucking bridges."

"Do you think he knows what he's talking about?"

"No."

Click. Clog. They could hear Higgins locking his front door after them as they walked down the stairs.

"He's so frightened."

"It's natural for Americans to take things personally. It saves them thinking."

They crossed the river and strolled along the Boulevard St. Germain. Here and there the paving blocks had been torn out of the streets, a tree blackened by fire, a street light sawn off at its base. But the cafés were full, the crowds coming up out of the Métro as stolid and aloof as homeward-bound residents in any other city. It wasn't until they reached the Rue Monge that they saw any immediate signs of unrest.

The metal shutters of the cafés around the Place Maubert had been lowered. The adjoining streets were blocked with young people. Bascombe was struck by their look of respectability. Many of the young men wore jackets and ties, the girls neat blouses or sweaters.

"Let's go and hear what they're saying." Venus was leading him across the square.

"Can you understand French?" She had given no indication in the taxi that she could.

"It's mostly a development of Frankish and Latin." From the way she dismissed the question, he knew that within a few hours, a day at most, she would be speaking it far more fluently than he did.

They paused at the edge of a group surrounding a boy in a light raincoat. He was holding a transistor to his ear and translating its static-broken sounds into terse, high-pitched announcements. Now that he was among them, Bascombe could sense an anxiety in the listeners; it reminded him of the atmosphere in college corridors just before a test.

"If you get your demands, if they release the arrested students?" Venus had got into conversation in English with a dark-skinned girl.

"That's only the beginning. We're challenging the principles of our whole present society."

"It has no principles."

The girl laughed. She had one of those faces that are neither ugly nor pretty, only themselves.

"It has force."

"Will you fight?"

"We won in Algeria."

"The police have warned the students to clear the streets." Bascombe had caught a scrap of information from the boy with the transistor.

"Are you a Canadian?"

The hell with it. They could only lynch him.

"American."

"I've got a brother in Montreal. He wants to go to America, but he's afraid they'll mistake him for a Negro and send him to Vietnam."

"No. No. No." The boy in the light raincoat had lowered his radio and was waving his left arm up and down. "No. No. No."

The students around him took up the refrain. "No. No. No." Soon the whole gathering of three or four hundred were caught up in the same rhythmic ritual.

A boy wearing a red armband brushed past Bascombe and headed into the crowd. He could hardly have been over eighteen, but there was a brisk authority about him that would have been impressive in a senior officer.

"He's from the *service d'ordre*," the Algerian girl told Venus. "Now we'll see what they want us to do."

"They?" Venus was still seeking exact information.

"The action committee."

The chanting had ceased as the boy reached the center of the crowd. For a minute there was a waiting silence, and then suddenly, without a word of direction, the whole gathering began to migrate up the Rue Monge.

"Come on." Venus touched Bascombe's arm. The Algerian girl fell in on the other side of her and they moved with the rest.

Bascombe was quite happy to take his direction from Venus. He had not questioned her decision to come to France. She was impelled by aims that were beyond his experience. At best he could only understand them in human terms: she was seeking some hope, some fulfillment in Paris.

The Algerian girl asked her where she had bought her sweater.

"Marks and Spencer."

"Please?"

"In London."

Venus had changed her style lately—loose sweaters and skirts, low-heeled shoes. Bascombe found this new modesty wildly provocative. He hadn't had a chance to make love to her since noon.

"I find the English very sympathetic." For a revolutionary, the Algerian girl had a quiet line in conversation.

"I found most of them barbarians," Venus admitted.

"The consumer society makes everyone barbarians."

"Who made this society?"

"The colonialists." Like the authorities she opposed, she still clung to the reassurance of familiar ideas.

Mysteriously, without a word of command, the students were splitting up into smaller groups now, choosing different routes toward wherever they were going. They were hurrying, breaking into a run, darting from one sidewalk to another. For the next few minutes Bascombe lost all sense of his own identity. His impressions were as static as snapshots. Doorways dotted with faces; upper balconies striped with legs; the hunched shoulders of the girl in front of him; a window full of surgical trusses; Venus' cool hand clutching his.

As suddenly as it had begun the onward rush halted. Venus

pulled her hand free and dropped to the ground. He knelt quickly beside her. But it was not breathlessness that had brought her to her knees. A boy in a leather jacket had produced a screwdriver and was prying a paving block out of the street. Venus using one of her shoes as a hammer, was helping him. Bascombe found the heavy hotel key in his pocket and began hacking away with it. A car glided forward pushed by several boys, a girl leaning in through the window and steering it into place across the street. Another car was pushed in behind it. A park bench appeared, a sawn-off street light, planks and tubular scaffolding from a house under repair. The paving blocks were piled into the gaps. Within half an hour a barrier six feet high stretched from the metal shutters of a fish shop to the wall of the house facing it.

Doorways, windows, and balconies were thronged with spectators. They might have been watching some circus act: impersonally approving, expecting more. The sole dissenter emerged as they were capping the barricade with a one-way-street sign. He arrived breathless in pajamas and dressing gown, but he had paused long enough to put on socks and shoes. Heading straight through the students, he stopped a foot from the park bench and, hands on hips, stared at it with disbelief.

"*Voyons,*" he appealed to the nearest group. "Now look." In spite of his agitation he still believed in what he thought of as reason, the orderly precedence he had relied on all his life.

"Now look," he repeated. "That's my car."

"Where?"

"My Peugeot! Under the bench!"

"We won't do anything to it." The boy in the leather jacket hastily pocketed his screwdriver as though to prove this.

"I tell you, that's *my car!*"

"Why should you have a car when the workers who made it can't afford one?" The dialogue was spreading.

"Now look. Now look." The woolly arms flapped in a new appeal. "That's to say, it doesn't altogether belong to me. I haven't even finished paying for it yet."

"We don't believe in the credit system."

224

"It's usury."

"You should be glad to help the revolution," the Algerian girl pointed out earnestly. "You're a victim of the consumer society, too."

"Give him back his car."

"Let him take it."

"Throw him out." Friends and enemies on the balconies were beginning to join in the argument. For several minutes individual opinions were lost in the general clamor. The man in the dressing gown finally quieted it by climbing onto a pile of blocks and standing with his arms raised until he had gained attention.

"If you don't give me back my car at once," he announced from the barricade, "I'll call the police."

The howl of laughter that answered this was too much for him. Abandoning every aspect of reason, he began to burrow through the piled wood and ironware that separated him from his property in a wild attempt to liberate it single-handed. The students made no move to interfere. They watched him with polite embarrassment as he heaved and raged, letting him exhaust himself in indignity until he was tired enough to be led away.

"We won't harm your Peugeot," Bascombe heard one of them say as they escorted him back to his own door. "We'll come and help you get it tomorrow."

A few minutes later came the first explosions.

Bascombe learned afterward from the newspapers that those explosions—the first barricade being attacked by the riot police—came from at least a quarter of a mile away. That wasn't the way it seemed at the time. The t-o-o-nk of the gas canisters, the crack of the concussion grenades, the startled chants of *"De Gaulle—Assassin,"* the yells of defiance and pain sounded like something in the same room.

They were all the more frightening to listen to because there was nothing to see. Flashes and beams of light, a sudden glow: it was all as impersonal as the glare of a freeway. Only the sounds, the screams were happening. All the rest remained imminent. As the Algerian girl said, there was nothing to do but wait.

For long periods Bascombe found himself sitting on the curb

with Venus, their arms around each other's shoulders, her cheek against his. At some time he was handed a bottle of wine from a doorway. They both took a swallow and passed it on. Later it seemed so long since Venus had moved he thought she had fallen asleep. Her eyes were open, tranquil and expectant. *"De Gaulle —Assassin. De Gaulle—Assassin."* The chanting had lost its startled quality. It had become a sullen repetition of hatred.

"Les flics."

That was the moment the waiting ended. There was no beginning to what came next. He was on his feet with his arm still around Venus. Something detonated at his feet, striking his ankle. The stab of it was more frightening than painful. He lost his hold on Venus' shoulder and found her hand. For twenty yards around them the street was filled with eddies, spreading and merging like the smoke of burning leaves.

It was impossible not to run. Somewhere back down the street, out of the crowd, was the irresistible promise of air. Pulling Venus along with him, he fought his way toward it.

They were leaning in a doorway, choking and sobbing from the gas. He had never seen Venus in pain before. He held her against him as he might have done a child, stroking her hair, trying helplessly to comfort her.

"Come on." She had stopped crying. He started to lead her off down the street.

"No." A few yards away a dozen students were reassembling, tying handkerchiefs over their mouths. He didn't argue with her; he felt it himself: the unworthiness of abandoning his own kind. They weren't her kind, but she apparently shared something of their point of view, and to her any act of indignity was impossible.

She lifted her skirt and tore at her slip. Even at that moment the sight of her legs stirred him. He helped her rip off a strip of silk and knotted it behind her head. She did the same for him with his handkerchief.

The gas hung like foliage between them and the barricade. It was pierced here and there by a beam of light from beyond. Arms, bodies, triangles of white cloth, appeared and receded and darted about in it. Gradually a pattern that was almost order emerged. Students were racing forward into the gas, vanishing, stumbling out of it, weeping.

It was not until he reached the barricade himself that he saw there was not only order but purpose. He seized a paving block, too, hurled it, and ran.

Venus was beside him as they came out into the air again. They leaned against each other, their heads down, their hands on each other's shoulders, waiting for their sight to clear, the choking nausea to pass. He felt no sense of accomplishment, no pride. He was too scared to feel anything but defiance. He was afraid for Venus. That ache to protect her had always been an essential part of his feeling for her. But he was scared for himself, too. He was afraid of being injured, suddenly deprived of youth by some damage to his body.

On their fourth trip the defiance changed to hatred. As he threw his paving block his eyes were level with the top of the barricade. He caught no more than a glimpse, but it was as detailed as a Bosch painting. Shields, helmets, goggles, gas masks, truncheons, grenade launchers, carbines. Searchlights and steel-plated trucks to back them up. The wooden paving block slipped in his fingers. He had held his breath too long to reach for another. He grabbed Venus' hand. They fled again.

There was an explosion behind them. As they bowed, gasping in the air, the street was flooded with light. A concussion grenade had hit a gas tank. A car had gone up. The Peugeot? It was doomed now anyway.

"This way." A boy in a red armband pointed impatiently away from the fire. A girl was kneeling, retching at the curb. Venus pulled at the girl's shoulder, trying to raise her to her feet. They lifted her between them. It was the girl from Algeria.

"This way." There was another red armband at the corner. The whole group from the barricade was running now. In all the confusion, his own fear, he was struck by how light the students' footsteps were.

He stopped, holding the Algerian girl upright by her waist. The *service d'ordre* had made a mistake. Sixty yards away a line of helmets and goggles, of round shields and truncheons, stretched across the street.

To the right was an archway to a courtyard. The Algerian girl was still quietly retching. It seemed the only effort her body was capable of making. He lifted her in his arms. Once off her feet she was as light as a husk. The courtyard was in darkness, the windows shuttered.

Venus ran ahead of him. She found a door. He heard the sound of a bell through the shutters. Half a dozen students had followed them in through the arch. As they waited for an answer to the ringing, they held themselves so still they seemed barely alive. A light striped Venus' face. He couldn't hear what she said but the light broadened. A moment later they were all inside.

He thought at first the place was a furniture store. Tables, sideboards, sofas crowded every foot of it. Then he saw a square of lace, a stuffed canary under a glass dome, framed photographs on the mantelpiece. It was the living room of a French flat.

The woman who had admitted them closed and bolted the door. She was about fifty, in a bulging skirt and an unevenly stretched cardigan. Her face had a look of stubborn ill temper.

"She's hurt?"

He was still holding the Algerian girl in his arms. He looked for a place to put her down.

"It was the gas."

"Here. Put her here." The woman had a way of talking as though she were alone, muttering to herself over her dusting. He worked his way across the room and settled the Algerian girl on the sofa.

"Would you like some coffee?"

Venus glanced around at the students. They nodded politely.

"It's very kind of you, Madame." For the moment she was the leader; none of them would have questioned it. It brought into Bascombe's mind something that had been on the verge of it all evening. Since they had joined the students, no one had paid particular attention to her. In contrast to London, where she had shown she could hold any crowd fascinated at will, she had deliberately muted her personality to merge with the group. He wondered if that was why she had taken to those modest skirts and sweaters: she wanted to remain unnoticed in Paris.

The woman returned with the coffee. The Algerian girl had recovered a little. She was sweating, her skin like wet brown paper, but her breathing was almost normal. He held her up while she drank.

"Turn the lights off." Venus was at the window, listening. A girl near the door clicked the switch. The brusque footsteps in the yard outside, the voices giving and answering orders, the hammering at doors were like the sounds of locks, shutting them in. He wanted to get to Venus. It was as though they were all going to suffocate in a moment, and he wanted to be with her when they did. He felt his way to the table and started carefully around it.

"Open."

The hammering was at their own door.

"Open. You're sheltering rioters."

He reached the window and found Venus' hand.

"I'm alone. There's no one here. I'm alone." There was the same muttering sullenness in the woman's voice. The light clicked on. She was standing by the switch.

"I'm alone," she repeated. "I'm alone."

Something crashed into the door from outside. The woman turned briefly to Venus. She shrugged. There was a whole life-time of experience in the gesture: it was a good door; doors were expensive. She pulled back the bolt.

The door was thrown open. No one entered.

"Outside." The police weren't taking any chances.

"Thank you, Madame." Venus accepted leadership again. Holding Bascombe's hand she stepped through the door first. There were perhaps twenty of them in the courtyard. Dark blue battle dress, those round Gaulish shields, helmets shaped like hermit crabs, carbines slung across their backs, long pale truncheons in their hands.

Three of them hurried eagerly forward. Bascombe tried to draw Venus toward him, to protect her with his arms, to get himself between her and the raised clubs. She shook her head quickly and led him straight on.

They let her pass. One of the men's faces almost brushed his own. There was no surprise in it, no indication he was acting against his will. He struck at Bascombe in passing as though to get him out of the way. Then three of them fell on the first student behind him.

He knew in some fragile way he ought to feel guilty, but he didn't. He felt nothing but relief as they reached the arch untouched. Venus stopped there and looked back. He had never seen her so moved. It was no longer an emotion commanding her. She was fury itself. He looked back, too.

Three of the students were on the ground, the helmeted men leaping around them, competing with each other for room to swing their clubs, bringing them down on the boys' inert shoulders, heads, faces.

The Algerian girl came out of the doorway. He caught the word *"Négresse,"* soft as a promise. Four men closed in on her. They had her by the hair, dragging her into the open, away from the shelter of the wall. Her dress was torn down to her waist. He saw her bare shoulders, frail as wishbones.

He knew it was useless: there was nothing he could do. He started toward her. Venus held him back.

"I can't help her." There was no defeat in her voice. It was like a command.

"They'll kill her."

"I can't help her." It was an ultimatum this time. She led him into the street.

It was going on there, too, the same eager cruelty. As the students filed out of the doorways they were clubbed to the ground, beaten helpless, then tossed like game into the waiting police vans. Venus guided him quickly away from it. Her fury seemed to have given way to a determination, not so much to escape as to withdraw herself at once, decisively, from this savagery.

To reach their hotel in St. Germain directly they would have had to pass through the thick of it. They circled in the opposite direction until they came to the river.

It was dawn by then, the sun gilding the gargoyles of Notre

Dame a mile away to their left. They had heard from a radio outside a café that Cohn-Bendit had ordered all the students to get off the streets and go home, but the police vans were still holding the bridges. Chuck Higgins was still safe. They found a bench and sat down.

Bascombe was suddenly helplessly exhausted. He sprawled back, yawning, incapable of speech or thought. Gradually some feeling returned to his body. His left foot was wet. He looked at it. The sock was sodden with blood from a gash above his ankle.

"What the hell good was it?" He was incensed with himself for bleeding: it didn't even look like real blood. "What the hell did we do?" He didn't mean Venus; he meant himself, all those others of his own kind. "We built a goddamned barricade. We waited behind it like a lot of schmucks in a bread line. Hours and hours. Then they took it away from us in twenty minutes. A lot of poor bastards got their heads beaten in. And that was the end of it. We might just as well have got off the streets at once. Last night. We might just as well never have been there at all."

He started to tie his handkerchief roughly around his ankle; he couldn't stand the sight of that inane mark on himself. Venus took it away from him, folded it, and bound it neatly in place. She didn't speak until she had finished. He was terrified she was going to agree with him. But she was more consistent than he was.

"It was better than nothing."

"Why?" He wanted her to tell him: only someone with her timeless perspective could.

She leaned back and rested her head on his shoulder.

"Something terrible's happened to you. To so many of you here." She was avoiding the distressing word *mortal* again. "All this talk about the pressures of society. The rat race. Your bosses. The authorities. Your superiors. There was even a man at one of those parties in London who talked about his masters in the government. You've reduced yourselves to the attitudes of slaves. Free men have no superiors except their own gods. The Greeks knew that. So did the Celts. And some of the people we met in

Ireland. I think these students know it, too."

They stood up and started back along the quay toward their hotel. Venus took his arm. She was her usual cheerful, affectionate self again.

"It was better than nothing. You'll see."

She was right. In a small way they began to see what the students had done before they reached their hotel. They stopped at a pharmacy to buy some antiseptic for Bascombe's cut. From their disheveled appearance the owner of the shop guessed at once they had come from the rioting. There was a strained diffidence in his manner as he showed them a bottle from the shelves. He tried to hide his feelings with chatter.

"It's a new preparation. An improvement. Better than iodine. You see. It's Swiss."

Bascombe held out a fifty-franc note. The man's eyes slid away from it.

"It's shameful." He used the French word *ignoble*. "The police. To act like that. It's shameful." The unfamiliarity of his own indignation embarrassed him. He refused to accept payment for the antiseptic.

He was not the only Frenchman who felt that way. When Bascombe and Venus woke up that Saturday evening and walked out into the streets, they found thousands of middle-aged Parisians wandering around St. Germain. They all appeared to be wearing their best clothes, but there was no gaiety in them. They paused and stared at the burned-out cars, the charred remains of the barricades. They might have been visiting a military cemetery, paying a pilgrimage to the ruins of Verdun.

The detonator had set off the explosion. The three weeks of asking why had begun.

Why should we go on making things we don't need to earn the money to buy them?

Why do we talk about progress, tradition, power, order, without ever asking what we mean by these words?

Why don't we take a look at the whole absurd mess and decide what most of us want?

"Why doesn't Charlie get off the pot?" Chuck Higgins turned

away from the windows. The police, sick of being apologized for by the government they were paid to protect, were sulking in their mobile cages along the quays; the bridges were empty.

"What do you want De Gaulle to do, Mr. Higgins?"

"Do? Quit screwing around. Is this any time to go off on a state visit to Rumania? There were eight hundred thousand Reds marching down the Boulevard Sebastapol this afternoon. With that mother Cohn-Bendit leading them."

"I know." Venus and Bascombe had watched them file past, mile after mile, an incredible flood of disparate individuals who appeared to have nothing in common except that they had chosen to come there together.

"Do you think the strikes'll continue?"

"Damn right they will. You'd better stock up on American cigarettes, that's all." Higgins slumped down on the sofa beside Venus. "Or don't you smoke?"

"No."

"No vices?"

"What would you call a vice?"

"You're as bad as those fucking students, asking questions all the time instead of answering them."

It had been Bascombe's suggestion to come here this time. He had been entranced by the events of the past few days. All the public liars who had driven him all his life into that clammed-up indifference with which he had protected hope against them, had suddenly shut up like a switched-off P.A. system. There was a great stillness waiting to be filled with imagination. It seemed possible that what Venus had suggested in London—"You should try to organize things so you can live, so you can forget everything except living"—might actually be given a try at last. Anything seemed possible. He found it so exciting he had felt a need to control his enthusiasm, to get a whiff of prison air again, to remind himself that all the screws were still there, only waiting for their opportunity to refill the silence with shouted orders, specious rules, their own self-importance.

"The whole country's gone crazy. A few kids get what's coming to them, and everyone's on their side." Higgins was doing a great job of reminding him. "What the hell's wrong with this consumer society they're all yelling about? It works, doesn't it?"

Click. Clog. The front door was locked after them again.

Clang! Higgins had had a new bolt installed since last Friday.

"It's funny. It's like being back with Mr. Mitchel." They walked across the bridge to the Ile St. Louis. "Everything he says is a sort of second-hand lie."

"Let's go back to the hotel." Venus took his arm with one of her sudden changes of mood. He forgot Higgins, all the problems of society instantly. Making love to her had always been a new experience each time.

"I'm afraid there aren't any taxis."

It was the only time during those three weeks in Paris that either of them regretted any of the consequences of the May Revolution. It took them half an hour to walk home to bed.

They walked a great deal during the next few days, and each day Paris became a pleasanter place to walk in. As more and more service stations closed, there were fewer and fewer cars on the streets. There was less of many other things, too: less waste, less boredom, less presumption. Old words reappeared like laundered flags. *Commune. Participation. Contestation.* Every order, every authority was to be contested. Signs appeared everywhere: "It is forbidden to forbid."

It wasn't only the students who discovered the excitement of exploring what had always been taken for granted. On street corners, at café tables, middle-aged men and women, often total strangers, examined each other's preconceptions as though searching their own minds for reflections of them. "You think that, do you? So did I." The French had always enjoyed talking to one another, playing a kind of intellectual Breakfast. Now they seemed to be listening to each other, too.

With another factory, another office or department store closing every hour, it was extraordinary how normal life in Paris seemed. There was no mail, no public transportation, but the ambulances kept running. Food was brought into the city. Butchers, grocers, cafés stayed open. Electricity was cut off for several hours every day, but never during those hours Frenchwomen were home cooking. The automatic telephone worked. It was even possible sometimes to get the operator, some girl who had decided to go to work that day, and now decided as an action committee of one whether to help you or not. This spontaneity made even the banal fascinating. You could never be sure whether anyone would choose to do anything, or for how long. One afternoon Bascombe and Venus were sitting in a café. A young waiter was writing the evening's menu on a blackboard. Using a thin brush and a pot of poster paint, he was painstakingly spelling out *"Soupe du jour," "Hors d'oeuvres," "Jambon de Parme"* in that rococo script, the secret national code taught to all French children. He was blindly absorbed in what he was doing until he got to *"Fil"* (*Filet de Boeuf?*) halfway down the menu. Then he suddenly got bored with it. He washed his brush, put his poster paint away, sat down at a table, and began reading a newspaper. The enigmatic *"Fil"* was still uncompleted when they came back for dinner that night, but the young waiter was still there and served them cheerfully enough.

It was hard to guess what Venus thought of it all. She was interested in everything, the occupied factories, the incessant discussions and demonstrations, the almost continuous debate in the amphitheater of the Sorbonne. Like an informed antiquarian touring the ruins of Pompeii, she observed it all eagerly but impartially. After that first night at the barricades she participated in nothing. She expressed few opinions.

One of the few she did express was after listening to a heated discussion on the function of religion—still, presumably, Christianity—in the socialist state at the Odéon one evening.

"You're always talking about love," she accused Bascombe afterward as they walked over to the Sorbonne; again it was evident she didn't mean the "you" personally. "You seem to imagine everything'll be different if you *love* one another."

"Won't it?"

"Of course it will." She pushed a strand of hair from her cheek with an impatient gesture. "But only if you feel it, express it in your lives. You can't keep your whole physical existence out of it. You can't separate love from your bodies, the way those

Christians think you can. How can you love anyone so long as your religion believes in trying to suppress your only natural way of showing it?"

"Shame is the only perversion," one of the dozens of grafitti applauded her as they entered the great court of the Sorbonne. "And cruelty" had been added as an afterthought beneath it. Anarchist flags hung limply over the statues of Victor Hugo and Pasteur. "The more I make revolution, the more I feel like making love," someone had written in red chalk, and in the shadows several couples were testing the truth of this. The amphitheater was packed, but after a few minutes Bascombe and Venus managed to find two seats together.

There were perhaps a thousand students there that night. Like a crowd on a holiday beach, even those who had found chairs had spread themselves out, each in his own patch of sunlight. Others basked in the aisles and all over the stage. They came and went, climbing over each other's legs as though on their way to the ice cream stand, the sea.

"The verb 'to be' must be outlawed from politics." A young man in bifocals was on his feet. "Why should we pay politicians to advance their own careers? Why should we give them power so they can use it to keep it?"

Venus was sitting upright with her hands in her lap, apparently absorbed in what the young man was saying. Bascombe had never seen her look bored.

"Is it progress if a cannibal uses a knife and fork?" A girl had the floor. "Has any civilization ever honestly tried to define progress—"

Bascombe leaned toward Venus. He was caught by a longing to know what she was thinking.

"Why don't you speak? Why don't you tell them?" He meant, tell us what we're here for, what we should do with our lives.

She didn't answer. For a moment he could feel her withdraw from him as deliberately as she had withdrawn from the savagery of the police after the night of fighting in the streets. Then she slipped her hand into his. She shook her head.

"Are you an American?" The girl in the seat next to him had turned and was smiling at him.

"Yes." Bascombe had lost his timidity about admitting it. In spite of Chuck Higgins there was little active prejudice against Americans in Paris.

"A student?"

"No."

"A tourist?" She covered her ugly little face with her fingers. She evidently thought tourists were hysterically comic.

"I'm an engineer."

Surprisingly that sobered her at once. "Do you know anything about radios, loudspeakers?"

The chief thing Bascombe knew about them was that he loathed them. He nodded.

"Can you fix them?"

"Yes." Reluctantly.

"Come on." She stood up, all hips and shoulders. Her body had the same animal frankness as her monkey face. She grabbed his arm and tried to pull him toward the aisle.

"Where?"

"The revolution needs you." Like the Algerian girl, like many of the students, she had no shyness about high-sounding phrases. "Come on."

"I can't. I can't now." Bascombe lifted his hand, which was still holding Venus'. He didn't need to explain any more clearly than that. Personal involvements had a high priority among rank-and-file revolutionaries.

The girl sat down again. She groped in her bag and found a pencil and a scrap of paper.

"You come to this classroom tomorrow. Tomorrow morning." She had written a number on the paper which she pushed into his hand. "Understood?"

"Understood."

Without his knowing it, it was what Bascombe had been looking for. The opportunity to cease being a spectator. Starting the next morning, for hours every day, he was up to his neck in wires, cannibalizing transmitters and public address systems. He spent one whole day rigging a truck which was later found to have had its engine removed. Lack of foresight was not a monopoly of the capitalist system. But for the first time in his life he felt useful.

He had never for an instant since he had known her cut off his attention to Venus or replied automatically to anything she said to him. It was a new experience for him to spend whole hours consciously engaged in his work. The wires he handled were like living things to him. Connecting them had a purpose he could actually respect. They would be used to try to encourage in others some of the protest he had had to stifle against the mindless futility of all his previous employment.

He went back to the hotel around one every day. He and Venus had a quick lunch together, half a bottle of wine. Then for an hour or two before he returned to his wires they would share that intimacy which had for so long seemed to him the single sensible aim of living. Now this aim had widened to include other possibilities. The hours with Venus were no longer an escape. It seemed conceivable there might be other sensible, even realizable aims. It seemed possible they might all be connected in some way. Making love and making a revolution might be one and the same thing.

While he was at the garage, Venus continued to spend her time walking around Paris, listening to discussions, attending meetings, buying each irregular issue of *Le Monde,* and absorbing every word of it in five minutes at a café table. In her own enigmatic way she still seemed encouraged by the way things were going.

This in itself was encouraging. Venus might have reasons for her optimism: whenever she wanted to she could take a look at the future and see what was likely to come of it all. At the same time Bascombe was worried by the occasional glimpses he was getting at the garage into what was going on behind the scenes. The trouble was that although the students had managed to paralyze the government and might even be able to bury it, they could not take its place. Quite apart from their youth, they were caught in the web of their own principles. Opposing all authority, they mistrusted all leadership, even their own. They could skirmish, organize demonstrations, issue slogans and manifestos. They could not take charge.

There was no one they could trust to take charge for them, either.

"They keep talking about Mendès-France." Bascombe and Venus were having dinner at a family restaurant near the hotel.

"I know." She pushed her plate away from her. For once she seemed to have no appetite.

"At least De Gaulle's gone."

"Where?"

"Nobody knows." He had heard all about it from the monkey-faced girl at the garage that morning. Her father was a secretary at the Élysée Palace. "The weekly cabinet meeting was cancelled at the last minute. And he just drove off with his wife. He was very irritable and kept telling her to hurry. People at the Élysée think he's decided to resign."

"Do they?" She did not look at him, staring into her wine glass. He had never seen her so withdrawn.

"Do you think Mendès-France would be any good?"

"He won't change anything."

He knew she was right. People working in shops and factories would have a little more money to spend until inflation caught up with them. The toilets would be cleaner, the coffee breaks longer. No attitudes would be changed: expediency would always overrule imagination. The bright mad promise of these past few weeks, the possibility that there was another way of living would be lost again in the usual jargon of self-interest. It would be the same old shit, even if there was a little less of it.

What was the alternative? Where could the students find a leader, someone with that hard-headed belief in dreams which was the only hope of change?

It was so obvious it frightened him.

He was aware of several things at once. He saw the personal loss it would mean to him. It would be like London; much worse; she would be a full-time public figure, continuously occupied without him, surrounded by petitioners, acolytes, worshipers. He saw what it would mean to others, a renaissance of dignity, truth, all the things she meant by the word virtue. He knew she could do it. He was suddenly convinced she intended to do it. It was what she had planned all along. This was why she had come to Paris; why she had studied the present-day world so diligently. It was why she had sprung from his head, reborn.

It had all been for this.

"The first step is to take over the government radio station. You'd better do it tonight." He was so carried away that his enthusiasm, the idea itself, the means of carrying it out had all become one. He spoke as much to himself as to her.

"You'll need a small striking force of students. We'll recruit them from the *service d'ordre* at the Sorbonne. The police won't resist *you*. You can—" He hesitated for the right word. Infatuate? Enchant? "You can influence the police and lead the whole group of us into the building. There's only a skeleton staff working there now. You . . . influence them to set up a national television appearance for you. Then you can tell the whole country—"

"Tell them what?"

"What you think, what you want us to do. How we ought to live . . ."

Venus was no longer listening to him. She was walking away from the table, slipping between the chairs of the other diners, out of the door. He hurried after her. The patron stopped him. He found a hundred-franc note. The patron was a scrupulous man: the bill would be much less than that. By the time Bascombe had forced the money into his hand and reached the street Venus was no longer in sight.

He thought for one moment she might have gone to the Sorbonne, to start putting the first part of his plan into action.

Then he went back to the hotel and lay down on the bed.

He remembered the day he had returned to the apartment in London and found her with the razor blade. He had always underestimated her. For months he had closed his mind to the truth of her identity. He remembered what she had told him the

240

night of the barricades when the police were beating the Algerian girl. "I can't help her." She had not been excusing herself. She had been affirming a truth that was obvious to her but that he was too blindly human to see. She had once tried to put that truth into words he could understand. As far as people were concerned, gods were ideals. They weren't judges or messengers. They couldn't interfere, tell us what to do, put things right for us. The moment they did they ceased to be gods. They became our servants.

He was furious at his own stupidity. He hated himself for his callousness. Within the limits of her human condition she had fought on their side. He remembered her leaning against him, choking from the gas. He had accepted that and expected more. He had wanted her to do conjuring tricks for them. "Influence the police." He felt sick when he thought of the way he had talked to her: not asked, told her to clear up the mess they had made of their own world.

He wasn't lying on the bed any longer. He was walking up and down the room, hurrying to the window at every sound from the street, to the door at every creak of the stairs. There were three of her skirts, two sweaters on hangers in the closet. She had always been neat. He didn't blame her if she never came back to him. He decided to kill himself if she didn't.

It was after midnight when he recognized her footsteps in the corridor. He was too relieved to do anything but stand looking at her. She was carrying her shoes. She put them down and slipped out of her sweater.

"It's all over."

There was a sadness in her voice. He shook his head stupidly. How could it be over? She was back. Standing there naked, less than an arm's length away from him. Was she telling him to leave?

"De Gaulle's returned."

He began to laugh.

"Why have you got your clothes on?" She sat down in front of the dressing table. "He's got the army behind him. Their tanks are closing in around Paris." He nodded, kicking off his shoes.

There was no need to ask her how she knew. She had looked at the future and seen defeat there.

"It won't all have been useless." She was thoughtfully combing her hair. "Some people have been changed for the rest of their lives by what's happened. They'll go on believing in me. In other countries, too." She stood up. "Even in America."

He stepped toward her. She raised her hands to his chest.

"I'm sorry the students lost."

"It doesn't matter."

Nothing mattered except this. What she was. What he believed in. Her tenderness and affection. Her laughter. Her power to heighten his awareness of her and himself to this pitch. He ceased to be one consciousness. He became part of hers. He felt, breathed with her body as familiarly as with his own. Nothing mattered except this. This understanding. This accord. This empathy. Perhaps it was only a beginning. It was as much as anyone had ever achieved.

"Send the students to Dachau."

Bascombe watched them march past down the Champs Élysées, rank after rank, with their sashes and their medals. The victors. There was a fanaticism in these faces he had never seen at the barricades. They had the true fervor: to hold on to what they had.

"Shave their heads."

They did not believe shame and cruelty were the only perversions. They believed they were virtues.

"*Vive De Gaulle.*"

Imagination had been crushed by a vain old man who had never believed in anything but symbols.

"*Vive l'armée.*"

Bascombe started slowly home. The army had gasoline as well as tanks. All over Paris service stations were opening like faucets. Traffic was blocking the streets again, cars fleeing for the *autoroutes,* the beaches. In a month of riots two people had been killed. Sixty-eight were to die violently on the roads that weekend. The consumer society was back at the wheel. The cannibal had his knife and fork out again.

"*Vive la France.*"

He turned off into a side street. "History has to repeat itself," someone had chalked on a wall. "No one ever listens to it."

He found a travel agent open on his way back to the hotel. There were no trains running yet, but he managed to get two seats on a private bus leaving for Cannes the next day.

Venus was sitting cross-legged on the bed when he entered the room. She was naked. He leaned over and kissed her shoulder. She had a needle in her hand and a skirt spread across her knees. She put them down as she stood up and touched her mouth against his. She was as tall as he was now, over six feet. He picked up the skirt. She had been lengthening the hem. It had fitted her perfectly last week.

16
CHAPTER

THERE WAS A high stone wall around the garden but it gave them little protection because the road to the house wound along the side of a hill above it. From the nearest bend, fifty yards away, anyone could look down over the whole property. Only the narrow walk between the rows of plane trees was screened from view of the hill, and to reach it Venus had to cross the open yard in front of the door. Behind the house the land dropped steeply to a stream; there was nowhere she could stroll or rest there.

Bascombe walked up and down between the plane trees. Each time he turned at the bottom of the garden the road came into sight above the wall. There were only a dozen people, most of them children, waiting there this evening. The children were playing their French version of hopscotch, making the best of the road as they would have climbed and played tag over the benches of an empty stadium. In a little while if Venus didn't appear they would go home to their soup. They would have lost nothing by spending the day there instead of somewhere else. Tomorrow, if she did appear, they would have something special to talk about and prize. The adults were more impatient. It annoyed them to spend hours waiting and then leave without a glimpse of her. At first each of them had only wanted to be able to say it was true, he had seen her for himself. Now, by the middle of August, their curiosity had grown. They wanted to be able to hurry into the village, to nod, to whisper, "It continues."

As he walked up and down beside the wall he was listening for the sound of a car. Nolan had phoned the day before to say he was staying nearby. After some hesitation Bascombe had invited him to dinner. They had had no visitors since the end of June. Two or three times a week he drove into Grasse for food and wine, loading the back of the Renault like a truck. Twelve miles away were the fuming traffic jams; the barely separate bodies on beaches that had to be watered and swept every morning; the aircraft carriers at anchor in the bay: the Riviera in August. They had stopped going into Cannes after the first few days of their stay here. Venus hadn't left the grounds since then. Except for the watchers on the road she had seen no one but him for six weeks.

They had been lucky to find the house, with its tall arched doors, its high-ceilinged rooms. It belonged to the parents of a boy Bascombe had known at the garage. They had rented it for the summer. An hour at the casino in Cannes with Venus soon after their arrival from Paris had more than paid for it.

There was a sound from the hill. A tiny Fiat turned off the road and plunged down the drive to the house. Nolan barely managed to stop the car short of the wall. Bascombe unlocked the iron gate. They shook hands.

"How are you both?" Nolan glanced about him as they crossed the yard. He was obviously nervous: longing to see Venus again, afraid of the renewed longing seeing her would cause him.

"She's in the living room." Bascombe led the way across the hall and opened the wide double doors.

He had prepared everything very carefully for this moment. The curtains were drawn, softening the room in a pale orange light. Venus was lying on the sofa. She was wearing a blue sari that covered her from her shoulders down, hiding even her feet under its loose folds. A chiffon scarf was draped over her arms. Her hair hung loose on either side of her face. As Bascombe paused with Nolan just inside the door, her beauty caught at him like a hook in his flesh. He heard Nolan gasp. He looked at him sharply. There was no dismay, nothing but admiration in Nolan's eyes.

He started forward. Bascombe touched his arm.

"You'd better stay away from her. Venus is just getting over a cold." He tried to make a joke of it.

"I've been in bed all day. I still feel rather tired."

He was relieved to see she was smiling. She had cheerfully agreed to all his preparations, deferring to him in the way she had lately, but he had been afraid outside, waiting for Nolan, that she might find the actual meeting with him disconcerting.

"Would you like a Scotch?" He took Nolan to the drink table he had set up in the corner of the large room farthest from the sofa. "Sit down." He had placed an armchair near the table. He knew, of course, that he couldn't hope to keep Nolan at a distance from Venus all evening. He wanted him to grow so familiar with her loveliness first that later, dazed by it, he would be unable to see anything else.

He gave Nolan his drink and poured a highball glass full of wine for Venus. Handing it to her he stood directly in front of the sofa so that Nolan couldn't see her arm, bare for a moment as she reached for it. Venus took the glass and rearranged the scarf over her elbow and wrist. Leaning back on the piled cushions, she sipped the wine without exposing any more than her hand. Her hand looked quite unremarkable clasping the tall glass.

Bascombe got himself a drink. Nolan was sitting on the edge of his chair, staring at Venus.

"Where are you staying?" Bascombe tried to get Nolan to look at him instead.

"Near St. Raphael." His eyes didn't move. "My sister's taken a villa for a month. Her husband's there, too. He's a vet. His name's Daniel." He seemed to find it difficult to look at Venus and talk at the same time. He chose silence.

"I know. I met them." He was going to distract Nolan's attention from her even if he had to embarrass him to do it. "You remember Nora, don't you, darling? That party we went to in California."

"All those sofas." She cooperated with him at once. "And the hungry camel."

That did it. Whatever exact image her words created in Nolan's mind, he found it impossible to endure it while faced with her actual presence. His head jerked to one side. He began to talk hastily about London, the Labour government, the latest follies of that shit, as he called him—"he thinks Johnson *likes* him"—about anything except Nora's parties.

Bascombe saw to the dinner. He had cooked a roast of veal on the electric spit. He carved and served it in the kitchen, putting his own and Nolan's plates onto trays so they could eat on their laps. Venus' plates he loaded onto a trolley which he pushed in front of the sofa. She could reach everything on the lower shelf, the dishes of meat and potatoes and salad, the loaf of bread, the wheel of camembert, without raising herself. The upper shelf, over which he had draped a napkin, partly hid her from Nolan while she ate.

They finished their meal before she was halfway through hers. It was another of the precarious moments he had anticipated. Venus paused and rested her head on the cushions, as though she had eaten all she needed. He stood up and asked Nolan if he'd like to see the house.

"It's supposed to have been built by Pauline Borghese." He led the way across the hall into the vast, almost empty room which had once, supposedly, been her library.

"Are you actually married to her?"

"No."

"God, if I—why *not?*"

"She doesn't believe in it." He hadn't really expected Nolan to be interested in the house. He wasn't interested in it himself. He kept him out of the bedroom, with its oddly arranged double beds.

"Will you bring her over to St. Raphael one day?"

"I don't think we'd better."

"Because of Nora?"

"It might be difficult." Bascombe avoided an outright lie as they entered the living room. Venus had really finished eating this time. He managed to get the trolley out to the kitchen without Nolan seeing the number of empty plates on it.

"Would you like—will you have dinner with me in Cannes one evening?" Nolan had drawn a chair closer to the sofa. He was leaning forward, his elbows on his knees. His hands kept plucking at each other like startled squirrels. "Just the three of us, I mean, without—anyone else."

"We don't go into Cannes very much." She had never been able to be cruel to be kind.

"I could pick you up in my car."

In that tiny Fiat? Bascombe glanced at Venus. She still loved laughter, even when it was self-mocking. She was pressing her lips together, struggling to control it.

"I've been very busy. There's still so much I haven't read."

"The encyclopedia?"

She seized the chance to let out her suppressed laughter. Bascombe walked over to the table in the corner to get them all another drink. It was going to be all right. Nolan was beyond noticing anything but his own passion. He felt a sudden sympathy for him and poured him another inch of Scotch. Then he remembered the last evening they had all spent together. Nolan among the mink and the vicuña. It was an hour's drive back to St. Raphael and it was impossible to ask him to stay the night. He tipped some of the whiskey back into the bottle.

"Anna Karenina."

"Did you like it?"

Bascombe waited with the drinks to give her time to reply. He wanted her to talk, to get whatever pleasure she could from Nolan's attention. He had invited him more for her sake than his own.

"If a woman finds herself snubbed by a particular social set. If she can't get divorced, and remarried in a church. It isn't a human tragedy. It isn't a problem to concern an intelligent person. It's only a tragedy that she should think it is."

"Do you think Tolstoy believed it was a tragedy?"

"How do I know?" She was laughing at herself again. "Tolstoy was a Christian. He believed all kinds of things that I don't."

She started to talk generally about form and content, Dickens, Balzac, Flaubert, "your writers," as she called them. It surprised her that they all seemed more concerned with the form of the social order than the content of the human condition. The Greeks—

"Christ, you're lucky."

"I know." He walked Nolan out to his car.

"I can't imagine. I mean, I can't even try to imagine what it must be like. Living with her. Seeing her every day."

Bascombe didn't answer. In spite of his relief that Nolan was leaving, he felt a return of his old affection for him. He couldn't think of any way of expressing it.

"If you change your mind about having dinner one night . . ."

"Yes." There was nothing he could say. He could never tell him the truth. He fell back on the usual lie. "I'll call you."

He locked the iron gate in the wall. The lights of the little Fiat swept across the hill. The last of the children had left hours ago. It occurred to him as he walked back to the house that he would probably never see Nolan again.

"It was all right, wasn't it?"

"He's madly in love with you." He sat on the edge of the sofa and kissed her cheek. "Are you tired?"

"No."

"Did you have enough to eat?"

"You arranged everything beautifully."

"He wasn't very interested in the house."

That amused her. She was smiling as she pulled the hem of her sari aside and swung her bare feet to the floor. They both stood up.

His head no longer reached to her shoulder. He had to raise his eyes to unfasten the brooch that held her sari in place above her breasts. She unwound it and, dropping it over the sofa, stretched herself, relieved to be naked again.

He waited until she was at the tall arched doorway before following her into the hall. It was only when he was standing close to her that he was aware of his own smallness. For all her height she was so perfectly proportioned that walking a dozen steps behind her up the wide stairs he could still feel their bodies were as equal, as serenely matched as they had been in Paris. Long before they reached the bedroom he wanted her as wildly as he ever had.

They had arranged one double bed across the foot of the other. When she had had a shower and combed her hair she turned out all but the shaded light over the dressing table. She lay back with her head on the pillow, her feet stretched gratefully onto the second bed. Her breasts were still perfect half-spheres, the nipples set slightly above the center. Leaning over her he touched her left breast. His extended fingers could no longer quite span it. It was as delicately firm as the tiny rounded cone she had pressed against his cheek in that clearing in California. He kissed it with an eagerness that was like a vow. Half his pleasure in making love to her had always been in the pleasure he could give her. She responded to him now with a frenzy that moved him to rouse every sense in her body, to torment her with tenderness until her sensuality stretched her to the breaking point and she cried out in protest.

She cried out again and again. She turned her head from side to side on the pillow.

Not yet. His mouth was against her breast. Not yet. There was still more he could give her. More she could experience. There was no boundary to what he could make her feel. Her cries rose to a final cry of acceptance.

He kissed her gently on the mouth. He was filled with incommunicable tenderness for her. She stroked his hair back from his forehead. He found the sheet and covered her with it. A minute later she was asleep.

He turned off the lights and lay down beside her. It was the time of dread. The anxiety he had felt before the races in Ireland would have been a respite to the hours of terror he experienced every night now before he could get to sleep. He tried to fight it with whatever reassurance he could find. Her body was growing with perfect uniformity. Although he had measured her height that morning as seven foot six, she was still slenderly proportioned, with a thirty-inch waist. There was no grossening of her limbs. That plump secretary on the crosstown bus had had fuller, surely *heavier* thighs than Venus had now. If Venus seemed to tire more easily than she had in Paris, it was the heat, the closeness of the Riviera summer.

The terror remained. A few days ago he had discovered an old weighing platform in one of the barns and had managed to repair it. Venus weighed almost three hundred and twenty pounds. He didn't need a pencil and paper to work out what that meant. As he lay there sweating in the dark the figures raced through his head. The answer was like an inexorable damnation. Although she was less than one-third taller than she had been in Paris, she was twice as heavy. The cubic relationship between size and weight, which had once made her so light that she could float on the surface of milk, was now working against her. If she grew one more inch it would increase her weight by ten pounds. Two inches by a little *more* than twice ten. There was no sign she had reached her full height yet. She seemed, on the contrary, to be growing a little faster than she had in Ireland, in London. In a month she would be over eight feet tall. Then she would weigh . . . The merciless figures raced through his mind again.

"Oh god," he pleaded, "oh god, oh god, help her."

"Bascombe."

He realized he had spoken aloud. He turned to her, stroking her cheek.

"I'm sorry. It's so hot. I was—"

"I know." She took his hand and held it. He felt a longing to look at her. He reached for the light switch.

"No." She pressed his fingers. "I like the darkness. It's like that night on the beach in Ireland. Who were you praying to?"

"Your father."

She sighed.

"Can't he help you?"

"I don't know." She was silent until he wondered if she had fallen asleep again. "Perhaps. If I talked to him."

17

CHAPTER

"Passaporto, per favore." His uniform was very smart and fitted him perfectly. He obviously enjoyed wearing it, but with a childlike, not an officious pleasure. He would have been equally happy in doublet and hose. Bascombe handed him both passports. He returned Bascombe's at once. He opened the other and looked at the photograph.

"Dov' é la signorina?" His eyes livened with interest. *"Signorina Hannah Cooper?"*

Bascombe knew no Italian. "She is in back," he explained in French. "She has driven all night. She sleeps."

It was the wrong tactic. The Italian's eagerness to see her (in bed? in her nightdress?) increased at once. He followed Bascombe to the back of the truck parked outside the inspection station.

There was very little of Hannah Cooper to be seen. She was lying curled up on the mattress that took up most of the floor space. With her long hair tangled over her face, her head looked like a great golden tumbleweed. She seemed to be a husky, broad-hipped girl. It was hard to tell under the shapeless heap of bedclothes. The official shrugged, disappointed but tolerant. It had been a good summer: Swedish, Danish, American, Dutch, English, French, German: more bra-less, bare-thighed girls than he had expected to see in a lifetime as a boy in Salerno had passed his appreciative inspection since April.

He nodded politely and handed back the English signorina's passport.

Bascombe climbed into the front of the truck and drove on. Venus was safely across the first frontier, into Italy.

It was almost the end of September. Hope had delayed them for another month in the house near Grasse. Hope that Venus would stop growing; then hope that despite her human body she would not be bound by its physical laws. After both had failed it had taken him another week to make the necessary preparations for the journey. Buy the truck and equip it as comfortably as he could as a resting place for her. Provide it with emergency supplies of food, cold water. Change his money on the black market in Nice (there were currency restrictions on the franc since May). Prepare the fabric of disguise he hoped would get her across the three frontiers between France and Greece. He hadn't expected any difficulty with the Italians, but after Trieste was the Yugoslav border; Communist inspection would probably be less relaxed. The passport Venus had obtained in London by showing a copy of Hannah Cooper's birth certificate gave her height at that time. Five feet eight inches.

It had taken over two hours to drive the fifty miles from Grasse to Ventimiglia. For another forty miles he crawled on through the seaside suburbia that stretched unbroken along the southern coast of Europe. Then suddenly he was on the *autostrada*. He pushed the light truck up to the limit and kept it there. Kilometers replaced minutes as a unit of time. A hundred kilometers to the hour, twelve hundred to a day. How many days to Mount Olympus?

Venus had grown an inch in the past four days. With that inch she had gained sixteen pounds. Unless that appalling progression were halted at once it would be too late. It took all her strength to stand upright now. The strain on her heart of every movement she made terrified him.

Past Piacenza he pulled into a service area. He got the gas tank filled, then parked the truck as far from the other cars as he could. He opened the back of the truck and climbed in. The heap of bedclothes had been thrown aside. He could see the outline of her body under the sheet; Venus was lying on her side with her knees drawn up. He knelt beside her.

"Are you all right?"

"Yes." She had combed her hair back from her face. She smiled.

"It's not too tiring for you?"

"No."

"Hungry?"

"A little." Her tongue showed between her lips. "Thirsty."

He opened the small electric refrigerator he had fixed up in a corner of the van and took out a wine jug filled with water. He held it to her mouth. A few swallows and it was half-empty. She let her head rest on the pillows. A skein of hair had fallen across her cheek. He smoothed it back behind her ear. It had once been so fine that it looked in the mass like a single strand. He could feel the texture of each hair now, like a thread. He closed his eyes and kissed her forehead.

"I'll get you some food." He stood up before looking at her again. From even this distance, the six feet of his own height, he could no longer see the pores in her skin.

The restaurant was combined with a supermarket. He loaded his basket with salami, bread, cheese, fruit, wine. Venus had always had a healthy appetite; she needed three times as much food now as she had in Paris. He searched the shelves for something she particularly liked and found a basket of fresh strawberries.

He did not wait while she ate. He helped her sit up against a big leather cushion he had bought in Cannes, the food and an opened bottle of Chianti beside her. For half an hour he kept his speed down to forty; then he felt the balance of weight shift slightly in the van behind him. She was lying down again. He accelerated to sixty.

He had determined to drive through the night, but when he stopped for food and gas at another service area about eight o'clock, he could see she was too tired to stand the vibration of the floor of the truck much longer. He had chosen the mattress with care, the thickest, strongest foam rubber he could find in Nice. He had thought at first of buying two of them, laying one on top of the other, but in all his preparation he had had to

254

weigh her comfort against the fear of drawing attention to her. He wished now he had risked that. Where her weight rested on it the mattress had already flattened until it had little more resilience than a quilt. He turned off the *autostrada* and explored the byroads until he found a quiet place to park the truck on the grass verge.

"Where are we?"

"Near Venice." He turned on the light inside the van and began to arrange her supper for her. He hadn't been able to vary her menu much. Ham instead of salami. A jar of olives. Sardines.

"Venice?" She was intrigued. "Have you ever been there?"

"No."

"You could leave me in the truck—"

"No." He had no intention of leaving her for a minute. He smiled, trying to make up for his curtness. "I've got the rest of my life to see Venice."

He wished instantly he hadn't said it. The future, his own, hers, theirs together, was an area, as the past had once been, it was best not to examine. They would get through the next few thousand kilometers. She would talk to her father. He would not think beyond that. He opened the wine and filled a pint glass for her. There was a taste of lead in his mouth. He took a drink from the bottle. He had started smoking again in Grasse. He was hardly ever without a cigarette now.

They ate in silence. He had finished long before she had. He opened the back of the truck and jumped to the ground. When he looked back she was resting for a moment against the leather cushion, her eyes half-closed. In the amber overhead light she was like some perfect close-up: all the women whose projected beauty had relieved the drabness of his childhood for an hour or two, idealized into a single flawless face. He closed the door softly and walked a few yards down the road.

Her father would help her. He believed that. He would restore her strength. They would find some place, some island in Greece, perhaps, where they could live privately, undisturbed together. He didn't ask that she should be restored to his own human size. Only that she should be freed from her helplessness.

She had finished her meal when he returned. He got out the metal basin she had had to use lately and knelt beside her. He lifted the sheet. She was lying on her side, her hips turned toward him. He saw the gentle sweep of her belly, the joints of her thighs. He put his arm under her waist to lift her.

"No. Please." It was the first time he could remember she had shown any sign of human vanity. "Go away, please, Bascombe."

"All right." For a moment he was afraid he was going to cry.

He walked a hundred yards from the truck, out of hearing of her breathless struggles as she lifted herself without his help. When she had finished he emptied the basin into the ditch and washed it carefully with water from the tank under the front seat. He had turned off the overhead light and left the back of the truck open so that she could stretch her legs out full-length while he was doing this. She pulled her feet up onto the mattress as he closed the door after him.

"Don't turn on the light."

"Don't you want me to bathe your face?"

"I did it."

He took off his clothes and lay down beside her. She was on her back, her knees raised. He felt for her breast, caressing it with the tips of his fingers.

"You needn't—"

"I want to."

"Poor Bascombe."

"No."

He couldn't keep the protest—it was almost anger—out of his voice. He couldn't stand her pitying him because of her. He leaned over and kissed her, forcing his tongue between her lips. She responded at once, all gentleness. She stroked his chest. He remembered how she had once wandered there, smaller than a single joint of her finger was now. She was still the same Venus: this woman beside him, taller than he was by the length of his own arm, so that standing he could barely touch her face. She had not grown old, or gross. She was the same Venus, no different in any way except for this illusion, this human prejudice, size, the accompanying helplessness his own natural laws had imposed

256

on her. She was the same Venus who had lain with her head on his shoulder in Ireland and taken him into her body with such blithe affection.

He had to move down until his face was below her breasts. He could not quite span her hips with his arms. His hands followed the soft oval between her waist and her thigh, the graceful swelling between thigh and loin. He changed the angle of his body to hers until that familiar plucking each time he moved in her assured him that in a moment her breathing would begin to quicken with expectancy.

He lay panting on top of her for a minute after her last accepting sigh, then slipped quickly away to the corner of the van. He drank, pressing the mollifying coldness of the wine jug against him until it was safe to return to her. It had been easier in Grasse to keep her from knowing he hadn't come.

"Passport."

The man was about the same age as the Italian, with a broad face and intelligent gray eyes. His voice was curt, almost hostile. He wasn't wearing a uniform.

Bascombe handed him both passports, his own on top. The Yugoslav looked at the cover.

"American." It was like a reproach.

"Yes."

"You have a visa?" He spoke perfect English, with a flat mid-Atlantic accent. He still hadn't opened the passport. "You obtained a visa from a Yugoslav consulate?"

"No."

For all his preparations he hadn't foreseen this. No one at the travel agency in Cannes had told him he needed a visa for Yugoslavia. A visa implied forms, photographs probably. Venus would almost certainly have to present herself in person, sign her application in front of some official.

Damn Yugoslavia. They would have to manage without it. Lose all this time. Drive back to Venice, get the car ferry from there. It was one of the alternatives he had originally considered and rejected. It meant hiding Venus in the back of the truck for two days—in effect, stowing her away. There was no choice now. He started to reach for the passports.

The Yugoslav had opened the top one and was looking through the entries at the back. He picked up a rubber stamp, inked it, and slammed it down on a blank page.

"Five dollars."

Bascombe handed it to him. It was still not too late to withdraw. The official was filling in a printed form. When he gave it to him to sign he would say he had changed his mind. The paper was passed across the counter to him. Bascombe picked it up with his passport. It was a receipt in English for five dollars.

The Yugoslav turned to the second passport.

"For the British no visas." He handed it back unopened. "You want tourist coupons?"

"Thank you."

"For fifteen dollars, twenty dollars worth of gas."

"Thank you." Bascombe gave him the money. As he pushed the little book of coupons toward him, the Yugoslav was looking directly into his face. His left eye slowly closed and as slowly reopened.

"In the end you get your five dollars back."

"Thank you." Bascombe suddenly found himself smiling. The man reached over the counter and punched him softly on the shoulder.

"Good trip."

Bascombe thanked him again.

They were all rather like that.

The girl in the tiny restaurant in Senj where he stopped to buy food. He tried English, French, and German on her. She shook her head brusquely at each of them in turn. With her fists on her broad hips she stood silently watching him as he drew a loaf of bread, a fish, a sausage on the paper tablecloth. "You get funny with me and you'll get a clout on the ear," her whole manner warned him as he glanced up from the uncompleted sausage. She raised her hand to her mouth and rubbed her even white teeth thoughtfully with her thumb. She was obviously strong enough to knock him through the window if she felt like it. He hastily rounded off the second end of the sausage. She lunged forward and tore the whole cover off the table. A last appraising look; she disappeared into the kitchen with it. It was only after she had brought the food and wrapped it for him that he got any reaction from her except that challenging stare. As he paid her and turned to leave, she gave him a sudden friendly grin and shook hands with him.

The man in the service station who tore out his coupons as though they were weeds; they all seemed to have the same good-humored pugnacity. By the time he pulled the truck off the road for the night Bascombe decided he liked Yugoslavia.

He felt more hopeful than the evening before. The Yugoslav border was the one which had worried him the most, and it had turned out to be even easier than the Italian.

There was an emptiness about the landscape that was reassuring. He had decided for Venus' sake to take the coast road. She had developed a longing for the sea the last few weeks in Grasse. From the foot of the tall cliffs the Adriatic stretched out, blue as the sky, to a distant haze of islands. On the other side the mountains rose steep and wooded to a high flange of rock. He managed to get the truck down a bouldered track to the edge of a cove. Except for a rare car passing on the main road half a mile away there was not a light to be seen.

Venus seemed to be feeling stronger. She asked him to walk off alone down the beach. When he got back she was lying on the sand; she had managed to climb out of the truck unaided. He hauled the mattress down beside her. She made him turn away again while she lifted herself onto it. He didn't dare light a fire, it might bring someone down to them, but there was enough of a moon to see by. He had managed to buy two roast chickens at a cafeteria in Zadar. They both drank a good deal of wine with their picnic. For the first time in weeks Bascombe found he had spent a whole waking hour without smoking.

"We'll get to Dubrovnik tomorrow afternoon. Then we're practically in Greece."

259

He had brought the leather cushion out of the truck. She was leaning back against it, the sheet wound loosely around her.

"Is it awful for you, making love to me like that? Like last night?"

"No. Of course not. What—" He stopped himself. He had been going to say, "What are you talking about?" They had never been dishonest with each other. "No," he repeated.

"Before. When I was too small for us to fuck together. We used to find other ways."

"Yes." He remembered that evening in the apartment in London; they had made each other come without any conventional sexual contact at all; they had done the same thing in varied ways many times after that.

She had raised herself on her elbow. Her hand slipped inside his shirt. He felt her fingers move softly over his chest.

"Close your eyes."

She was leaning over him. A tassel of hair brushed his cheek. He let his eyes close.

He thought of her naked, standing by the mirror in London, moving to the bed. He recalled the first breathless contact of her body against his. He began to move his hips in response to her image in his mind. The need to touch her seized him. His hand found her shoulder and moved on to her neck. He was suddenly exultantly happy. She was no longer touching him at all. Only there, close to him. Nothing had changed between them. They could still make love out of nothing but the stimulation of their awareness of each other. He thought of the flawless skin of her breasts, the small poignantly delicate nipples, her marvelous buttocks, the tender opening between her thighs. The movement of his hips quickened. His body arched. Wave after wave of feeling spread outwards from its center, calming, relieving. He let himself surrender to it.

A great weight was pressing against his legs. He opened his eyes. For a moment he could see nothing but the moon, the gleam of her hair. Gradually normal sight returned. She was lying with her head across his knees, the tip of his cock still resting between her parted lips.

"You're sure the road's all right?"

"Yes."

"All the way to the Greek border?"

"It's an excellent new highway in first-class condition." The girl in the government tourist office in Dubrovnik was smaller and slimmer than the one in the restaurant in Senj, and she spoke perfect English and probably German and French, too, but she had exactly the same look of good-humored pugnacity. Bascombe opened his road map on the desk in front of her. Between Titograd and Skopje the black-bordered red line was broken here and there by white dots. He hadn't noticed it himself until this morning. It scared him a little. He had decided to check it before going any farther. He pointed out the white dots to the girl behind the desk.

"That is an old map."

It was copyright 1968 by Kümmerly and Frey, Bern, Switzerland. He pointed that out, too.

"The new highway has been completed since it was printed."

One of the things he liked about them was the way they all looked straight at you when they talked to you. There was none of that impersonal blankness you got from girls behind desks in other countries. Meeting those direct gray eyes it was impossible to doubt she was telling him the truth.

Venus had been asleep when he parked the truck near the harbor. Trying not to wake her, he kept his speed down to thirty as he wound on along the coast road and then turned inland. It was early evening when he reached Titograd. Spread over a wide plane between two mountain ranges, it seemed to be less a town than a blueprint for one. Long broad avenues crossing each other at exact right angles, but with few buildings, and leading to nothing except their own ends. Here and there a stark concrete wall marked the government's intention to build—a factory? A hotel? A palace of the arts? It was impossible to tell.

Beyond this asphalt plan of a city the road narrowed a little as it climbed into the foothills, but for another five miles there was still a road. Its end appeared as suddenly as the edge of a cliff. Bascombe braked the truck and climbed down. It wasn't as bad as he'd thought. There was something ahead of him, at least, a sand-colored track with the rock face on one side of it and a sheer drop on the other. Every few yards sharp white stones had pushed up through its dusty surface like pimples. He kicked at one of them. From its solid resistance he guessed it was part of the rock itself. The track had been blasted out of the cliff, roughly leveled, and then covered with a few spadefuls of loose soil. He thought of the girl in the tourist office in Dubrovnik. He wished he had asked if Titograd had been completed yet. He had an uneasy feeling she would have told him with that same level confidence that it had. "An excellent new city in first-class condition."

Venus was awake. She touched his hand as he knelt beside her. "What's wrong?"

"The road. It's pretty rough ahead." He told her how rough. "It might be only a sort of interruption in the new highway, an uncompleted stretch." He tried to sound hopeful.

"I'm quite comfortable. Don't worry about me."

"I'll stop if you're tired."

"No."

"All right." He knew what she was thinking. If they pushed on they could cross into Greece in the morning, reach Mount Olympus before tomorrow night.

He switched on the headlights and pushed on.

He kept his speed down to ten miles an hour. The track kept climbing in steep twisting turns. There were no markers, no protecting rail. Each bend was the edge of a precipice. It began to seem at first probable and then obvious he had misled Venus. This was no interruption. It *was* the new highway. There was no reason why any construction gang thrusting out from Titograd should skip a few miles. They would have blasted this track through and then started to surface it. They might with luck have worked from both ends. There might be another surfaced stretch out from the next town. The next town on his map was Peć, a hundred and fifteen miles over the mountains.

He had to keep pushing on. It was impossible to turn back. The track was only a few feet wider than his wheelbase and there was no verge to back onto for a U-turn. Only the rock face on

262

one side and the cliff edge on the other. The cliff increased in height with each bend. Occasionally, six or seven hundred feet below, he caught a glimpse of a dark wooded slope. He tried not to think about it, to keep his whole attention on the sand-colored strip twisting toward him in the beam of his headlights.

It was dark by the time he reached the boulders. The moon which had lighted the beach the night before hadn't risen clear of the mountains yet. He saw what looked like a rough stone wall —much like the walls that had divided the fields in Ireland—across the road ten yards ahead of him as he rounded a bend. He braked hard and climbed down to look at it.

It was a small landslide. A trail of boulders, most of them about the size of his head, had come bounding down the mountain and piled up there. He picked up the nearest of them and heaved it over the edge of the track. He counted to six before he heard it crash into the trees. He dimmed his headlights and set about heaving the other boulders, one by one, after it.

"*Stop.*"

He stood with a boulder cradled in his arms. He was afraid for a moment the voice had come from below, from some woodman's hut he had been unintentionally bombarding. A shower of stones pattered around him. There was a rushing sound, a yell. A man leaped from the top of the rock face and landed on the road.

"*Stop?*" The man stepped forward into the glow of the head-lights. He was wearing a dark double-breasted suit, a blue shirt and tie and a black felt hat. He looked like a small-time boot-legger from the nineteen twenties. "*Stop?*" he repeated in that questioning way.

Bascombe was still holding the boulder. He heaved it aside. He could see the man's face now. It was not reassuring: heavy and aggressive, with the padding of muscle around the eyes that prize-fighters develop. He had the build of a boxer, too, and the huge dangling hands. The silence between them had lasted too long already.

"I'm just trying to clear the road," he explained in English.

"*Da. Stop, huhn?*"

"Stop?"

"Da. Stop?"

They obviously weren't getting through to each other. Bascombe resorted to action to explain himself. He picked up one of the smaller boulders and slowly, explicitly, carried it to the edge of the road. He dropped it into the valley.

"Da. Da. Stop?" The man picked up a larger boulder. Bascombe reflexively stepped out of the way. He was glad he had. As carelessly as though discarding an empty bottle, the Yugoslav sent the boulder spinning over the cliff. It would have hit Bascombe in the chest if he had stayed where he was.

"Da. Stop!" A cheerful madness had seized the man. He was throwing boulder after boulder into the valley, yelling "stop" after each one. He had tossed half the obstruction away before Bascombe suddenly understood what he was yelling about. *"Stop"* was the French, the general European word for hitchhike. The bootlegger wanted a lift.

There could be no question of refusing him. Between them they finished clearing the road. The man leaped into the front of the truck; all his actions were performed with the same exuberant energy; every word was a yell, every movement a feat. Bascombe drove on.

"How far are you going?" He had no hope his passenger understood English. He hoped only to interrupt him. He was now bawling the words of some tuneless song, kicking the tank under his seat in accompaniment. Trying to follow that narrow twisting band as it unwound into his headlights, Bascombe found the kicking distracting.

The song broke off. The man shouted something at him in Serbo-Croatian. Bascombe assumed it was Serbo-Croatian. He shook his head.

"Anglish?"

"American."

"America." The man took off his hat and thoughtfully rubbed his head. "America—Vashington."

"Yes."

"Francia—Baris."

Bascombe nodded vaguely.

"Angland—London. Espania—Madrid. Italia—Roma."

"Yes."

"Svaden—Stockhom." There was no stopping him. This was his own weird version of Breakfast, and he was as intent on playing it as the man from Westwood on the flight to Los Angeles. He continued to shout out the names of the countries of the world and tell Bascombe their capitals. It was no more boring than dandruff as a subject of conversation. After a while Bascombe began to join in.

"New Zealand—Wellington."

"Ganada—Ottava."

They almost came to grief over Germany.

"Deutschland—Berlin."

"Deutschland—Bonn." Bascombe wasn't contradicting him. He was only adding to the list. There was a heavy silence.

"Amerikanische Deutschland—Bonn." He punched Bascombe persuasively on the shoulder. "Demokratische Deutschland—Berlin."

"*Sie sprechen Deutsch?*" The way he said *demokratische* made Bascombe think he might.

"*Ja. Ja. Sie? Sie sprechen Deutsch?*"

"*Ja.*"

They were both exaggerating. Bascombe hadn't spoken German since he was a child, and although he was surprised how much of it—whole phrases of his grandparents—returned to him, it was a clear example of the medium and the message. The language dictated not only the limits but the subject of his conversation.

"Where are you going?" He didn't know the German for "How far?"

"*Ja.* To work."

"Where?"

"*Ja.*" The other's medium was even more limited than his own.

"You have the wife?" he asked.

"No."

"*Ja. Ja.* I have the wife too."

Bascombe remembered how easily he and Venus had understood each other, writing messages in a dead language. There had been so little they needed to say. He felt a clutch of guilt. He had scarcely thought of her once in the last hour, since he stopped at the end of the surfaced road.

"Where do you work?" He was shouting to silence his self-reproach.

"To work. Work. *Ja.*"

"Denmark—Copenhagen." It was better than trying to find out about each other. It was better than thinking.

"Boland—Varszava."

"Turkey—Ankara." They were off again.

He saw the beam of light several bends ahead of him. It was the thing he had been half-consciously dreading since it had grown dark. He drew in as close to the outside edge of the road as he dared and waited. If it was a car, a small car, there was a chance they would be able to pass each other.

It was an oil truck. It came to a shrieking stop five yards from his front fender.

The hitchhiker leaned half out of his window and yelled something in his own language. There was a shouted reply.

"*Zurück.*" Bascombe remembered that word at once. It meant "back."

He looked in the rear-view mirror attached to the outside of the door frame. He could see about ten feet of the inner section of the road stretching out behind him in the red glow of his tail lights. He couldn't see the outside edge of it at all.

He pushed the gearshift into reverse. Watching the rock face in the mirror and keeping so close he was almost scraping it, he ground backwards at a walking pace down the steep winding track. He remembered there had been places where the road had narrowed until it had been difficult to squeeze along it coming up. He could not remember any place where it had widened.

Momentarily glancing ahead he was appalled to see how near his right front wheel kept veering to the edge of the cliff. The desire to stop was as urgent as thirst. He was afraid if he did the oil truck would slam into him, canon him playfully into space. Its driver was goading him down the track, advancing with whoops of encouragement and laughter as Bascombe retreated.

"*Recht.*" The hitchhiker was half out the window again.

"*Recht.*" He grabbed the wheel and pulled it hard over to the right. Bascombe snatched on the hand brake.

"*Zurück.*" He waved his hand impatiently. "*Mach schnell. Zurück.*"

Oh Christ, Bascombe thought. He supposed this madman knew what he was doing. He straightened the wheel and backed another ten yards.

"*Alt.*"

Bascombe obeyed him at once. As he braked, he looked over to the left. There might be just room for the oil truck to edge by.

Its driver had no intention of doing anything so tame. With a final mule-driving yell, he switched on his brights and shot forward. He took Bascombe's rear-view mirror with him and, grazing the rock on the other side, left a hail of stones in his wake. Bascombe closed his eyes and sat quite still for a minute until he felt well enough to drive on. Changing into low gear, he eased off the hand brake fraction by fraction as he let out the clutch. Nothing happened. He accelerated a little. He could hear the back wheels churning up soil and gravel now. He grabbed at the brake again, switched off the engine, and climbed down.

The truck was resting on three wheels. The rear right tire was a clear foot out over the edge of the cliff.

"*Oinye!*" His passenger had joined him. "*Oinye!*" He gazed down into the dark valley a thousand feet below. The word appeared to be a Serbo-Croatian expression of surprise. There was no dismay in it.

"You dumb bastard." Bascombe had had enough of their reckless Slavic fatalism. "You stupid idiot, why didn't you shout *alt* before?"

The outburst relieved his tension a little. It didn't seem to have offended his passenger in the least. He was already gathering stones and wedging them under the wheel that was still on the road.

There was no decision to be made. It was like that afternoon in London when she had climbed naked into the elm tree: he

267

was willing to face the threat of any curiosity. He was going to get Venus safely out of the truck now, at once. He opened the back of the van.

She was sitting, resting against the leather cushion. Slowly, tentatively—the slightest movement might alter the precarious balance of those three wheels—he climbed in and crawled toward her.

"What is it?" She was obviously very tired but there was no complaint in her voice. He took her hand and held it as he crouched beside her. He explained what had happened.

"You want me to get out?"

"Yes."

"I don't know if I can." She was smiling, mocking herself. She might have been telling him she had done something silly. He pressed the palm of her hand against his face. It wasn't altogether an act of contrition for his lack of thought or concern about her these past hours. It was a renewed understanding of her courage and generosity, of all she had been, all she still was to him.

"*Eine Frau!*" The boxer's eyes under the black felt hat were peering excitedly into the truck. "*Oinye! Eine Frau.*"

"*Meine Frau.*" Bascombe emphasized the "my." "Be careful," he continued in German as he crawled back along the floor of the truck. "She's ill. We must get her out. Come on. And be careful."

Whether the man understood the words or not, the sharpness in his voice impressed him. He stopped grinning.

"Can you turn on your side, darling? Very slowly." Bascombe dropped to the ground and faced her.

Venus started to lower her knees. He felt the floor of the truck tilt under his hands. He doubled forward, throwing his weight onto it.

"The other way!" He was shouting with terror. "Keep over on this side. As far as you can." He turned his head toward the figure behind him. "You! Here! Hold it!"

Whatever his eccentricities, the Yugloslav was not a man to ask questions in an emergency. He clutched the side of the truck and hung from it. The rear left wheel settled slowly back to the ground.

Venus tried again. A minute later she was lying on her side, her back against the wall of the van.

The sheet had slipped down to her waist. Bascombe saw the soft curve of breast below her arm. She reached down and pulled the edge of the sheet over it. Her modesty was like a reminder of suffering. Three months ago she would have walked proudly naked anywhere.

He gestured to the Yugoslav. Together they grasped the end of the mattress and began to pull it toward them. By the time Venus' legs were out of the van, her weight was over the left rear wheel. There was no longer any immediate danger of the truck toppling over the cliff, but they could not pull the mattress any further out. Another few inches and she would fall into the road.

He crawled back into the van and knelt behind her head.

"Can you sit up, darling?" He held her under the arms, trying to help her raise herself. They strained together; she lifted her head and shoulders until she was resting on her elbows. He shifted his hands, pressing against her back. Another straining movement: she sat upright, her legs and the bottom half of the mattress hanging over the end of the van.

She was tall enough to touch her feet to the ground. Her breathing was frighteningly quick and shallow. He jumped down onto the road beside her and put his arm around her waist. If he could get the mattress out from underneath her, spread it flat, she might be able to lower herself onto it and rest. She raised her hand to the top of the open door. The sheet slipped to her feet. He felt her body tighten. Supporting herself from the door she stood upright, naked, in the red glow of the tail lights.

"*Oinye!*"

There was dismay in the exclamation this time. The Yugoslav had backed away from her step by step. He was crouching with his hands on his knees twenty feet down the road. With a frightened movement he snatched off his hat and, still bowed forward, clasped it over his chest. He moved his other hand from right to left in the Orthodox gesture of crossing himself.

"Come here. Come here. Help me." Bascombe realized instinctively that it was fear, superstition, that was the greatest threat. If he could convey his own acceptance of Venus to the man, he might still be coerced into making the kind of practical, self-protecting adjustment with which he would have reacted to a sudden burst of gunfire, pain.

"Pull this down." He tore the mattress aside. "Spread it out over there."

The Yugoslav hesitated, still bowed in that intent, wary attitude.

"*Raus!*" Bascombe shouted at him. "*Raus!*"

It worked. As he snatched up the sheet and put it over Venus' shoulders, the man hurried forward and grasped the mattress. He did not look at Venus as he spread it out at her feet. Bascombe drew her arm around his neck. She lowered herself slowly to her knees on the mattress. She was panting as she sank onto it. He pulled the sheet over her.

"I'm sorry, darling. I'm sorry you had to go through all this. It's my fault." He touched her cheek. Her breathing frightened him. While he was helping her to her knees, her side pressed against his cheek, he had heard the uneven thundering of her heart.

The Yugoslav was still determined not to look at her. He got his shoulder against the back of the truck. Bascombe climbed in and started the engine. The rear wheel churned the loose soil. A quick heave from the man behind it. The lightened truck lurched forward. It settled on the road.

"No. Please. Let me try alone." She could not stand the indignity of being helped again.

"Come on." He grasped the Yugoslav by the arm and led him forward into the glare of the headlights. He gave him a cigarette. They stood there in silence, smoking. The man's face was impassive, like a rubber image, the padded cheekbones shadowing the eyes as the light struck them from below.

Bascombe walked forward to the edge of the cliff. He tried not to listen to the sounds behind him, the rasp of her breath, the straining gasps, the creak of the truck's springs.

The Yugoslav's silence continued as they drove on. They were still climbing, twisting upward over the rock-strewn track. The moon came into sight; patches of pale snow showed on the slopes above them. The Yugoslav sat huddled against the door. He might have been stowed there.

What could the man do anyway? Bascombe decided. Talk? Tell everyone in Peć about the American, the giant woman in the truck? They would be clear of the town before a crowd could gather. It was nothing for the police to concern themselves with. The only real danger was that news of their approach might reach the next town, Skopje, before they did. It seemed unlikely with these primitive roads—unless some reporter, the telephone . . .

"Italia." His passenger had sat up. He pushed his bootlegger's hat to the back of his head and rubbed his short blond hair.

"Italia—Roma" Bascombe reminded him hopefully. At least it would stop the man thinking about Venus for the moment.

"Italia—" He shook his head, correcting Bascombe. "Italia—lire." This was a variation on his Breakfast game. "Angland—pounds. Russkia—roubles."

"America—dollars!" Bascombe shouted gratefully back at him. "Holland—guilders."

"Espania—pesetas."

The road leveled. A few minutes later they started the descent.

They had run out of countries and were repeating themselves before they parted. It was getting light. They were across the mountains, in thick forest country, still fifteen or twenty miles from Péc, when the hitchhiker clapped Bascombe on the shoulder.

"*Alt.*"

"Here?" There was no sign of human life. Firs, rocks, a clear narrow stream.

"*Ja. Ja. Danke.*" He climbed down and slammed the door. He stood looking up at Bascombe. He straightened his black hat.

"America—" A wild grin: wait for it. "America—Johnson," he shouted triumphantly. "Angland—Vilson. Francia—De Gaulle." There were whole areas of conversation they hadn't even approached yet. He turned and bounded off into the forest.

Bascombe drove on.

The man had put the whole incident, that sudden vision on the mountain road, from his mind like some unwelcome appointment. In a day or two his thoughts might return to it. In a week it might be a story to be recalled and repeated. Perhaps in the telling Venus would grow smaller. It would not be her size but her naked beauty he would remember.

"Passport."

Bascombe handed them both over with a smile. This was Greece. *Never on Sunday, People of Poros, Zorba, the Greek*—that was the extent of his associations with modern Greece. They were all encouraging. The Greeks were a kind of super-Italians, a warm, laughing, dancing, bazouki-playing people. Excitable, passionate, with a streak of stern courage when they were pressed.

Everybody adored the Greeks.

"Where have you come from?" The Greek official spoke formal, classroom English. He was a small, slender man with carefully tended hands and a neat moustache, like a chevron, under his nose. The American army officer's uniform he was wearing had a stiff padded look across the shoulders.

Bascombe waved his hand vaguely toward the door of the inspection station, the truck parked outside, the Yugoslav customs shed twenty yards away.

"From over there. Yugoslavia."

"Yes." Patiently. "Before that?"

"Italy . . . France."

"Albania?"

"No."

"Turkey?"

"No."

"Hungary?"

Hungary—Budapest, Bascombe thought. He had slept for an hour outside Skopje and then driven straight on to the border. He was feeling a little lightheaded.

"Hungary? No."

272

The Greek opened the passport to Bascombe's picture. He rubbed the tip of his dainty finger across it, as though smoothing a leaf. For the first time he looked straight up into Bascombe's face. His eyes had a bruised olive shadow beneath them, like those of a child who had learned wariness too young.

"Where were you born?"

"St. Louis, Missouri."

"When?"

Bascombe told him. It struck him for the first time in his life that 1943 seemed like a long time ago.

"How old are you?"

"Twenty-five."

"When were you twenty-five?"

"September the tenth." Venus had been eight feet tall that day: he had done nothing to celebrate it.

The Greek was still looking at him with those watchful eyes. What the hell was this all about? A joke? He smiled. There was no answering friendliness. The official pushed the still-open American passport to one side and picked up Venus' British one. He looked at the name through the slit in the cover.

"Miss Cooper?" He glanced around the bare office as though expecting her to answer him.

"She's in the truck. Outside."

The Greek put Venus' passport on the counter. He did not place it in front of Bascombe but slightly to the left, as though it no longer directly concerned either of them.

With fastidious care not to smudge his fingers he opened an ink pad, found the right stamp, and stamped Bascombe's passport. He put it on the counter a foot from the other one. Bascombe picked them both up.

"Thank you."

The inspector did not raise his eyes. He waited until Bascombe had started to move away.

"Miss Cooper will have to present her own passport."

He started to check through a list on his desk, holding his pen a half-inch from the paper and following the lines with it. Bascombe watched him until he got to the bottom of the page.

"Miss Cooper's asleep in the back of the truck. She—"

"All passports must be presented in person by their owners."

He looked up again then. There was a warning in those dark eyes, but more evident was the flicker of hope. Bascombe suddenly understood him: the patient questioning, the padded shoulders, the neat moustache. He hoped Bascombe would start something. He would enjoy dealing with that, here, on his home ground.

The one lousy Greek in the whole country and he had to show up at the border.

"She can't get out of the truck." He kept his voice quiet. There was only one thing that could possibly work with a bastard like this. Diffidence. Let him have his power. "She's sick. She can't move."

"If Miss Cooper is ill she cannot be admitted to Greece."

"She had a stroke. On the road. In the mountains. I didn't know what to do with her." It was a version of the story he had prepared in case he had trouble at the Yugoslav frontier. He altered it now to fit the new circumstances, telling it awkwardly, without shame at his own helplessness. "I thought if I got her to a heart specialist in Athens. I don't see what else I can do." He looked down at his feet. "I mean, I feel sort of *responsible* for her."

It didn't seem to be working. The official paid no attention to him. He picked up the list he had been checking and carried it over to a stout, hairy woman at a typewriter by the window.

The two passports were still in Bascombe's hands. They wouldn't get five miles before they were stopped. At least they'd be across the border, in Greece. Then? Explanations. "Open the back of the truck." Venus. A freak to their prejudiced eyes. It was the same threat he had faced so many times this past year: the reaction of unimaginative people confronted with the inexplicable. Here, in this fabled country, Greece, would they at least try to understand? Would they let him drive on to Mount Olympus? He wished he'd had more sleep before approaching the frontier and this prick of an inspector.

"Here." The prick was standing ten yards away down the coun-

274

ter. Bascombe hurried toward him. "Miss Cooper will have to be examined by a doctor before she can be admitted to Greece."

"Great! Will you really, honestly get a doctor for her?" He'd better watch himself: he'd be saying "gee whiz" in a minute. "She's in the truck."

"We are not here to provide free medical treatment for tourists."

"I see." It was the answer he had expected: they didn't have a doctor to provide. He waited. The prick went back to his hairy typist.

He waited ten minutes, smoking, trying to hide his anxiety, watching the truck.

"Here." It was like the police in Paris with their "Open," "Outside," "Forward." All shits were alike. They loved being obeyed. Bascombe obeyed him.

"What is the matter with her?"

"I don't know. She was okay until we got to Peć, and then, suddenly, I don't know. I guess it's her heart. The doctor in Skopje said she didn't have any fever. He said I ought to get her to a specialist in Athens."

"Wait here."

Bascombe watched him go out to the truck. He watched him get his hands dirty opening the back. He would see no more than the Italian inspector had, a heap of bedclothes, a tangle of hair. Bascombe was sure he wouldn't risk getting his uniform dirty climbing inside. He didn't. He came back into the office. Of the two, Bascombe thought, he preferred Chester Voigt. Voigt had loped. This one swaggered.

"Wait."

Another cigarette. The window again. The prick went off into another office. The hairy typist was yelling something in Greek. Bascombe approached her. She snatched Venus' passport out of his hand. She found the right rubber stamp. She pressed it down on the blank page like a brand, holding it there, waiting for the scream.

Venus was in Greece.

The highway was excellent, in first-class condition. There were shits everywhere. In every country. The military regime which had taken over last year had probably had to comb the whole of Greece until they found that inspector—one of their own kind. Wait till he met the *real* Greeks.

He met some of them in Katerini when he stopped to buy food. The dim shop smelled of rope and olives. A small brown man with pitted cheeks and a wrinkled forehead appeared out of the dusk. Bascombe showed him the drawing he had prepared. Bread, cheese, a half-opened can of sardines. He had gone to some trouble to make it representational. The brown man looked at it; he looked at Bascombe. His eyes were the color of varnished mahogany. There was an unmistakable hatred in them. He shook his head. He did not return the drawing; he pushed it aside. He jerked his hand at the shelf of canned apricots and tomatoes behind him. He was obviously finding it difficult not to lose his temper.

They were all rather like that in Katerini. Going from shop to shop, Bascombe finally managed to collect a reasonable meal for Venus. In each of them they snatched the money out of his hand; they slapped his change, always exactly the right change, down on the counter like a curse. They could hardly wait to be rid of him.

He had had enough experience of foreign countries not to take it personally. It was just this part of Greece, Macedonia, the north. The real Greeks were down south.

"We're there."

Venus was sitting up in the back of the truck. He started to climb in to help her out.

"I can manage."

"Do you want me—" He was going to ask her if she wanted him to walk away and leave her alone until she had managed to get down.

"Give me your hand, Bascombe."

He reached out and she clasped his wrist. A single straining movement and she swung her feet to the ground. She stood beside him. He hauled the mattress out for her to rest on. She remained standing. They both looked upward.

He had pulled off the highway, down a byroad, along an unpaved track until it narrowed to a footpath leading into a grove of olive trees and he was forced to stop. He had turned the truck then so that it would be the first thing she saw when she stepped onto the ground. There was still just light enough. Above them rose the slopes, the summit of Mount Olympus.

He stared at it. He wasn't sure what he had expected: something awesome, majestic. He thought he had never seen a less impressive mountain in his life.

It was curiously shapeless, long and irregular, its peak slightly off center. There was nothing striking about its color either: it reminded him of an elephant that had had a roll in the grass. The dwelling place of the gods was such an anticlimax he couldn't take his eyes off it.

"Does your father live up there?"

"Of course not."

"Then why—?"

"He doesn't live anywhere in the way you mean." There was a hint of amusement in her voice.

"Then why—why did we have to come here? All the way to . . . *that*?"

"Millions of people all over the world still think of him as living there. Somewhere at the top of Mount Olympus."

"You don't."

Venus sighed. He wasn't sure whether she was sighing because of his obtuseness or out of sudden fatigue.

"Do you want to lie down?" He put his arm around her. He could hear her heart. Its beat sounded reassuringly even.

"You needn't help me." He took his arm away. She bent slowly to her knees and sat upright on the mattress, her feet drawn up under her. He felt an inexpressible happiness. Already, she seemed restored. Simply from being here, she had found some source of renewed strength. He dropped to the ground beside her and pressed his cheek against her naked thigh.

"What I'm asking my father is a human demand, Bascombe." She stroked his hair. "I want him to free me from the human laws that have made me so helpless. I've got to approach him as a—"

She paused, still avoiding the word *mortal*. "As anyone would, anyone who believed in him."

He raised his head hopefully. "Which laws?"

"It's a condition of human life that nothing's ever at rest."

That was easy enough to understand. People, mortals grew, decayed. The intellectual, emotional cycle might not match the physical one. But there was no single fraction of a second in a man's life that could be isolated as the still peak of his existence. It was like a stone thrown curving into the air. Throughout its whole flight it was either ascending or descending.

"It's a condition of my life that I can't grow old."

The implication of what she was saying didn't strike him at once. Then the familiar terror of those nights in Grasse returned. If she could never decay she *must* keep growing. He seized her hand.

"Your heart." It was like pleading for his own life. "Your human, physical heart. It won't be able to stand the strain soon. It can't. You won't—"

"I won't be able to move." It was not in her nature to be afraid of the truth.

She had never seemed so beautiful to him. He pressed her hand against his mouth.

"What are you going to ask him, then? How are you going to ask your father to help you? What can he do?"

"Free me from this human condition."

"To stay as you are—exactly as you are now?"

"Are you sure you want that?"

He was. All the struggles of these past few weeks, her heart-breaking dependence on him, the responsibility of feeding, tending, hiding her, were a reprieve compared to the thought of her condition worsening, her increasing helplessness, the final vegetable immobility, the thought of her dying.

"Yes. Yes. We'll find somewhere, Venus. Somewhere, darling. A Greek island. Anywhere. Yes."

She touched his cheek with her free hand.

"Can I? Would it do any good—" He meant if he stayed with

278

her now, prayed to her father, anything to help secure that reprieve.

"No." As always she had understood him at once. "No you'd better leave me here alone until—"

She broke off. There was the sound of footsteps on the path, approaching through the olive grove. He realized she was naked. The sheet was still in the truck. He scrambled in and found it. By the time the figures came in sight she was lying on her side, her knees drawn up, all but her head covered by the sheet. Bascombe walked forward into the grove to meet them, to stop them, if possible, from coming any closer.

There were three of them, a man and two women. They were real Greeks, all right. The man was wearing a rough knitted jacket and dark trousers. His feet were bare. The women had black cotton shawls over their heads. They were all elderly, lined as raisins, their eyes startlingly dark even in contrast to their brown skins.

They stopped the length of his shadow from him. One of the women was carrying something wrapped in a cloth. She passed it to the man. He spoke a few, soft, hesitant words in Greek.

Bascombe raised his hands: I don't understand. The women were peering past him at Venus. He wanted to seem friendly without letting them any nearer.

The man turned and pointed to the mountain behind him. He spoke again in that low, faltering way. Bascombe shook his head, smiling.

"They live up there in the hills. They saw the truck." The language had changed very little in two thousand years; Venus had no difficulty understanding modern Greek.

She called out something to the man. Suddenly they were all three smiling. It was the first time Bascombe had seen a Greek smile. Their smiles explained to him at once how the Greeks had earned so much regard, their reputation for being such a warm, natural, straightforward people. He would have trusted these three with his life at that moment.

The man raised his voice, speaking directly to Venus, more confidently now. He lifted the bundle he was holding, offering it to Bascombe.

"They brought some things for us."

Those quick, enchanting smiles again. Bascombe took the bundle. Venus thanked them in their own language. The man clapped his hands, sharply, twice. There was something profound, perfect in the gesture. It was an act of art. As he watched them walk away, Bascombe felt he could ask nothing more than to live the rest of his life in this country with Venus among people like that.

He took the bundle to her. They unwrapped it together.

A small round loaf of bread, a lump of goat's cheese, a dozen olives.

"Ouzo?" Bascombe ignored the irritation in the waiter's eyes, his curt impatient movements. He knew better now. That was just their surface manner. Everybody was right: the Greeks were a magic people. He had never been swayed by sentimentality, but he was sure the gift, the food those three old Greeks had brought them, was an omen, a reassurance from the gods of Olympus.

He had left Venus on the edge of the olive grove. He had left her water and food for the night and had driven into the nearest town in the truck. By the time he returned to her in the morning, her father would have granted her request. They would plan their lives together from there.

For the first time in weeks Bascombe could think about the future.

She would remain as she was now. She would never recover her full, active strength. He would have to wait on her, protect her. They would have to find some place, some house out of sight of curious watchers. They would live there alone.

It occurred to him only briefly to worry about money. If she felt like it, Venus could gamble on the stock exchange. She could visualize next week's market quotations as clearly as she had seen Semolina stumble home the winner. If that tired her too much, he would get a job. He didn't care what—house painting, carpentry, work in a garage. He had never had any ambition career-wise, as Mr. Mitchel would have put it. He had none now. As he saw it, all ambition had ceased to have any meaning with the end of the last century. The concept of doing, making, had been possible to the Victorians. Most of them (including Karl Marx) had lived early enough to be able to believe in material progress. To build a railroad, a bridge, larger and faster ships, had seemed to them indisputably constructive.

It was now clear the opposite was more likely to be true. More ships, more bridges, more highways only succeeded in threatening more life.

It was practically impossible under the present conditions for politicians, heads of state to *do* anything either. (It had been a long time since any of them had tried.) Ambition had been demeaned to the level of a competitive game: "to be"—as that student at the Sorbonne had put it. "Being" was rewarded with envy, servility, and various toys—a private helicopter, a personal washroom—and with that celebrated thrill, the exercise of power, which was nothing, when you thought of it, but a monotonous form of sadism. To Bascombe, the final insanity of ambition was illuminated by the fact that there were actually men who had worked and schemed and fought all their lives to *be* premier of Northern Ireland.

He had wanted once to take part in a revolution, to change things as they were, as Nolan had expressed it. It hurt to remember Paris. It had been naïve to hope a new kind of society could come of it. The glow of his own hope was painful to recall now.

Those three weeks aside, he had never cared about anything in his life except making love.

Sitting there in the dirty, noisy café, drinking the ouzo the sullen waiter had brought him, Bascombe was looking forward to the future.

He understood now, at last, what Venus had tried to teach him long ago. Everything they did together could be a way of making love.

18

CHAPTER

THERE HAD BEEN a terrifying five minutes on the highway when he thought he had lost the turnoff. He had hurried on, driven back, found it at last. The track was beginning to narrow now. In a moment the olive grove would come in sight.

He braked quickly. People were approaching, walking in the center of the path. He recognized the old man, the two old women, the bearers of gifts last night.

They stopped in a line facing him. Even at a distance he could sense concern; it was almost an agitation in them. He jumped down and ran forward.

The man raised his arm and said something in Greek. His eyes looked even darker in the morning sunlight. He had a small scrap of paper in his hand, holding it above his head like a challenge.

"What is it? What's happened?" In his anxiety, Bascombe scarcely realized he was shouting, shouting uselessly in English.

The man shouted back. In the flood of Greek, *ohi* and *oreste* were the only sounds that stood out separately. Bascombe had an idea that *ohi* meant no. The old man was still challenging him with that scrap of paper. What did they want? Could it be a message from Venus? Why didn't they give it to him?

The Greek shouts continued.

"Give it to me!" He was, after all, being no stupider than they were. He couldn't understand them either. "Give it to me!" he demanded again. He held out his hand for it.

The shouting abruptly stopped. The paper was thrust into Bascombe's fingers. He straightened it. It was blank. He turned it over. There was nothing on the other side either. Only a few scrawled figures.

The Greek was shouting again. The women joined in. It was the first time they had spoken. Their voices were as sharp as quarreling rooks. Something in their tone reminded him of the shopkeepers in Katerini, the hairy typist at the border. He suddenly got it.

They had gone back this morning and found the truck gone. They had hurried in pursuit of him. Even now that they had caught him, they could not shake off the anxiety the discovery of his disappearance had caused them. The scrap of paper with its scrawled figures was the bill for the bread, the goat's cheese, the olives.

He found a fifty-drachma note and pushed it at them. Climbing back into the truck he was quick with fear. If they had gone back this morning they had evidently not found Venus there. He raced the truck forward along the narrow path. The three old people scattered before him. He was rewarded as he passed with their wonderful Greek smiles.

The mattress was still there, the sheet, the water tank, some scraps of food. Venus' handbag was in the center of the mattress. He remembered buying that handbag together in London. He picked it up. He looked up at Mount Olympus. There was nothing to worry about, he told himself. It was a long climb to the summit. She had eaten before she left last night, perhaps rested for an hour or two. It was still early morning. There was no reason to expect her back before noon.

He wandered into the olive grove. The ground here was so dry its surface was like fine sand. He could see the impress of her bare feet in it, clear as footprints on a beach. He started to follow them.

They were lost here and there where grass had found some life in the bare soil, but there were enough of them for him to see she had been hurrying. There was more than a yard between the footprints. The rounded depressions in the gray dust brought

283

a vivid image of her to his mind, striding naked through the twilight, the great golden plume of her hair swinging about her shoulders.

He walked on. She had begun to tire. He had gone less than a mile before he noticed how much shorter her stride had become. He stood looking down at her footprint on the path, feeling her panting fatigue in his own body, longing to help her.

He bent down. It was a clear complete print, not merely the impress of the ball of her foot and her toes. The mark of her heel was quite plain: she must have paused here.

He straightened. He tore off his shoe, his sock. He fitted him own foot into the print in the ground: it fitted almost exactly. The impress of his foot was, if anything, slightly larger than hers.

He was running back down the path toward where he had started. There was a clear, full print in a pool of dust between two rocks. He pressed his bare foot into it. The marks of her toes overlapped his by a good two inches.

He dropped to his knees, staring at her footprint in the dust.

There could be only one possible explanation. She had not tired. Her strides had shortened for a different reason.

Without pausing to replace his shoe, carrying it in his hand with her purse, he raced on. He stopped again at the place where he had first measured his foot against hers. He ran on again.

The path was rising now, the soil harder, the stones and tufts of grass more frequent. It took him an hour of desperate, scurrying search before he found another clear, complete footprint.

It was less than three inches long.

The ground was as soft here as back in the olive grove. Seeing how much shallower the impress of her foot had grown, he realized how light she must have become to leave such a faint print. No heavier than that morning in London when they had gone shopping for clothes for her and he had carried her in the Mexican basket.

Although he searched for another hour he found only three more traces of her. The last was no bigger than the joint of his finger. He could just see the tiny impressions of her toes, like delicate brush strokes in the dust. He knelt for a long time, staring down at them. He thought she must have been less than twelve inches tall, small enough to perch again on his shoulder, when she left that last record of her journey up the mountain.

A mile beyond it Bascombe came to the bank of a stream.

He sat there long into the afternoon, hoping, waiting, remembering. It was her courage he remembered best, her laughter and her indignation. But she had lacked nothing; she had been complete. Although the time of her human ripeness had been so brief—a month in London, three weeks in Paris—little more than a tenth of her whole human life—every instant of her existence had enriched him. She had engaged his total interest and affection every second he had known her. She had given him everything he had ever wanted.

Although he had already begun to think of her in the past, he did not finally bring himself to face the possibility that he would never see her again until he found he was still holding her purse and looked inside it.

There had been a time when she had written to him constantly. Notes of her needs and desires. They had always been brief. Her last message to him was on a single sheet of paper, a half dozen lines in her firm clear hand.

"Bascombe." She had never been one for endearments. All the affection and tenderness she had shown him had been in her actions, rarely in words. "There is only one way I can free myself from the conditions of my human existence. I must go back now. If you take the shell to my shrine on the island of Kythira and place it between the two columns that are still standing there, you will receive my gift."

She did not end with love. It was not a word they had, either of them, ever needed to speak. She had simply signed her name, Venus.

The shell was the only other thing in her handbag. Bascombe held it wonderingly in his hand. It was impossible to be sure: he thought he recognized it. That night on the beach in Ireland when he had finally admitted her identity to himself, she had been fondling a shell, stroking her cheek with it. She had slipped it into the pocket of her cardigan. Had she kept it all this time?

285

He knew at once what she meant by her gift. He remembered the afternoon in the British Museum, looking up references to Aphrodite, the phrase in one of the books the attendant had brought him.

"She had the power to bestow the gift of irresistible charm on any mortal she chose."

"Irresistible charm." It took Bascombe some time, sitting there by the stream, to realize the full implications of those words.

He thought of the girls on the Earl's Court Road, his longing to know each of them in turn, the yearning fantasies that had filled his life before Venus. He could realize every one of those fantasies now.

Tall girls, short girls, plump girls, slim girls. Vague-eyed girls. Girls with direct, knowing glances. Girls in saris and girls in jeans. Mysterious girls with skirts down to their ankles. Proud girls with thighs bare up to their hips. Girls with bellies like Buddhas and girls with waists like greyhounds. Girls with great round pumping bottoms and girls with deft evasive little rumps . . .

He could discover, explore, experience, *know* them all.

The vivid meeting, the exchange of confidences, the mutual searching out of past and present, the caresses, the first long-anticipated, always faintly startling contact of nakedness. The act: prolonged, savored, repeated, varied. The languor, the gratitude, the waking together, no longer strangers.

All this would be his for the wishing as long as he lived.

He could grow old, fat, dirty, decayed; they would still greet him with eager glances, take him gratefully into their arms. He could ignore them, bully them, betray them, abandon them; they would return to him, enraptured, at the curtest invitation.

They would cook and wash up for him, serve him, wait on him. They would support him. They would defer to him endlessly. He could be stupid, repetitious, boring; they would cherish every word he spoke to them. They would beg him for his favors. They would bare their marvelous bodies for him, welcome him into their gentle cunts.

They would ask nothing but to belong to him forever.

It was getting dark. If he didn't start back soon, he would have trouble finding the truck.

Before he left, Bascombe performed his last act of respect and devotion to Venus. She had always loved laughter. He was laughing with her as he did what he knew she had hoped of him.

He fitted the shell carefully between his thumb and forefinger and threw it as far as he could into the dark tangle of trees on the other side of the stream.